The Emerald and Crimson Chronicles

A Dream of Fire

The Emerald and Crimson Chronicles

A Dream of Fire

By

Rhys W Morgan

Quantum Dot
Press

DEDICATION

To my dear husband, who has always had my back. Thank you for always believing in me and pushing me to make this book possible.

ACKNOWLEDGEMENTS

To my grandfather who was always a father, I hope this makes you proud.

To my mother and grandmother, my two favourite women in life, thank you for always supporting me also.

To the Walker clan who I married into, thank you for making me feel part of the family.

Edwin, thank you for making this a reality and helping me publish my book.

Contents

WHERE LOVE STARTS

HUMAN REALM
YEAR 318 ID

TRISTAN

Twigs crunch beneath my feet and drops of water are kicked before me as I make my way through several muddy puddles.

The wind lashes and howls, I pull my cloak tighter around me as I carry on down the undulating pathway; tall green trees soaked in rainwater loom over each side.

I exhale and my breath turns into a soft mist.

I have not done this for a while, I have to be careful, of course.

There are always people watching.

So many people.

I have to be careful, always.

To hide myself, who I am.

How I wish I could show everyone, show the world, but I simply cannot.

YOU SHOULD NOT HAVE TO BE CAREFUL!
YOU ARE INCREDIBLE!
YOU SHOULD NOT BE SCARED!
THEY SHOULD!

THEY ALL SHOULD!
YOU ARE ONE OF A KIND!

Yes, that I certainly am.
No one like me has existed before, and I doubt anyone ever will again.

I come to a stop, my boots caked in mud, my cloak drenched.
I'm cold, incredibly so, but that does not matter.
No, only what I came to do matters.

Practise makes perfect after all, does it not?

I can do this.

I reassure myself confidently.

Think upon good thoughts, happy thoughts.
Warm thoughts.

I remind myself.
I think about my bed, the warm sheets and soft pillows.
How I long to be there now, warm and cozy under the covers.
The hot milk served by one of the many servants or slaves.
And finally, my thoughts turn to fire.
I picture the hearth, its embers shining brightly, slowly growing and growing.
I outstretch my hand.
I focus on the heat, the intensity, the smell.

I can do this.

That's when I hear it, the sound of small sparks.
It crackles and snaps.

I open my eyes, and to my astonishment I can see a small ball of fire, raising ever so slightly above my hand.
I stare in wild wonder and awe.

I did it!

A smile spreads across my face, I can't believe I actually managed it.
I feel immensely proud of myself.
It's just a small, burning, ball of fire, yet it is better than the mere flickers I had Cast before.

YES, IT MAY BE ONLY A SMALL FIRE.
BUT A SMALL FIRE CAN TURN INTO A MUCH BIGGER ONE.
YOU NEED ONLY TO HONE YOUR POWER...

And that's when it comes, the one thing I cannot shake, no matter how hard I try, and I try often.
It is a fear, a deep and never-ending fear which haunts me.
Plagues me.
Day in, day out.

The flames continue to flicker above my palm, they burn brightly despite the rain.
Yes, I should be proud, but my joy turns sour as I realize the daunting truth.
I have known it for a while, that I am different.
In more ways than one.
But I honestly thought perhaps I had been mistaken, that the small embers I could Cast were nothing but a trick of the mind.
But here I stand, flames in hand, it comes to me then, that I do indeed possess the ability to Cast, and the heavy cloud which that itself brings looms over me.
The ability to Cast is not good for anyone.
Especially not in the Human Realm.

Especially not in the Capital.

Especially not here, on the island that hosts the Imperium.

And especially not for someone like me.

IF THEY FIND OUT, YOU WILL SURELY BE KILLED.
PERSECUTED AND MURDERED LIKE SO MANY BEFORE YOU!

I look upon the ball of flames once again and in the flames, I see myself, for surely if I am caught, then the flames would be my fate.

For the best way to cleanse a witch's soul is with fire, to burn away the darkness and let in the light.

At least, that's what Claudius says.

Claudius being a holy man who resides within the Imperium, the castle which my family have lived in for nearly three centuries.

He has however only recently returned.

He had been sent away by the High Pope some years ago for his dangerous propaganda and hateful speeches.

The High Pope is a kinder and more gentle man, although growing old and a very sickly man.

And missing...

He has not been seen for some weeks, as if just vanished.

The Imperium is therefore under heavy watch right now.

I barely managed to escape tonight.

I had to slip out, dressed head to toe in black.

Black shirt, black trousers, black cloak and black boots.

With the High Pope gone, they say Claudius is next to take over, which I sincerely hope is not true.

He likes to preach and condemn witches and magic more than anyone I know.

He has a fever of fury when it comes to these matters, and his only resolution is immediate death.
And here I think the God Of Light is about acceptance and love; perhaps not.
But then, perhaps yes.
After all, we have had an uneasy peace with the witches for centuries.
The good witches, anyways.
And uneasy being the preferred word.
In truth, there is much prejudice and hatred.
More so the humans against the witches.
The witches merely want to live in peace, humans however cannot accept what they don't understand, and magic is not something easily understood.

And with men like Claudius preaching their hatred, it only festers and rots in the mind of others, the hatred spreading.
I only hope that Claudius will be sent away again, and the High Pope found safe and sound.

Witches, good or bad, are branded 'Soulless' by the many.
But that isn't true, it couldn't be.
Could it?
There is only one true Soulless creature in this cursed country, and that is the Red Eye Demon.
They think witches are bad, but that pales in comparison to what can really hide in the darkest, depraved parts of the country.
Those creatures are really the Soulless ones, not witches.
But then, many disagree, many see witches as a plague also.
For not just witches lurk in the shadows, for something else even fiercer resides there.
Those dark creatures who possess red eyes and sharp fangs.
Everlasting youth and beauty.

Vampires.

Truly, if anyone deserved the title of 'Soulless' it would be them.

Whilst witchcraft is technically legal in the Human Realm, and some do Cast openly, it is heavily frowned upon.
Many witches are beaten, raped, tortured and murdered.
Of course, those who do these vile crimes are duly punished.
Which in turn only breeds more hate.
Humans don't understand being punished for murdering what they assume are freaks, for murdering what they and the rest call 'Soulless'.

With all the prejudice and hatred many wonder why the witches even bother staying in the Human Realm and yet they I suppose they are too proud to be shunned away to run and hide in the Black Woods, the Black Woods being the entirety of the Magic Realm.
I longed to go there one day.
To see their amazing City Of Bridges.
Truly it must be fantastical, and the witches who live there must be even more so.

I can't fathom how they would be called Soulless.

But is that even true?
Am I or others really without a soul just because I possess magic?
Without a soul just because I can make some flames appear in my hands.
It did not make sense.
I feel feelings and emotions, then how can I be Soulless?

THE PEOPLE SHALL TURN AGAINST YOU!
YOU SHALL BE CAST OUT!
YOU'LL LOSE YOUR FAMILY, YOUR STATION AND TITLE!

Especially me.

I was not just anyone, no, and therefore must be more careful than anyone.

Had I been blessed to be born a commoner then perhaps I would have been able to be freer, to practise happily and away from scrutiny.

Yet that was not the life I was blessed to have, for I had a thousand eyes upon me at all times.

Slaves, servants, lords and ladies, every person in the Capital surely knows me by face and name.

And further throughout the Human Realm, I am well known.

And no doubt my name has been mentioned in the Magic and Dark Realms.

For alas, sadly I was not born a commoner.

I did not have that luxury.

> *FOR I AM TRISTAN IMPERIAL.*
> *SECOND BORN SON OF THE KING.*
> *NOT THE HEIR, BUT THE SPARE.*
> *THIRD IN LINE TO THE IMPERIAL THRONE.*

For centuries my family have ruled.

And for centuries we have been at war.

The Human Realm and Magic Realm joined against the Dark Realm.

Locked in an endless time of death and misery.

Although it appears to have been stagnant for some years now.

Ever since he left the battlefield, the most feared of them all.

Known for his insatiable, crazed bloodlust.

And for his war crimes, his extremely violent and psychotic tendencies.

And most recently, famous for what he did... Eighteen years ago. Something truly vile, something that nearly wiped out the Imperial Dynasty itself.

Thankfully, he did not succeed.

But since then, he has all but disappeared.
Hidden somewhere, no doubt in the Dark Realm.
Some say he is even hiding under the skirts of his sister, who is none other than the Witch Queen.
The darkest and most powerful witch to have ever lived.
They both hide in their Crimson Castle.

Located deep within the horrors, monsters breed nothing but death there.

And sadly, they too have aid of their own witches.
Known as 'Dark Witches' and it is because of witches such as them, magic as a whole gets a bad reputation, and those who can Cast an even worse one.
Humans naturally assume all witches are 'Dark' no matter what.
And for that reason alone, I must always hide.
I have to deny that part of myself which I most covet.
People fear magic and those who Cast it, yet what is there to fear?

Do they not see the ball of fire?
How it glitters and shines?
The beauty of it.
And the power that can come from it...

THE CHAOS IT COULD CREATE!

BEAUTIFUL CHAOS!

I push the dark thought aside.
I don't want to create chaos.
I simply want to have fun.

BUT WHAT IS MORE FUN THAN CHAOS?!

I shiver at the thought.
Oh, how wonderful it would be to be free.
To be free from titles and obligations, duties and responsibilities.
To be able to not be Tristan Imperial.
To not worry about the war, the country or the throne.
But just to be Tristan.

Simply Tristan.

BUT YOU SHALL NEVER SIMPLY BE TRISTAN!
BUT YOU SHALL BE POWERFUL!
MORE POWER THEN YOU COULD POSSIBLY IMAGINE!

Did I really crave power though?
I suppose as a second son, mayhaps it was normal to want to seek what the elder shall inherit.
After all, he is destined to have everything.
The throne, the crown, the entire Human Realm.
Everything at his desire, unlimited power.

Yet, despite what my elder brother stands to inherit, he does not possess what I do.
He does not possess the ability to Cast magic.
His power is nothing like mine.
No, this power is mine and mine alone.

***A POWER THAT RIVALS ANY TITLE OF KING!
LET YOUR BROTHER INHERIT THE THRONE!
AND YOU SHALL INHERIT THE EARTH!***

It's a dark thought, one that I should not have.
He is my brother after all, my blood and future king, and yet despite all that, this dark thought still stands.
After all, is he really suited to be King?
He may be the Crown Prince, but he is the furthest thing from a maiden's fantasy.
Sure, he is classically handsome and youthful, being only two years older than me, but as handsome as he is, he is equally as vile.
Maidens do not run to him; instead, they are known to run from him.
Usually bleeding, screaming, and terrified.
And that is who is supposed to be King?

When I could be so much better…

More dark thoughts envelop my mind.
However, they do not frighten me; instead, they offer comfort, making me feel safe and secure.
The flames themselves even grow darker, going from bright yellows and oranges to dark reds and purples.
They must be getting darker with my thoughts.

Soft drops of rain fall all around me.
And yet the fire does not extinguish.
It crackles fiercely as I continue to stare blindly at its beauty, my thoughts chaotic.

Just then, something happens.

A vision comes to mind.
It's me, apparently crowned and throned.

The crown and throne are unlike anything I've ever seen.

Certainly not the crown of the Imperial Kings my father and his forefathers have worn.

Neither is the throne the one which my father and his ancestors have sat upon.

The crown is beautifully made.

Black with huge gems consisting of green and red.

The green I can assume was emeralds; it matched my eyes.

And the red I can assume were rubies, a deep and bright crimson.

And me… I look beautiful…

And all around me there is fire.

It swirls and dances around me.

The fire, the way I look, everything looks chaotically beautiful.

And just like that, the vision ends, and I snap back to what I assume is reality.

I take a step back and begin panting hard.

The flames I had Cast soon cease.

My mind is awhirl with thoughts.

Will this be my future and fate.

Is the fire friend or foe?

Will I really be consigned to the flames or shall I conquer them.

And if that is the case, will I be King?

Would my soul finally then feel free?

Would I enjoy the eternal feeling of the Light's love?

Or would my soul be damned regardless?

Will I be forever consumed to be tortured and burned in eternal hellfire for my sins.

I begin to control my breathing and start to focus.

Palm outstretched again; the flames appear instantaneously.

I did not even need to think about it… Perhaps I am getting stronger?
And perhaps I'm losing more of my soul?
But surely this is a gift.
A gift from the Old Gods.
To make us special and unique.

The Old Gods being the ones witches follow, the Lord of Eternal Light for the humans.

Yes, surely, I had been given these gifts from the Old Gods themselves.

I had been so lost in thought that I did not notice the approaching footsteps, yet I was pulled from thought when I heard a loud and clearly audible gasp.

Startled, I turn to leap back, my concentration once again spoiled. The ball of flames immediately disintegrates into nothing but a pile of ash, dissolving in the puddles beneath.

A single thought envelopes me.

Am I about to die?

Fear consumes me as he stands there, staring directly at me. For the person standing before me is none other than the boy who owned my heart.

Kaleb.

My feet are firmly planted into the ground, sunken into the mud.
I want to move, to run.
To talk, to deny and plead.
To tell him what he saw wasn't what he thought.
That it was just a trick, not real magic.
To try to persuade him this is all just a dream.

Neither of us speak, the only sound is the gentle rain drops, the sound of rustling leaves drifting in the wind and the nearby hoots from owls.

My eyes, like my body, are frozen.
I look at him intently.
Out of anyone who could have caught me, it just had to be him.
It could not have been a slave or servant or even a commoner, all of whom I could have persuaded or bribed to keep quiet.

OR THREATENED TO KEEP QUIET.

I push the thought aside as he takes steps toward me.
He is one year older than me, being seventeen, but as he approaches closer, I realise that he looks older than me, a man completely grown.
His frame already hulking and bulging past men twice his age.
His height towering over nearly everyone.
He has always been big.
Thick stubble already appears upon his face, and poking from out of his tunic, a thick mallet of dark chest hair.

He is certainly tall, dark and handsome.

Not to mention strong.
Incredibly strong.
He stood there, wrapped in a thick dark cloak, a mighty long sword hung from his sword belt.

Every inch the warrior.

And why would he not be, after all he is famous.

His father is none other than the General of The Imperial Army.

A fast friend of my father, the King.

Not to mention that the General's younger brother, Kaleb's uncle, is the Lord Commander of the Slayer Syndicate.

The Slayer Syndicate being infamous, created shortly after vampires came into the world.

They are men and women who take special oaths sealed in blood.

They may take no wives or husbands or have children.

They have no worldly goods.

They have to renounce their former lives, completely.

They are warriors meant to hunt the creatures of the dark.

And Kaleb, to the shock of many, stunned everyone by taking his vows as an Initiate.

Shocking for two reasons.

Firstly, he was meant to follow in the footsteps of his father, the revered General.

Especially since him being the only son and heir, he stood to inherit everything of House Umpire.

Secondly, he had not done the deed required to be an Initiate in the first place.

He had not slain a vampire.

He spent most of his time training, however.

Always training.

He started training young in the castle courtyard and still to this does.

And now he even trains at the Grand Spiral, the home of the Slayers, which is situated in the heart of the Capital, just over on the other side of the water.

Yes, he trained constantly, and he had the strength and muscles to proof it.

Kaleb and I grew up together, being similar age and social standing.
The firstborn son of the General, he was supposed to be best friends with my brother, the firstborn son of the King.
My father and the General, best friends wanted their sons to be the same.
However, it was not meant to be.
From ever since I can remember, Kaleb and I shared a bond.
And not just any bond of friendship, it seemed to run deeper.

At least I hope it did.

BUT HOW COULD YOU HOPE FOR SUCH A THING?
A WITCH AND A SLAYER?
DON'T BE RIDICULOUS!

The Syndicate had no quarrels with witches, however witches who lived in the Human Realm nonetheless had to be reported and noted, and regularly checked upon so that they do not go dark.
Syndicate members have also been known to brand witches with silver, and not just any silver.

But Saerillian Silver, made from what legends say was a fallen star.

Such a star has not fallen for some years, however.
It leaves an awful, terrible scar and shows the world that they are a witch.
Some Slayers have even been known to kill witches on sight, sometimes for the sheer pleasure.
They are caught and reprimanded of course, sent into exile and even executed.

Yet there have been some who have gone unnoticed and unpunished.

Yes, Witches may live and travel throughout the Human Realm, yet they are feared and hated, spat on and stones thrown at them.
Branded and murdered at whim.
It was horrible.
Because of this they mainly try to stay hidden in small villages throughout the Human Realm, staying away from towns and cities and especially the Capital.
Yet there were surely witches here, hidden.
 I could almost feel it.
Yet some care little about what humans think, they Cast out of wilfulness in public.
Which in truth just breeds more fear and hate.
He comes to a stop and stands directly in front of me.

"What are you doing here?
Why are you following me?"

He says nothing, simply looking at me.

"Should you not be with Theodore?"

I imply sarcastically.

He looks me up and down…

And then a wicked smile appears across his face.

A wicked and cheeky smile.
A smile he only reserves for me.
It makes my heart flutter.

"You have magic."

It was not a question, instead he was telling me.

My voice became lost again.
All these years, I had been so careful.
Always sneaking outside of the castle in the late hours, to perform and
Cast at my hearts delight.
Or try too, at least.
Tonight, being the best I've ever actually accomplished.

And yet I always knew this day would come, and here it is.

I simply nod, confirming his words.

"I knew It."

He tells me.

"I've known it for a while."

He mutters, that wicked smile still on his face.

All I can do is blink; how did he know?
I had been so careful… However, I am sure I will not stand here
speechless, if this was to be the end then I shall face it with my back
straight, my chin held high and my voice clear.

REMEMBER WHO YOU ARE!

Yet somehow, I did not feel like this was the end, not the way Kaleb
is smiling at me.
I look away from him, my cheeks burning in embarrassment and awe.

"Are you going to report me…"

I mumble.

He looks hurt by this question.

Instead of answering, he simply smiles again and asks in rapid succession.

"You had fire in your hands!
How did you do that?!
Why did you do that?!
How long have you been able to do that?!"

His voice was not harsh or accusatory, like how I would expect it to be from that of an Initiate of the Syndicate.
But rather sweet and full of excitement.

Did he really want me to answer this questions?

OR HE IS LURING YOU INTO A TRAP, FORCING YOU TO ADMIT YOUR CRIMES AND SIN.

But what crimes or sins have I committed?
Surely none.

And besides Kaleb would not do that.
He had honour and had never been deceitful, neither to me nor anyone else for that matter.

I decide to relax, the muscles in my ridged legs thank me for it.

"Technically, the fire was above my hands."

I tell him.

"If it was actually in my hands, I think it would burn"

I say with a coy smile.

He still seems amazed, so I continue.

"How I did it, well I just focused.
On warm thoughts, happy thoughts"

I dare not tell him about my darker thoughts, or how the flames changed colour with it.
The thoughts that plagued me, that said awful things.
And that vision… Me throned and crowned, so beautiful and regal.
Surrounded by beautiful fire.

No, I dare not tell him that.

No, that would not be wise at all.
Best to keep him amazed rather than scare him off.

"As for why, well because I wanted to see if could.
Plus, I find it fun."

DON'T FORGET POWERFUL!
SO POWERFUL!

Be quiet.

"Just fun."

I state again.

"And, as for how long"

I continue.

"Well, I suppose I've always been able to… Yet never when I want too."

A twinge of sadness is in my voice.
Kaleb notices this and places his hand on mine.

I freeze.
I had felt the touch of his hand before, either playing games as children or training together in the courtyard, practising our sword skill.

Yet this was different.
We were not playing games or training with swords.
No, we were just two young men, holding hands in the rain.
It was tender and caring.
It made my heart beat fast.
We look at each other deeply.

We had shared looks before, looks of deep longing.
But I never really knew if he felt the same way.
How could I?
It's not exactly a question you just ask.
Especially not here.
Or anywhere, I suppose.

"I guess… Keeping apart of yourself hidden, that can be a pretty heavy burden to bear."

As he says this, he squeezes my hand, stroking it with his thumb.

I had not expected to hear these words, yet they comforted me.
He sounded like he understood, like he too carried a secret…
But what could that possibly be?

Intrigued, I decide to press upon him.

"I have answered your questions, now answer mine."

The authority in my tone evident.

"Oh, why at once, Your Highness."

He jests, before taking a step back to curtesy.

I roll my eyes at his evident sarcasm, turning my face away ever so slightly so that he does not see me smiling myself, bemused by his humour as always.

"In response to your first question, you could not pay me to hang around with your brother,"

He says matter of fact.

This came as no surprise, my brother's… tendencies… were apparent from an early age, and it drove most people away from him in disgust and fear, including Kaleb.
Instead, he was and always had been mine.
Ever since before I could remember, we have always been inseparable.
Yet despite that closeness, despite that inseparability, despite the fact I've known that I've loved him since before I could remember, I had not shared the fact with him that I am a witch.

And it seems it did not matter, for he already knew and clearly doesn't mind.

"As for what I'm doing here, you're not the only one who walks the castle grounds, wanting to be alone with their thoughts.
Especially here, amongst the trees, where a man can just relax and think."

His answer is honest.
But his words are heavy.

"So… you weren't following me?
You just happened to be here, in the same place as me, at exactly the same time?"

I ask again, not finding it believable.

He smiles that smile again, the smile that I loved

"Well… I…"

He doesn't finish the sentence, he's too busy chuckling.
He holds his hands up, palms outward.

 "Okay, maybe…"

He runs a hand over his shaved head, the hair growing back already.
He is clearly thinking on what to say next

"So…, So, I noticed that you sneak out of the castle… You've been doing it a while.
Always when the castle is asleep.
You come always under the cover of darkness.

And well… I wanted to see what you were doing… And why I wasn't doing it with you"

The way he said the last part of that sentence made me catch my breathe.

If only he had known how much I really wanted him to **'do it with me.'**

I push aside the comment.

"Did you not think maybe I wanted to be alone?"

I snap at him, not meaning too.

He ignores the anger in my tone and speaks.

"To practise your magic?"

I instantaneously fall silent.
Perhaps it was not best questioning him back after all.

"Turn around."

 His tone firm.

I stand there, looking at him.
Why does he want me to turn around?
My eyes flash down to his longsword hanging there.
Did he mean to use it?

DON'T DO IT!
FIGHT BACK!
USE YOUR POWER, UNLEASH YOUR CHAOS!

I ignored the voice completely.

I would never harm Kaleb.
Not now, not ever.

He was too firmly placed within my heart.

"Don't you trust me?"

He coos.
That same arrogant, smug wonderful smile
I hated how he made me swoon for him.
I do as he tells me.
I turn around.

WHAT ARE YOU DOING?!

I trust him!

I can hear him rustling about behind me.
The crunching of his shoes, the clanking of his belt.

HE IS GOING TO USE HIS SWORD!
HE MEANS TO SLAY YOU!
USE YOUR POWER!

I continue to ignore.

I do not yet hear the sound of Silver.

I'm fine, he's fine, everything is fine.

I reassure myself.

I feel something cold against my neck.

I shivered as I contemplated whether it was his sword at my neck.

No, it wasn't his sword I realised as he begins to tie something behind me.

He releases his hands, and something falls gently on my chest.

I look down and see a necklace.

It's handmade, that's easy to spot.

Being made from wood and string.

Yet the wood was beautifully handcrafted, into the shape of a small sword, with an intricate crown for its pommel.

And it is clear that it was made from Black Oak.

The very wood Slayers of the Syndicate use to stake and kill vampires.

Of course, Saerillian Silver worked just as well to harm if Black Oak was not available.

It is small, fitting into my hand, and feels sharp also.

A small dagger.

I think playfully.

So, I did feel a sword at my neck.

I jest to myself internally.

I turn to look back at him, my eyes are warm, whilst his seem terrified.

"Thank you... I love it."

It is the truth.

He seems less terrified upon me saying that I love it.

Yes, it might not have been gold or jewels like that which I used to wearing as befits my station as Prince, yet nonetheless it was perfect.

Perfect because he was the one who gave it to me.

I cared not that it did not cost money, or was worth money, because to me it was priceless.

Yet seconds of silence pass us.

He is clearly not a threat to me, not when he presents me with a gift…
But then again, I had to be sure.

"Please, please don't say a word."

I say to him.

He looks hurt again.

"You wound me my, My Little Prince"

'Little Prince' being a nickname, a playful mocking of the fact that despite our close ages.
And yet called it because Kaleb easily towered well over me, as he did most people for that matter.
However, usually when he had referred to me by this nickname, it was always playful. However, this too was tender, his strong voice surprisingly sweet.

He continues to look at me, his eyes full of curiosity.

"Can you do anything else?
You know, magic wise."

I want to say yes, yet I stop myself.
I do not want to give too much information over, I still have a fear inside me.

"Why do you ask these questions?
Why are you not trying to report me, or brand me?
Why are you not running and telling others.
 Reporting me to —"

"Reporting you to whom exactly?"

He cuts in.

"Shall I run around shouting about the castle that the King's own son, a Prince of the Imperial Dynasty can Cast magic?
That you are a witch?"

He shakes his head.

"No thank you.
 I rather like keeping my head."

This saddens me.
Whilst he makes sense, his accusations would probably bring about his death, or both of our deaths, yet however I thought that maybe for a brief second that he wouldn't tell anyone due to our… **Connection.**
He seems to notice my sadness once again, using his hand he ever so softly brushes my cheek.
He had never done this before.
I feel my whole body tingle with unparalleled joy.

"Do you really think I would ever put you in harms away; My Little Prince?"

Once again, his voice so tender.
The way he said it makes me feel like melting.
Just like the ashes did in the puddles.

His lips are right there.
He has thick stubble surrounding them, and although the hair looks rough and fierce, his lips however looked supple and soft.

Do I dare?

YOU ARE POWER ITSELF!
IF YOU WANT SOMETHING, TAKE IT!

Our faces grow closer, our eyes lock on each other.
He's so handsome, and strong.
He has always made me smile and feel at ease.

DO IT!

The voice screams.

I do not get the chance, for Kaleb wraps his strong arms around the small of my waist.
The feel of him, masculine and dominant.
He leans down, I find myself standing on my tip toes to meet him, and our lips touch.
My world collides and colours spark inside my mind.

I see a range of colours.
Blues, reds, greens, oranges and violets.
I feel something grow beneath me,
And the raindrops; they feel ever so colder, as if touched by frost.

Kaleb pulls away, his eyes widen, and he gasps.
For a moment I think I have done something wrong.
That it has been a terrible mistake, that I should never have kissed him nor answered his questions.
How I should not have opened myself so easily.

That's when I notice he has a wide smile, his eyes full of admiration.

"LOOK!"

His voice loud and full of excitement.

Beneath our boots, which had once been wet with rainwater.
We were now standing on a bed of flowers.
The same colours I saw in my mind.
Blues, reds, greens, oranges and violets.
It surrounds our feet.
They are beautiful and vibrant.
And above us, the rain has turned to snow; it falls softly.
Collecting all around us.
I am stunned.
How did I do that?
I've never been able to Cast so effectively before…

Kaleb looks at me with pure wonder.

"You're incredible."

He breathes.

My heart soars as if it has burst from my chest.

He thinks I'm incredible!
I could not be happier!
So happy that I kiss him again.

He does not resist, instead he wraps his arms around me tighter and kisses me passionately as the snow continues to fall and the flowers grow even more and spread around us further.

It's intense, and wonderful, and everything I had wished for.
When it ends however I feel sadness.
Yet I somehow know in my deep subconscious that this has been the first of many, many more kisses to come.

"I've wanted to do that for a very long time."

He admits to me.

"I've wanted you to do that for years too."
I admit as well.

"I was scared".

He answers.

This shocked me.
Kaleb is the epitome of a man.
Strong and brave and excellent with a sword.
I did not believe a man such as he could be scared of anything.

"I was scared because I wasn't entirely sure that you would feel the same.
 I had a feeling you might, but I couldn't be quite certain.
I had hoped our mutual fondness and years of growing up with each other would help my cause, and I glad that it has.
I'm glad that you feel the same.
And the fact that you, of all people could like me back... Well, that is a great honour."

"Me liking you back… Is a great honour"

I question, sceptical and yet flattered.

"Of course it is, you are –"

"The prince."

I interrupt him, sighing deeply.
I hated being a Prince, you never knew if people liked you for who you were, or what you could do for them with your power and status.

"It's nothing to do with you being the prince."

He says to me.
I remain sceptical.

He smiles at me, and then says.

"Don't flatter yourself, your head will grow."

He then finishes with a wink which brings laughter from my lips.

"And then that pretty crown you like to wear won't fit your pretty little head."

He jests again, laughing.

The crown in question more of a silver band, nothing special or grand. The Imperial Crown worn by the King was simple too, albeit made of gold and bigger than my own.
Nor was it the beautiful crown I saw befitting me in the vision.

No, that crown had been the darkest of blacks and encrusted with green and red jewels.

I decide to playfully punch his shoulder, but with quick reflexes befitting that of an Initiate in training, he quickly grabs my arm, and pulls me close.
His laughter is gone, he looks at me with seriousness in his eyes.

"It's because ever since we were young, you have always been kind.
You treat people with decency, you care not if their nobility or slaves, you treat them like humans."

His face comes even closer, his lips nearly once again on mine.
The look in his eyes is intense, and the deepest of browns.

Like acorns in autumn.

"It's because every time you've smiled at me, it feels like I can't breathe.
When you're near, I can't think or focus.
You're always on my mind.
You always have been and always will be."

His words make me burst with profound happiness, perhaps this really was a dream.
Perhaps I was actually back in my chambers, in my comfy bed with warm sheets.
Perhaps I would wake any moment, and I would kick myself at how pathetic and stupid I had been.

"I just wanted to tell you how I feel…"

He trails off, his voice getting sad.

"I'm going to the frontlines soon… I may be an Initiate for the Syndicate, yet my Lord father, the General, has commanded I come and see him."

A knot forms in my stomach.
I had not known this, and I wondered why.
Me and Kaleb shared everything; we told each other everything.
But then again, I had hidden magic from him, so I suppose that wasn't necessarily true.

"He wants me around the men."
To get to know them better,
To get them to start respecting me.
Silly really, I'm never going to command them.
Not now."

His voice trails off, uncertain.
Yes, I suppose since he promised himself and begun his Initiation, and of course if he completes his training, which I certainly have no doubt he will, then he will be a fully-fledged Slayer of the Syndicate, and thus he will never be General of the Imperial Army, nor hold lands or titles.

He will inherit nothing.

I hold back tears that mean to sting my eyes.
I shouldn't be shocked, and yet I was.
It was true, a man such as he and with his familial background would surely be on the frontlines.
After all, whether he be a captain for his father or a captain for his uncle he was born to be on the battlefield.

All that training he did in the courtyard, practising with knights twice his age…

And winning too.

He really is strong, perhaps that would benefit him on the battlefield.

It makes me feel good that he is strong, but perhaps if I was not scared for his safety then his strength would have excited me and surely my manhood would be hardened.

He will hopefully win fame and glory.

After all, one day it is sure that he will surely one day become Captain, maybe even Lord Commander like his uncle.

And yet, a small part of me had hoped that when he took his Initiation only weeks ago that he would be staying a lot longer.

INDEED, HE WILL FIGHT!
INDEED, HE WILL GO TO THE FRONTLINES!
INDEED, HE WILL DIE!

I turn away, wishing the voice to stop.

And yet there was truth to it, there was every chance he could die.

I will not let that happen.

I will keep him close.

Keep him safe I decide.

YOU CANNOT PROTECT HIM FOREVER.
HE WILL DIE!
HE WILL DIE AND IT WILL ALL BE YOUR FAULT!
YOUR FAULT, YOUR FAULT, YOUR FAULT!

The tears I had try so hard to fight back from stinging my eyes are let loose, flowing down my cheeks.

He notices this and cups my face.

"My Little Prince, do not weep.
Nothing shall happen to me."

"You cannot promise that"

I tell him.

The tears continue to flow.

"Why can't you ignore your fathers command?
Perhaps ask your uncle?
Surely if you express how dedicated you are to your training at the
Syndicate, then maybe."

"Maybe I won't go the front lines?"

He scoffs.

He sighs deeply, taking a step back.
He composes himself and then tells me.

"Even if I did speak with my uncle, it would only buy me a few short
months at the best.
Regardless, I would still be going."

"But even a few months, isn't that better than nothing.
At least then you can stay"

I realise I sound like a whingeing child.
I try to rein myself in, yet I cannot.
My feelings spill from me.

"You cannot follow me here, in the rain and darkness and give me this."

 I touch the necklace he made me with my fingertips.

"You can't do that and then simply just leave"

 I finish.

"I don't have an option!
My Lord father, he has commanded it… And my uncle agreed too!
He thinks it's a good idea.
To be honest, as do I.
I was born for battle, it's in my blood.
I cannot escape from it; I cannot run from who I am!"

His voice rises, I can sense anger.

I have seen Kaleb angry before.
With many things.
Many times, in the courtyard.
His blood runs hot.
I must admit, one of the many reasons I like him.
Not to mention that when he's angry I find it rather exhilarating, a deep sense of attraction to his primal anger.

"I need to do what I must.
I have to get to know the men on the frontlines, the ones who sacrifice and die for us every day.
Imperial soldiers and fellow Slayer alike.
The ones who stop the hordes of nightmarish creatures invading the Human Realm.

I have to fight with them, earn their respect!
If I have any chance whatsoever of leading my own men into battle one day or sending them to die in my stead.
I have to battle them, Vampires and Witches!
Soulless abominations!”

Even in his anger, Kaleb catches and stops himself.

He takes deep breathes.
I can tell he is stressed and angry.
I know Kaleb.
I know that he is also scared of going to the BorderLands.
The Borderlands being the common term for the outskirts of the Magic Realm.
It sits between the Realm of Magic and the Dark Realm.
It is where the fighting carries on even as we speak.

“I’m sorry, My Little Prince…
I don’t want you to think…
I did not mean too…
Please, forgive me!
I would never hurt you!
NOT EVER!”

I can tell what he said was true, he would not harm me.
And his words were not aimed at me, he merely said them out of anger, as we all do sometimes.
He wanted me to forgive him yet in my heart there was nothing to forgive him for.

“Please don’t think for a second that I think that about you!
Because I don’t!
Not for a second!

I never have!
I see you, Tristan.
And you have more soul than anyone I know!
I SEE YOU"

He shouts.

All the time I have known him, all the time we have spent together, all those longing looks and playful remarks, yet he has never spoken as he has this night.
It overjoys me.
Yet he is a warrior, and a dutiful man.
He will obey his father's command.

Yet I do not want him to go.

IF HE FOLLOWS HIS FATHERS COMMAND, WHY NOT YOURS?!

But I did not want to command him.

ARE YOU SURE ABOUT THAT?!

Yes, because commanding someone is not love.

YOU DON'T WANT HIM TO LEAVE!
THEN DON'T LET HIM!
MAKE HIM STAY!

The inner turmoil is too much, and yet against my better judgement I listen to the latter.

May God and Old Gods forgive me.

"Please, I understand your duty, I understand you need to befriend your fellow men, I understand you have a duty to your father and uncle but what about."

"ABOUT WHAT?!"

He shouts.

He looks at me, ashamed.

"Forgive me, I did not mean too."

"It's okay."

I soothe him as I reach for him, my hands clutching his.
His lip quiver, it looked almost as if he would cry too yet he does not.
He shuts his eyes tightly and then reopens them; the tears forced away.

"It's just… We are both slaves to our responsibilities."

He sighs

I know he is right.
We are no ordinary people.
And yet I still do not want him to leave, regardless.
I know it is wrong, but I want him to stay.

THEN DO WHAT YOU NEED TO DO!

I continue to soothe him, my hands rubbing his gently.
They feel hard and rough, no surprise from someone who practises with the sword every day, not to mention an assortment of other weapons.

"I know that you must go… But please, please just speak to your uncle. Please, please just stay for a few more months."

I plead with him.

He shakes his head and tries to back away, yet I hold onto his hands firmly.

"Please don't, Tristan."

He asks of me.

"Why not."

I retort as I hold onto his hands and continue,

"Please, I need you here.
Just a few months, just for me.
Then you can go and do what you must, I just need you for a while longer."

THAT'S IT, REEL HIM IN.

I do not want to reel him in, I simply just want more time.

"Please, Kaleb… I – I love you."

I stutter, stupidly.

The words escape my lips.
I had not meant to say them, I wish that I could suck the words back into my mouth and never release them again.

His eyes widen, and he chuckles warmly.

"Only you."

 He says with his gaze on the flowers and snow beneath us.

"Only me, what?"

 I inquire.

He looks up and long into my eyes again.

"Only you… Only you would be able to get me to dismiss my duty."

 He remarks, his voice heavy.

THERE YOU GO, IT WORKED!

I feel instantly bad.
I want to continue speaking but before I get a chance he whispers to me.

"I have never seen eyes such as these… Beautiful emeralds."

He remarks.

It is true that I was known for my eyes since birth, high lords to the lowest slave had many a time commented that I had two emeralds for eyes.
How it accentuated my beauty.
Yet how out of all the people who complimented me for it, none of their words compared to the words Kaleb just uttered.
I had seen him staring at them hundreds of times over the years, and now I realise it's with the same longing he shows me now.

How had I never realised it before… I had been so madly in love with him that I failed to realise he was madly in love with me too.

"So beautiful."

He whispers.

> *BEAUTY AND POWER!*
> *YOU SHALL BE WORSHIPPED!*

I want the voice to stop, so I kiss him once more.
I am more desperate and rougher this time.

The voice does not seem to stop.

> *BEAUTY AND POWER!*
> *BEAUTY AND POWER!*
> *BEAUTY AND POWER!*

It chants, over and over.

> *YOU SHALL BE WORSHIPPED!*

It finishes.

Kaleb gently pulls away from me,

"Calm yourself, My Little Prince."

He whispers to me.

For a second, I feel as if I had gone too far, and offended him, yet he merely does that cheeky wink of his at me and I know he is not offended in the slightest.

"As much as I have enjoyed this. and shall certainly continue to enjoy this."

He winks then.

"We must head back.
 After all, I have to speak to my uncle."

He smiles at me as he gestures back to the castle.
High in the sky the full moon was descending, and the sun would surely rise soon.
The moon, getting lower is partially hidden by thick clouds, yet the sound of birds had started, and sure enough the sunlight would creep through, presenting itself as the morning dawn.
Not that the sun was ever bright anymore, nor the country.
It grew ever darker and colder these last three centuries.

But breathless anyways, I agree with him.
He leans down and picks two flowers.
One a brilliant forest green, the other a dark but bright purple.

He presses them into my hand.

"Green to match your eyes, and purple because it's your favourite colour."

He tells me.

Gods, if I hadn't loved him before, I did now.
He turns to walk toward the castle, but he looks back at me and with the same wonder on his face.

"By the way, I love you too."

He utters with his cheeky smile, and then another wink.
I could not believe it.
The two things I hid for so long, and now I find that I can share them in another individual.
Maybe now I won't always feel so alone?
A part of me still continues to think perhaps that it truly was a dream indeed.
A marvellous, beautiful dream.

And if it was, I truly did not want to wake.

He turns to walk back, up along the pathway and back towards the castle.
I look down at the green and purple flowers in my hand, smiling warmly at his loving gesture.
I place them gently inside the pocket of my cloak.
Looking up, happy at how the night had turned out, I begin to follow him, both our feet crunching in the small circle of snow that laid around us.

Kaleb had just stepped over the last bit of snow, his foot making a splash as it goes over a puddle when we hear it.
An awful, shrieking noise.
One I had never heard before, and yet Kaleb stops dead in his tracks.

Without hesitation, he pulls his sword from its scabbard.
 A longsword, yet not the common swords that Slayer Initiates were given during their training years, but rather it had an intricate handle made of orange jewels, his favourite colour.
And the pommel in the shape of a sun, the same for all Slayers.
And the metal which the sword is made, none other than Saerillian Silver.
It glistens and shines against the fading moonlight.

Silver said to be made of a star itself, Saerillian being the word for Starlight in the language of the Old Gods.

A language used by witches… Yet not by me.

For that I would need a teacher and that's scarce to happen here.

He turns to me and shouts.

"GET BACK!
 GET BACK NOW!"

The seriousness in his voice was strong, yet I still do not realise what is happening.

Is it some sort of animal?

THAT'S NO ANIMAL!

The awful shriek rings out again, and then I see it.

At first all I see is the trees, but there it comes, the sound of its feet heavy as it comes stumbling out.

Through the branches, leaves, and puddles.

It steps out onto the pathway, approaching closer, closer to us.

Closer to the flowers and snow.

Upon closer inspection, its feet aren't feet at all.

Not completely anyhow, they seemed elongated and twisted, with jagged razors, the same which matches its hands.

Sharp, razor talons.

They glistened against the rainwater.

The creature is not like I had ever seen before.

It looks a mixture of human and bat.

It has a head, torso, arms and legs yet it also has huge wings jutting out of its back, they too look sharp, not to mention sunken black eyes and grey skin.

It has scraps of clothing on its body.

Yellow robes… Tattered and torn… They seemed familiar.

At another glance, it looks to be male.

Kaleb holds his sword high, points toward the creature.

His other hand goes backwards, extending towards me.

"Stay back."

He says, panicked

His head does not turn back to look at me, instead looking firmly ahead, his gaze locked on the creature.

It is so ugly and terrifying, yet it is also incredibly and unbelievably fascinating.

What is this creature?

I can sense immense power from it

It almost sings to me.

> *YES, YES, YES!*
> *YOU HAVE ALWAYS BEEN DRAWN TO POWER!*
> *YOU CRAVE IT, DON'T YOU?*
> *YOU CAN'T DENY IT.*
> *NOT TO ME!*

Why does this voice plague me so?

Why can't you just leave me alone?

It repeats, getting louder and louder.
I can't take it.
I end up shouting involuntarily.

"BE QUIET!"

I roar.

I instantly regret it.
I had not meant to shout; I simply just want the voice to stop.
Yet shout I did.

The creature springs to life, his huge wings span out around it, its arms rise too, showing the true length of its long and razor-sharp claws.
Using its huge legs, it propels itself upward into the air, shrieking as it does.
It begins to swooop down upon us, I watch almost as if in slow motion as it gets closer and closer to the ground.

Towards us.
Towards me.

Quick as a flash, Kaleb pushes me hard.
So hard I fall back several feet, the only thing breaking my fall is luckily landing in the pile of snow.
Or had Kaleb purposely pushed me here, making sure my fall would be soft?

I only have enough time to sit up as I watch the creature land, right next to Kaleb!

He quickly jumps aside, swinging his sword back.
It hits the creature directly in the arm, black blood sprays through the air, landing and ruining some of the pretty flowers.
It looks even more disturbing against the white of the snow.
The creatures screams in pain before swinging at Kaleb who artfully dodges it.

He is quick, that is evident.
And so strong.
Watching him battle this creature, it is exhilarating, the way he shows no fear, the way he protects me.

He really does love me.

Through the fighting, in the distance, more noises.
Human noises thankfully, not those of monstrous beasts.

They grow closer, shouting as they do.

"PRINCE TRISTAN!"

I hear one call.

"MY PRINCE, WHERE ARE YOU?"

A second calls

The voices distract the beast, who swings in the direction of the incoming noise.
With it's back turned, Kaleb takes the chance and plunges his sword deep into the side of beast, it goes straight through one side and out the other.

It lets out a blood curling howl.
Full of pain and rage, it sweeps forth with one of its huge, sharp wings.
So fast and powerful that this time Kaleb does not have a chance to dodge.

The wing hits Kaleb with full force, shooting him across the muddy pathway and smashing directly into a tree.
He hits it hard, and lands on the ground beneath.
He is instantly still.

My breathe catches in my throat.

Please don't be dead.

I plead to both the Old Gods and the God of Eternal Light, whoever will answer.

The creature is still full of fury, black blood sprays from its wound.
It goes on all fours, snarling and biting as it begins to make its way to Kaleb.

IT MEANS TO KILL HIM.

I will not let that happen!

YOU HAVE THE POWER!
KILL IT!

I don't know how!

UNLEASH YOUR CHAOS!

Is the answer I receive.

I raise my hand at the creature, knowing I must protect Kaleb no matter what.
I think back to earlier, to the ball of fire I had ignited.
It is not warm and happy thoughts that I think of, however.
No, it seemed the fire got bigger the darker my thoughts got.
So, I let dark thoughts enter my mind.
Horrible, awful thoughts.
My thoughts are on.

DESTRUCTION, DECAY, DEATH.
BLOOD AND FIRE.

A fire appears spontaneously above my palm.
It's flames the darkest of reds.

YES, DO IT!
UNLEASH YOUR CHAOS!

I let out an almighty scream, the fire shoots from my hand, it travels at an almighty speedy and hits the creature directly.
It lets out an otherworldly shriek, but I do not let that stop me.
I continue to Cast fire directly at it.
Its skin begins to crackle and burst, the fire consuming it.
It falls to the ground, letting out a final death scream as its body flails and shakes.

The fire continues to rage from my hand, blasting the creature with such ferocity that its skin begins to wither and melt, showing bare bone underneath.

A heavy feeling of tiredness comes over me, my head feels sore, and my vision begins to blur.

BE CAREFUL!

TOO MUCH CHAOS CAN DRAIN YOUR LIFE FORCE!

I'm still full of anger, however.
Anger at this creature for appearing.
Angry at it for ruining what was a perfect night.
Angry for hurting my love.
Angry for thinking it even stood a chance against me!

Does it not know who I am?
Does it dare defy me?

POWER, POWER, POWER!

My vision continues to blur, black spots envelope my vision.
The fire drains away, ceasing to appear.
I fall to my knees, weakened and tired.

Is this what it feels like to die?

Kaleb is just up ahead; he still lies there unmoved on the ground.

Please, please don't be dead.
I say another silent pray.

My body is so tired, yet despite this, I still crawl towards him.
Intent on helping him.
Saving him.
The voices in the distance get closer and closer.

"YOUR HIGHNESS, WHERE ARE YOU!"

I ignore the voices.
I continue to crawl.
I drag and pull myself.

Crushing flowers, wading through mud and snow.
I'm coming my love.
I pass the dead creature, now nothing more than a charred corpse.
The smell of burned flesh fills my nostrils, I gag at the smell yet will myself to continue on.
Just a little more…
I continue to drag myself.
Finally reaching him, I place my hands upon him.
Shaking him, I try to get a response.
None.

Please gods, don't be dead.
Please be alive!

He is lying on his stomach; I can see his back.
A large gash is going from his left shoulder to his right side.
It bleeds profusely.
I place my hands the wound.

YOU ARE ALREADY WEAKENED!
I WOULD NOT CAST ANY MORE.

I ignore and focus on the wound.
Closing my eyes I focus not on the wound and the blood, but instead on what it should look like.
A strong, smooth back.
I focus harder and harder.

Heal.

I think constantly as I will the wound to heal.
I reopen my eyes and smile wryly as I see it happen.

Am I seeing it?
Or am I dreaming?
My vision is so blurry.

The skin begins to knit itself together, slowly but surely weaving itself together until it is sealed completely shut, leaving a long haphazard scar.

Wound healed; I push with all my might.
I only manage to get him onto his side, I quickly lean down and place my ear to his chest.
I listen for what feels like a lifetime before finally I hear it.
The thumping sound of a heart.
Yet it is weakened, and depleting.

I will not let this happen, I have not finally found acceptance and love only for it to be taken away.
I place both my hands on his chest and begin to focus on his heart.

STOP IT!
YOU WILL KILL YOURSELF!

I ignore once again.

Beat faster, beat stronger!

I think.

WHAT ARE YOU DOING!

Saving him!

YOU'RE WASTING YOUR POWER!
YOUR CHAOS!

YOU COULD DIE!

I don't care!

I continue to focus.

Beat faster, beat stronger!

I will his heart to listen to me, to take heed of my command.
My eyes narrow even more, I can feel myself slipping away.
I don't care, I continue.

Beat faster, beat stronger!

I think one last final time with my remaining strength.
The world begins to close around me then, darkness surrounding me.
But then I feel it, that soft heartbeat begins to pound away.
Strong and healthy.
It thumps away with force.

Thump, Thump, Thump!

It worked!

I think gladly, finally letting the darkness overtake me, the voices of
men that seemed so close now seem so distant.
I slip into the darkness with a smile knowing I saved him; I saved my
love.

A FEW MOMENTS LATER

CLAUDIUS

I shake my head in frustration and say a silent prayer, hoping that everything goes to plan.
If I arouse suspicion, if I get caught, I surely will be killed in the most brutal of ways.
I had enjoyed the warmth of the castle, it was true, yet I am wide awake.
Wide awake with worry.
Worry if the plan will succeed or fail.
Worried if I am doing the right thing.

But there is one question that is foremost in my mind.

Why did she want him dead so badly?

After all, he is just the spare, not the heir.
And yet, he is the beloved Prince with the Emerald Eyes.

I think on this as I quickly wrap my cloak around me, and shove on my boots.
Imperial Guards are already outside, waiting on me.
And surely the others have released the creature. . .

Prayers to the needy.

That is what I had told them and will be my answer of anyone that asks.

I leave my room, and several Guards stand there.

I nod to them, and they nod back.

I walk hurriedly down the steps, the men with me.

The castle is cold, I pull my cloak tighter around me as I weave down corridors.

The cold bites even harder as I make my way out to the castle courtyard.

A large, sprawling space.

It is late at night, nearing the early hours of the morning.

The moon hangs still in the sky, yet it will not last too much longer.

Guards stand sleepily by.

Slaves walk about, like at all hours of the day and night, going about their duties.

The courtyard also being where the stables are located.

Rain comes down hard, the moonlight emanating from the puddles collecting on the cobblestones.

YES, IT HAS TO BE A FULL MOON.
JUST LIKE SHE SAID.

There was power in such things as full moons.

I push the notion aside as I nod to the men closest to me who nod in return.

A couple of them quickly make their way to the stable to get my horse, as well as any other spare that does not belong to any Lord or Lady.

I stand there impatiently when I notice another guard walk over, having taken an interest.

I stay calm as he slowly but surely makes his way to me.

"Everything ok, here?"

He asks, his voice hard.

I look at him and smile warmly.
He is middle aged, and on the heavier side.
His plain silver tunic barely fitting.
The only thing of colour being an orange sun with a simple gold crown
encircled on the breastplate.

"Yes, everything is fine."

I respond.

I had hoped that would be the end of it.
It should have been the end of it.
Yes, it seems as if this particular guard does not know his place.

"A bit late to be out for a ride, sir."

 He mentions.

Before I have a chance to respond, a slave comes running down the
steps bounding straight towards us.

This is unexpected…

His skin matches the night sky.
Coming to a halt, he gasps and pants hard.

"What do you want?"

The same annoyed Guard asks.

I too wanted to know, but I also need to leave.
And I need to leave, NOW!

The slave keeps his head to the floor.

"The Prince, the Prince is gone."

He speaks frantically.

Damn you!
Damn you straight to the hottest hell!

Of course, I knew the prince was gone.
It was not the first time he had snuck out the castle, in fact, it's why I
too had planned on leaving tonight.
I had been planning this for weeks.
Ever since I came back to this soulless and sinful place.
Everything had to be perfectly planned.
And now this stupid slave has messed things up.

"The prince?!
What do you mean he's gone?"

The same disgruntled Guard asks.

The slave still keeps his head hung low.

"He is not in his rooms."

The slave answers.

Before the Guard gets startled and alerts everyone, I quickly step in.

"Do not worry.
I'm sure he is not far.
After all, we are on an Island."

 I chuckle, trying to defuse the situation.

This was true enough, the Imperium was built on an island, at the highest point of the cliffs.
Below was a vast woodland area, with many pathways, with the main one leading straight down, to the very bottom where several small fishing villages wrapped round the island.
The guards who had walked me from my room chuckled around me.
This seems to calm the inquisitive individual guard who dared to question me.
After all, he suspects nothing.
And why would he?

The Guards around me all look the same.
And why would they not?
Yet not is all as it seems…

Let's just say, these particular guards who stand with me shared…
Well, shall we say familiar ideologies.
The questionable guard still looks uncertain, so I assure him once more.

"I would not worry.
I was just about to go for a ride, anyhow.
I can look for the prince."

The guard does not seem satisfied, his eyes narrow at this.

"Yes, it's late though, isn't it?"

He questions, once again.

Inside, I am angry.
How dare this insignificant little man question me.
I want to slap him, hard.

Does he not know who I'm about to be?
The power I shall wield.
But I simply smile, keeping my cool.
The answer already thought of.

"Yes, but with The High Pope missing recently, may the Eternal Light protect him."

"May the Eternal Light protect him."

The other men around me chime.

The guard looks startled, but quickly recites the prayer.

"Yes, yes.
May the Lord of Eternal Light protect him."

 He stutters.

"With him missing, I have taken it upon myself to keep up with his duties.
I was going to ride to the fishing villages below, and share words of comfort in these uncertain times
It shall be dawn soon enough."

I answer.

The guard seems satisfied with this.

"Uh… Okay, sir.
Well, if you were going already."

"Yes, and as you can see, I have plenty of guards."

I gesture to the men around me.

He nods, satisfied.
Finally, my horse and a couple others are brought forward.
I am about to take my leave then; everything having gone to plan.

ALMOST.

Another slave comes stumbling down the stairs.
Upon seeing us, he makes a beeline towards us.

You have to be kidding me?!

"Guards, there is someone missing."

He pants hard.

I wave him away, smiling.
Although I am furious at a slave speaking without being spoken to first.
Does he not know his place?
I take a quick look around, making sure no other idiot slaves come forward.

"Do not worry, we already know the prince is not in the castle."

I say light heartedly.

How I wish I had been wrong; however, I was not.

"No, sir, it is not the prince.
I have been sent by Lady Umpire; she says her son is missing from his bed.
Kaleb Umpire is missing."

He pants.

Damn it!

All my planning, and yet this I had not planned for.
Despite the fact I should have!
The Prince and Kaleb were inseparable after all, always had been.

The prince had been known for his nightly wandering in the past.
He seemed to have kept these strolls to himself, Kaleb never accompanying him.
Yet tonight, of all nights, it seems the blasted warrior child has gone with the prince or followed him at least.

Damn it!

"It looks like I'll be looking for two boys, then."

I jest.

The guard does not seem amused however, he goes back to being concerned.

"Sir, with the prince missing and now Kaleb, perhaps we should put an alert out."

I wave this suggestion away, my smile still in place.

"I'm sorry, I didn't quite catch your name?"

I ask of him.

"Uh, oh, it's um, it's Todd."

He stutters.

Todd… An insignificant name for an insignificant man.

"Well Todd, I do not see the point of alerting everyone in the castle?
And the King?
No, I doubt that would be a good idea.
Especially when I highly doubt they're missing.
It is just two boys out, most likely having fun.
They won't get off the island anyhow, too many Guards down at the Grand Bridge."

I note.

The Grand Bridge being a bridge that sprawled some several miles, connecting this island to the mainland.

"And I have Guards with me, so no doubt we will find them easy enough."

I speak.

This Todd fellow seems to nod in agreement, his face slightly softening.

Thank the Light, I have wasted too much time on this fool.

I go to take my horse then, when a third interruption happens.

Another thing I had not planned for.

A soft, high voice rung out.

"Did I just overhear that Kaleb is missing?"

I swear to the Lord above, if this is another slave I shall have them whipped to death.

I turn and my smile goes immediately.

I should have prayed to the Lord of Eternal Light for another interrupting slave.

A slave would have been better.

But no such luck was to be found.

Instead, I find myself stood in front of a Slayer of the Syndicate.

A surprisingly youthful young boy, yet a Slayer nonetheless.

Dressed fully in black armour with a black cloak.

They hunt and slay vampires after all, and their grim and dark attire helps them blend into the shadows to fight the demons.

On his breastplate, a bright red sun with a Black Oak stake through it.

And yet despite his youth, it would be foolish to misjudge him.

After all, to be a fully-fledged Slayer you had to of passed the rigorous Initiation process.

An Initiation process that requires you to slay a vampire to even be asked to join the ranks.

Yet, it seems not everyone has to slay a vampire around here to become an Initiate as of late.

A sore spot I could surely count on in the future.

"He is not missing."

 I answer.

"He has simply gone for a walk, no doubt.
I am heading to find him now, with these guards."

 I gesture around me.

I go for my horse again, when I hear him speak up.

"I'll join you."

I stop dead in my tracks.
Turning around, I have a wryly smile fixed on my face.

"I thank you, but I doubt I will need your presence."

 I assure.

"And yet I shall come anyways."

 He answers back, immediately.

"Kaleb is an Initiate of the Syndicate, and the beloved nephew of the
Lord Commander.
It is my duty to check that he is ok.
If I do not, the Lord Commander would surely use my bones as a
toothpick."

He smiles at this, and the men around all share various chuckles.

Yes, Kaleb Umpire.
The prized warrior child.
Beloved by many.
Almost as much as the prince.

I look up at the moon, it is beginning it's descension already.
I should have left by now, already on my horse riding through the woods below.
I have to leave now, before it's too late and real alarms go off.

Surely it would happen soon, or even any moment now.
Yes, I had to leave.
Before the screams start.
Or maybe there would not be any screams?
Perhaps it would be over quickly, before they even had a real chance.

Yes, she wants the prince dead and gone…
A Prince that was meant to be alone.
And now he has Kaleb with him, an Inititation of the Syndicate!
And now you have a fully-fledged Slayer coming with you!

I want to scream.
I want to dismiss him.
To just get on my horse without these damned, unplanned interruptions.
I know however I cannot outwardly refuse a Slayer of the Syndicate.
Not without risking suspicion.
So instead, with my teeth held tightly together, I smile and speak.

"Of course.
Ride with us."

Damn.

PERHAPS YOU SHOULD ABANDON THIS PLAN NOW.
YOU NEVER INTENDED ON THESE UNEXPECTED CHANGES.

No, I cannot back down now.

I have planned this for months, even before returning to this wretched Capital.
I've been working for years… Under **her**.
And I cannot back out now.
No, if I do, then everything will become undone.
All of God's work.

YOU ARE NOT DOING GOD'S WORK.
YOU ARE DOING HER WORK.

God spoke to me, as he did so often.
Yet I did not always understand.

No, I did God's work.
Only God's work…

IS IT GOD'S WORK TO BE OUT IN THE PISSING RAIN RIGHT NOW?

No, it indeed was not.

BUT YOU HAVE TO CHECK IF THE PLAN WORKED!
HER PLAN!

God's plan!

Her plan or God's plan… Regardless I knew I would be riding out.

Even if now I am accompanied by this Slayer.
It was true after all, I had to see if the plan worked.

IT'S DEFINITELY HER PLAN!
YOU SAY YOU DO GODS WORK!
BUT REALLY IT BE THE DEVIL!

No, God has a plan…
And this is part of the plan.
It has to be.

BE TRUTHFUL, GOD HAS NO PART OF THIS!
HER PLAN, HER PLAN, HER PLAN!
YOU DO IT FOR WHAT SHE CAN OFFER YOU!
YOU WANT TO BE THE HOLY POPE!
TO HAVE COMMAND OF ARMIES!
SHE IS EVEN ALLOWING YOU TO DO YOUR CLEANSE!
AND PLAY KING!

Allowing me?!
No one allows me!
I have used what she had to offer and now I make my own plans.
Yes, a Cleanse shall come indeed like she wanted, but it shall be who carries it out!
And she thinks I'm loyal… Ha!
Perhaps for years in the past, but no longer…

BUT WHAT ABOUT YOUR PRECIOUS GOD?
I THOUGHT THIS WAS FOR HIM?
ADMIT IT, YOU'RE JUST AS SELF SERVING AS EVERYONE ELSE!
YOU CRAVE POWER AND HIDE BEHIND GOD!
WHAT IF THE CREATURE DOES NOT SUCCEED,
SHE SHALL NOT BE HAPPY!
SHE MAY HAVE YOU KILLED, OR WORSE!

Red eyes come to mind, the eyes of a demon.

I had been given the poison, and the blood.

Yet the creatures' eyes had been black, after all it had not been fed for weeks… as per her command.

SEE, IT IS HER THAT COMMANDS!
NOT YOU!
NOT YOU!

"You! Come with us,"

The Slayer says to Todd.

The Slayer then turns to me and adds.

"One more guard couldn't help."

I could curse till I was blue in the face, yet I know I do not have time to argue.
I have wasted enough time already.

"You two."

I point to the slaves.

"You will follow on foot."

I command.

They will be dealt with indeed.

"Let us leave."

I then snap, saddling my horse finally.

I waste not an iota of time, before my backside barely hits the saddle,
I immediately let out a loud shout and ride hard, straight out of the
open gate, leaving the rest behind me.

Despite riding hard, the Slayer caught up on his horse in no time, the
rest follow behind on their own horses.

I wind down the many undulating paths, before finally taking a sharp
right, the sound of waves crashing can be heard all around.

I know the creature had been left close by… Sleeping and drugged,
waiting to awaken.
I only prayed it did not awaken and see us instead of its intended target.
As I get closer an awful smell hits me hard, the smell of burning flesh.
That was something unexpected… What in the name of Light?
I am indeed worried, of course.
I do not like changes, they worry me greatly.
And yet I kicked myself for not expecting it, for having not seen these
unexpected changes.

I knew the boys were extremely close, and I should have made plans
for the fact that Kaleb could have joined or followed him at any time.
After all, some would say that they are too close…
But that was a conversation for another time I suppose.

Yes, always together.
Hardly ever apart.

And indeed, too close…

And I was not the only one it seemed that had noticed.

After all, whispers have already spread around the castle.

Even when they were younger these whispers started.

I had not been here for years of course, returning only weeks ago…

And yet the rumours had stayed.

And I had seen it myself.

I of course had to stalk my victim, and I saw much more than I intended when watching the young Prince.

After all, they shared longing looks at each other.

And when they would practise swordplay together in the courtyard, it usually ended up with them wrestling playfully.

And when they did wrestle, it seemed to go on longer than it should, usually ending up on the ground and sometimes the wrestling even seemed inappropriate…

I had even seen that they would brush their fingertips against each other when they thought no one was looking.

And they also shared long looks with one another, their eyes giving away their love.

Yes, I saw much, as did others, and people whispered in secret, and yet no one dared breathe it out loud.

Yes, the Prince with the Emerald Eyes, and the Prized Warrior child.

And they were both completely, madly in love with one another.

And now I'm riding with a Slayer and that pesky guard named Todd who dared question me.

And of course, the two slaves who somehow managed to keep up with the horses.

They are fast indeed, despite being chained.

I suppose they have their uses.
And yet, I could hardly leave them back at the Imperium.

Not a chance.

There could be no loose strings.
But it certainly was not the plan.
I said silent curses.
Curses at this stupid Todd who questioned me, riding behind me.
Silent curses for the unexpected slaves who had said both the Prince and Kaleb were missing.
Silent curses for the damned Slayer who decided to join.

Yes, I was seething, and my mood incredibly dark.
I will punish them all.

Yes, the slaves had ruined it, certainly.
If they had never run up to us, mentioning the prince or the warrior brats name then I would have surely been left alone to my own business and a damned Slayer would not be riding with me.
No, nothing it seemed thus far was going to plan.
Yes, the slaves had ruined it, and for that they shall pay with their lives.

That I would be sure of.

I continued to ride hard, I had to act like I was worried for the two boys.
The Slayer managed to keep pace, he rode his horse alongside me, the rest flanking us.
I looked over to him, he was young.
Incredibly young.
That may yet work in my favour.

He will not have years of battle experience, so he should be easier to dispose of.
Regardless, I still have to do what needs to be done.

The men called out the name of the prince, the name of Kaleb too.

We received no answer.

And then it happened…

A loud, otherworldly scream comes from further up in the woods.

The horses buckle and neigh nervously.

The Slayer comes to a halt, before shouting

"QUICKLY, WE MUST GO, THEY ARE IN DANGER."

He kicks hard and rides ahead with a wild fury.
I only hope he rides straight into the creature and is killed swiftly.
We hear another shriek, this one worse than before… A scream of death?

And what felt like… **Heat?**

It is still raining and yet the air around us suddenly feels very warm.
As if the very air itself has dried up.
Just through the thicket of trees, I can see smoke undulating upwards into the air.
And the smell… The burning smell of flesh.

Peculiar…

The prince was not seen carrying a torch when he left, and doubtful Kaleb had one either.

After all, torches brought too much attention, and if you are sneaking from a castle the last thing you want is attention.

And that creature certainly could not muster fire.

It assaults my nose, yet I continue on.

I get an overwhelming sense that the plan did not indeed work.

God be damned!

NOW, NOW.
I THOUGHT THAT THE LORD'S NAME SHOULD NOT BE
TAKEN IN VAIN.

My horse neighs and brays as we get closer, as if it senses my anxiety that the plan has failed, that these two boys were to be found alive and well.

The guards call out several times for both Tristan and Kaleb, yet no call is answered.

My horse continues to neigh and bray even louder.

Or it senses danger…

But how could it?

My mood already darkened at having to find these two foolish boys.

Whilst I could do nothing to his Highness, Prince Tristan, I could remand Kaleb.

After all, he gave up any lordly right he had ever possessed, now being an Initiate.

And even if he still retained what power he had, being the son of the General, there was no higher power like that reserved for the Imperial Family.

Not in the Human Realm anyway.

As I continue to ride, I notice something peculiar.

The pathway turns from muddy puddles to that of… **Flowers?**

Flowers of all different colours, flowers that had no right being here.

Neither the weather, the season or even the area where they are surely from.

No, these flowers were vibrant and wild, appearing as if from nowhere.

And… Is that what I think it is?
Is that snow?!
How in the name of God?

It is melting away, due to the rain, yet some still remains.

And that's when I see them.

Three bodies lay on the ground.

Two are that of humans, the other a nightmarish creature.

The two that are humans I can only assume are Tristan and Kaleb.

For a moment I have hope that the plan indeed did work.

DID HER PLAN WORK?
OR WAIT, WAS IT GOD'S PLAN INSTEAD…
OR WAS IT YOURS?

I shake my head at the thought.

The Slayer had already jumped from his horse, looking around at the ground, examining it heavily.

My own horse comes to slow trot as I come to a stop.

The men come to a halt too, and they quickly dismount.

The slaves surprisingly somehow manage to keep up the pace with the horses, even though their chains rattle heavily at the hands.

Yet they pant hard.

And they looked tired… **Good.**

The more tired, the less able to fight back.

"What is their condition."

I shout out to the Guards as I unhorse myself.

The men do not answer me.
Nor do they go to either the Prince or Kaleb.
Instead, they stand transfixed upon the corpse of the inhuman creature.

The Slayer pulls his gaze away from the flowers and what remains of the snow, and begins to push past the men, kneeling low, assessing the burnt remains.

I say a silent curse at the child, his black cloak spread around him.
I really wish he had not come along, yet I could hardly have said no to him.
No, not in a courtyard with other slaves and servants walking around, and guards standing at their posts.

No, slave and servants and even guards talked.

THEY WOULD NOT TALK IF THEY HAD HO TONGUES…

He kneeled there, a mere boy amongst men.
The men stood transfixed, surrounded behind the Slayer and the corpse.
I suppose they had never seen such a corpse.
It was shocking to look at.
It appeared almost as if it is a huge bat, however it was so badly burned that all you could see were bones, sharp claws and a set of sharp fangs.

"WHAT DO YOU THINK YOU ARE DOING?
ATTEND TO YOUR PRINCE AT ONCE!

I shout.

"AND PRAY THAT HE IS WELL."

I also shout, feigning ignorance.

Several guards dutifully do as they are told; they walk several paces and crouch down to check upon the prince.
Meanwhile the Slayer stays crouched, examining the creature.

This angers me, they should ALL listen when commanded.

> ***BUT WHO ARE YOU TO COMMAND ANYONE?***
> ***WHAT ARE YOU?!***
> ***YOU DO NOT GIVE ORDERS!***
> ***IT IS YOU WHO IS ORDERED!***
> ***BY YOUR PRECIOUS GOD AND YOUR DARK QUEEN!***
> ***YOU ARE NOTHING!***

Maybe not yet… But I shall be.
I shall be the one who brings the Light.
I am resolute in this.
Yes, the time is coming, a time where I shall take command.
A time where God's glorious Light will finally shine on this darkened land.
It shall cast the shades and shadows away, and in its place a burning brightness.
This land has been godless for too long.
Allowing disgusting, filthy witches to roam the land.
But not much longer, no, the time is drawing near.
A glorious cleansing will come.

My men will only grow in number.
They already reach thousands.
The love of God will grow.

I shall cleanse this Capital of sin and spread throughout the Human Realm.

And one day, one day I will even march on the cursed Magic and Dark Realms themselves.

And further still.

YOU REALLY THINK WILL HAPPEN?
THAT SHE WOULD NOT FIND A WAY TO SLIT YOUR THROAT
IN YOUR SLEEP IF YOU DARED THINK OF BETRAYING HER?

She has no idea what my plans are, my real plans.

Yes, the splendid light will reach all.

BUT WHAT ABOUT WHAT SHE WANTS?
DO NOT LIE TO YOURSELF, YOU ARE NOT BRINGING LIGHT!
YOU ARE BRINGING DARKNESS!
YOUR STILL JUST A SERVANT!

The Slayer looks at me, and goes

"This is clearly the corpse of a vampire."

He states.

You do not say!

I think, annoyed.

I look at the corpse myself then, a real hard look.

It's more bat than human, with the remnants of huge wings still.

The filthy rags he had been wearing had once been beautiful, yellow robes.

He has been missing for weeks… Except I knew where he was.

I had my men take him after all.

It was his own fault, old idiot disagreed completely with my own views.

He honestly thought these Casters were harmless, and therefore let them be.

Just fellow humans with **'Gifts'** he thought

But I saw these **'Gifts'** for what they were… **Power.**

And the only one who should have power should be God.

AND YOU!
POWER WILL BE DANGEROUS IN YOUR HANDS.
ANOTHER THING YOU DID FOR HER…

I did it for me.
She may have told me to kill him, but that was no command.
No, I killed the silly old fool for sheer pleasure.

ANOTHER MURDER…
AND MORE TO COME.
YOUR HEART BLACKENS.

I did what I had too.

The Slayer looks around then, gazing at his surroundings.

"These flowers, they have no right being here.
And they travel along the footpath."

He gestures to where we rode in.

"And even behind us."

He gestures the other way.

"They are all full bloom, and some I have never seen before.
They aren't local to this region of the Human Realm.
And this snow…"

He looks around, amazed and confused.
The men had taken notice of the Slayers words, and they follow his gaze, all looking around at the flowers and snow.

"THE PRINCE, IS HE OKAY?"

I shout once again, hoping to get attention away from the Initiate.

"Still breathing."

 Shouts one of them, examining both the Prince and Kaleb.

"Yes, the Prince, he's alive."

Shouts another.

"And Kaleb too!"

Says a third.

DAMN!

My plan has failed miserably… I have failed.

YOU'VE FAILED, YOU'VE FAILED, YOU'VE FAILED!
SHE SHALL NOT BE HAPPY!
SHE SHALL SURELY ORDER YOUR DEATH!

All the men seem overjoyed.
The prince is well loved.

It irritates me greatly.

The General's son too…

I had plotted on the prince's life and failed… But I still have one idea in play.

SHE WILL KILL YOU!

No, she would not dare get rid of me, not when she knows that she needs me and my influence to even carry out her plans in the first place. And she would not waste all these years of hard work, of that I am sure.

After all, it was her who sought me out.

It was her who came to me with her devilish plans.

She needed me.

The Slayer does not move, he still looks around, his eyes feel of scrutiny.

"Where in the name of Light has this snow come from."

 He mutters out loud to himself.

"It's not snowed for a while."

He goes on.

"And it's been raining for weeks.

By right, there should be no snow.

And it's only in one area, although nearly melted."

He points around our feet.

It is true, the more he speaks, the faster it melts.

The answer is quite simple, and I know that the Slayer is about to say the answer any moment.

The answer is simple.

This had been done by magic.

I knew it the second I saw the flowers and snow.

Witchcraft wasn't exactly easy to hide.

It stunk heavily of magic, I could smell it almost as well as the burnt corpse, its white bone sticking out from melted flesh.

This was another unexpected change.

The flowers, the snow, and the burnt-out creature… Only a witch could do this.

And a witch certainly was not part of the plan.

Or was it?

It comes to me then… A horrible realisation.

One even I had been blind to.

But there was only one explanation for it.

The prince was able to Cast…

I know it was not Kaleb, his pesky uncle would have made sure of that years ago.

It was a simple test of course that was carried out by Slayers, at every Spiral throughout the Human Realm.

All those promised to join the Syndicate were tested before even being allowed to become an Initiate.

They merely placed a chunk of Saerillian Silver on one's skin.

Usually using their swords, all made from Saerillian Silver also.

If it burned; you were a witch and disallowed from joining.

However, if your skin did not burn, you were human and therefore allowed to join the Syndicate.

Not only that, but if you were a witch, then you would be branded for life, so everyone knew.

They may live amongst us, but their burns mean they cannot hide so easily.

They are well documented also.

The Grand Spiral keeps thorough records of all known witches.

Something which if goes to plan, it will prove extremely useful.

After all, it's only the witches I want dead.

However, the Prince would have received no such test, and why would he?

They were above the laws of man after all, being closer to the gods.

I had always wondered why.

There was nothing special about them, they were flesh and blood like the rest of us.

Yet because of their royalty they supposedly were closer to gods.

Ridiculous if you ask me, there is only one God.

The true God.

The God of Eternal Light, whose Light shines upon us all, cleansing us and making us whole and empty of sin.

THAT'S WHY SHE WANTS HIM DEAD!

But why him though?

Witches infested this Human Realm, whilst it was not prohibited or illegal to Cast magic, it was deeply frowned up and they were thankfully persecuted, thus not often revealing themselves.

Humans did not trust witches, yet they did walk amongst us.

It made me sick.

The High Pope did not see the dangers of these witches, nor had his idiotic predecessors.

They could be your neighbour, your best friend, brother or sister, even a lover.

It sickened me how easy they could hide, pretending as if they were real humans and not Soulless Abominations.

Focusing instead on God's light being about unity and friendship, when really it should be about exterminating those who do not believe, who do not possess Souls.

AND THAT IS WHAT MADE YOU COME UNDER HER GAZE.
ALL THOSE YEARS AGO...
YOU WERE A MERE YOUNG MAN THEN...
NOW YOU ARE MIDDLE AGED.
A LIFETIME OF WORK...
YOUR PREJUDICE, YOUR HATRED... YOUR BLACK HEART.

I suppose my views could be misconstrued as hatred, yes, but there is only one good thing for a witch and that's immediate death.

And the men who followed and believed in me had the similar frame of mind.

And not just the men I recruited here within the Imperium and islands surrounding it, but men and even women spreading out into the Capital, and further throughout the Human Realm.

I had humble beginnings it's true, but I rose quickly when I shouted and cheered my views of witches.

Is it my fault the crowds I gathered agreed?

Is it my fault they too have hatred in their hearts?

I had even managed to come to the Capital, I had a wife and three children.

That was years ago, however.

I had been here for months, and my words grew many numbers of people.

Big crowds would form wherever I went.

I was winning power, that was evident.

And just like that I was sent away.

The High Pope and the blasted council got involved, and I was sent packing.

I had to leave my children here.

In fact, since my return a few weeks ago I had not seen any of them for years.

My mission and the open road too dangerous for mere children.

And I shall make that damned council pay for that.

The High Pope already got what he deserved.

The rest shall pay soon.

And yet, it seems this worked in my advantage.

So I went, exiled, and once again I travelled far and wide just as I had before.

I went back to the same villages, towns and other cities where I had once travelled before and the crowds came running to me, eager at my return.

And during those years in what I could call exile I found countless who shared my views, who knew the truth about these Soulless creatures.

Yes, I spent many meticulous years growing my faction of like-minded men.

I spent my time as a Holy Man, a real Holy Man.

Once I saw the threat and danger they possessed.

Yes, I indeed travelled far and wide spreading God's Light to those that needed it most, even the desolate small villages along the coastlines to those growing just outside of the Black Woods.

Witches were prominent there, and I nearly got killed once or twice.

But God kept me safe.

Yes, I had indeed dared to go as far as there, I wanted the witches to know I showed no fear, nor did I appreciate their ungodly ways.
Yes, in all those places I spread my words and views that God's Light is not about love, but about cleansing one's soul.
And that the soulless are God's abominations, that those without souls are not worthy of God and his Light, that they need to be exterminated so that those with souls can truly be saved.

I believe in God's cleansing Light and that alone.
And anyone who does not accept the cleansing Light shall be pulled out root and stem until there is none left.

So yes, I saw these 'Gifts' for what they were… **Power**.

And the only one whom should have power should be God.

AND YOU!
POWER WILL BE DANGEROUS IN YOUR HANDS.

I look over to the prince, still laying in the muddy puddles and flowers.
The snow now finally gone.
But why this certain witch…

Was it because he was an Imperial?

It was true she vehemently hated the Imperial Dynasty with a passion, determined to extinguish their line, and has proudly has killed many Imperial members over the centuries…

But he is just the spare, not the heir.
He would not be King nor hold any real power.
He was the second son, not worth much other than to be a Lord with his own castle and lands one day.

I am pulled from these thoughts as the Slayer finally stands straight, and loudly proclaims.

"This is a feral vampire."

He says out loud.

You don't say.

I think once again, equally annoyed.

It is obvious this creature is not from our Realm, and only one creature looks like this.
A vampire turned feral.
The rest of the men mutter between themselves.
He then takes it a step further, trying to pull out commands.

"We should report back to the castle at once.
We need carts to transport the prince and Kaleb, and the healers.
We also need to send messengers to the Grand Spiral."

"Why does the Grand Spiral need to be involved."

Todd stupidly speaks.
The rest of the men being dutifully and deathly silent.
I do not want the Slayer to answer so I do it for him.

"Because you fool, Kaleb is the Lord Commander's nephew.
Not to mention the son of the bloody General.
Are you a bloody idiot?!"

It was not a question; it was an insult.
He hangs his head in shame and the rest of the men snigger.
The rest shuffle around nervously.

I pull my own cloak around me, trying to keep what warmth I can.

The Slayer turns to me.

"Actually, it's because this is a vampire and anything to do with vampires needs to be seen directly by the Syndicate.
How in the hell did it even get here?
We are on a bloody island.
This clearly needs investigating and investigating immediately.
We also need to ascertain how in the name of Light this vampire was killed"

The Slayer says.

For a moment I think he's stupid, it's clear how the creature died until he says the following.

"It was killed with fire, yet I see neither the prince nor Kaleb with a torch.
And even if they did…"

He leans down, touching the creature's arm.
As he does ash falls away, so badly burned as it is.

"What torch do you think could have fire this hot?

He looks around again.

"And the flowers… Even the snow… There's only one logical answer."

He has been dancing around the question, yet now he wants to address it.

Silly boy, does he not know he's signing his own death warrant.

HOW GODLY IT MUST BE TO KILL AN INNOCENT.

Yet he wasn't innocent, was he?
None of the Slayers are or their Initiates.
I'm sure this one is as sinful and destructive as the rest.
They don't adhere to the laws and regulations of men, of our Faith, they deal with demons and witches and thus becomes half soulless themselves.

BUT HE IS JUST A BOY.

A boy, yes, however this particular one is far too inquisitive besides.
Never did I like someone who talked too much or asked questions.

And this boy is doing both.
Shame but true.
He had to go.

He stands up, looking around again.

"This is magic.
Clear and simple."

The men prick their ears up at this.
The men secretly under my command do not have knowledge of the kidnapping of the High Pope, nor this assassination attempt.
And yet they know if we have any chance of bringing about the Cleansing, I promised then the Syndicate can surely not be sniffing around.
Neither had they anything to do with the kidnapping of the High Pope.

No, the beasts who had helped me kidnap the old fool had been slaves, already killed and dealt with.

I may have persuaded some Imperial Guards to agree with my hatred of witchcraft, but this was due to a deep hatred of magic which spans centuries and runs deep in many humans.

However, if they thought for one moment that I wanted to kill an Imperial they would surely turn on me also.

The love for the Imperial Family is strong.

And I certainly cannot have my own men questioning me, not when I'm just starting to build my… **DEFENCES.**

The Slayer stands.

Being brazen, he points to one of my men and says again, louder and clearer this time.

"You there, get back to the castle immediately.
Bring carts, and the healers.
And alert the Syndicate.
Do it now."

The man remains unmoving.

The boy looks affronted.
As if he genuinely suspects that his so called **'orders'** would be followed.

"Did you not hear me?"

He tries so hard to sound in command, yet the high tones in his youthful voice say otherwise.

The men remain unmoving.
All apart from Todd who looked around quizzically.

"Uh… I could go."

He volunteers.

Silly fool, if you had not stopped to question me, you would be safe back at your post right now.

"They are not yours to command."

I say silently to the Slayer, yet filled with detest for thinking that he could have commanded anyone.

"They are Imperial Guards and will do as told when lives are at risk!"

Yes, they were indeed Imperial Guards.
But as I said earlier, not everyone is as they seem…

The Slayer's footsteps make slushing sounds across the mud as walks toward me, trampling the flowers as he does, his face growing angry.

"What reason would they even have to be here other than to serve?"
And what reason do you even have here?
Are you planning on praying them better?"

BLASPHEMY!

"The reason they are here."

I speak through gritted teeth.

I take a step forward, and the guards take their positions.

Todd and slaves do not notice.
They have been so distracted by the Slayer and my own conversation that they do not realise what is about to happen.

YES, YES!
DO IT NOW!

I look at the Slayer and smile.
An evil, delicious smile.

"Why, they are here to kill you, of course."

The Slayer scoffs at me, only for a second however, as the guards, MY GUARDS, all brandish knives.

They stab and thrust wildly at Todd and the two slaves.
The young Slayer turns around, pulling his sword, the Saerillian steel shines bright as what's left of the moonlight hits it.
He faces them, shocked and confused, I'm sure.

However, his mistake is turning his back on me.

The rest of my plan may have failed, but this shall surely not.

Brandishing my own knife, I quickly step up behind him and thrust hard into his back.

Over, and over again until blood drenches my hand.
He yells out in pain and falls to the ground.

THIS IS NOT WHAT SHE TOLD YOU TO DO!
YOU WERE NOT SUPPOSED TO DO THIS!

SHE SHALL NOT BE HAPPY!

But what can she really do?

She wanted me to attempt to kill the prince, and the plan did not work. And I can't let this silly boy alert the whole damned Syndicate, especially not right before I'm about to start the greater plans.
No, this was not my fault, but hers for underestimating her enemy.

But why is the prince her enemy?!

The sound of the dying boy brings me back, I calmly take out a cloth and begin to wipe away the blood on my blade.

He manages to roll onto his back, facing up at me.

"Why… Why…"

He cries, choking on his own blood.
He weakly reaches for his sword, but I kick it away and kneel.

"Because your silly Syndicate shall ask too many questions, carry investigations, and well, I simply don't have time for that.
I have great plans you see. I've been growing a faction.
For years now… I hadn't at first meant too, I was simply preaching.
But the faction grew all the same.
A faction of like-minded, God-fearing, Witch hating people.
Good people.
Godly people.
People who believe the witches need to be wiped out, like I do."

"But the Slayers… We hunt."

He coughs blood.

"You hunt vampires, you only kill Witches who you have to.
Meanwhile hundreds upon hundreds of them live in the Human Realm,
acting as if they were real humans."

"They… They are humans."

He coughs, more blood pours from his lips.
He is clearly a sympathiser.

BLASPHEMY!

"And yet whom are we at war with?
The Witch Queen… And who are her armies?
Bloodthirsty, bloodsucking monsters.
Monsters those witches brought upon us.
Summoned them from some unimaginable hell.
They should be held accountable, all of them.
And I shall see that they do."

He takes a final breath then, finally dying.

"God has spoken to me. |He has presented me with instruments to bring
about his Cleanse…
Not just witches, but sympathisers too.
Those who share your… view of them as **'humans',** shall be taught
the right way of thinking.
And those who cast shall all see God's Light; they shall see it in the
fire when they die.
Soon every Witch in this Realm shall be dead."

I am talking to a corpse.

I begin to pant hard; I had not killed someone so brutally before.
The High Pope was poisoned… And then reborn.
And technically it was Tristan who truly killed him.

I looked down at the Slayer, lying dead, covered in blood.
It pooled around him.
He looked so young… I push away the pang of guilt.

It had to be done, he would have talked.
They all would of.
That could not do.

"What shall we do about the prince?"

Asks one of my men, pulling me back to the present.

I glance at my men, and they all proudly move their cloaks aside from their chest, revealing their hidden pins on their tunics.

A white sun with a sword through it.

The white sun being the sigil for the Faith for these last few centuries, however I added the sword myself.
To show that now we are armed, and now we meant to do what God really intended, and that's the destruction of the damned witches.
The emblem of my men, of the Defence of the Lord and his Eternal Light.

I take a final look down at the dead boy, before stepping away from him and walking over to the prince.

He lay there, almost as if he was asleep.
Blood pours from his nose, mouth and even ears.

I have seen it happen in witches before.

The prince has drained his Chaos… I have seen and heard of it, witches who Cast too much, thus exerting themselves physically.

So much so that they are rendered unconscious or even dead.

Yes, he put himself in a comatose state.

He is alive and will wake, although when he wakes will be a matter of guessing.

Could be days, could be weeks.

Kaleb on the other hand was a different story, laid on his side.

I could evidently see the back of his tunic ripped, with blood soaked around him.

And yet blood did not continue to pour.

Odd, a wound like this would usually continue to bleed and surely mean death.

I crouch down and examine the wound… Miraculously it's healed.

The skin is already knitted back together, and the blood completely stopped, leaving a huge scar which would stretch across his back.

Something like this would take weeks or even months to heal properly, that's if infection didn't set in and kill, which happened with most.

And yet the wound was completely healed…

I look back the prince, and I soften.

I do not know why I soften; I have just murdered a boy after all and had my men slaughter Todd and two slaves, yet soften I did.

I may not have been here to see it happen, yet I can only assume that Kaleb protected the prince… **And lost**.

Grief and rage taken over, the prince cast a fireball at the feral who was once our High Pope.

Casting magic from what I've seen is heavily based on emotions after all.

I'm guessing whatever strength he had remaining after igniting the feral, he used to heal Kaleb… his lover.

Yes, this only proved they were lovers…

Only love could spell this much hatred.

I lean over place my hand on the prince's chest, I can feel a heartbeat.
A soft thump, yet there all the same.
But waning fast, he would die soon if not treated.

> *IT IS A GOOD THING HE EXERTED HIMSELF AND PUT HIMSELF IN A SLUMBER.*
> *MAKING FLOWERS GROW AND SNOW FALL…*
> *SETTING A FERAL ON FIRE AND COMPLETELY HEALING A WOUND THAT WOULD OTHERWISE MEAN CERTAIN DEATH.*
> *AND THE FEROCITY OF THE FIRE WHICH KILLED THAT FERAL…*
> *AND ALL AT SUCH A YOUNG AGE!*
> *THIS IS AN INCREDIBLY POWERFUL WITCH!*
> *YOU WOULD NEVER HAVE KILLED HIM IF HE WAS AWAKE…*
> *BUT HE IS SLEEPING, RIGHT THERE ON THE GROUND!*
> *SO JUST SLIT HIS THROAT.*
> *DO IT QUICKLY!*
> *DO IT NOW!*

"Are we killing him?"

Asks one of my men.

A silly mistake.

I had not revealed my plans to kill Tristan.
These men had been told exactly what I told the dead guard and dead Slayer.

I meant to go and pray to the fishing villages at the bottom of the Island.

Yes, they may be under my command, and they may have just partaken in the murder of a fellow guard, two slaves and a Slayer, but that's because they believe wholly in my plans for the witches.
The plan that I've told all of them is from God.

But they would never be part of the death of an Imperial.

Not right now at least.

Not with the King still alive…

But maybe… Maybe soon they will change their mind.
Perhaps even help me end the Dynasty…

But not right now.
Too much had gone wrong.
Right now, I need to keep my cover, and more importantly cover my tracks.
I may not be liked by the Council or even the King, but so far they do not know of my treachery.

And if I'm the one to save the Prince and General's son… Surely that would make them soften towards me, not to mention make me a hero… Albeit, temporarily.

Standing up, I look to one of my other men.

"You would attempt to kill an Imperial?"

I say, pretending to be utterly shocked.

"Kill him."

I command pointing to the man who asked the question.

The guards duly do so, they will not stand a threat against their Prince after all.

He looks startled as he is quickly stabbed and killed, his startled expression still fixed on the face of his corpse as he falls to the ground.

"Let me make one thing clear.
We were never here to kill or harm the prince."

LIES, LIES, LIES!

Some of them look as if they knew it was lie and yet said nothing.
I look at their faces, to see what they are thinking.

Another speaks up.

"Sir… Is this allowed?
Killing these people…"

He seemed nervous, and once he has mentioned this so do the others.

"Remember the reason you are here!
Remember that this is God's work!
God has spoken, he has shown me the great Cleansing to come.
Witches will finally be free of this land!
So yes, this is allowed.
These men had to be killed, for the sake of making sure the eradication of witches happens! Finally, the Human Realm will just be humans, and soon, the entire country!

You are warriors of his Light,
You are defenders of the faith!"

That's when it hits me.
The perfect name for my new army.

DEFENDERS.

"Tell me men, are you God's Defenders?"

They begin to cheer.

"Are you, my Defenders?
Will you help me Defend God, will you help me kill these witches for once and all?!"

They cheer even louder.

Good… I have them under my control.

"This it to be kept quiet, no one shall speak of this.
Not about the feral, nor this Slayer, or even the guard and slaves."

I point to their dead bodies.
I then point to that of the Prince and Kaleb.

"We have saved the Prince and Kaleb Umpire!
Those who do as they're told, shall be rewarded handsomely.
I shall speak to the King and make it so.
And then the Cleansing!"

The men nod their heads enthusiastically, eager as the mere thought of being rewarded.

Eager at the thought of finally cleansing our land and killing these vile witches.

The sudden sound of men in the distance unnerves me.
Men crying out for the prince and for Kaleb, and even myself.

Damn!

I had mere moments, if that.
I take one final look at the prince.
I know that I should kill him, that way there is no ramifications from her…
And yet I simply cannot do it.
Not just because I have guards surrounding me, guards who for all intents and purposes still obeyed, followed and loved the Imperial Dynasty.
But because for some reason, I find the prince protecting his lover oddly touching.

A rare thought indeed.

As two boys in love, it goes against everything I believe in, I find it disgusting even.
And I hate magic with a furious passion, and I should certainly kill the prince…
But not right now.

SHE WANTS HIM DEAD!
KILL HIM AND RUN!

No, I will not run.
Not now, not ever.
I have amassed an army and given them a name.

Yet oddly enough, I do not, in this moment, care.
 I really, really do not.
The boy had battled a feral and lived to tell the tell, God clearly did not want him dead.
And what threat is he to me?

But he is clearly a threat to her!
Why else would she want him dead so badly?!

The fact the Witch Queen feared anyone was ludicrous…
And betraying her like I was planning on doing…
Well, you had to be crazy to do that.

Yet, she seemed very eager for these plans to be fulfilled with urgency, and it had to be fulfilled under the full moon.
A full moon which has now gone.
The land begins to lighten, but not by much as the sun is hidden by thick clouds.

Yes, she fears this boy… she has to.
She had instructed me to return a couple of moons ago and get to work quickly and quietly.
I knew I still had men who shared the same thoughts in the Capital, and despite my absence these last few years, they quickly found and rallied to me.
It was easier than I thought to get them to wear the pins and have their loyalty.
Yes, the hatred for witches runs deep.

AND YET IT IS HER WHO BROUGHT THE PLANS TO PURGE
THE WITCHES OF THE HUMAN REALM.

That in itself is odd…
She clearly has a plan, and that part I am not privy too.
That's fine, she is not privy to mine either.

WE ALL HAVE SECRETS IT SEEMS…
BUT IF SHE FEARS HIM, YOU DEFINITELY SHOULD!
DO NOT BE A FOOL, KILL HIM!
KILL HIM NOW!

I ignore this as the voices get closer and closer.
More men will be here any moment.

I shall spare the prince.

After all, if the Witch Queen truly does see him as threat, then that could be an asset to me.
Especially as I mean to betray her myself.
Indeed, she may have come to me in the dead of night and whispered sweet nothings into my ear, she may have ignited the fire which has taken hold of me and made me vie for power to begin with…
It was her who made me realise that I didn't have just followers, but an army.
It was her who told me to return to the Capital with her dark deeds.

Foolish really.
She should have realised that I would never be her servant, not really.
But if I get to pretend and have the power to purge witches, then I shall play the servant for now.

I look at the prince, still sleeping peacefully… And dying too.

You had best be worth it.
You better be a damn good asset.

You can still be killed along with your lover.

I thought firmly.

"Quickly, drag these bodies through the woods there and chuck them over the cliff side.
Get rid of those pins too!"

I gesture to the thicket of woods, the sounds of the sea nearby.

"Quickly, go and let the sea take care of them."

They do as I tell them, grabbing the corpses.
It takes two to drag the overweight Todd.
The slaves are taken too, and I give one last look at the young, dead Slayer as he too is taken.
I didn't even know his name…
They heave and drag them off.
They just need to get off this damn path.
They continue to drag, getting closer to the tress.

I can hear the sound of the men approaching, I can hear the stamping of hooves coming directly for us.

"FASTER!"

 I shout.

Thank the Light, they finally disappear through the trees, bodies dragged with them.
Not a second later, horses and men appear.

"QUICKLY!"

I shout.

"The Prince and General's son, they are wounded."

I muster as much emergency in my voice as I possibly can, the men swing from their horses and quickly run to the boys.
They stop dead in their tracks however when they notice the corpse of the charred feral.

"A VAMPIRE!
AND A WITCH!
THE WITCH RAN THAT WAY!"

I shout, making it up on the spot and pointing in the opposite direction.

Guards quickly run off to investigate whilst others gather around the Prince and Kaleb.
Nothing seemed amiss to them as they tended to the boys, this was good.
And my men by now had surely thrown the bodies off the cliff side.
To let the sea hopefully wash their bodies away to somewhere distant and far from here.
They shall return any moment and help.

YOU MAY HAVE GOTTEN RID OF THE BODIES.
BUT HOW SHALL YOU EXPLAIN THEIR DISAPPEARANCE?!

Simple, they ran after the witch and perished.
I push this thought aside, for there is still plenty to do.
With the boys' injuries and the body of a feral the Council will have too much on their hands to be bothered about the insignificant deaths.

I have to act quickly and create even more diversion.

And what bigger a diversion then a Great Cleansing… And the death
of a King.

I look upward, back to the Imperium and smile evilly.

God is coming to the Capital.
Me, God, Me, God… Are you God?
Yes, yes… I am God.
And I shall bring about a Cleanse.
The likes of which the Human Realm has ever seen!

THREE YEARS LATER

THE DARK REALM

YEAR 321 ID

BLOOD AND PLOTS

MARCUS

More darkness, more despair, more death.
And another moon high in the sky.
How utterly dull.

I have been shrouded in darkness now for centuries.

Sure, I have on occasion enjoyed seeing dark grey skies in them Magic and Human Realms, yet even there the sun did not shine brightly, perpetually hidden behind clouds, storms and heavy rain.

And in the Dark Realm there was no light whatsoever, it was nighttime all the time.

She enjoyed it that way.

I remember when I first came to this land, the sun always shone.
The weeks I spent before my death had been full of sunshine.
Not as bright or clear or hot as my home country, yet it did shine.

   Then that fateful night…

When Red Eyes first entered the world… **My eyes.**

And over three hundred years later here I still sit.

Still cursed.

I had been innocent once… Just a boy.
And she had been just a girl.

And now look at us both.

A dark witch who enjoys pain and misery, and a murderous, blood-crazed monster.
Mother would surely turn in her grave.
Except she did not have a grave.
She burned with the rest of the village.

I wonder how long her bones laid there…
Never properly given a decent burial or any last prayers, the prayers of our Ancestors.
No one to place coins on her eyes and give her last rites.

No… Her bones were left there in blood and fire.
Maybe it was good she had died, so that she did not witness what her children became.
My sister, hell-bent on getting revenge on the Imperial Family, who has taken control of parts of the country and shrouded it in spells and magic, darkness covering the lands she took, now known as the Dark Realm.
And me, her brother, a plague on humanity.
How many hundreds of thousands have I killed over the years?
And how many have I turned into Red Eyes?

How many souls had I ripped out of people's bodies, turning them into monsters such as myself?

I am nothing but a plague on humanity.

My sister disagrees, tells me that what I have is a gift from the Ancestors, that they surely blessed me to help take revenge and free our people.
But I have not freed anyone, especially not our people.
Most of them are monsters like me now, the rest enslaved in the Human Realm.

And what did I do?
I just created more slaves…
Except our slaves are white.
They enslaved our people; only fair we enslaved them.
Or so I had thought to begin with.
But the truth is, no one should own anyone.

People are people, not objects.

Not only captured white slaves, no.
I had taken it further, imprisoning hundreds of them in what is now called Blood Camps.
I walk to the window, and I can see it.
Huge camps where humans are bred, born, and grown for slaughter.
This of course is one of many.
They spread out throughout the Dark Realm.

They live cramped and desolate lives, knowing only death.
It was my idea… After all we needed blood… Constant blood.
Yes, I was a plague on humanity.
All I've brought to humanity is death… And yet I cannot die myself.

The gods do enjoy their cruel games.

YOU AND YOUR SISTER ARE GODS!
YOU ARE FEARED AND WORSHIPPED!

But we are not gods, we are monsters.

GODS AND MONSTERS ARE ONE AND THE SAME!

No, only monsters hide away in the shadows.

This was true, I had long left the battlefield.
I had had enough of the death.

Hundreds of years of it.
And thousands upon thousands of dead, their bones litter the land's undergrowth.
And the need for blood… The never-ending blood.
I had drunk and revelled in more blood than I dare to imagine.
Yet it was glorious.

As much as I despised it, I also loved it.

And yet I could not go without, the thirst was always there, a constant scratch in one's throat.
A slight knocking of the door begins.
Odd, everyone knows I do not like being disturbed.
Whomever was knocking that door must have a death wish.

"Enter."

A young man opens the door, a collar and chain around his neck and hands.

He was light skinned, tall with dark hair and comely, yet that was normal.

My sister and I liked beautiful things, and therefore we fill our castle of horrors with beauty.

Beauty And Blood.

Therefore, even the slaves are carefully picked out, always to made sure they are good looking.

The blood camps are inspected regularly, for anyone who has any beauty, to be brought to the castle.

Pitiful humans jump at the chance, anything to get out of the Blood Camps, after all they wrongly assume it's a chance to escape from the horror.

Yet this is not the case, instead they go from one horror to another, for they are more than just drank dried here, they are used as our playthings.

Yes, he was indeed comely.

And I had no doubt who had sent him.

My sister…

No doubt she thought sending him would soften me to whatever she no doubt wants to ask of me.

No, I will not do it.
I shall remain in the shadows.
Hidden away in my rooms where I belong.

YOU HAVE SAID THIS BEFORE!
YOU KNOW YOU SHALL GIVE IN!
YOU KNOW YOU SHALL YES!
YOU ALWAYS SAY YES!

No, this time is different.
I will stay where I belong.

WE SHALL SEE...

The young man looked utterly and perpetually terrified.
But then again, I must be a terrifying sight.
Sitting here in the shadows, the corner of my room with various books, maps and scrolls.
I had to do something after all in my self-imprisonment, and what better then reading.
It keeps the mind sharp after all.

BUT WHAT ABOUT YOUR FANGS AND CLAWS?!
ARE THEY STILL SHARP?!
OR ARE THEY AS DULL AS YOUR LUST FOR POWER HAS
BECAME...

But I never had a lust for power.
That was her.
Always her.

AND YET YOU FOLLOWED EVERY SINGLE ONE OF HER
COMMANDS, LIKE A GOOD LITTLE DOG.

"What do you want?"

I ask of him, annoyed that I've been disturbed.

He stands there looking as if he is about to wet himself.

He blinks, and in the half a second his eyes are closed I flit towards him.
By the time his eyes have reopened, I am stood before him.

He gasps, falling backwards on his backside.
And yes, he even wets himself.
I can smell it strongly, unfortunately.
I probably shouldn't have done that, but I have to find my small enjoyments from somewhere.
And it has always been fun using my super speed to sneak up and terrify people.
Who doesn't love a good scare, after all.
He begins to stutter and whimper on the floor; I can't help but smile.

"My sister wants me, yes?
Was that what you came to tell me?"

He doesn't answer, he continues to stutter and whimper, the smell of urine growing even stronger.

"Well, don't just sit around all day.
Go and do whatever servants do!"

 I say cheerfully.

I quickly lean down towards him then and give him a wide, open smile.
My fangs protrude, I cheerfully shriek.

"AND DO NOT FORGET TO SMILE!"

I shout.

The sight of my fangs sends him scrambling to his feet and fleeing, screaming down one of the many hallways.

I stand there laughing hard.

Oh, it is fun to tease.

THAT WAS FUN AND CRUEL, HOW WONDROUS!

Yes, it was cruel, but it was funnier.

At least for me, anyhow.

My laughter ebbs away as I stand there alone.

My sister wants me… I could go back inside my rooms and close the door.

The slave surely won't be knocking again anytime soon.

I wonder if he's still running.

I let out another laugh and begin to subconsciously walk towards my sisters' chambers.

TOLD YOU, YOU'RE GOING TO HER LIKE ALWAYS!

Damn!

My feet move.

Left, right, left, right.

I walk along the various hallways and as I do the screams become evident.

They're thick and heavy in the air.

I know that the screams are constant, however I cannot hear them in my rooms, my rooms being magically sound proofed.

I know that behind each room I pass, there is either a dark witch who Cast dark spells or a vampire torturing a human.

Not just the sounds of pain, but of pleasure too.

There were sounds of sex also, both consensual and non-consensual.

Screams of mercy and screams of delight.
Consent and rape.
Life and death.

And blood, always blood.

This truly is a castle of horrors.
And yet what else are we supposed to do?
When you can live for hundreds of years, either as a vampire or witch and you have lust for blood or power or both you naturally fall into depravity and darkness.

Walking swifter, I get to my sisters' chambers.
Guards in Red armour with black bats on their breastplates stand there.
Vampire soldiers, loyal and strong.

Otherwise known as **'Scarlet Soldiers.'**

They stand to attention at my approach, and shuffle nervously out of my way.

They know who I am.
What I'm capable of.
No one in this castle dares interfere.

I enter her chambers with ease yet brace myself all the same.

WHAT SHALL BE HER NEXT ORDERS?
WHAT HORROR SHALL SHE COMMAND ME TO DO THIS TIME?

No, I shall take no commands.

Maybe command was a lie, she had never really commanded me. Merely implied what she wants, and loyally, I have always done it. Sometimes even gleefully.

I remember my days on the battlefield, centuries of it, conquering lands to add to the Dark Realm, the fights with the Imperial Army, aided by that damned Council of Covens and their armies of Protectors.

Yet there's an uneasy alliance.

Witches may have been safe at the Magic Realm, and yet it was not the same for witches in the Human Realm, and there was deep distrust between them.

I suppose witches are safe here in the Dark Realm also.

Well, most of them.

Only the strongest survive around here.

However, there is mutual hate for me and my sister it seemed everywhere.

Even here in our own Realm we are feared and hated, yet too powerful to be stopped.

Upon entering the chambers I smell the scent of oils and sweat in the air.

And upon a huge bed lay my sister, writhed and tangled with some slave boy.

I stand there and let out a deliberate cough.

The slave lets out a yelp of fear before jumping off both my sister and the bed.

A comely young man, he attempts to grab his clothes and scurry out of the room.

My sister quickly grasps hold of a chain and pulls back hard.

The slave is pulled back to the ground, the chain connected to a collar around his neck.

I look upon my sister, who smiles wickedly at me.

"I wasn't finished."

She complains.

"I'm sure you can always get him to come back later."

I reply.

"No, he's a boring lover, I shall have him executed and a new boy brought forth.
Or perhaps a girl this time."

She ponders out loud.

The slave's eyes widen as my sister so nonchalantly declares his death. I remain silent as she pulls a purple silk robe over herself, she gracefully moves from the bed and takes a step toward the naked, kneeling slave.
He doesn't even get a chance to plea for his life when she snaps her fingers and his neck snaps with it.

He slumps to the floor, dead.

She lets out a musical laugh as she walks towards me, her naked body apparent beneath the thin silk.
She shows no mercy, evidently.
And her beauty is apparent.
Dark alabaster skin, with dark curls hanging down to her lower back.
An hourglass figure and an ample bosom.
And her eyes… The deepest cerulean blue.

"Brother."

She declares happily as she embraces me.

She wraps her arms around me and places a kiss upon either side of my cheeks.
I do the same to her and she takes a step back.

"I hope your slave pleased you better."

She remarks as she wanders over to her black table, adorned with various maps and letters.

"I fear I sent him running from my rooms screaming."

 I answer.

She turns back to me, a wicked glee in her eyes.

"It's not like you to hurt the pretty ones, not their faces anyways."

 She remarks.

She laughs then and as she does, I am reminded of more of my past misdeeds.

Yes, I had indeed hurt many young men… All beautiful… All dead now.

"I fear it was the sight of my speed and fangs."

I point out.

"Ahhh, you flitted and bared your fangs.

Hilarious, I always love it when you scare them."

She tells me, another musical laugh escaping her full lips.

There was a time I enjoyed scaring people too, but I had long had enough of it.
I want to change, to be better.
Yet it seems as if I cannot.

WHAT MADNESS!
YOU ARE A MONSTER!
A PLAGUE ON HUMANITY!
A RED EYED DEMON!
YOU HAVE TOO MUCH BLOOD AND DEATH ON YOUR HANDS
FOR ANY CHANCE OF REDEMPTION!

Yes, I was certain that I was damned.
And yet I had to try.
To create even a shimmer of light.
To try and apologise for all the darkness I have wrought.

The clicking of her fingers and the entering of servants brings me back to the room.
I am handed a jewel encrusted golden goblet, filled with blood.
My sister is handed a similar jewel encrusted golden goblet, although hers no doubt contains strong wine.

"Remove this."

She tells the slaves present and gestures to the dead body.

"And bring in the *Girl...*"

The way she said that made me get an uneasy feeling as the body is dragged from the room.
I take a sip of blood, it's fresh and sweet.
My sister likewise takes a sip of her wine before setting her goblet down on the table.

"You're probably wondering why I sent for you."

 She asks.

This was true, even my sister has respected my choice of my self-imprisoned exile in my rooms.
She of course has entertained herself with other distractions and being Queen to really care that I was refusing to leave my own chamber.
Yet now she calls upon me.

AND YOU CAME RUNNING LIKE A WHIPPED DOG.

"What is it."

My voice stern and annoyed.

I do not like the fact that I truly had come running to her as usual.

"Now, now, is that any tone for your Queen?"

 Her voice tentative.

"Queen my backside, I'm your brother.
Now cut the bullshit and tell me what you want."

 I state simply.

Her eyes widen with joy and another laugh escapes from her lips.

"Ah, sweet brother.
 You're lucky I love you so, if you were anyone else, you'd be dead right now for speaking to me like that."

She says it as a threat and yet she smiles the entire time, I can't tell if it makes it more amusing or frightening.

I smile back at her.

"Well, it's probably good that I'm not someone else then."

 I reply coyly.

She removes a letter from the table and hands it to me.
It bears the seal of the High Pope, an evident C on the torn wax.

C standing for cunt of course.

"Why would I want to read this?
He's your pet, not mine."

 I answer, unamused and uninterested.

"A pet that has infiltrated the very heart of the Capital, on my request."

 She answers.

"A cunt who has his own designs of power, on the Imperial Throne and you even gave him permission and years to grow an army of fanatical witch hating cunts.
They're even worse than the damned Syndicate."

My voice is angry, I remember now why I had exiled myself to my rooms in the first place.

"A cunt he may be, yet a cunt that has helped turn the tide.
When you came forth, reborn as you are, and turned others into glorious creatures such as yourselves, the silly Syndicate was made, and their ugly Spirals were created.
Besides, who cares about the witches who have been killed.
They turned against me, against us, and your kind.
I fought for you, to keep you safe, and your creations."

This was true, from the second I unleashed this plague on humanity I was immediately hunted, a whole order of Vampire Slayers created.

"And how exactly has he turned the tide?"

"Gods."

 She moans, exasperated.

"This is why you shouldn't keep yourself in your rooms for years, your brains go to shit.
Witches fought against us, helped the humans!
Yet despite that humans have always distrusted them, scared they would go Dark like those of us in this beautiful Realm we've created.
An uneasy alliance between them for hundreds of years, and yet I took that uneasy alliance and shattered it.
I unleashed upon the Human Realm a fanatical, zealous god-fearing cunt and he has put to death hundreds upon hundreds of them, him and his so-called army of Defenders.
And guess what, little brother?
Those who have escaped have come where?"

"The Realm of Magic."

I answer.

"Not just that, they came here!
Do you know how many recruits we have acquired these last three years?
How many witches have fled to our ranks!
Surely you noticed?!"

She sighs deeply and rubs her temple with her forefingers.

"The fighting at the frontlines is on the verge of collapse, for hundreds of years those pesky Protectors have guarded the BorderLands between our realms, that peace of dead land, but now with the humans turned against them also, they are all but finished.
And the Imperial Army is all but gone."

"And yet the BorderLands remains.
The fighting continues."

 I say truthfully,

"For now."

 She says as she flicks a curl behind her shoulder, clearly getting bored.

"The General created a stupid amnesty with the Council of Covens."

The mention of the General keeps her a moment pause.

I awkwardly stay silent.

She then continues.

"No infighting between humans and witches within the Realm, it's the last safe haven for witches now.
Aside from here.
And yet the witches who stay good have lost families in the Human Realm, and surely, they won't want to protect them for much longer.
Not when they can join me, free from all persecution."

She smiles a wide smile.

Funny how she mentions free from persecution when she orchestrated the largest purging of witches I'd ever seen.

She had told me this years ago, all of this.
The pain of hearing it once again drives me to anger, my sister has done many evil things in her life but the killing of her own kind…

Even that I could not fathom.

I take a step towards her.

"And if anyone found out you did this?
You are the Witch Queen, and yet you single handily unleashed a purge on them the likes of which I've never seen.
And in such a short amount of time…"

I trail off.

She becomes annoyed.

"Why do you keep sulking about this?!
You are going to grow a conscience and take the high road?!

After everything you've done?!
All the misery and death you've caused?!
And don't tell me you didn't enjoy it, some of the happiest times I've ever seen you is drenched in the blood."

"HUMANS!"

 I shout, not worried about anyone hearing.
Her rooms are magically sound proofed too, after all.

"Humans who brought us here, who imprisoned us, who beat and raped us!
Yes, I killed hundreds of thousands, but that was to-"

"TO WHAT?!"

She shrieks back.

"Free us all? Save our people?! Return home?!
We have no home to return to!
They made sure of that?!
Why do you think I carved out a kingdom within their kingdom?!
Because they took our lands and lives, brought us here as playthings.
So, I got my revenge, I took their lives in return, and I took their country.
I still remember that glorious day when that foolish King died beneath my feet.
It may have been centuries ago, yet I remember it like it was yesterday.
And you, you were right there beside me.
And guess what, you were drenched in blood and loving every moment!"

I want to argue back when she simply waves her hand.

"Enough!
I did not bring you here to fight?!"

"Then what have you brought me here for?
Spit it out so I can say 'no' and return to my rooms."

Anger still bubbling within.

"It's time."

She says quietly and solemnly.

I stand frozen, I look at her and know she means it.

"Why now."

I ask of her.

She turns from me.

"I need you to go to the Human Realm,"

This shocks me, and trust me, I am not someone who is easily shocked.

The last time I left…

YOU FAILED HER…

But there was so much blood… And the children, they were so young.

It was just over twenty-one years ago…
The last time I had left the Realm.

When I was sent to execute the whole Imperial Family
They had travelled to the Realm of Magic
They were on the cusp of entering the Black Woods when I attacked.
It was late in the year was 299ID… Only days before the start of the new century.
The reason for their travel was to celebrate the Year 300ID with the Council of Covens.
A show of unity between man and witch kind.
And I had swooped in and destroyed it.
I had stayed hidden for weeks…
I murdered the Imperial Family apart from one…
And the hatred between humans and witches grew more.
Humans automatically blamed the witches, despite not a single witch having attacked the carriage.
Sure, Dark Witches had travelled with me and a retinue of Scarlet Soldiers, to help keep us hidden.
But it was me who butchered them.

"You didn't kill all of them."

She must know what I am thinking.

I look at her and she looks back at me, her eyes angry.

"I could have been sat on the Imperial Throne these last decades…
That was the closet chance we got…"

Her black throne not being enough for her, no, she wants the Imperial Throne.
She is obsessed with it.

"I tried, but…"

"You grew a conscious.
And why?
It's not like you hadn't killed children before."

The way she says it, without a hint of remorse or pity in her voice, rather boredom.

"Never on purpose!"

 I cry!

"Only when."

"Only when the bloodlust took over and you could not control yourself.
Yes, yes, you've said before."

Her voice more bored than ever.

"You've done enough skulking and moping around.
You are my brother, General of my armies, it's time you step up and become what I know you can be."

She seems almost proud.

Proud that I'm a monster,
Proud that she can call upon me whenever she chooses.
Proud of the horrors I can unleash in her name.

"Why should I?"

"Because you want to be left alone, yes?
In peace and quiet?

Do this for me, and I shall never ask you for another thing so long as I
live.
Do this last thing for me, brother, and you shall be set free."

In over three hundred years, she had never spoken like this.
And she certainly never said before that she would set me be free.

But should she keep this promise?
Begrudgingly, I do what I've always done.

"What is it you need me to do?"

I sigh deeply, once again I am under her command.

YOU'VE ALWAYS BEEN UNDER HER CONTROL…

She smiles sweetly at me, and her eyes have a sparkle.
Her eyes have always captivated me, captivated others.
For centuries, since we were young.
Sometimes, she looks just like mother.

Another time.
Another land.
Another life.

And for the briefest of seconds, it reminds me of who she used to be.
Before all of this.
Back when we were children running free through the tall grass, back
when we weren't monsters.

"I need you do go to the Human Realm; you need to do so under
complete discretion of course.

Across the BorderLands, through the Magic Realm and its Black Woods and straight to the Human Realm when there I want you to do two things.
Firstly, I want you to deliver something to Claudius.
Two things, actually."

She then hands me a small, yet intricately crafted vial and a letter with her own seal.

"And secondly… I want you to bring me the prince."

The prince?!

"The prince?"

 I repeat out loud.

"Yes, but after you've delivered this letter and vial to Claudius.
And don't bother opening it, only with his blood will the ink reveal itself.
And the same goes for the vial.
It cannot be unlocked unless Claudius drips his blood on it.

Ahh yes, blood magic.

She outstretches her hand, a letter and vial in hand.
I take them from her and slip them away in my pocket.

"Forget about him, what do you want with Theodore?"

I could scarcely remember the Crown Prince, yet from what I had heard about him he was vicious, stupid and cowardly.

"I have no use for that insipid fool.
 He shall never be King; besides he is not the prince I speak of."

She pauses for a second, before finishing.

"I want you to bring me Tristan, the younger brother."

This confuses me further.
Why would she want him?

And yet, it brings back the whisper of a memory.
It was three years ago… News from the Human Realm.
The prince being attacked by some feral, the General's son too.
I found it odd… And assumed it was my sister of course, yet I never gave it a second thought again, nor asked anyone about it, instead sticking to my seclusion and books in my dark tower.

"Sister, if you're saying it's finally time to bring down the Dynasty…
Then I think it would be best to dispose of the heir, not the spare?"

"They shall all be killed of course, but first I want you bring me the second son.
Bring him to me, and you shall be set free.
To do whatever you wish, you can live the rest of your immortal life doing whatever makes you happy.
No more war, no more death, you can return to your own castle.
You can be happy there, for I know you are certainly not happy here."

"It sounds almost as if you want rid of me."

 I half jest.

And yet, it would be nice to return to my own castle and lands.

Some leagues away from here, a part of land always covered in deep snow.

Albeit, they are much smaller than here, but I missed having my own space.

I half wondered why I had not exiled myself there to begin with, but I knew my sister wanted me kept close so instead I stayed in my rooms here.

She takes my hands then and looks at me both sweetly and equally seriously.

"Brother, it's no lie that you have done unspeakable things, we both have.

But if we do this, if I finally can crush our enemies completely, then I can make the world anew.

Witches and vampires will rule this land, it will be beautiful."

A world without humans?!

No, humans would still be around… They would of course be in Blood Camps.

The whole of humanity enslaved.

And I would be the one to help bring it about…

"But why the second prince?"

I ask once again.

She pushes away from me, all sweetness gone.

"I offer you peace and freedom and you ask me questions?
Me?!"

She gets louder. Louder and angry.

"I am your queen!
You will do this for me, and you shall not fail me!
I shall be Queen of the whole country, not just some of it!
And you will be free to as you wish!"

I stand there silently.

Where did she go?
My sweet sister?
Why did her innocence have to die.
Why did mine have to die too.

She grabs her wine goblet and drinks heavily, the whole cup.
Slamming it down in the table, she turns to me.

"You will be leaving with a guard of Scarlet Soldiers.
And a small group of Dark witches, to help you pass undetected throughout the BorderLands and into the Magic Realm."

That could potentially be harder said than done.
The BorderLands were a thin stretch of land where, during the last three centuries the war has been fought.
It's between the Dark Realm and Magic Realm.
It is nothing but darkness and decay.
Sometimes there is nothing but fighting and other days it could go weeks without a single drop of blood being spilled.
However, nothing grows there.
No plants or tree, and animals dare not go near it either.
It is soaked deep in blood and death.

Perhaps keeping to the outskirts would be the safer bet.

"Once there, you need to travel through the hundreds of miles of Black Woods and get to the Human Realm.
Reach the Capital and do what you need to do.
Once you have the prince, you contact me.
So, make sure you take your mirror."

The mirror in question is special.
The glass being made from Saerillian Silver.
The handle being a different material, usually wooden.
After all, neither vampires nor witches can touch Saerillian Silver, it burns greatly.
It does however allow witches and vampires to communicate with each other from far distances.

"I shall send you a portal and bring you straight back here."

She continues.

"Can you not just portal me there, I can grab him for you now and be done with this."

"No, if I portal you to the Human Realm the portal will most likely be detected, especially in the Capital.
The Defenders are everywhere, and they hunt magic like dogs with bones.
The witches I send with you are not to Cast either once in the Human Realm.
I want no attention brought to any of you.
This mission needs to go without a hitch, it cannot fail.
Do you understand me?!"

She has left me with more questions than answers, yet I cannot help but say I am intrigued.

And perhaps it will be good to get out of this castle, out of this cursed Realm.

I have not left for so long, and staying here has not been doing me any good.

And if I do this, finally I will be free.

AND SHE SHALL RULE EVERYTHING…
THE WHOLE COUNTRY PLUNGED INTO DARKNESS.
THE END OF A DYNASTY…
THE END OF HUMANITY…
AND YOU WILL BE THE ONE HELP BRING IT ABOUT!

But perhaps it is time to give up on humanity.
After all, it was humanity that turned me into a monster.
It was the Imperial Dynasty that brought me here.
I should have every reason to hate both.
And yet, I do not.

I am pulled from my thoughts by the doors opening.

A young girl enters, a teenager.

Yellow straw hair and brown eyes, wearing a grey tattered dress.

A slave girl, and yet… I can smell magic.

Her eyes widen with fear.

Makes sense, she's standing in a room with two of the most powerful beings to ever walk the Earth.

"Come here, child."

My sister says sweetly.

I know the girl is going to die, that is obvious.

I should tell her to run, to even protect her.

Yet I stand there and do nothing.

The girl walks towards my sister, she begins to tremble as she gets closer.
My sister cups her face with her hands and begins to make soothing noises.

"What is your name, sweet child?"

She asks, her voice like honey.

The girl is too terrified to speak.

"No name?"

 She coos.

"Oh well, your name matters not."

This time her voice sharp.

She grips the girl tighter and begins to inhale inwards.
The girl begins to shake before finally becoming still, as if her body has become stone.
My sister inhales deeply once again and a light emanates between them.

A soft, golden glow.
She is sucking out her soul.

It's humorous almost, humans have long called witches Soulless, branded along with us vampires.

However, what they fail to realise that witches have more soul than anyone.
For you have to have a soul wild and free to be able to possess the ability to Cast.
After all, what is magic but if not wild and free.
And this is what the zealots and fanatical god-fearing folk don't understand, they want everyone to conform and be what they consider 'normal' and yet they fail to realise those that are different are the best people of all.

No, it's only my kind that is truly Soulless.
For how can a walking corpse, who craves blood, possibly possess a soul.

The golden glow turns to a ball, and it appears from the girls' mouth, it travels from her mouth and into that of my sisters who continues to inhale and swallows greedily.

Once released, the girl falls to the ground, dead.
Not just dead, but her soul stolen from her.
A fate worse than death, she will never know peace.
Trapped forever in hell.

My sister now having this poor girl's soul, she has gained beauty and youth.

But she already had beauty and youth.
Why take more?

I really have been in my rooms too long.

I wonder if she has been Cleaving anyone.

Cleaving differs from Soul Stealing.

To Cleave means to take one's magic completely, leaving the person nothing but an empty shell.

For witches, it is a fate worse than death.
My sister has done it before to Cleave powerful witches who were enemies from their magic.
But she never took the magic, merely allowed it to dissipate into thin air.
After all, she does not need more magic… **Does she?**
I have seen Cleaving first hand, and it is torturous and terrible.
Stronger witches have been known to Cleave upon weaker witches, however it is frowned upon even here in the Dark Realm.
Not that my sister cares, and why would she?
She is queen after all.
At least stealing someone's soul was quick and painless, even if it did send you to hell due to not having a soul anymore.
She is and has been the greatest and most powerful witch for centuries…

Hasn't she?
Isn't she?

May the gods have pity on the poor girl.

And may the gods have mercy on my sister for this vile act.
Her body shudders in delight as she turns to face me, her face almost aglow.
She seems somehow younger, more vibrant, more beautiful.

BUT SHE IS ALREADY ALL POWERFUL…
WHY DOES SHE NEED EVEN MORE…

MORE MAGIC?!

It seems as if I have been I seclusion for too long and let too many years and questions pass me by.
But not any longer, I intend to come out of the shadows and shed some light on what's really happening.

An ecstatic giggle comes from her lips.

"That was wonderful, as always!"

She shrieks happily.

I can't stop looking at the poor child on the floor.
So young, so innocent.
She did not deserve a fate like that.
And I just stood and watched and did nothing.

A plague on humanity.

No doubt when my time comes, I shall burn in the hottest part of hell.

"Do not feel guilty for her."

 She sighs.

"She served her purpose in life.
Most people who have life don't even have purpose.
At least she did."

If this is meant to be words of comfort, they do not work.

"Prepare yourself, you leave tomorrow.

Those accompanying you will meet you tomorrow night at the gates.
Don't worry, you shall be leaving here in the comfort of a carriage.
But once you get close to the BorderLands, I'm afraid it's either horse
or foot for you.
Your choice, of course."

Like I have ever bad a choice in anything.

She then says with ice in her voice.

"And make sure you do this quickly.
I want him in my hands as soon as possible."

Before I can question why, she waves me away.

"Leave now!"

She commands, fixing herself another goblet of wine.

I take one final look at her before leaving disgusted.
Disgusted at what my sister has become.
Disgusted at myself for following her commands as always.
Disgusted yet determined to find the prince.
And yet, not for her.

No, the Prince was clearly valuable, and I intended to find out why.
Bring on tomorrow's full moon and the start of my journey.

And finally, my freedom.

THE NEXT NIGHT

THE HUMAN REALM

FORBIDDEN LOVE

TRISTAN

Kneeling on the bed, I look eagerly upon the hooded figure before me, just out of the way of the illuminating moon, hidden by the shadows.
The figure finally takes a step forward, the moonlight from the balcony shining upon them.
It exposes their impressive and hulking frame.

It is the early hours of the morning, yet it's still dark out and the moon shines brightly.
I was not sure he would come; it has been several days after all.
A shiver travels down my spine and goosebumps cover my naked body as the hooded figure finally pulls his hood back, revealing themself.

Standing before me was none other than Kaleb.

My love, My life.

Fierce warrior and a proud Captain of the Slayer Syndicate.

My Brave Captain.

He unclamps the buckle of his cloak and it falls to the ground beneath him.
He wears a thin tunic, his muscles evident through the material.
And his tight pants do not leave much to the imagination either.
Not being able to stand the suspense any longer, I reach forward cupping his rugged face and pulling him in for a rough kiss.

It's a deep, long kiss.

The kind that leaves you feeling ravenous.
He pulls away from the kiss and I let out a breathless sigh.
That is until he pulls his tunic over and throws it across the room.
My breathless sigh turns into an excited squeak of delight as I drink in his looks.

A hard squared chest and toned stomach, covered in a thick pelt of dark hair which starts from his chest and travels all the way down to his manhood.
Arms, strong and thick from years of handling various weapons.
Dark stubble covers his face, and he has dark eyes.

He pulls down his pants, and his hard member stands tall and proud to attention.
Like the rest of him, it too is thick and large.
He takes me in his arms again and we fall backwards on to the bed, our bodies entangled, and our lips locked in a fierce embrace.
His kiss trails from my lips down to my neck, and he bites down.
I let out a small yelp as he releases his bite, his kisses trailing back up to my ear.

"Tell me you want it."

He whispers, his voice rough.

"I want it, I want it so badly!"

I gush, unable to contain my excitement.

Bending my knees to my chest, I hold my legs in place as he spits
several times into his hand and begins to rub his manhood.
He lines it up with my entrance and begins to push.
Resistance at first, yet slowly inch by inch he dives deeper inside of
me, until his sword is all the way to the hilt.

We both let out moans of ecstasy.
He leans down and whispers once again.

"I've been waiting all week for this."

I had been waiting too.
Waiting eagerly, waiting painfully.
It was not often we were able to do this after all, and we took our guilty
pleasures in whatever chance we got.
His pace begins to quicken, I wrap my legs round the small of his back
and pull him in closer.
His thick chest hair tickles my bare skin as he thrusts into me, over and
over again.
I begin to kiss and nibble at the side of his neck and his hips begin to
buck faster, his thrust becoming rampant.

He is like a man possessed.

My moans turn to squeaks, he quickly and strongly puts his hand over
my mouth, silencing me.
Force of habit, of course my room is soundproofed thanks to my
Casting.

His breathe becomes ragged as he keeps thrusting fast.
I quickly place my own hand over his mouth too as he lets out a loud groan and one final thrust, his seed deposited deep inside of me.
He lays completely on top of me, spent and tired.
Our bodies are covered in sweat, it glistens in the moonlight, our breathes are erratic.

He pulls out of me and rolls over.
I miss the feeling of him inside me immediately.
He rolls off me and I quickly snuggle into his furry chest.
I listen to his heartbeat, loud and strong.

A heart that belongs to me.

A HEART YOU HAVE POWER OVER!

The thought sent a shiver down my spine.

"What is it?"

He asks, concerned.

"Just cold."

I lie to him.

I simply wave my hand across the room, and as I do the candles dotted around in various places suddenly come alight.

Reds, yellows and oranges flicker around us.
The shadows of the flames dance across the room.
But not just any candlelight, these were brighter and fiercer.
My magic is strong.

"TRISTAN!"

He scolds.

"Kaleb."

 I whisper back seductively, blinking my eyes at him.

"Don't even bother, that sweet voice and puppy eyes won't work on me."

"Are you sure about that?"

 I whisper again, reaching for his manhood.

He grabs my hand and sits up, his face serious.

"Yes, Tristan, I'm sure.
You know how I feel about you doing that, it's not safe."

He tells me, for probably the thousandth time now.

I roll my eyes and pull my hand from his grasp.
The romantic atmosphere of the room quickly changes.
There used to be a time where he found me wonderful.
He was in awe of my abilities, but over the last three years his awe has turned into fear.
He says it's through fear of me being caught, but sometimes I wonder if it's really because it was fear for me.

The last three years he had progressed from Initiate to Brother to Captain of the Syndicate.
He had rose quickly through the ranks, his prowess remarkable.

He had fought on the frontlines as well, something I had tried my hardest to stop from happening, yet I could not forever.
Three years ago, he had promised that he would stay with me for a few months longer, I had managed to extend that to two whole years.
It was wrong of me; he had wasted two years not getting to know his men and gained two years of his fathers' wrath.

But after two years, he finally went.

That was last year, and I hated every moment of it.
From what I can gather he was impressive on the battlefield, killing several vampires – a feat not easily achieved – and he also killed some twenty witches.

People like me.

It was three years in total now since we professed our love in the woods that day.
And yet those three years had been long on both of us.
It felt more like ten.

"I'm sorry."

 I say, regretting instantly for apologising.

AND YET YOU APOLOGISE EVERY TIME, AND WHY IS THAT?
BECAUSE YOU DENY THE POWER YOU HAVE!
IF ONLY YOU COULD CAST FREELY, YOU WOULD BE
UNSTOPPABLE!
A LIVING GOD!

I shake my head, as if trying to shake the thoughts from my mind.

I feel Kaleb's hand on mine.

"No, it's me that's sorry.
I didn't mean to upset you; I just want to protect you."

 He explains.

The same explanation he always gives.
That he just wants to protect me.

> *YOU DO NOT NEED PROTECTION!*
> *YOU WILL BE THE GREATEST WITCH THIS WORLD HAS*
> *EVER SEEN!*
> *YOU WILL OWN VAST LANDS AND CONTROL ARMIES!*
> *THOUSANDS WILL BE YOUR SUBJECTS!*
> *AND YOU WILL HAVE A THRONE AND A CROWN!*
> *YOU ONLY NEED TO UNLEASH YOUR CHAOS!*

The thoughts that plagued me for years plague me still.
It scares me, I do not want to unleash chaos.
I want to help people, help humans and witches alike.
Get us to live in harmony once again.

But then again, I don't see how that's possible.

Claudius and his army of Defenders make that impossible.
A man from nothing somehow rose and became High Pope.
And it all started that day, the day I saw the Red Eyes.

I do not remember much from that night.
It had been a full moon however, much like tonight.
I had snuck out... I had been Casting... And behind me Kaleb
appeared.

I can't remember all our conversation, but I do remember being given the handcrafted wooden sword attached to string.
A necklace I wore to this day, having never taken it off.

A simple necklace, yet I loved it all the same.

I wore it around my neck right now, the only thing I was wearing for that matter, being completely naked otherwise.
We both told each other we loved each other; he was full of those cheeky smiles and winks that made me swoon.
I had got him to promise to stay longer… And as we left, a foul screech and red eyes.

After that, I don't recall much.

I had a dream of anger and fire… And crawling towards Kaleb… But how could that be?

Was it not he who saved me?

But whether that was true or not, I could not be certain.

After that, I had awoken to find several weeks had passed.

Rumour was, me and Kaleb were practising early sword play in the woods, a rumour I was grateful for, for the truth would have got us killed, when we were attacked by a feral vampire and witch.

A vampire I remember clearly… The Red Eyes seared into my memory.

But a witch?

That I could not seem to recall, yet it must be true.

Mustn't it?

Kaleb was celebrated for having killed the feral and saving me.

Yet did he?

And the witch?

Well, the supposed witch was what helped Claudius launch his paranoia and terror upon the Human Realm.

The fact a witch would attempt to kill one of the Imperial Bloodline was a matter of great controversy.

Claudius apparently fed this witch story to my father, the late King.

And my father had always been a proud man, and he too had his own negative views upon the witches, and the attack on me led him to his final decree before his death.

A decree to purge all witches.

The ink had barely dried on the parchment when he died.

Yet Claudius was all too keen to keep the late King's final command, he raised an army of fanatical witch hating bullies that spread throughout the entire Realm.

'Defenders'

They were named.

Supposed Defenders of the Eternal Faith of Light, yet all they were was bigots and cruel murderers.

In the last three years thousands of them had been hunted and murdered, people like me.

Claudius and his Defenders were full of nothing but hatred.

"What are you thinking about?"

He asks of me.
I ignore him but he grabs my arm and pulls me into his chest.

"I really am sorry, My Little Prince."

He soothes to me.

I know he is no longer angry, yet I am the one who now has anger.
I hate this, hate how everything has turned to shit.
Outside these castle walls, my people died.
I called them my people, not just the humans but the witches too.

I was an Imperial, an Imperial with magic.
I could be the one to unite the people.

To stop the violence and hate.
To work together in harmony once again and finally defeat the Witch
Queen, and her monstrous brother the Lord of Darkness.

BUT HOW CAN YOU DO ANYTHING?
YOU ARE UNDER CLAUDIUS CONTROL LIKE EVERYONE
ELSE!
AND YOUR BROTHER IS NEXT IN LINE FOR THE THRONE.

Thoughts turn to my elder brother, Theodore.

He would never rule.

YOU SEEM CERTAIN OF THIS...

I was certain.

Theodore could not do anything.
Not to better the Crown, the Capital or the Country.
He is a foolish, vicious monster and would make an awful King.

BUT HE IS STILL THE HEIR, AND YOU ARE JUST THE SPARE!
IF YOU WANT TO RULE, IF YOU WANT POWER, IF YOU WANT
TO CHANGE THE WORLD AND UNITE THE PEOPLE, THEN
THEODORE WOULD NEED TO BE DEAD.
THEODORE AND CLAUDIUS!

I would happily murder Claudius without a second thought, but Theodore…

He was stupid and vicious and a drunk, yet he was my brother.

My own blood.

BUT HE HATES YOU ANYWAYS, AND IT WOULD BE A
KINDNESS TO KILL HIM.
A KINDNESS FOR THE REALM.

The war has been going worse than ever, Claudius' tyranny extends all the way through the Human Realm, witches who aren't caught and killed flee to the Magic Realm for safety, some travel further and joined the Witch Queen, becoming Dark Witches.
However, in the Magic Realm, The Council Of Covens decreed that if Claudius or his Defenders dared enter their land, they would stop aiding us and grant the vampires access to the Human Realm.

Despite Claudius' tyranny and violence, he dare not risk vampires invading our lands.

Besides, the loyal council that was left behind after my father's death also stepped in and told Claudius he would not be supported in the

Human Realm or within the Capital or castle if he dared bring vampires to the land.

So, Claudius let them flee to the Magic Realm and beyond.
And he dare not step foot there, neither do his armies.

Instead, they stay here and continued to kill any witches within the Realm.
You would doubt any remain after three years of purging, however some do.
And some are here in the Capital…

There is a rumour these last years that there is a Secret Court.
Witches who are hidden somewhere.
And it has to be true, I can feel it.

I can't quite describe it, but I can feel magic stemming from the Capital.
Indeed, witches hide there somewhere.

Yet neither Claudius nor his Defenders or anyone else for that matter have been able to find it.
Witches that are caught are tortured in horrendous ways and even promised freedoms if they only give up the location of the Secret Court and to this date not one witch has spoken a word.

Choosing death over betrayal.
They truly are loyal.

AND YOU PLAN ON FINDING THIS SECRET COURT!
HOW SCANDALOUS AND DANGEROUS!
AND KALEB, YOUR PRECIOUS LOVER HASN'T A CLUE!
NO, THAT IS SOMETHING I HAVE NOT EVEN SHARED WITH KALEB.

THAT'S BECAUSE YOU NO LONGER TRUST HIM!

I again snuggle deeply into his chest, breathing in the smell of him.
The smell of sweat and seed.
I can trust him.
I love him, I can trust him more than anyone.

ARE YOU SURE ABOUT THAT?
THEN TELL HIM, SEE WHAT HAPPENS…

"Are you thinking about the execution tomorrow?"

The mention of this brings fresh thoughts to mind.
Yes, tomorrow shall be another prime example of Claudius tyranny.
Over a dozen people are condemned to die tomorrow, weather permitting.

FOR THE ONLY WAY TO TRULY CLEANSE THE SOULLESS IS WITH FIRE.

The words ring in my head, I have heard them enough times over the last three years.

"It shouldn't be happening."

I state, matter of factly.

"And yet it is, my love."

 He replies grimly.

I turn to face him, and he sits upward on the bed.

"Your Uncle should stop this."

I say to him.

He sighs exasperated

"Tris, we've been over this.
 My uncle can't do anything.
The Syndicate-"

"The Syndicate cannot interfere in the Realm Of Men."

I interrupt, for I too have heard those words thousands of times.

"Well, it's true, the Syndicate cannot help.
 We have all took sacred oaths, we are Vampire Slayers".

"And witches."

 I add.

He sighs again.

"Tristan, yes the Syndicate have killed witches, but."

"I do not care about the past."

 I snap at him.

"What I care about is the last three years the Syndicate has stood by
whilst the Defenders kill innocent people.
Even children!
They are burned alive."

I continue

"We cannot help them.
And at the same time, we do not persecute them.
 In fact, myself and many other Slayers I know do not seek out witches,
we turn blind eyes."

"And yet you have done it.
You did not turn a blind eye!"

I snap once again.

It was not an accusation; it was the honest truth.
I had not meant to see it of course; I had snuck out into the city like I
had done so many times before.

And that's when I had seen it… My love killing a witch.

It was a middle-aged man, he begged for his life, Kaleb stood there as
did several Defenders and I watched.
He struck off his head with his Saerillian Silver Sword.
Claudius might be obsessed with fire, yet Saerillian Silver worked just
as well.
After the deed was done, Kaleb spotted me.

He always did say he could spot me from any crowd just by my eyes.

I had been appalled, it was one thing killing witches at the frontlines,
that I could understand, they were Dark witches after all.
But killing an innocent man in the street like a dog… And afterwards
I had seen the man's family dragged from their home, all of them
accused of witchcraft also.

They were burned alive shortly afterwards.

And Kaleb did nothing… He says the Syndicate do not take part and
yet he beheaded a man.
Thankfully, with his uncle being Lord Commander nothing happened.
This has caused ire as of late from other Syndicate members who have
been exiled or even executed for such a thing.
Kaleb tells me not to worry, however.
Whilst I am thankful he did not get into trouble, to tell the truth, it has
created a rift between us as of late.

That was several weeks ago now.

How I wish I had never seen it.

"I should leave."

 He mutters to himself.

I feel a stab to my heart as he says this.
I did not want him to leave, not like this.

"Stay."

 I tell him.

He sits on the edge of the bed, as if debating whether to leave or not.

"I should probably get going.
It will be morning soon; people are most likely going to wonder why
I'm not yet back at the Inner Spiral."

The Inner Spiral being the name for any Spiral built within a castle such as ours supported.

The Inner Spiral was made specifically for the Captains and Lord Commander, yet neither the Lord Commander nor any of the Captains stayed there within the Imperium.

They abandoned it when Claudius started his Cleanse, they were disgusted by his actions and no longer wished to live here.
Thus, the Lord Commander and other Captains left and have stayed at the Grand Spiral in the Capital ever since.
Kaleb would have left too, to sleep at the Grand Spiral within the city, yet I had once again persuaded him to stay.

YOU HAVE POWER OVER HIM!

Be quiet!

"The execution is tomorrow; it was dangerous me coming here tonight. I've stayed long enough."

He stands from the bed and begins to pick up his clothes.
I can see it then, his huge scar, it is evident in the moonlight.
It starts from his left shoulder, travelling diagonally down his back to his right lower side.

It had happened that fateful night…When the Red Eyes appeared.

Yet it healed very well.

Claudius had spun some half-baked story how the witch who was present must have realised who Kaleb was.

Not wanting the wrath and the power of the Syndicate cast down upon them, they tried to heal him.

Despite the story and its many irregularities, it was quickly brushed past due to the Cleansing.

But surely that Caster must have known that attempting to take the life of me, an Imperial, would bring down the King and the Imperial Army down upon them…
My father had decreed the death of witches and him being a king his word was final.
But most of the Imperial Army was stationed in the Magic Realm, and fighting at the BorderLands, and therefore they did not get involved.

However, many Imperial Soldiers garrisoned at the Capital also committed these atrocities.
Not real Imperial Soldiers, not anymore.
They joined Claudius army of Defenders instead.
Thankfully, we did retain many loyal men still here who did try and help the witches…
At first, at least.

No one can help witches anymore.
Not unless they want to taste the fire also.

No, it was only Claudius and his Defenders who really were the driving force behind the Cleansing.
Yes, a lot of it did not seem to fit… And yet no one dared to question anything.
No one really got a chance, too distracted with my father's death, and then Claudius assuming near ultimate power as the new High Pope…

And with me and Kaleb still healing at the time and wondering if we would live, it was easy I suppose it was easy enough for Claudius to step in and take the reins.

The Human Realm would have surely descended into chaos had he not, and yet it already is chaos and yet the Council should have known better…
They should have acted, instead they stepped aside and let him take over, to start his tyranny and cruelty.

If only I had not been in my sick bed… Perhaps I could have done something.
The Council should have done something, yet they all simply stepped aside like kicked dogs and let Claudius have near enough ultimate control.

But neither of us did do anything, except hold each other and cry.
We had made love for the first time shortly after all of that happened.
It had been amazing, like tonight… Until now, anyhow.

I watch with a dismal grimace as Kaleb begins to pull his trousers and tunic on.
He never gets to stay the night; all these years I have longed to just spend one night asleep in each other's arms… And yet it has never happened.

We can never be found in one another's bed.

It would surely mean our deaths.

THESE PITIFUL HUMANS CANNOT KILL YOU!
YOU HAVE POWERS THAT SHALL STRIKE TERROR STRAIGHT INTO THEIR HEARTS!

But is this really true?

Yes, I have magic, and yes, I feel like my magic is strong, yet rarely being able to Cast and having to constantly suppress myself I have not a chance to really find out what I'm capable of.
What I need is a teacher, yet that is never going to happen.

Not unless I really do find the Secret Court.

I watch as Kaleb gets dressed, and feel despair.
Despair over the fact that my magic is not the only thing I have to suppress, but also my love for him.

It is not right.
The world is wrong.

YOU HAVE THE POWER TO CHANGE THE WORLD!

A vision of myself appears in my head.

Crowned and throned.
Emerald and Crimson.
I look regal and powerful…

I have had the same vision these last three years…

And then it changes.

I hear the sounds of bells.
I'm in the Capital.
Fire everywhere!
Buildings, homes, even people.
Fire everywhere.

And there stands me… **My green eyes burning brightly against the flames.**

The Capital, the streets and buildings, thousands of people screaming and dying.

And I am there, I look powerful.
The most powerful in the world.

The room comes back into view as my vision fades.
I pant hard and grab at my neck as I struggle to breathe.
I have never seen that before… I had seen myself crowned and throned and surrounded by fire before, but I have never seen the Capital burn like that before…

Was it… **The future?**

No… Surely the Capital could not burn, and why was I there?
I'm always there in the fire.
It seems as if no matter what I do or dream, fire is my fate.

"Are you okay?"

Kaleb asks as he reaches for me.

I turn from him and outstretch my hand; I have a desperate need to write down what I saw.
My mind still hazy, the nearby book shakes several times before shooting out, across the room and directly into my hand.
My very own journal or **'Grimoire'** as I've heard witches call them.

I smile widely, happy with myself.

Kaleb on the other hand looks even more pissed off.

"WHAT DID I JUST SAY!"

 His voice raised.

I rise from the bed, anger swelling within me.

I am sick of him always being annoyed whenever I Cast.
And I am sick that I keep having these visions… But the Capital burning is entirely new.

It frightens me, at least I think it does.

But I still looked so powerful… **And beautiful.**

No, I can't think like that.
The Capital and its inhabitants will not perish like that.

"YOU USED TO FIND IT WONDERFUL AND NOW YOU CAN BARELY STAND THE SIGHT OF IT!"

I shout at him.

"Lower your voice."

He gets up from the bed.
I am not too bothered.
I have sent the guards away for hours like I usually do, and they aren't expected back till the morn.
Besides, I used magic often to make my tower soundproof.
No one passing in the corridors and hallways outside would hear a thing.

At least I hoped so.

"Hear what?!
That I have Mag-"

I did not get a chance to say the whole word.
His reflexes amazing like any Slayer, he covers my mouth tightly with his hand and pushes me backwards on to the bed causing me to drop my grimoire.

He falls on top of me and I instantly begin to struggle.
Kaleb quickly grabs both my wrists with his free hand, he uses it to pin my arms behind my head.
His other hand remains tightly clasped around my mouth.

I do not feel any fear, I know Kaleb would never hurt me.
He merely wants me to listen.

"DO NOT SPEAK THAT WORD!
DO NOT EVEN THINK ABOUT IT!"

His voice is beyond angry, yet still low as to not draw attention.

"YOU KNOW WHO LIVES IN THIS CASTLE!
HOW SUPERSTITIOUS THEY ARE?
THE WALLS HAVE EARS, SLAVES REPORT EVERYTHING!"

I begin to attempt to talk, to remind him that no one can hear us, although it's muffled beneath his enormous strong hand.

"DO YOU HAVE ANY IDEA WHAT THEY WOULD DO TO YOU?"

I continue to muffle; Kaleb quickly releases his grip and pushes himself from the bed.

He is shaking with anger.
I rise from the bed and look at him.

"They would drag me from this room, imprison me in the dungeons
and I would be sent to the pyre.
I would be burned to death."

I answer solemnly.

Kaleb winces at this but replies.

"Exactly, they burn every day.
They have for three years.
I've seen it, you've seen it, we've all seen it."

He says in rapid succession.

"And you're worried I'll burn like the rest of them."

 I answer.

He grabs and pulls me from the bed, I fall into his strong arms.

He cups my face roughly and begins to tremble.

"No. That will never happen, do you understand me?"

His face grows dark.

"No!
It may happen to others, but it will never happen to you!
I will never let anyone harm you!

If anyone tries, I will kill them!
I would go to war for you!”

He is deadly serious, meaning every single word.
It makes my heart quicken to hear how much he loves me.
To hear what he would do for me.

YOU HAVE POWER OVER HIM!

“Kiss me.”

 I breathe.

His breathe is ragged, and he looks deeply into my eyes.

He kisses me.

Our tongues dance and I feel like I’m in heaven.
Abruptly he pulls away turns to and leave.
Before he does, he looks back at me and winks at me, my heart skipping a beat as he does.
He quickly pulls his cloak around him, making sure the cloak covers his face.
With that he sneaks out the door.
It closes and then silence.
He always leaves me wanting more.

I stand there, my naked body illuminated by the moonlight.
I outstretch my hand without looking.
My Grimoire flies into my hand as I continue to stare at the moon.

I may not have a teacher but everything about magic I have learned or thought or practised I write it all down, making sure not to forget anything.

It is enchanted…

Enchanted to look exactly like the Book of Light, the sacred book with all the texts and stories and commandments of the God of Eternal Light.

But really it was a spell book.

Claudius would surely drop dead if he knew.

Anyone who believed in God would surely drop dead also.

I smile widely at the thought of the deception.

A GRIMOIRE DISGUISED AS THE BOOK OF ETERNAL LIGHT! HOW DELIGHTFUL, THAT TRULY IS DARK INDEED.

I continue to smile at the thought.

I have used this book for years now, any sort of magic I Cast I write down.

From the smallest to the biggest.

Any magic whatsoever I can conjure, or any information I can learn whatsoever, I write it all down.

YOUR LOVER DOES NOT KNOW ABOUT THIS EITHER!

Yet it does not matter in that moment, for I can not stop staring deeply at the moon.

It is bright and full.

I look at it with intent and feel a shiver of something I cannot quite place my finger on.

It crawls up my back, my body tingling.

As I continue to look at the moon, I feel something coming.

Something dark.
Something dangerous.
Something powerful.

It lights me up with excitement.

DARK, DANGEROUS AND POWERFUL!
SOUNDS DELICIOUS!

Indeed, it does.

With power I can change the world, make it better.

YES, CHANGE THE WORLD!
BURN IT ALL DOWN AND START ANEW!

Flashes of the Capital burning again begin to fill my mind.

And then me, sat on a throne and crowned.

And fire.
Fire everywhere.

I am beginning to fear these visions less, the image of me on the throne
with that beautiful emerald and crimson crown burn deep into me.

I look so powerful… And beautiful.

POWER AND BEAUTY!

Yes, it is all about to come to pass…
Something is coming, it starts tonight.

I smile wickedly at the thought.

MEANWHILE ACROSS THE CASTLE

ANOTHER WATCHFUL NIGHT

ISABELLA

The blazing moonlight keeps me from sleep, I lay there wide awake on my bed.
The sea air pours from the balcony and various windows.
I can hear the violent crashing of the sea.

Feeling restless, I pull myself from my bed and walk straight to the balcony.
The cold air hits me hard.
I plead with myself that I'm not going to see it.
What I had seen before.

The lit candles.

But these were no ordinary candlelight, they shone so brightly that the light shimmers from his tower, the light itself bursting from the balcony and windows.

It was stronger and brighter… **Almost like glistening diamonds.**

I know the reason.
Yet dare not say it.

I know also that whenever I see these strong lights peering from his chambers that Kaleb is no doubt there.

It seems my brother is comfortable enough to… Cast… In front of his lover.

Indeed, he has two huge secrets, secrets I know clearly, however.

He never speaks directly about it; I'm guessing he is too scared.

And he has every right to be.

Two men having sex was enough to get you killed, but magic…

That got you burned.

I have seen it often before, these last few years.

Tristan's rooms were not within the Imperial Apartments, like where that of me and my eldest brother Theodore stayed…

No, Tristan had wanted to live separately…

He picked a small tower close to that of the Inner Spiral…

He did so shortly after the attack three years ago and after he woke up from his several week slumber.

And it's a wonder why.

I wished that it was him who stayed and Theodore that left…

His rooms are only a couple of hallways away, and yet when the wind and sea is quietened, I can hear the screams.

Plenty of girls walked in…
And not all of them walked out.

The candles may be lit, yet I do not know whether Kaleb is still there…

He would be a fool to stay of course, if they were ever caught together at this hour with the rising sun soon approaching, well, it would not end well.

The slaves and servants will surely start their duties now, not to mention the slaves and servants who work during the night.
They have surely seen it… They whisper about it.

Do they both not realise the danger they are in…

Blow out the damned candles!

I think angrily.

I have long had my suspicions, about his ability to Cast, and about his relationship with Kaleb.

Tristan is my twin brother after all, and I can always sense what he wants to remain hidden.
I have no judgement, I care not that he could Cast, or that he was having relations with another man… I care only for his safety.

I love him greatly, and do not want him to…

***TO BE BURNED LIKE ALL THE REST, LIKE THOSE
CONDEMNED TO DIE THIS MORNING!***

The candles do not go out, in fact, they shine brighter than ever.

They glisten and glow brightly, the light emanating fiercely, so much so that the entire tower seems as if it the sun itself.

If I can see them, then so must others.
I know for a fact I am not the only one awake in this castle right now.

I know for a certainty that guards patrol at night, and even servants and slaves go about their nightly duties.

How I wish Tristan would be more careful.
And how I wish I could get some real sleep.
But perhaps that's because like most nights, I cannot sleep.

Especially before an execution.

I know I have to be in attendance, it is mandatory of me as an Imperial…

PLUS, HE SUMMONED YOU; I WONDER WHAT GIFTS HE SHALL SEND THIS TIME.

It has been going on for a while now.
At first it started with compliments.
On my clothing, my appearance…

And then came the gifts.

Perfumes, oils, expensive dresses and even precious jewels.

I did not understand it.

Why was he sending me these things.

DO YOU NOT SEE?
HE CLEARLY WANTS YOU!

The mere thought made my stomach feel uneasy.

He is the High Pope after all.
And whilst the governance of the Realm fell to the stewardship of the Council, they were mostly puppets, it is Claudius who truly rules.

He had started as a Holy Man from humble beginnings; and he slowly gained a following for his particular views on witches.

He had been sent away when I was very young.
I do know he first arrived in the Capital a few years before the fateful year of 299ID, when the Imperial Family nearly was eradicated.
He stayed after too, but was gone and exiled before my birth, however. Myself being born in the early 302ID.
He had heard like so many others about the massacre of the Imperial Family, with only my father surviving.
He went full zealot apparently, spending the next months using the deaths and near extinction of my family to vehemently preach in both the Capital and around the Human Realm.
It was during those travels out in the Human Realm he returned with his adopted son, Connor.
He kept going on about how all witches should die, although it was none other than the Lord of Darkness who committed the atrocity.
He was sent away, however, shortly after his wife died giving birth to their natural son, Claudio. Because of this, he had to leave behind his children including his eldest daughter.

Not allowed to return to the Capital… Until he did.
Had to leave his three children behind, however.
Two born from blood, and one child he found and adopted on his previous travels.

And during those years he was gone, he went from village to village, town to town, preaching his hate.
He had been growing an army and no one even realised.
But he returned just over three years ago.

And when he came back, he quickly went back to preaching in the Capital and even castle.

And then the High Pope disappeared.

He was a kind man I remember; he believed that the God loved all.

Claudius did not.

No one knew what happened to him at the time, but many used to whisper that Claudius done something to him.

Of course, without a body there was no proof of that accusation.

And the attack on Tristan… On Kaleb… It was Claudius who found them… And it was Claudius who was alone with my father in his final days… The rest of the council having been sent away.

The feral was killed bravely by Kaleb by all accounts.

And he of course has that awful scar trailing down his back to proof his fight with the foul beast.

And talks of a Dark Witch, a witch never found.

It remains a mystery to this day.

Claudius was apparently appalled by the attack though.

The Grand Bridge had been immediately sealed off, and I remember the commotion the days after.

Tristan was unconscious and would not wake.

He was treated and attended too by many healing men.

Kaleb was taken care of too… Although thinking back on it I do not remember many worrying about him…

Not as much as Tristan, anyways.

No, Kaleb was kept somewhere else…

I feel a pang of guilt as I realise, I had never even bothered to go and check on him.

With them being treated, Claudius entered the Throne Room when my father and Council members, debated what to do.

Claudius simply walked in and began with a fever like usual condemning witches.

I was not permitted inside of course, being only a girl, and yet I could hear the fever in Claudius voice as he called for the immediate death of all those who could Cast.

From what I gather, the council and many other disagreed.
My father had sent them all away however…
Only my father and Claudius remained…
I had to run and hide then, leaving as the others came out, as I did not want to be found skulking on private matters.

I can only guess what happened or what was said between them.

My father died then, suddenly.
Apparently from a broken heart over what happened to Tristan.
My father always did love us dearly.
But with his death, his last decree was to the begin the Great Cleansing.

It must have been rage, he must have done it in the moment of anger, it surely had to be.
My father would never have done such a thing otherwise.
It was written in his hand and the stamp was with his own personal seal.

The Imperial Seal.

With the previous High Pope having been still missing, and still is to this day, it seemed obvious he needed replaced.

But Claudius of all people…

And he gave himself that title.
And just like that, Claudius not only became the High Pope, but he was also at the very helm of the Great Cleansing, something he enjoyed greatly…

And all around the Human Realm, his men began wildly slaughtering without mercy.
Normal, typical commoners rose up and purged also.

Just because they were witches.

He just went about committing atrocities and war crimes.
And no one dared even stop him.
And even Imperial Soldiers and Guards did so too.
They are no longer within the Imperial service; however, no they became part of a different army instead.

They traded their signature orange suns with gold crowns for a white sun with a sword through it.
And if not on the breastplate of their armour, then emblazoned on their tunics, or even those silly little infernal pins.
An army of hateful people he had been growing for years apparently.

And yet they seemed to pop up out of nowhere.

Defenders.

That's what he called them.

Defenders of the faith.

And yet I did not believe that for a moment.

I had read the Holy Book Of Light, it had many great stories and fables and the condemnation of the Red Eye Demons, more commonly known as vampires.

It talked a lot about souls and the soulless…
Yet as much as I've read, I never saw any texts about the condemnation of witches.

Yet that did not matter.

Hate was hate.

And these Defenders did not just target those with the ability to Cast, no.
They targeted anyone.
Anyone who was different.

Who spoke different.
Who acted different.
Who thought different.
Who looked different.

Claudius and his Defenders did not just execute witches, but anyone deemed even remotely different.

Although the executions of witches always drew in the biggest crowds.

Everyone had to conform…
Conform or die it seemed were the only options.

I gasp as I see him standing then.

Tristan.

He stands there on his balcony, naked as the day we were both born.

What on earth?
What is he doing?
And why?
He does not seem to see me however, his gaze transfixed upwards.

He is starting intently at the dwindling full moon…

And… **What is that?**

He seems to be holding something.
Yet I cannot tell what it is, he is too far away.
I have half a thought to call out to him.
Yet there would be little point.
He wouldn't hear me, not over the sound of the violent waves that surround the cliffs on which this castle is built.

And even if he could hear me, that means others would too.

And I dare not draw attention.
Not to myself, nor to my brother.

I will not be the one to expose him.

I may have very little power, being the third born and only a girl, yet I wielded some power as an Imperial, I must do.

And whatever that power is, however small, I shall surely use it to protect Tristan.

I will not watch my brother burn.

YOU MAY HAVE NO CHOICE.
HE SIGNS HIS OWN DEATH WARRANT WITH HIS OWN
ACTIONS!
HE SENDS HIMSELF TO THE PYRE!

Then I shall have to protect him from himself, it seems.
The moon begins to lose its brightness, as it descends and slowly disappears.
In the east, I can see the beginning of day approaching.
No sun however, always hidden behind clouds.
Yet some light still pours through, however small, indicating daylight.
I looked over to my brother's balcony, he is no longer there.

And the glistening and shining lights are gone.

Thank the Light.

I have been stood here for quite some time, it seems.
The wind howls and the sea bashes against the rocks, yet I do not mind.
I watch as the castle around seems to come alive.

More noises are heard, candles and torches are lit.

The views are incredible.

Not only can I see part of the castle, but I can see the woods and ocean that surround the jittering cliff that the Imperium stands on.
And in the distance, the Grand Bridge and parts of the Capital.
The first Imperial King over three hundred years ago won the last battle between the last warring tribes where the Capital now stands.

But it was this very island he saw in the distance that day, and chose it for where we should dwell these last centuries.

The beginnings of the Capital were built first, and the first members of the Imperial Dynasty lived there whilst construction was undertaken.
Boats travelled back and forth for supplies and the beginnings of the Grand Bridge which connects the two.
The island itself being a piece of land jutting out of the sea.
An island which contained a forest and wildlife which still exists.
The bottom of the island several small fishing villages sprawled around it.
And on top of the island, our stronghold away from everything.
An island fortress, if you will.
The King back then had decided that it would be perfect for the castle to be built.
Safer for his family and future generations he said as he deemed it was only accessible through the Grand Bridge that was built.
Of course, ships and boats could travel, but the waters are so choppy it is unwise.
When supplies and construction had first begun many sailors in boats died during the small travels.

But that's what the first Imperial King had done anyhow.
And yet, construction so grand was timely, the King would not live to see it finished.
We simply did not have enough people to build at the speed in which the King wanted too.
So, before dying, in the Year 03ID he sent forth his son, who took ships and sailed to distant lands to see if he could hire others to help.
According to the histories, he returned with news of people black as night.
Strong and fast, he said he had made friends with them.

He had himself crowned and throned and stayed for several months solidifying his reign before he once again left with more ships.

And in the Year 04ID he came back.

However, apparently once these supposed friends who were dark as night were brought here, they turned against us and unleashed the awful Red Eyed Demons on the land.

A shiver runs down me as I think upon it.

A feral had already got onto this island once… What if more came.

I look at The Grand Bridge and hope those iron gates on both sides are strong enough.

One at the mainland, and one at the island.

The gates are open during the day, to allow lords and ladies to travel freely back and forth, as well as the servants and slaves.

BUT NOT YOU, IT WOULD SEEM.
NO, YOU ARE NOT ALLOWED TO MOVE FREELY.
EVEN THE SLAVES CAN DO THAT.

Not only was that cursed bridge made of iron and stone, but right in the middle it was crafted from wood however and huge chains were used which pulled the wooden part upwards, splitting it into two.

A Bridge with a drawbridge.

I loved the water however and swam there when I could, weather and water permitted.

We had many violent storms, and you could easily die in that water.

I had been stopped several times, but still, I remember sometimes escaping to swim anyways.

It was after all my only real escape.

Many villagers also swam for fish, their boats usually needing constant repairs.

Indeed, only brave people embraced those waters.

Am I brave though?
I cannot always tell.

So anyhow, it seemed as if the first Imperial King was correct.
Building the Imperium here was the perfect idea.

And yet I hate it.

It's certainly safe… And a prison.

A pretty prison on an island surrounded by water yet a prison all the same.
I look past the island and to the mainland where the Capital resides, I can just make out the various buildings.
The easiest thing to see of course is the Grand Spiral, a huge pointing tower that reaches the heavens, situated in the heart of the Capital.

The infamous Slayers Of The Syndicate reside there.

NOT ALL OF THEM THOUGH, IT WOULD SEEM.
LOOKS LIKE A SLAYER PREFERS YOUR BROTHERS BED!

He was not just any Slayer either, he was the Lord Commanders own nephew.

They were both indeed playing a dangerous game.
And yet, it made perfect sense.
Tristan and Kaleb have always been inseparable.
I remember us as children, always playing together.
But Tristan and Kaleb always had that special connection.

Tristan was my twin, we had a bond like no other, and yet it feels as if the bond between them is even stronger.

It always did make me feel jealous, I could not help it.

And here's me, a silly girl it seems obsessed with my own brothers love life.

Perhaps because I do not have one of my own.

And yet why would I want too.

Love does not exist for girls and women it seems.

I have seen girls married around the castle.

Daughters of noble birth sold off by their Lord Father or Lord Brother, usually to some old, disgusting man.

They are raped and impregnated over and over until finally they die in their child bed which is common for nearly every female.

It is no different in the capital.

I have seen and heard lowborn and highborn girls alike abused and killed by their husbands.

Females have little to zero rights.

To me it seems like love does not exist for the likes of us.

We are merely playthings to be sold at a whim by men.

For that reason alone, I decided I would never marry.

I would never be someone's property.

To use and abuse as they saw fit.

BUT YOU WILL NOT HAVE A CHANCE, YOU'RE NINETEEN ALREADY.
YOU SHOULD BE ALREADY MARRIED, ALREADY SQUEEZING OUT MORE IMPERIAL HEIRS.
FULFILLING YOUR DUTY TO THE DYNASTY LIKE SO MANY PRINCESSES AND QUEENS BEFORE YOU!
YOU DO NOT HAVE MUCH TIME LEFT; YOU SHALL SURELY BE WED SOON.
BUT TO WHO?!

Who indeed was certainly a daunting thought.

As a princess, the only living princess and female of the Dynasty, my hand in marriage was highly sought after.

Many lords, both mighty and small had already shown interest.
None of them actually interested in me of course, more interested about what I can bring them as the blood of an Imperial.
I do not want a man to marry me for my status or title, I want them to marry me because they saw me for me.

Not a princess but as just Isabella.

Only Isabella.

Yet it seems like that is not meant to be.
No doubt I will be sold off to marry some Lord with money or food.
And no doubt for extra men too.
Whilst humans are no longer allowed into the Magic Realm due to the Great Cleansing, most of our Imperial Army got stuck there and we are disallowed from sending reinforcements.
The rest of the army which had remained on the Human Realm fell into disarray and disbanded.
The Defenders taking over as our main military.
I suppose Claudius could try and sell me to some Lord in return for more men to become Defenders, however.
Or to keep the peace and stop any lords from gathering men to raise their own army.
His army numbers in the tens of thousands now and he has used these last three years to make sure no one else could try and overthrow him.

But why should I have to sacrifice my life?
My youth, my body.

All for a war that has been going on for hundreds of years.
And I shall be sold to some ugly, fat old Lord to secure any armies in that region.

Of course, what is left of the Imperial Army is loyal to the Imperial Dynasty only, and yet each Lord of course has his own men to guard his own lands.

And what does that make me?

IT WOULD MAKE YOU A CASUALTY OF WAR!
CASUALTY OF WAR!
CASUALTY OF WAR!
CASUALTY OF WAR!

No, I cannot allow that to be my fate.

YOU HAVE NO CHOICE!

As the dawn progresses, I know they will be here any moment.
They usually sleep in my quarters, yet I gave them leave last night to do what they wished.
Yet there was little they could do, of course.
They no doubt went to their home in one of the small fishing villages on the island.
Yes, they will be here any moment.
The large clanging of my doors proves me correct.
Yes, they always make sure to arrive early.

"Enter"
 I shout out.

I hear my doors open, and then close.

"It's cold in here."

I hear one of them say.

"Yes, indeed it is."

Agreed the other.

"Princess, where are you?"

I hear, yet I do not know which says it.
I can hear them walking around my chambers, looking for me.
I don't move, remaining on my balcony.
If only I could hide here forever.

A PRINCESS TRAPPED BY THE SEA!
ALWAYS LOOKING FOR FREEDOM, YET FOREVER
IMPRISONED!

I continue staring out at the views.

"By the Light!"

I hear one of them gasp.

"Princess! You must be freezing!"

Says the other.

I turn to face them.
It's twin women, slaves.
Dark skin, both young and pretty, however they still have silver collars
fitted around their necks.
And not just any silver, but that of Saerillian.

All slaves In the Capital and Imperium wore Saerillian silver.
Can't have any slaves suddenly realising they can Cast.
The lesser and poorer areas of the Human Realm however can only use normal silver.
And Saerillian not only burns witches, but it stops them from Casting altogether if they are chained.
However, it is evident that neither One nor Two had magic, for neither of them have burn marks.
Not that I can see, anyhow.
The twins looked completely identical too.
Although I know their names, I can never name them correctly.
They instead stitched initials into their clothing.

An O and a T

O standing for One.
And T standing for Two.

Therefore, they were referred to as One and Two.
Bad I know, yet it was the only way I can possibly differentiate between the two.

"Gods, you need to warm yourself immediately, Princess!"

Says Two.

"SHHHH!"

Hisses One.

"Do not dare mention the gods, not here!
There is only one God, the God Of Light!
Remember that, remember it well!"

Demands One.

I do not mind the mention of Two speaking about the gods, after all as
my friends I let them speak freely.
Only within my chambers of course, and only when it is just the three of
us.

Yet Gods or God, do any of them exist?

I mean, truly.
And if they do, why do they allow such horror to overtake the country?
Why so much death.
No, I doubt any of them really existed.

The Old Gods or The New.

Two simply rolls her eyes.

"The Old Gods existed long before."

She says.

"Don't make me slap you."

Threatens One.

"If you slap me then I'll slap you."

 Warns Two.

A giggle escapes from my lips.
They were always like this.

Forever arguing with each other, yet it is easy to tell they were inseparable.
It's a twin thing, after all.
One is the elder, she cares for Two greatly and often remands her.
Two on the other hand is more outspoken… Yet I do not think she means to be.
She does it without thinking.
They notice me giggling at them and their faces soften.

"Princess, please come inside.
You'll catch a cold."

Soothes One.

"Yes, a cold."

 Repeats Two.

I take both of their hands as they lead me back into my room, and away from the cold.
I hear the wooden doors close behind me, yet the wind still howls through them.
It's ferocity not able to be muted.
They wrap a shawl around me and begin to rub my arms and back, trying to warm me.

"We must get you bathed and dressed, Princess."

Says One.

"The execution is at midday."

She concludes.

I am dreading it.

I have seen many die by flame, and it never gets any easier.

Not once.

And the smell… I can smell it even when it's not happening.

"The execution, is it in the Capital?"

I ponder and wish.

Not wishing for the death of those poor people of course but wishing I might be able to get off this bloody island and across to the mainland and the Capital.

I have not left for weeks.

The Grand Bridge remains accessible of course, yet I am not allowed to travel along it.

As an Imperial Princess I am not permitted to travel freely, as a woman in fact I am not allowed either.

Neither are any of the other ladies here trapped here on this island?

Yet the men, including my elder brothers are allowed to travel freely.

Theodore leaves almost every morning with his group of… **Friends.**

A group of highborn men, who share… Similar interests such as him.

One of these men includes Claudius own son, Claudio.

He is a great burden on Claudius, a deep shame due to what they get up too in the Capital.

My brother, Claudio, and the rest.

Vile, vile things.

Aimed exclusively at women.

As a Princess, it is not deemed fit for me to mention the things they do.

Unspeakable things.

And he is supposed to be King one day.
A scary thought indeed, especially for any woman who is near him.
Tristan leaves too, yet he mainly leaves dressed in the clothes of small folk.
He likes to leave and come without being noticed.
Kaleb does this too I have noticed.

No doubt they met in secret in the Capital.
Claudius with his executions.
Theodore with his vile nature and Tristan with his secrets.
It seems as if men can do whatever they please.

"Yes, the execution shall be In the Capital."

Answers One grimly.

"But let us get you in the bath, Princess."

Says One.

"Yes, a bath."

Repeats Two.

Whilst I have my bath, One and Two go about their duties.
Cleaning, sweeping, dusting and wiping.
They also pick out my clothing for the day, not to mention my jewellery.

They know my favourites and I trust them with their choices.
Bathed, I stand out of the water and One and Two begin to dry me.
Once dried, they both begin to brush my hair.
It is wavy and yellow; it hangs to my hips.
They also apply scents and oils to my body.
About to get dressed, I hear another knock on the door.

All of us freeze.

Please do not let that be what I think it is!

One goes to the door.
I do not see who is on the other side, merely that something is exchanged between the two of them.
One closes the door and turns to me.
In her hands, she holds a fancy box.

IT IS EXACTLY WHAT YOU THINK IT IS…
A GIFT FROM CLAUDIUS…

One stands at the door, almost upset at the thought of having to give it to me.
Two rubs my shoulder, offering comfort.

"Bring it to me."

I say gloomily.

He will want me to wear this to the execution no doubt.
Yes, I do not believe there is Old Gods or a God Of Light.
Only this hellish nightmare I find myself trapped in.

"He should not be doing this, Princess."

Say One.

"I agree, he is overreaching his hand."

Joins in Two.

He may only have the title of High Pope, but it's evident that he controls more power than anyone else in the Human Realm.
It seems as if he can do whatever he wishes.
Which includes sending me expensive gifts.

A PRINCESS TRAPPED, LIKE SO MANY BEFORE YOU!

One gingerly walks to me and opens the box for me.
Inside, a beautifully made gold chain with an assortment of blue sapphires.

"Would you like me to put it on you, Princess?"

 She tentatively asks me.

POOR, TRAPPED PRINCESS.
THIS IS YOUR FATE, LIKE SO MANY BEFORE YOU.

As a Princess I was taught courtesy and ladylike behaviour from an early age.
To say my pleases and give thanks with a smile and grace.
To be quiet and obedient in front of men.
To always wear a smile and have a sunny disposition.
Yet all of that went out the window as I said the following.

"Let us get this over with."

I mutter miserably.

"The execution will be soon."

I finish just as miserably.

One and Two hold me then as I begin to weep.

Will this ever end?!

I think as I continue to cry.

THE INNER SPIRAL

MORNING TROUBLES

KALEB

The crowds cheer loudly and enthusiastically.
They holler and scream in happiness.

"BURN HIM!
 BURN THE WITCH!"

I can hear the crowds cry.

I can see him then; he is drugged and being dragged towards the pyre.
He looks groggy, but I can tell those eyes from anywhere.

Beautiful Emeralds, they shine so brightly even in his weakened state.
I become frantic then.
I shove and push my way through the crowd, harshly throwing people aside.
But it doesn't matter how many I push past; they are quickly replaced by more and more in front of me.

"MOVE OUT OF THE WAY!"

I scream as loudly as I could, and yet my voice is lost in the thousands of voices in the crowd.
He is further and further away from me, dragged closer and closer to the pyre.

"BURN HIM!
BURN HIM!
BURN HIM!"

They chant in unison.
Over and over again.
I begin to push even more wildly, pushing people as hard as I can.
I trample over them as I eagerly, desperately try to get to him.

They get to the scaffold.

He is dragged upwards and tied to the pyre.

"BURN HIM, BURN HIM, BURN HIM!"

They continue to chant, thousands of voices beaming with joy at the prospect.

Do they not know who he is?
He is their Prince?!
He has the blood of the Imperial Dynasty in his veins.

"NO!"

I scream.
It does not matter.
My voice is merely wind, a whisper in the storm.

I look up at him on the pyre, those beautiful emeralds meet mine through the sea of the crowd.
I can see the fear, the longing to be saved.
I pull my sword from its scabbard then; I slash and hack wildly and randomly, cutting down anyone in my way.

Cutting down peasants… For him.
Anything for him.

People all around me begin to scream.
They recoil and flee in terror.

But despite how many I slaughter, there's still thousands to travel through.
Tristan seems further and further away the closer I get.

I'm panting hard and, drenched in blood, I nearly slip on it as I continue to push forward.
The cobblestones beneath my boots are slick with red.
I look up at him, he's still looking at me, that same sense of dread in those gorgeous green eyes.

That's when I see the torch.
And just like that, the pyre is lit.

The flames take hold quickly.
Travelling upwards, towards Tristan's feet.

"No!"

My scream is so loud it burns my throat.

I see Tristan once more then.

The fear and despair that was once in his eyes a moment ago is gone.

Instead, they shine brightly with a fierceness…

And on his lips, a smile…

But not one of Tristan's usual warm, happy, make your heart pound fast and time stand still smiles.

No this is different.
A smile I have not seen before.
This is a smile that looks sinister.
It sends a shiver down me, and that's not something that happens to me.

The scene changes abruptly then.

The pyre, the cheering crowds, the fire, Tristan and that smile, they all disappear.
The vast Grand Square replaced by woods…
The crowds replaced by trees…

And the blood beneath my feet, it's now…

Flowers and snow.

Tristan is there, although younger.

I know the night instantly.
It's the night I followed him to the woods, and first saw him Cast.
I always had a feeling he could, a feeling of sorts.

He was special after all.

So special.

It was also the night I gifted him the wooden sword necklace I had handcrafted.
Made from Black Oak.
A necklace he still wears to this day.

It's also the night we professed our love for one another.
Something else I was overjoyed about.
We kissed that night, and it was the best thing that ever happened to me.
It's beautiful, a memory I cherish.

And it appears to be happening again.
Tristan's lips touch mine, and it feels glorious.

The beauty of that night changes however…

Red eyes appear.
And then the snapping of fangs.

I wake up then.
I shoot upright in my bed, panting hard.
Sweat covers me, my hairy chest is slick.
My eyes come into focus, and I find myself in my bed, one of several that surround the room.
The other beds are empty, I can hear noise from downstairs.
Lost in… A dream?... A nightmare… A memory?
Whatever it had been, it terrifies me.
A feeling I am not accustomed too.
Both dreams, and nightmares, they both involved Tristan.
And they were both of things I dread the most, his death.

No, whatever happens, he will not die.

BUT YOU COULDN'T SAVE HIM FROM EITHER.
NOT FROM THE FLAMES, NOT FROM THE FANGS.

But I saved him from the fangs… Had I not?

I do not remember much from that night.
I remember the good things.
Seeing Tristan Cast, and gifting him that wooden sword necklace he loves, the one that took me a week to carve.
I remember the kiss, our love.

All of the beauty.

But the Red Eyes and fangs…

They have always haunted me.
I think I had pushed Tristan out of the way… I fought it, didn't I?
I stuck it with my sword…

Then… **Nothing.**

I woke up a few days later, sore and groggy.

Yet I felt strong… stronger than before.
And my heart, my heart felt stronger too.

It was weird, but true.
I had been locked somewhere in the Imperium, the Imperium itself had also been on full lockdown.
I did not wake up in the rooms belonging to my family however, or in the bed I had always slept in.

No, I woke up in some dark, damp room.

And there were no familiar voices to greet me either.

Not my mother or sister, who had and still do reside in the castle.

And not my uncle either, I had later found out he was stuck on the mainland, the drawbridge of the Grand Bridge had been raised, keeping the island sealed off.

Only one Daughter tended to me, a Daughter being a woman of faith who had healing knowledge.

She at least made sure I was alright.

Apart from that however, I had been locked in a room.

Extremely weird I had thought at the time and still do.

My torso had been wrapped tightly.

And my back felt weird.

I could tell I had suffered a massive wound to my back, yet I could not feel a thing.

Nor did I have the fever most men got from a supposed wound.

I asked for mirrors, even a piece of glass to look at my back, yet I was not allowed.

And when the Daughter changed my bandages, I was not allowed to touch my back to feel it.

I had been locked there for days but it felt like weeks.

And then the bells…

The bells only rung if something important was happening.

I could hear them, all over the castle.

I was terrified something had happened to Tristan, so I broke down the door with my bare fists.

I ran through the corridors, blood dripping from my knuckles, and came upon Tristan's rooms in the Imperial Apartments.

He was surrounded by healing men and Daughters, it turned out he was in a slumber of some sort, and no one knew when he would wake.

I remember them all being shocked at seeing me.

Had they even known I had been locked away?

Or that I was there with Tristan, that I had saved him…

But the bells turned out to be not for him, instead the King had just died…

And that's when the Cleansing came.

MAYBE YOU DID SAVE HIM FROM THE FANGS?
MAYBE YOU DID NOT…
BUT WHAT ABOUT THE FLAMES?
WILL YOU SAVE HIM FROM BURNING…

I would do anything for him.

EVEN MURDER COMMONERS…
YOU CUT THEM DOWN WITH THAT SWORD…

No, it was just a dream… Or a nightmare… Or both.

DREAM, NIGHTMARE, REAL LIFE.
WOULD YOU DO IT… WOULD YOU KILL THE INNOCENT FOR HIM?

I sincerely hoped that I would never have to find out.

I shake my head.

Shake the thoughts, dreams and nightmares from my head.

I climb out of the bed, and hurry to the basin of water.

I quickly grab a sponge, soak it in the scented water and begin to vigorously scrub my body, removing away any traces of sleep and sweat… And seed.

Seed from last night, when I had made love to Tristan.

But as always, I had to leave.

And I left on an argument.

I should not have just walked off, but I did not want to continue the conversation we always seemed to have as of late…

HE IS VERY STRONG-MINDED… AND ANGRY, DOES IT NOT SEEM?
YES, HE DOES SEEM TO BE RATHER INTENT…
WITH THE THRONE AND WITH MAGIC.
AND THAT TALK OF REMOVING CLAUDIUS…

But that is just idle chatter, mere threats, he would never really murder anyone…

BUT DOES CLAUDIUS NOT DESERVE TO DIE?

I thought about that then, as I continued to wash and scrub my body.

Claudius is despicable, truly a tyrant.

This Great Cleansing of his, it's an abomination.

And yet so many people joined in for the cull.

Small folk, from the lowest to hard working, poor and better off, even the high lords and ladies, they all joined in for the bloodshed.

I knew humans always disliked witches being in our Realm, many believed they should have stayed in their own, and yet I had not realised that given the free pass to murder that so many participated.

It disgusted me and left me with little faith in humanity.

The Syndicate which I am a part of is divided on it.

Many Slayers even joined in with the cull, although my uncle the Lord Commander strictly forbade it.

Something I was thankful for, it made me realise he truly was honourable.

He once stayed in this very the Inner Spiral where I stand now, he even has a room strictly for the Lord Commander only above this room.
However, he left three years ago, when the Cleansing first started.
He was disgusted and would no longer live, stay or sleep at the castle.

I stayed however… Something which caused a great argument between me and my uncle.
He could not understand why I wanted to stay…

FOR TRISTAN.
EVERYTHING YOU HAVE DONE, EVERYTHING YOU DO, IT IS ALWAYS FOR HIM.

Body thoroughly washed; I glance at a mirror adjacent to me.

I have to stand back to see myself clearer, being taller than the mirror.
I am tall, incredibly muscular and my body covered in a thick pelt of fur.
Tristan loved to run his hands thorough it when we made love.

I quickly get to work putting on my armour, which I had left at the foot of my bed.
It is black as night, and recently cleaned.
It shone in the morning light.
A huge red sun with a Black Oak stake through it emblazoned on the breastplate.
And a thick, black cloak to match.

It takes me several moments to get myself together.
When I am finally ready, I quickly hurry down the stairs.

"Morning, sleepy head."

I hear a familiar voice shout.

It's that of Liam, a close friend.

He is tall, although not as tall as me.

Classically handsome with dark eyes, much like my own.

Yet he is clean shaven always.

Our hair is both cut short however, in the style that most Slayers of the Syndicate keep their hair.

We became Initiates at the same time and underwent training together.

He sits at a table breaking his fast with my other friends.

The table consisting of Boris, George and Luca.

Boris is heavyset and sometimes dumb but kind.

Then there is George; he is younger than me, yet he has a not-so-secret lover with three children who he keeps not so hidden within the Capital.

And then Luca, the newest and pluckiest of the group.

We are the only ones who regularly stay at the Inner Spiral.

And as of late, sadly Edgar.

And yet, we have all slain a vampire.

It is after all the only way to become an Initiate… Apart from me.

I had gotten to take my Initiation without having to slay a vampire.

I merely begged my uncle again and again until he relented.

He relented and some small part of me wish he hadn't.

It had caused great animosity amongst the rest of the Syndicate.

Every other member having earned their Initiation through slaying a vampire.

Whilst vampires live in the Dark Realm, many often manage to sneak and leak into the other Realms.

Older vampires of course; the newer ones do not have the best self-control.

They can hide and live amongst the Magic and Human Realms without getting caught.

At least for a while, anyways.
Usually accompanied by Dark Witches who help conceal them.
However, it is somewhat rare, and yet it does happen.
Thankfully, they are often found and swiftly killed.

All my friends at the table have come across and slain such a trespassing creature.
Of course, you always have the choice to say no.
And yet, many say yes.
Mainly because when you're a peasant with no chance of a good life, being part of the Syndicate which can always offer you somewhere to sleep and eat seems intriguing to many.

"Wish I could sleep in."

Liam hollers playfully.
I shoot him my middle finger and I give a nervous laugh, still wrestling with my thoughts.

They are already seated, and by the looks of things, they are finished eating.

"If you're going to eat, I'd hurry, we have to leave soon.
Our duties start."

He tells me.

I smile at him, and answer.

"Perhaps your duties, maybe.
I'm expected for another execution."

They all look at me, fallen silent.

It's true, no one likes these mornings.

We have all seen so much death these last three years… So many people burnt.

No matter how I try, I can never forget the smell of burning flesh.

"This shall be a godly day indeed."

A voice says from the corner.

I turn and see none other than Edgar… Anger rises in me at the mere sight of him.

He did not usually stay here, instead staying in the Grand Spiral back at the Capital, and yet for the last few weeks he had annoyingly stayed here.

The rest shift uncomfortably in their seats; they do not like him either.

He might be a fellow Slayer, and yet he is too feverish in his faith.

Many Slayers of course do follow the faith and yet they did so in private.

"I wonder if Claudius will give any speeches today.

It is always good to hear his wise words."

His voice was usually solemn and grave, but whenever he spoke of Claudius, he seemed happy.

I didn't like it, not one bit.

"Nothing about today is good, Edgar."

I tell him.

"Then you are foolish and cannot see that today is a day of God!

He will shine his Eternal Light on those soulless witches and cleanse them from their hateful nature."

"You shouldn't speak to your Captain like that, **your superior.**"

Comments Liam.

The rest of my friend's chime in unison.

I ignore it, I have never been one for commanding respect and authority.
The urge to lord over people was never for me.
Edgar does not answer, he simply continues reading from his miniature book of Light.

"The lords and ladies who are wanting to see the action are no doubt already ready.
Same for the Imperial Family."

Mentions George whilst gorging a piece of bread.

"Theodore will be already drinking."

Boris says

They all laugh together.

"And the Princess… She will no doubt look beautiful as ever."

Luca adds.

He was young and had a huge crush on the Princess.
I cannot say I blame him.

The Princess, much like her twin brother Tristan were both beautiful.

"And Tristan will no doubt argue with Claudius, that's always fun.
He always cries at the executions."

Replies Boris.

"Yeh, I would pay to see that."

George adds.

He's my friend, yet this annoys me greatly.

This was true, Tristan had made several incidents at executions before,
and he had even shed tears.

He had cursed at Claudius, even shouting that what's happening is
wrong.
Yet he had only ever done that in the castle, some executions taking
place in the courtyard.
He is largely ignored, no one dare go against Claudius in the castle.

"Nah, Tristan won't do anything.
It's not in the privacy of the castle, it's in full view in front of thousands
at the Capital."

Says Liam.

So, the execution is in the Capital then it seems.
I had half hoped that it would be done in the courtyard, at least that is
more private.
These executions in the Capital do nothing more than earn further ire
and spread more fear.

"True, he is an Imperial after all, he needs to behave in the public eye, more so the Capital."

Says Boris.

"He always seems tired."

 Remarks Luca.

I remember last night, the feeling of me inside of him.
How he had writhed and squealed underneath me, how he had nestled into my chest after.
It felt glorious and had certainly made me feel tired this morning.

"I heard slaves say he doesn't sleep… Spends hours in that tower with hundreds of candles lit, just reading or whatever he does."

Says Luca.

It is true, Tristan often spends many hours into the night reading by candlelight.

If we're not making love…

"He does not have hundreds of candles, that's nonsense.
That would burn down the bloody tower.
If the smoke didn't suffocate him first."

Answers Boris.

"No, it is hundreds.

I've seen the tower sometimes late at night, you should see the lights from his windows.
It's so bright."

Finished Luca.

My whole body becomes rigid at that.

Tristan always made the candles burn brighter with his Casting.
He did it for me… Back when I was in awe of his magic.
But now… Now I just want to keep him safe.

Every single time, even though I always tell him to stop.

To be careful.

But it seems he's been doing it more and more often by himself.

Does he not realise how dangerous this is?
Does he not care?

YOU USED TO FIND IT WONDROUS!
YOU USED TO THINK IT WAS AMAZING, THAT HE IS
AMAZING…

He is still amazing… I only want to protect him.

BUT BY PROTECTING HIM, YOU OPPRESS HIM.

I know this is right.
There had been a time when I really did think this was wondrous and amazing…

But ever since that Imperial decree…
To Cleanse all those who could Cast…
And with Claudius living in the castle, king in all but name, and his Defenders always lurking, I had to protect Tristan.
If he was caught… Claudius surely would condemn him.
Tristan thinks his name gives him protection, but it doesn't.
Maybe if the King had survived, if Tristan had been able to speak to his father…

Perhaps things would be very different right now.
But as they stood, magic meant death.
And I would not allow Tristan to die, not under any circumstances.
The image of him tied to the pyre appears in my mind.
I groan in pain at the thought of it.

Liam notices this.

Notices my discomfort.

"Perhaps we should get going, boys."

He shouts.

They call mutters various agreements and take their leave of the table.

Liam shares a look at me.

I would not openly say it or ask him, but I had a feeling that he knew…

About me and Tristan.

If he did, he has not mentioned it once.
I am thankful for that.

He takes his leave with the rest of them, one by one they leave the Inner Spiral.
The slaves immediately start to clear up and clean.
I too get up from the table and say a thanks to them.
They smile back warmly.
It's never sat right with me, the use of slaves.
People should not be owned, regardless of the colour of their skin.

I go to take my leave then, but Edgar stands too.

He approaches me and I have no option but to pause.

"Captain."

He says in a tone that doesn't feel like I'm his Captain whatsoever.

I know he looks down on me.
He is twice my age, and therefore feels as if he should be Captain instead of me.
In fact, many in the Syndicate think the same.
And the other Captains, well, they hate me.
To be a Captain is a prestigious honour, an honour many feel that I do not deserve.
That I had gotten due to being the Lord Commander's nephew, not to mention the General's son.

They deem me unworthy.

But I had I not slain a feral at age only seventeen?

I had protected the prince.

Tristan, my love.

"Perhaps you could enlighten me why you are here?
Again?"

I ask him.

It is odd, seeing him here this morning, once again.
Three years ago, when I had decided to stay here, my best friend Liam
and the others joined me.
I had at first thought I would have the Inner Spiral to myself, which
was a nice thought.
I thought perhaps it could have been a love nest for me and Tristan…
But the others joined anyhow.
Of course, sometimes they were not here, too busy with their duties,
and during those times me and Tristan had enjoyed each other's bodies
here, but always quickly.
It was easy dismissing slaves after all, but I could hardly stop fellow
Slayers and friends from coming and going as they pleased.

Things have been good though, I must admit, but these last few weeks
now Edgar has been here.
Showing up all hours of the day and sleeping here too.
Skulking around the castle like some rat.
And particularly skulking around Claudius chambers.
It did not sit well with me whatsoever.
And here he is this morning once again.

"Captain, the Inner Spiral is for any visiting member of the Syndicate.
To stay, use and sleep In as I wish."

He answers.

"Yes, I know.
But why are you specifically here?
You do not usually come to the island."

This was true, it had only been the last few weeks he had pestered us.

"Well, as you know, I have always had a love for the faith, and I have long admired Claudius."

He gushes.

The fact he admired Claudius spoke volumes.

"Well, I have spoken to him before, over the years, only ever briefly and in passing.
But I thought perhaps if I came to the castle more often, then I could speak to him more."

His answer is all sorts of wrong.

Whilst many in the Syndicate do have their believes in the Faith, this is kept to themselves, as when you become a Slayer you dedicate your life to the Syndicate, forsaking all else.

***HE HAS NOT FORSAKEN HIS RELIGION, JUST AS YOU HAVE NOT FORSAKEN YOUR LOVE FOR THE PRINCE.
YOU ARE JUST AS BAD...***

I push this aside as I ask.

"And... Why exactly do you want to speak to him so much?"

No, this does indeed not sit well with me.

"Well, because of his visions of course.
God speaks to him directly, and I would love to hear and share his thoughts on our Lord.
And where we can go forth with this Great Cleansing."

He answers, without so much as stuttering, as if he does not hear his own madness.

Another thing wrong with him, a Slayer who believes wholly in this Cleansing.
It is true that since the beginning of the Syndicates creation, we have indeed slain witches.
Witches who were known as Dark Witches, however.
Those who used their ability to Cast for eviler purposes.
We did not outwardly kill the innocent.
But there was, of course, over the centuries the odd Slayer here or there who murdered witches without cause, but they were always swiftly dealt with and executed.
And it pains me to admit, when the Great Cleansing began, some Slayers did partake in the violence and death, however they too were found and dealt with.

But three years later and here stands a Slayer who clearly and evidently wants to continue in the death.
It sickens and disgusts me, and I hate that someone like this even stands before me.

Wearing the armour of a Slayer.
It is the greatest dishonour.

I take a step toward him, towering over him.

He shows the slightest reaction of fear before it disappears as quickly
as it arrived.

"I think you should focus on your duties as that of a Slayer.
If you are to be here on the island, and in the castle, then I suggest you
focus on keeping a watchful eye and protecting those of the Realm.
Especially the Imperial Family who reside here."

He looks affronted at me telling him what to do yet says nothing.

He continues to stand there, in my way.

"Is there anything else?"

I ask of him, angrily.

He smacks his lips before answering.

"May I go to the execution."

He asks instead.

I scoff at him.
The brazenness of it, I could hit him.

"Do whatever you like."

I bark, then turn to leave then but he continues.

"You should really pray more, Captain."

He calls out.

I roll my eyes yet turn to face him anyways.

"If you don't pray, how do you expect God to protect you."

Is this a threat?

I take another step toward him, towering over him once again.

"And what exactly does God need to protect me from?"

I ask harshly.

"As I said, get on with your duties."

"But a moment ago you said I could do what I want, which is it,
Captain?
Your orders are confusing."

I sigh at this; he is clearly trying to get a rise out of me.

"Do your duties, and if you have free time, then go to the execution I
suppose."

 I tell him.

"Of course, I shall do my duties as soon as I have prayed again.
To ask God that I finish my duties and get to see the Lord's work today.
And of course, it's always good seeing Claudius.
Even if it's just from the crowd."

He speaks gleefully.

I can feel my anger rising, I clench my fists.

"As a Slayer, you should spend more time with your duties then praying constantly."

"Guarding the Realm, yes, but would you deny a man his faith?"

He knows I cannot outwardly say no, to talk against Faith is treasonous since Claudius came to control.

"Perhaps you spend more time praying for the poor bastards about to be set on fire."

I say through gritted teeth.

He looks confused at this.

"Why would I pray for them?
They're abominations and deserve death."

I could beat him to death.

I look at him in utter disgust and take my leave before I do actually beat him to death.
Leaving then, I walk down the few stairs that lead to the door.
As I walk away, can hear him start praying.

I open the door quickly and slam it shut behind me, shutting off the Inner Spiral and the sound of his prayers.

Sighing, I begin to walk the hallway.
I feel like I can actually breathe, being away from Edgar.
The audacity of him, I only wish I could ban him from visiting the Inner Spiral, however I simply cannot.

He is correct in what he said, as a Slayer of the Syndicate, he does indeed have the right to enter, use and sleep in any Spiral within the Realm.

Angry thoughts still swirl in my mind; it is people like him that brought a bad name to the Syndicate.
And just another Slayer who thinks little of me, does not respect my title of Captain.
I did not care, I did not care if it was true, if I only got my position as Captain for being the Lord Commanders nephew.
I did not care if I was just given the title, because despite what everyone else thought, there was one thing that I know has not been given to me or handed to me because of birth or blood.

And that is Tristan.
He is mine.

He loves me because he chooses to, and I love him too.
Yes, if anything in my life that I could say was truly mine, it is him.
I cannot wait to see his face again, even if it is at an execution.
Perhaps I should go to his tower and visit him beforehand.
Clear the air from last night, and make sure he is okay, and to beg him to behave today.

His tower is close, originally an abandoned tower.
Tristan originally lived in the Imperial Apartments, where Theodore and Isabella lived.
Yet Tristan had left, three years ago.
This was after the fight with the feral… and this supposed Dark witch?
And after the King died…
After the Great Cleansing began…

Yes, he had moved to the tower.

No one could understand it at first, why Tristan wanted to move from the Imperial Apartments and into an old, ugly, abandoned tower…
But it was because it was not only vacant, but closest to the Inner Spiral where I slept…
It was so we could stay closer to each other.
He had joked about it in his sickbed after the attack, trying to tease me.
He asked me if that would be such a bad thing, I had replied I couldn't wait.
And thus, Tristan moved into his tower and stayed there these past three years.
Close to me… How I longed to go to him now.

More thoughts of him surge in me.
Of us.

Of our love.

A LOVE YOU HAVE TO HIDE…
IMAGINE WHAT WOULD HAPPEN IF THEY EVER FOUND OUT?
EVERYONE WOULD TURN AGAINST YOU…
YOU WOULD JOIN TRISTAN ON THE PYRE, TO DIE IN THE FLAMES!

If loving Tristan meant the flames, then so be it.

I really do hope he will behave today; he was so angry last night.
He hates the world and wants to change it, and I love him for that.

But the way he is going about it, it's wrong.

I half think Tristan would really murder to get the throne… It's not right.
Even if Claudius deserves to die, there is no point now.

His power is coming to an end, and Theodore will be crowned…

Truly, I do not think that was better.

But with Claudius no longer in control once Theodore is crowned then perhaps the Council might finally grow their balls back and actually try to make things right.

To restore this Realm and make it better.

DO YOU TRULY BELIEVE THAT?
THAT CLAUDIUS WILL JUST WALK AWAY AND FADE INTO
MERE MEMORIES?
AND DO YOU REALLY THINK THEODORE WILL EVEN LISTEN
TO THE COUNCIL, OR ANYONE?
THE REALM WILL CONTINUE TO WORSEN, NOT PROSPER.

No, I cannot believe that.

I have to hope for the best.

Besides, I should not really be thinking about it all.

It is not my place, not as a Slayer, I cannot interfere in the Realm of Men.

The castle is cold this morning, the wind cuts to the bone.

I decide that I will visit Tristan before we have to depart, however, just as I'm about to turn in the direction of his tower, a young boy runs toward me.

A serving boy by the looks of him, fair skinned and dark haired.

By the look on his face, he looks terrified.

"Are you okay."

I ask him.

He comes to a halt, panting from running.

He looks incredibly small compared to my massive self.

"M – my L – Lord."

He continues to catch his breath, when he does, he says more clearly.

"My Lord, I have a letter for you.
From your Lady Mother."

 He answers.

I take the note from him, my mother's seal stamped in bright pink wax.

I open the note and read as follows.

DEAREST SON,

COME TO OUR FAMILY APARTMENTS AT ONCE.
WE HAVE URGENT NEWS TO DISCUSS.
DO NOT SHOW THIS LETTER TO ANYONE.

YOUR LOVING MOTHER.

Knowing my mother's usage of the word **'urgent'** could mean something as simple as that she ran out of pink fabric.

I shudder at the thought.

I realise then that the boy is still standing there, looking at me brightly.

"Are you really a Slayer?

You killed a vampire at only seventeen?
You torched him and he died."

He said all the words in a hurry.

I can't help but let out a booming laugh.

"Why, yes, I suppose I did do that."

 I say between chuckles.

Although, even three years later, I still do not remember anything about fire…

"You protected the prince and saved the day."

 He beams.

I smile.

"Why, I suppose I did indeed."

 I answer.

"When I grow up, I want to be just like you!
I want to have a Saerillian Silver Sword and Slay vampires!"

Sweet kid.

I tuck the letter in my sleeve and say to the boy.

"You know what, how about you come by sometime at the courtyard.

I'm usually there in the morning, come by and I'll teach you how to wield a sword."

He shows me a big, goofy smile then.

"Yes, yes, thank you so much my Lord."

With that he runs off screaming in excitement.

I end up laughing once again.

I debate still going to Tristan's tower.
I'm of two minds, I want to go to Tristan and speak soft words, and to hold him in my arms once more and put all of last night's nonsense aside.
Yet I know if I do not go visit my mother when summoned I will never hear the end of it.
Perhaps it is better to give Tristan more time to cool off anyhow, his mood can sometimes last longer than I would like.
So, I turn and walk the opposite direction, towards my family's apartments.

Arriving at the apartments, I am greeted warmly by the guards who open the doors for me.
Guards I had seen before many times.
Good men, and loyal.
I walk inwards and am in a large room.

There are chairs, desks, a big table, as well as plenty of other furnishings.
And on the wall, all across are various weapons.
Spears, swords, axes, maces and much more.
Mighty, historical weapons.

And every single one of them has a pink ribbon tied in a bow around them.

My mother is shameless, truly.

Weapons that had belonged in our family for centuries.
Weapons from our forefathers, and also weapons of my father, the infamous General.
Weapons from various battles and wars, each containing their own history.
House Umpire itself had lasted a century less than the Imperial Dynasty, we even shared blood, once, distantly.

There was a third son of an old Imperial King some two hundred years ago, with little prospects of course.
He however became distinguished in a battle long past and was granted great lands and a huge castle.
He decided to also forgo the name of Imperial and begun his own house.
Naming it Umpire, and thus my house was born.

This castle is to the north of the Human Realm, yet hardly used.
We have always been a house of warriors, and have always been on the battlefield, or in the Capital.

My grandfather grew up at our family castle however and raised my father and uncle for a handful of years, yet once they became slightly older, they were brought to the Capital and the Imperium, and we have resided here since.
My grandfather died before I was born, and my father married my mother young and sired me.
Whilst she was still pregnant with me, he began his campaigns at the BorderLands, and he rarely ever came back.

Not that he could anymore, anyhow.
Since the Cleansing began, any humans including the vast majority of the Imperial Army and therefore also my Lord Father had been held all but captive in name there.

Still, our House is proud, and I suppose it also means we share blood with the Imperial Family, and I guess, technically I am related to Tristan, as well as Theodore and Isabella.

However, very distantly.
I doubt if I even have one drop of Imperial Blood left to be honest.

Besides, it matters little, there are hardly any Lords or Ladies in the Human Realm that have not been attached to the Imperial Family either through marriage or blood at some point over the last few centuries.

I see my little sister, Violet, by the hearth, she sees me too and immediately runs towards me.
Her dark hair flows behind her in a mess of tangles and her blue eyes are sharp.
She jumps into my arms, and I swing her in the air.
She giggles and laughs as I set her back down.

"I've missed you!"

 She complains.

I have not been here for a few weeks.
Sadly, my many duties prevented me.
When I'm not busy as a Slayer, travelling to and from the Capital and the Island, I spend most of whatever precious time I have left for Tristan.

I always want to visit more, yet I never seem to find the chance.

"Sweetness."

I hear a shrill voice beckon from above.

I look upwards and my mother stands there, her hands on the wooden balcony.
She quickly makes her way down the stairs and rushes towards me.

"My sweet boy."

She coos as she embraces me, planting a kiss on either side of my cheeks.

"Mother, please."

I beg, feeling embarrassed.

"Do not **'mother'** me!
We live in the same damn castle, and you barely visit!
Your own mother, the woman who carried and birthed you!"

Me and my sister share the same exhausted look at each other, before then sharing a quick smile.

"I'm sorry, mother.
I'll visit more, I promise."

"You say that every time."

She retorts.

"You know, I'm sure there are plenty of other boys here in the castle that visit their mothers."

She continues.

And she wonders why I don't visit…

"Mother, I'm very busy with my duties, you know this."

She waves her hands away at that.

"You are the son of the General, you should not be this."

She gestures at my armour, the armour of a Slayer.

I sigh deeply.

"Mother, this is the life I chose."

"Yes, and I wonder why."

She barks back.

The way she says this concerns me slightly.

She knows the reason.
I want to rid the land of evil and the demons that inhabit it.

"Mother, I've always been a fan of the Syndicate since I was a child.

And uncle, he is a great man to follow."

"And your father is not?"

 She replies.

"I did not mean it like that, mother, I meant…"

"Meant or not, we both know it's not why you joined the Syndicate."

Her voice seems angry, but only for a second.

I want to press the question, to ask her what she means, but I do not get the chance.
Just then, my little sister gives me another cuddle.

"Sweetheart, go back over there and play."

She points back to the hearth, and the collection of dolls sitting on the floor.

"Yes, Blossom,"

'Blossom' being my pet's name for her since she was a babe.
Her actual name being Violet.

"Why don't you go and stay warm by the fire."

I say to her as well.

Once she in out of earshot, I turn to my mother and speak.

"I have to go, mother.

The execution,”

I remind her.

“Ah yes, awful business.
I don’t know why you bother going.”

Truthfully, it is to forever keep an eye on Tristan.
Yet I will not reveal that.

“Mother, the urgency you mentioned.”

I say firmly.

My mother purses her lips then, before saying.

“It is about your future, my son.”

She sighs.

“My future?”

I reply, confused.

“Yes, your role within the castle, and the Capital, the Human Realm.”

“Mother, I already have a role.
I’m a Slayer, I protect the Realm of Men and all its people, I protect them from the Red Eye Demons.”

“And yet, you do not venture out past the Capital, and you do not go out into the Human Realm.
You are a Slayer who stays in a place where there are no vampires.

You don't go and hunt them or fight them, you simply stay here.
For the sake of Light, when you were seventeen you were called to the front lines by your father, and you didn't go."

"If I had, it would have been as an Initiate of the Syndicate."

 I reply to her.

"As I said, I already have my role."

"Open your eyes."

She spits.

"How many Initiates do you know go to the front lines?"
Your father wanted you there to persuade you to forget the silly thought of being a thought of being an Initiate."

I had suspected as much, and her revealing this proved it.

"I had already made a promise to train and become one.
So, if I had gone, it would have been pointless."

"It would not have been.
 After all, you had not done the ceremony, nor took your final oath.
Besides, you were not a real Initiate anyways."

She brushes off.

This irks me greatly, yet, it has some truth to it.

Another reason why many other Slayers dislike me.

I was made an Initiate without doing what every other person did to even become an Initiate.

Slay a vampire.

You see; to become a Slayer, it has to be something you have the stomach and strength for.
Many young, brave and foolish boys and girls sought out the creatures.
Before the Great Cleansing, and the ability to roam freely between the Realms many simply went and found them out.
For often they managed to slip into the Magic Realm and even into the Human Realm, yet they are always swiftly found and dealt with.
Thankfully, there has never been a serious case of the disease having ever taken hold here, remaining in the twisted Dark Realm.

And yet these monstrous creatures being most people's nightmares, many eagerly raced to find them and even ran into the frontlines directly and prayed for the best.
They did so for fame and glory, or simply because they were from an extremely poor background and the chance of becoming a member of the Syndicate meant a bed and food for life.
They were however always certainly ripped apart.
Many had died trying to slay such a creature.
Yet of course, there had been the odd few who had lived to tell the tale and become an Initiate.

I however… I did not slay a vampire before being named Initiate.
Something that had never been done in this history of the Syndicate before.

Yet it happened anyways, did it not?

I realise my mother is still waiting upon a response.

"It was an honorary role…"

I bluster.

"Uncle said until I did slay one."

I finish.

"Son, please, it was all a ruse.
It was never meant to go this far; your father was supposed to persuade
you otherwise."

She tells me.

I am shocked and confused… It had all just been a ruse.
No, it could not be…

"Well, it doesn't matter what any of you thought, does it?"

I say, getting angry.

"I did slay one!
I protected the prince!
I became a hero, and I damn well got the scar to proof it!
Which my I remind you is why I didn't go to the damn frontlines; I
was injured!

My voice getting louder.

"Hush yourself, your sister!"

She begs.

I look over to my sister, playing bored with her dolls.
I take a deep breath and try to calm myself.

"My role is sealed mother, and it's not changing!
 Goodbye."

I turn to take my leave then; except something my mother says stops
me dead in my tracks.

**Surely, she did not just say what I think she said?
No, I am surely hearing things.**

I turn slowly, dreading to face my mother.
Dreading to hear those words again.

Finally turn, I stand straight and look her directly in the eyes.

"Mother, what did you just say?"

She folds her arms, and repeats.

"You are going to be married,"

She says again, firmer this time.

Surely, she must be joking…

Perhaps she has recently hit her head or is becoming sick with fever.

MARRIED?
SHE IS SURELY JOKING, CORRECT?
YOU CANNOT GET MARRIED… YOU DO NOT EVEN LIKE
WOMEN…

No, she cannot be serious.
This has to be a jest, a silly joke.
Surely, she will start laughing.
Please, please, start laughing.

Yet she does not.
She still stands there, arms folded.
Her face is deadly serious.

"Mother… Mother, I can't… Slayers do not get married."

She waves her hands at this too.

"Enough with that nonsense.
There are plenty of Slayers married.
Married before they join the Syndicate, you think they simply just give up their wives?
No, they usually complete their training, take their oath, then return to their wives and even children.
They then guard that area, only leaving when and if they have too, or are called to the frontlines of course.
And plenty of Slayers marry in secret after they join, also.
You may think I am simply a woman who knows not much, but I know more than you think.
And do not bother to tell me this is not true, for I know it is."

I am utterly dumbfounded.
Yet what she said is true.
Many who begin their Initiation are already married, and upon completion of their training many do return home to their wives and children and indeed they do guard that area.

And many Slayers once established do also marry in secret.

"Besides, never mind all that nonsense.
 None of that matters because you will not be a Slayer anymore."

The way she says it, so nonchalant it is unnerving.

Does she not realise what she was saying?
I have taken my oath, an oath not so easily broken.

ARE YOU SURE YOUR OATH IS NOT SO EASILY BROKEN?
WHAT ABOUT THE PRINCE?

Many Slayers have lovers.

YES, BUT USUALLY WITH THE OPPOSITE SEX.
NOT THE SAME SEX…
AND THEIR LOVERS ARE COMMONERS, CERTAINLY NOT
PRINCES!
HE IS THE PRINCE OF THE IMPERIAL DYNASTY,
AND YET YOU FUCK HIM OFTEN!

No, that is different… I love him.
I love him more than life itself!

AND MORE THEN YOUR OATH IT WOULD SEEM…

I feel so confused and conflicted.
Why?
Why is this happening?

Is this another dream?
Another nightmare?

My mother takes my hands then.
They are soft, and her smile is now warm.
My mother was a great beauty back in her day by all accounts.
She still is beautiful, but small signs of age have become evident.
A few small lines here and there, yet beautiful all the same.
Her dark hair flows down to her elbows, her body still slim despite birth.
Her eyes a sharp blue just like my baby sister.
My own dark eyes however I got from my father.
And she is dressed in a bright, pink dress.

"Precious boy, you are twenty years old.
You are young and do not yet know what life holds for you, but the life of a Slayer…
Well, that is always a short life."

 She remarks.

"So instead, you'd what?
Turn me into a knight?
An Imperial Solider?
They die young too, anyone who goes to the front lines is guaranteed a short life.
Besides, I went to the frontlines, I met with father and met the men.
I fought on the field of battle, and I killed several vampires.
Not to mention some Dark Witches."

"Yes, but you went two years after you were supposed to.
Your father called you at seventeen and you did not go until last year."

"I was injured mother as you well know.
And then the King died, it did not seem suitable to leave."

My mother once again pursed her lips.

"But two years son?
I understand you were injured; I understand the King died, and this nasty business with the Great Cleansing began, and yet when all the dust settled you still waited two whole years.
And during those two years, he wrote to you and asked that you would visit.
And yet, you did not go, and in doing so you spat on him.
And the men who fight and die under his command.
They were all expecting you, the prodigal son to make an appearance, to boost morale, and you waited two years."

Before I can reply, she continues.

"And then when you finally did go, you were only there for three weeks."

"Mother, I."

"And then you just left!"

She shouts.

"You left and returned here and haven't left again.
Three years have passed son!
Three years and only three weeks on the frontlines... Only three weeks!"

She halts as she realises that Violet is looking at us.

My mother sighs, regaining her composure.

"You may have accomplished yourself on the battlefield during those three weeks my sweet boy.
But anything you gained, any love or respect, you lost it all the second you ran like a thief in the night.
And your father…
You no doubt diminished his reputation."

"He hates me."

I mumble.

"He does not hate you; he merely is angry that you have defied him for so long."

"I have not defied him.
I stayed true to my oath and to my duties as a Slayer."

 I shoot back.

"Also, may I remind you, perhaps being a Slayer was the best thing that happened to me!
If I had not been a Slayer, then I surely would have not been allowed anywhere near the Realm of Magic!
I would not have been able to visit at all!
Not only that but say I did go three years ago.
Say I forwent my Initiation and gave it up, say I stayed at the frontlines with father and became a Captain of the Imperial Army instead, you realise if I had, then I surely would have been imprisoned all these years due to the bloody Cleansing!
Three years and I would not have been here at all!"

I speak with urgency in my voice, and my mother has fear in her eyes.

She knows what I say is true, and I have no doubt that the thought of me having been gone these last three years would have been agony for her.

Her fear quickly dissipates however, replaced with anger.

"You only ever became a Slayer because of,"

"Because of what, mother?!"

She looks at me then, her face deadly serious yet still somehow warm.

"Sweet boy, when I became pregnant with you, I was so happy I screamed.

Many women say they fall in love with their child when they first look upon them, but for me, I loved you since the moment I knew you were growing inside of me.

I prayed and counted down the days until your arrival.

And when you did come, I screamed and bled in agony for hours.

You were a very big baby, and I nearly died.

But I did not care about that, I only cared that you lived.

Do you know, the healers did not think I could do it.

They even said that I might have to choose to lose you to spare my own life."

I had heard all of it, except the last part, she had not spoken of this part before.

"I told the healers to get out of my room.

I sent them away, and I pushed hard.

Harder than I ever could, and finally… Finally, you were born.

And you let out a loud cry, and I was overjoyed.

I nursed you at my own breast, for I could not imagine you in the arms of someone else.

I raised you, I loved you, and I know you, my sweet son.”

She takes my hands again then.

“And as your mother, I have always known that you were…
Different.”

My body stiffens.

Did she know?

“I know, my son, about you… And the…”

I abruptly step back then and shake my head.

“We are just friends.”

 I confirm.

She places her hand gently on my cheek.

“Darling boy, ever since you were children you’ve been inseparable.
And as you grew, I saw the way you looked at him.
The way you played together… You were always so gentle.
And in the courtyard, when you wrestled and laughed on the ground…
And I have seen you disobey your father for three years for him.”

I do not know how to respond.
I simply, stand there with my mouth open.

“You love him, my darling boy.”

Her voice sweet like sugar.

"But loving him will mean your death."

Her voice suddenly sharp, the sugar gone.

I look at her then with all the seriousness I can muster, and I take her hand off my face.

"Then I will die, and I will die happy,"

 I answer.

My comment shocks her.

She takes a step back then, her face now fully angry, she points her finger at me.

"No, you will not.
You will dismiss this silly Slayer nonsense, and you will marry and become the next Lord of the House of Umpire.
You will do this, and you will live a long, full life."

"You cannot promise me a long life; I can still die on the battlefield."

"You won't be going to the battlefield."

 She answers flatly.

"Mother, look at me, I am a warrior."

"Yes, you are, but yet you have given that all up for him anyhow.
 So, what does it matter if you never see the battlefield again, you only went there once anyway."

This was true, and yet in those three weeks, I had loved every moment of it.

I was born for the battlefield, and I felt so alive when I was there, in the midst of life and death.

But, despite my love for it, my love for Tristan was stronger.

I remember it so well.

I had missed him greatly, and the time it took me to get there in the first place, and staying for the three weeks, and then the time it took me to get back.

All in all, it had nearly been two full moons away from him, and it was too long for me to bear anymore.

I remember leaving in the dead of night, without saying a word to anyone.

I remember riding hard out of the BorderLands though the Magic Realm and back into the Human Realm, over the various lands all the way to the Capital, racing through until I got to the Grand Bridge, and then once on the island, riding up and up the many roads leading to the castle gates.

I nearly threw myself off my horse, and I ran straight inside.

Up the many stairs, through the many corridors and hallways, lefts and rights, until I finally reached his tower.

I did not care about all the people that passed me; I ignored them.

Getting to his tower, I rushed inside and there he was.

Sat reading, looking beautiful as ever, he did not know I was coming, I had left in a hurry and without sending a letter ahead of time.

Although I am sure my father certainly sent letters of my abandonment.

The look on Tristan's face when I surprised him, he instantly cried.

I locked the door and grabbed him then.
We made love right there on the floor.
It had been glorious.

"Mother, you cannot force me."

 I answer.

"And besides, if you really know about me… And him… Then you know that I'm not interested in women.
Not in the slightest.
And I will not… I will not betray him.
Not now, not ever."

I say firmly.

My mother huffs at this.

"Son, I mean it, you shall be married.
Even if that marriage is only in name, you will be married.
And you will do this, and you will… You will stop this insipid obsession with… Him."

"He… He is precious to me."

"He will be your death, child.
Let's be honest, you are both getting older.
And with every passing year there are more rumours about you two…
I only thank the Light that these rumours have not seemed to go past the Grand Bridge."

"Why, because you are ashamed?"

She looks hurt by this.

"Son, sweet child, my darling boy, I could never be ashamed of you.
I do not care… That you… Have relations with… well, other boys.
You are still my son, and I still love you."

This warms me greatly… This conversation, my mother knowing,
telling me she loves me anyways… My heart swells, but at the same
time, she still doesn't understand how much I love him.

"Mother, I love you too, but I've never been with anyone but Tristan."

I keep my voice low at having mentioned his name.

"I… I love him.
More than I've ever loved anything or anyone.
When I look at him, it feels as if time itself has stopped still.
He is… He is the world to me, the very reason I breathe.
I will not give him up, not now.
Not ever.
Forgive me, mother.
But I will not go through with this."

"And what future do you think you shall have?"

 She replies.

"What future do you think either of you are going to have?
That you'll love and grow old with one another?
Son, please, see reason."

"I do not know what the future holds, mother.

But one thing I do know, as long as that future has Tristan in it, for however long my life shall be, then I will be happy.

And if loving him truly does mean that one day I will die, then I will die, and so be it."

"Theodore will be crowned soon; you know there is no love lost between them.

I genuinely believe Tristan will be sent away anyways, on order of our next Imperial King."

"Then I will follow.

I'll follow him anywhere."

I answer back.

With that, I take her hand and kiss it gently.

There are tears in her eyes.

"Marriage offers you protection, a stop to the rumours.

Take your place as the next Lord of Umpire.

With time, you may even fall in love with your wife, and I'm sure if you try, you'll have no problem having your own heirs."

A wife?
And children…

If only I could marry Tristan.

If only I could have children with him.

A silly thought, one that could not happen, and yet, one that filled me with happiness.

"Goodbye, mother."

 I answer her curtly.

I walk away from her then, and towards Violet who still plays bored with her dolls on the floor.

I kneel down to her.

"I have to go now, Blossom.
But I'll be back real soon, I promise."

She nods her head, but I can tell she is distracted.
She looks at the walls decorated with the various patterns instead.

I pull out my dagger.
A small, yet beautiful blade, made from Saerillian Silver.

"Here."

 I say, passing her it.

Her eyes light up as she delicately takes the dagger from my hands.

"Now be careful, it's incredibly sharp.
Do not use it unless you feel as if your life is in danger, do you understand?"

She nods her head quickly.

"Good, and keep it hidden from mother,"

I glance backwards, I can see my mother looking at us, but she can't see anything over my huge frame.

"Practise in your room.
When I come back, you can show me."

Then I wink at her, and she smiles warmly.

"I'll be a warrior princess,"

She beams excitedly.

I chuckle at this.

Then I think of a perfect name for her.

"How about a Fatal Blossom?"

 I tell her.

She gasps in wonder at this.

"Fatal Blossom?!"

She gushes.

"I love it.
I sound like a real warrior."

I chuckle again and rub her head as I stand.

"Yes, a real warrior."

I smile down at her.

I wait for her to discreetly hide the dagger in the sleeve of her dress,
before I step up and simply take my leave of the apartments.
Not a word or look at my mother.
I find myself walking back through the many corridors.
My head is reeling.

*SHE KNOWS ABOUT YOU AND TRISTAN; SHE KNOWS AND
WANTS YOU TO GIVE HIM UP.
THE LOVE OF YOUR LIFE, TO MARRY SOME GIRL AND
BECOME THE NEXT LORD.
TO GIVE UP BEING A SLAYER…*

I can feel tears sting my eyes, I quickly brush them away before they
take full effect.

No, I will not cry.
And I will not give up Tristan, **never!**

*YOUR MOTHER IS RIGHT.
YOUR LOVE FOR HIM WILL MEAN YOUR DEATH.*

Flashes of Tristan tied to the pyre come back to mind.
The flames licking upwards, ready to engulf him.
The crowds cheering for his death.

**That is something I will never allow to happen.
I shall stay here and protect him, always.**

*THIS LOVE WILL BE YOUR DEATH.
LOVE, DEATH, LOVE, DEATH.
BOTH SURROUND YOU, BOTH DOOM YOU.*

Then so be it.
It is not nothing I did not know already.
I knew, ever since we were but children.
I have always loved him.
And I always knew that love would mean my doom.
But loving him… Being loved by him… It is worth a thousand
deaths.

My mind unchanged, my love confirmed, I carry on walking.

Towards an execution
Towards my love.
And towards one day,
My own death.

MEANWHILE

PRAYING FOR THE LIGHT

EDGAR

I continue to pray out loud as Kaleb leaves the Inner Spiral.

Pray for Claudius.
The Faith.
The Light.

That today, a holy day, will surely be blessed.

And most importantly, they will get what they deserve.

I'm speaking of witches.

Cursed and soulless, they were being executed by fire.
Yes, today is indeed a good day.
However, Kaleb, the silly boy who had tried to dampen my mood, and
yet I would not let him.

This boy that would play Captain.

A truly despicable mess of a situation.
He is all but twenty years of age!

How dare he think for a second that he can command me.

I am twice his age.

I have slain more vampires and witches then that boy could count!

And not only that, but unlike him, I fought on the frontlines for over a full year.

I was under the command of the previous Lord Commander of the Syndicate, before our current Lord Commander, which is none other than the General's brother!

This was in my younger days, of course, some years before the Great Cleansing.

I had been in the Magic Realm and further on that strip of land known as the BorderLands.

Nothing grew there, the very earth was dead.

I had to sleep and fight alongside witches; I had to eat and bathe with them.

Treat them like comrades when really, I saw them for what they were.

Monsters.

I also saw Kaleb's father, who is every inch a warrior, of course, tall and strong and formidable.

I saw him many times during that year.

He stayed in the infamous City of Bridges too, and went there to and from the battlefield often, garrisoned there at the Borderlands, trying his best to keep the peace between witches and humans.

I did not know why he stayed there, he rarely left.

Not that he had a choice now, but when he did, he still stayed there.

He did not need to, of course.

He could have left his command under a trusted Captain and came and lived comfortably in the Capital, taking his place as a council member, and with his Lady Wife and children.

His wife… She is a beauty; I could not understand how any man could leave behind such a woman.

And yet stayed away he did.
Not that he had a choice now, being trapped in the Magic Realm since the Great Cleansing begun.

And it seemed Kaleb, whilst looking like a warrior and being the spitting image of his father, he however did not ever leave.
He stayed firmly in the Capital…

He only left once, and that was when he left last year.
He was gone nearly two moons, and yet had only stayed at the frontlines for three weeks by accounts.
He came rushing home, tail between his legs.
His father apparently was furious, and so was the Lord Commander.
I remember how he bellowed and shouted when he found out Kaleb had run away.
We had all been told to keep lookout for his return.
I could not wait for Kaleb to come back to the Grand Spiral, I prayed he would throw himself in front of the Lord Commander and apologise.
Yet, he did not return to the Grand Spiral, not instantly, however.
No, by all accounts he instead he rode furiously like the wind, past the Grand Spiral and straight over the Grand Bridge.

Straight to the island fortress.

No one knows where he disappeared too, it's as if he just vanished into thin air.
He was found shortly afterwards, by Slayers sent to bring to him to the Grand Spiral, by all accounts he was found walking near the Inner Spiral… And also, suspiciously close to Tristan's tower.

I had been lucky to be present when he had been finally brought to the Grand Spiral, we all saw him brought in.

We were all in the Great Hall, and many of us had expected him to be banished there and then.

Yet the Lord Commander forgave him.

He hugged him and welcomed him back.

This brought the ire of many of us, including myself.

Kaleb did not belong with the Syndicate, and his uncle was blinded to this.

And both of them were blinded to the fact that witches are abominations.

I have seen them, lived with them, seen the things they can do…

With their hands, their minds, they don't even have to speak, and they can unleash uncertain terrors.

Many are fooled, thinking it is beautiful and wonderful, however I see the darkness in it.

No one should be able to do those things… Only God has the power to change the world, to perform wonders.

Not these Casters.

I hated them deeply and was more than overjoyed when this Great Cleansing started.

Claudius truly was a visionary.

He saw the truth, and so did God.

That these abominations should never be allowed to walk freely.

Yet they had, for centuries.

They lived in our Realm, they took our homes, our lands, they even bred with us!

And now we have even more of an infestation.

At least we did before Claudius and his glorious plans came to fruition.

I remember three years ago when the Imperial Decree was made.

At first, I was sure it was a jest, and yet, it turned out it was correct.

As a Slayer, I was immediately forbidden from partaking in any of the murder and mayhem, even though I really wanted too.

I remember it so clearly.

Most had been sleeping, it was nighttime after all.

That's when the screams from all around the city erupted.

Thousands of them dead, hundreds of homes and building burnt and destroyed.

Many took part in the slaughter from the lowest peasants to highest lords.

Men of all sorts, even men who were once Imperial Soldiers.

They killed without discretion.

AND THEY KNEW EXACTLY WHAT HOUSES TO BURN.
WHAT PEOPLE TO MURDER.
IT IS ALMOST AS IF THEY HAD A LIST…

I push the thought aside immediately.

I had not thought of it for three years… And would not now.

THEN WHY ARE YOU HERE?
WHY DO YOU WANT TO SPEAK TO CLAUDIUS SO BADLY…
DID HE NOT TELL YOU TO STAY AWAY…
AND IF THE LORD COMMANDER FOUND OUT…

No, that certainly would not be good.

The Lord Commander was fervently against it.

Yet there was nothing he could do when it started.

He could not interfere in the Realms of men, so instead we simply closed the doors of the Grand Spiral.

When morning finally came, they were opened.

The city half destroyed and the Human Realm burning throughout.

The Lord Commander went straight to the Imperium where I now stand.

No doubt to shout how the witches who fought for us and protected us would turn their backs on us.

Yet the Cleansing continued anyways, onwards and throughout the Human Realm.

And yes, it did nearly cost us the aid of the witches.

Nearly.

But in my opinion, we did not need them anyway.

Many died, all around the Realm.

In the streets, in their homes, in their beds.

Villages, towns and cities all around the Human Realm were cleansed.

Fires burned for weeks, and the land was drenched in blood.

The Lord Commander could not stop or prevent it, so therefore ordered that the Syndicate would take no part whatsoever.

Some Slayers did not listen.

They privately or even openly murdered and took part.

These Slayers were executed because of this.

And yet our Captain Kaleb beheaded such a Caster mere weeks ago and the Lord Commander once again looked the other way.

I had been slightly proud of Kaleb for killing such a Caster, but I know he had a soft spot for them and did not want to actually kill the Caster so that slight proudness soon disappeared.

And there were also Slayers who tried to aid the witches, to protect and save them.

Fools!

I did consider joining in the bloodshed too… Yet I stayed my hand, for now.

Most witches who escaped ran back to the Black Woods, seeking the protection of their fellow sinners.

They should have stayed in the first place.

The Council of Covens was furious.

They threatened to attack us.

Threatened to switch allegiance and allow the Red Eyed demons through their land and kill us all.

Thankfully, God be good, that did not happen.

The new Head Witch, the previous conspicuously dying the very day of the Great Cleanse, sought more peaceful resolutions.

Witches would stay in the Magic Realm, in their own Realm, and humans were to stay the Human Realm.

The only humans who were permitted entrance were Slayers.

Slayers who were needed to help kill vampires.

But no others.

Not even more Imperial Soldiers were allowed to come as many joined in the Cleanse.

This meant that for the last three years, the Imperial Army stationed there has received no more fresh Soldiers.

No, they are banned entirely.

Rumours has it, what Imperial Soldiers remain are dwindling fast, and sure enough, the witches will not be able to hold out much longer, not without our help.

This means they must call for aid soon or simply perish.

And I doubt if there is even an Imperial Army left.

So be it, let them die.

No, the only army we seem to have remaining is the Defenders, a great army of faith.

Yes, Claudius and his army of God, the Glorious Defenders can fight them off.

And Claudius has only grown his Defenders these last three years; they numbered tens of thousands by now.

I hope that the only reason to be growing an army that large is surely to march it towards the Black Woods and cleanse those damned witches!

And hopefully, and finally cleanse the Dark Realm also.

Yes, God was good.

And who needs an Imperial Army when we have an army of God.

YOU SHOULD JOIN THEM…
BECOME A DEFENDER.
YOU ALWAYS DID LOVE GOD…

And yet, I could not.
I was a Slayer.
I had taken the sacred oath.
Drunk the ceremonial wine.
I had worn the black armour and black cloak.
It was all I knew.

YET THIS WAS NOT THE LIFE YOU WOULD HAVE CHOSEN.
NO, YOU WANTED TO FOLLOW A LIFE OF LIGHT.

Yes, I had once wanted to be a Holy Man…
To pray and love and share the Light with others.
Until my Light was quenched.
And Darkness took over my life.

YES… YOU HAD BEEN YOUNG ONCE, FULL OF KINDNESS
AND LOVE…
THEN THE MONSTERS CAME…

There was so much blood...
Blood everywhere...

No, no, I will not think on this.

BUT IS THAT NOT WHEN ALL THE DELICIOUS HATRED
STARTED?
WHEN YOUR HEART DARKENED...

May the Light Cleanse these dark thoughts.
May the light Cleanse these souls today.

I say another prayer before taking my leave of the Inner Spiral.

Kaleb and his group of friends have lived here permanently, there being five of them.
At first it was just Kaleb, then his friends came one by one.
The Lord Commander deemed that suitable enough to guard the island and the Imperium which it sat high upon.

And yet, that did not mean other Slayers such as me were not allowed to visit the island.
In fact, we were allowed to roam freely through the Human Realm, we often travelled to the Magic Realm to aid in the fight at the Borderlands.
Or we simply toured throughout the Human and Magic Realms to keep a forever watchful eye.
Dark witches and vampires alike have snuck past before.
I myself had ventured out many times.

BUT NEVER HOME.
YOU HAVE STAYED AWAY FROM THERE AS IF IT WAS A
PLAGUE.

YOU LEFT BEHIND EVERYTHING…

There was nothing left for me to return too.

YOU STILL HAD FRIENDS, NEIGHBOURS…
AND HER… YOU LEFT HER…

I did not want too.
But I had to become a Slayer

NOT TRUE, YOU HUNTED THE BEAST DOWN.
AND ALSO KILLED THE CASTER…
YOU CHOSE THIS LIFE…

I have always chosen God!

YOU CHOSE REVENGE AND HATRED!
IT IS STILL INSIDE YOU, IT ROTS AND FESTERS

I ignore these as I go about my duties, walking along the many hallways and corridors.

Checking on lords and ladies, making sure they are safe.

Many brush me aside, too busy getting ready to travel over the Grand Bridge.

Pretty pointless, and yet I have to do something to not look so suspicious just hanging around.

Other Slayers hate me.

Even though some of them share my love of God and the Light, yet they think me too feverish about it.

They think I do not take my responsibility to the Syndicate serious enough.

Ludicrous, I have slain more monsters than I can count.

I have toured the Human Realm and always protected it.

I have stayed in the Realm of Magic, guarded it and fought at the frontlines.
And yet, that is not good enough.

It need not matter, I know God loves me, he shines his everlasting Eternal Light upon me, and it keeps me strong.

And truthfully, even when touring the Realm, I do not usually stay in Spirals.
They are dotted throughout the Human Realm, and used for Syndicates to sleep, gather, train and rest.

But I never stay in them.
Instead, I stay in Temples dedicated to God.

Holy men and women live in them.
Temples have usually practised love and acceptance, things I have always admired.
Things that first drew me to God.
Because God did of course love us all.

And yet, they have also warned us of the dangers of the Red Eyed Demons.

But now, now the Temples are very different.
Love and acceptance are little mentioned now, instead fear and terror is institutionalised within the Temples.
They do not only warn us of the dangers of vampires, but they also feverishly pray daily and nightly about how these Casters of magic should be burned.

Every single one of them.

That is certainly new.

That there is no such thing as a good witch, they always have been in sync with the vampires.
Not only that, but anyone who is different.

Yes, this persecution extends to humans too.
And as such humans have been executed for things such as speaking out of turn as of late.
Claudius does indeed rule with an iron fist, and although talks of love and acceptance are a thing of the past, I still hold Claudius in high regard for at least opening the eyes of everyone and exposing these Casters for what they actually are.

Demons in human form.

After all, at least with a vampire you know what you are getting.
They do not hide; they show their true colours.
Their red eyes and elongated fangs evident.
Their beauty and everlasting life also evident.
They drink blood, murder and rip apart humans.
But at least they show what they are.

Witches on the other hand, they hide among us.
They pretend to love nature and balance, pretending to be peaceful.
They try so hard to be like us.
They pretend to have feelings and consciousness, yet they are dark and twisted.

All of them.

YOU JUDGE THEM ALL BECAUSE OF ONE WITCH, THE WITCH WHO BROKE YOU…
WHO TOOK EVERYTHING FROM YOU…

AND YOU BECAME THIS...

IT NEED NOT MATTER NOW.
THIS WAS YEARS AGO.
TIME TO FOCUS ON THE PRESENT...

And presently, I am bored.

Bored of this life, I want more.

I am sick of the Syndicate and their lazy views on the Cleansing, they need to help, not hide away in their Spirals.

Yet the Lord Commander's command still holds firm, and there is nothing we can do.

Yet I despise this.

Witches are monsters, they should be Cleansed.

And I certainly hate the Lord Commander.

He may be a formidable warrior but he's also a fool, he has given too much to his nephew.

Forgave him for what he has banished and executed others for.

There is even talk that he plans on making Kaleb the next Lord Commander.

That he is training and poising him for that position.

And if he is, then I hate him even more.

The position of the Lord Commander should be based on experience and what is best for the Syndicate itself.

It is not a throne you can pass off as a succession.

No, when a Lord Commander dies, they may indeed name a successor, however it is always put to a vote by those of the Syndicate.

Ever Slayer gets a vote, yet not all decide to vote.

Many aren't present when the naming of a Lord Commander is chosen, it is usually based upon the minority of those present at the Grand Spiral.

Lost in thought, I find myself subconsciously close to Claudius apartments.

I had not meant too, at least I do not think so, yet I am close.

Defenders are very present in this part of the castle.

Their yellow robes and White sun with a sword through it brazened on their tunics.

Yet, even though they are an army of God, I am not entirely sure that they are wholly faithful.

Indeed, Claudius has been building his army at an increasing rate, and with the increasing numbers of men, there is a decreasing lack of morals.

Many from the lowest parts of the Realm have been recruited.

Even rapists and murderers.

AND THIS IS YOUR SUPPOSED ARMY OF GOD?
THEY ARE THE LEAST GODLY MEN I HAVE EVER MET.

It does not matter.
God is the only thing that matters.

I turn to leave, I do not want to be seen sulking around this part of the castle, people would talk, however before I get the chance, I hear a familiar voice.

Turning round the corner, it's him.

Claudius…

Short, cropped hair, muscular yet neither big nor small build and wearing the yellow robes of the Defenders, a White sun with a sword emblazoned on it.

He is walking with several Defenders, and also his adopted son.

I always feet a shiver when I see the boy.
Connor is his name.
An abandoned child found sometime in in the year 300ID.
He is not often spoken about, that is usually reserved for Claudius' son by blood.
His son by blood being a truly disgusting boy named Claudio.
He was friends with the equally disgusting Crown Prince.
Neither were present, thankfully.
But Connor was.
As I said, not someone often spoken about.
He is a quiet young man, already had his twenty first name day.
Slightly older than Theodore by some months, who's own twenty first and coronation fast approaches.

*YOU LOVE CLAUDIUS AND GOD BUT LOOK AT CLAUDIUS'
SONS!
ONE BY BLOOD, ONE BY NAME,
AND BOTH MONSTERS IN THEIR OWN WAYS!*

God tests his most loyal, his most devout.
Surely, he is merely testing Claudius, his messenger here on earth by giving him truly godless sons.

They all stop in their tracks when they see me.
I too stand there, awkwardly.
Not knowing if I should walk away or speak.
Instead, I merely stand there.

An awkward moment passes, and it is Claudius who first speaks.

"Look, it's a Slayer.
Always so wonderful to see them walking in the halls."

His men snigger and laugh at that; however, Connor does not make a
sound.
He stands there, emotionless and expressionless.

"Your Holiness, forgive me.
I did not mean to intrude…"

Claudius looks at me sceptically.
In truth, he is angry, but he hides it well behind other forms of facial
expressions.

"I have seen you before… You have been here these last few weeks.
My men have reported that you do not usually come here, to the Island.
Tell me, has the Lord Commander resorted to spies now?"

His men immediately all put their swords on their hilts.

Even now, three years later, it is still a weird sight to see the Faith carry
weapons.

**They had been once peaceful.
Not anymore.**

These were not the same.
The holy men and women of before are long gone.
The ones of peace and love fled or dead.
Replaced by fanatics and even nonbelievers, anyone who wishes to
fight in the army really.
As Defenders, they can do as they choose.
Kill without question or reprimand.

AND THIS IS WHO INSPIRES YOU?

So, his army may not be completely faithful.
And they may not all follow the Faith.
And yet, God works through them.
It does not matter what they do… Because of them, tens of thousands
shall bring God and Light back to the world.
I have to believe that.
I will believe that.

THIS SPELLS DISASTER!
HOW DELIGHTFUL!

"I am not a spy, your Holiness."

Or perhaps I was… But he knew that already.
Claudius shows me a fake look of weariness, as do the others.

"Then why do you keep skulking around here?
And only these last few weeks."

"Your Holiness… I would very much like to accompany you to the
execution."

A pretend expression of shock comes from him, as well at the others.

"You think I would trust you?
A Slayer of the Syndicate.
Go back to your Lord Commander and tell him to try better next time."

They go to leave then, but I take a step forward.

Each and every Defender stands before Claudius, as if to guard him.

I hold my hands up, palms outward, trying my hardest to show I mean
no harm.

Claudius pushes through.

"Enough, enough!
I will not have bloodshed in the castle walls."

A lie of course, much blood had been spilled in these castle walls and far beyond.

"I meant no disrespect, your Holiness… I only meant to accompany you.
I have a great respect… For what you are doing.
And the Faith… I am a firm believer.
And the Great Cleansing… A great idea."

He looks confused at this; I can see he is trying to debate whether I am telling the truth in his head.
He should know all this already.
Was it not him whom sought me out?

AND YOU HAD OBLIGED WITHOUT QUESTION…

"Well… The Lord does work in mysterious ways."

He chimes.

"Many Slayers have faith, your Holiness."

I answer.

"Indeed, they do.
As do the highest lords to the lowest sewer rats.
All are free to follow the one true faith.

But you… You seem different."

I feel elated that he notices this.
He can see I am no ordinary Slayer; I am a firm believer.

He has always known.

"Slayers are not permitted to partake in the Great Cleansing."

 I mumble.

"An egregious mistake.
What is a Slayer?
We are supposed to protect the realm, yes?
From monsters, from soulless.
Well, what is not a soulless monster then a witch?
They brought the vampires to this land.
They all should be held accountable."

I had realised that I should not have said any of this.
Not out in the open like this.
As a Slayer, I should be faithful to the Syndicate, and I should not be
so openly talking about my true feelings on the Great Cleansing, or
today's executions.

Claudius looks at me, a smile appears slightly over his face, yet he
hides it from the others.

"Your name?"

 He asks of me, yet he already knows.

"Edgar."

I reply.

"Well, Edgar, if you wish to watch the execution I cannot stop you.
And I'm sure God shall be glad of your faith.
However, I think you should stay with your faction.
As for accompanying me, as you can clearly see, I have men around me."

He then whispers to his men.
Some talk of getting the carriages ready.
His men depart then, including Connor, and take their leave.
Each and every one of them eye me closely as they passed me.

And now we stand.

Just me and Claudius alone in the corridor.
It would be deathly silent if not for the sound of harsh winds and
violent waters that surround the island.
Claudius walks towards me then and stops right in front of me.

We are of equal height, yet not equal standing.

I am merely a Slayer, whilst he is the High Pope himself.
And thus, God's representative and messenger here.
He is the closest to God you can get.

"You are indeed intriguing, Edgar.
If you really do feel how you feel about the Great Cleansing, perhaps
there might be other things we agree upon?"

He ponders.

He already knows how I feel about the Great Cleansing, and he already
knows that I followed him once and would again.

Even with the men sent away, and it just being us, he still keeps up this pretence of pretending not to know me.
No matter, I happily play along to be close to God.

"Yes, yes indeed."

I almost shout back, responding too quickly, too happily.

He stifles a chuckle at this.

"Hmm, yes, I could have use for you in the future."

 He speaks.

> *DO YOU NOT HEAR THE SINISTER TONE?*
> *HE WILL USE YOU AND SPIT YOU OUT!*

> **Be quiet!**
> **He is the closest you can get to God!**
> **He is the Pope himself!**

> *AND WHO HELPED HIM BECOME THE HIGH POPE?*
> *YOU BETRAYED THE OLD ONE, HE TRUSTED YOU.*
> *YOU STOLE FROM THE SYNDICATE.*
> *HE AND YOU ARE THE FURTHEST THING FROM GODLY.*

"Your Holiness, is there a problem?
Within the castle? I can of course help you.
Anything for God."

He smiles at this.

"I think we shall have a good friendship, Edgar.
But perhaps…"

He looks around then, before moving even closer, he whispers to me harshly.

"Are you a fool, coming to me like this?
Skulking around these last weeks."

His abruptness feels like a slap.

"I have enemies everywhere, and the last thing I need is your Lord
Commander or the whole bloody Syndicate coming down on me!"

"I – I'm S – sorry," I stutter.

 He smiles at my unease, before speaking once more.

"I told you before, if I have need of you then I will send for you.
Unless I do, then stop skulking around and drawing attention to yourself.
May I remind you, if you're found out for what you did you will surely
be executed.

I gulp at the prospect but nod respectfully.

"Yes… If you have need for me.
After all, your enemy is my enemy,"

I tell him, reassuring him of my loyalty.
He smiles then, reassured of me I suppose.

"Well then, I'll see you at the execution."

He says happily before departing.
I hear his footsteps recede as he walks off, my brow covered in sweat.
I begin panting.
Had that really happened?

Had I angered him and lost all connection.
To him, to God.
I cannot bear the thought.

I merely wanted to be his loyal servant, and God's.
To help purge the country of witches and demons.
I need him to know I am his friend.
But for now, I shall do as he asks and stay away.
I only pray he has need of me soon.
Anything for God.

THIS WILL NOT BE GOOD.
I CAN SEE THIS ENDING TERRIBLY...

Nonsense!

DO NOT SAY I DID NOT WARN YOU...

I did not care, nor mind.
Despite Claudius' anger, I am incredibly happy.
After all I had still been close to him and spoke to him.
As if I was close to God, as if I spoke to God himself.
And for that, nothing could ruin today.
Surely God has smiled on me, I can feel the warmth of his Eternal Light.
It feels loving and amazing.
I positively skip with happiness as I head towards the castle courtyard to start the travels with the rest to the impending execution.

YES, THIS WAS A DAY OF GOD.
A DAY OF CLEANSING.
PRAISE THE LIGHT!

THE GRAND SQUARE

THE CAPITAL

HEADS WILL ROLL

KALEB

I stand there with a great feeling of unpleasantness.
I have been at countless executions now, yet nothing can change the vileness of what is about to transpire.
The weather is as usual, grey and gloomy, yet a couple of hopeful rays managed to break through.

The rain is off, which I know Claudius will be happy with.

And Tristan… Tristan would be angry.

And seeing as he was already angry to begin with, I imagine it would only build into a rage.

YES, HE CAN GET QUITE ANGRY.
THAT TEMPER… MIXED WITH HIS CHAOS…
HOW BEAUTIFULLY DESTRUCTIVE THAT COULD BE…

No, no matter Tristan's anger or subsequent rage, he has never used his Chaos to do bad things.
He makes flowers grow and the snow fall.

He creates light in a dark room and summons books with his mind or a mere flicker of his hands.

He is good.

And his smile… His beauty… Oh, how I loved him.

I let these thoughts warm me as I take in my surroundings.
The execution was originally meant to be on the castle grounds, secluded and away from the crowds.

And yet Claudius changed his mind at the last moment.

He usually does it within the castle grounds, at the Council's urging of course.
There had been problems in the past after all…
Commoners rushing up, trying to free the condemned witches.
Friends and families most like, or even sympathetic people I suppose.
Yet the Defenders loyally held them back, killing them often.
We are in the Capital Square, a huge open space in the heart of the Capital.

A massive courtyard which holds the Temple of Light; once a place of piety and love it is now used by bullies and villains known as Defenders.

It is a mere speck however compared to The Grand Spiral which also lives here, the biggest building in the Capital.

It shoots out towards the sky, the biggest Spire in the Human Realm and can host thousands of Slayers and Initiates.
Made from red stone and jutting out of the earth like a giant spear, it is never at full capacity, however.

Most Slayers are either at the frontlines or roaming freely, keeping guard of any potential threats that might arise.

The building intimidated most, including the damned Defenders.

Because of it, the Temple of Light is almost abandoned, the Defenders too scared of the Slayers being right on the same Grand Square.

There had been some infighting, plenty of deaths, over the years.

And yet the Defenders dare not take on the Slayers.
Not fully, anyways.
Sure, there have been quarrels and killings between the factions, but the Defenders are made of commoners mostly.
Whereas Slayers are battle hardened and put through rigorous tests and trials.

We are bred for war, death and monsters.

One of us has the strength of ten ordinary men, easy.
And the more battle hardened and experienced, the more vampires you've slain, you only become more and more lethal.

We are as quick and strong as vampires themselves; we have to be to begin with, to kill them.
Trained constantly in the art of slaying monsters, we are not to be easily trifled with.
Whilst the Temple of Light has been all but abandoned, Claudius has started the construction of several other smaller Temples of Light around the Capital.
He also started on construction of a bigger Temple of Light.

This being away from the Grand Square and the heart of the Capital and more inwards, closer to the Grand Drawbridge in fact, and thus closer to the Island and the Imperium.

He wants his men close… And he wants them to surround us.

I look at the Temple, white marble and stone.
The new ones being built are smaller yet similarly built from the same materials.
Claudius commissioned it to bring more people closer to God.
More Temples meant more worship he said.
These Temples were supposed to be about God's love…
Yet God only loves a select few it seems.
And Claudius is the one who speaks for God.
He tells us who God loves.
It's wrong, God is supposed to love us all.

No matter what.
And these Temples are surely meant to host the ever-growing faction of hate.

There was no love anymore, which God is meant for.

And yet, it was not God who had turned evil, instead it was men who did evil in his name.
And it seemed less and less godly things happened every day.
In fact, today shall be just another page in this book of travesties.

The Grand Square also hosted the Magnificent Markets,
Rows upon rows of wooden stalls, where hundreds worked selling various items, and where thousands poured in to buy.

However, the Magnificent Markets were closed today.

Yet there were still thousands gathered.

They stood there, motionless.

All eyes forward.

We stood on a wooden construction, a huge platform built upon the steps of the Grand Temple.

By *we* I mean myself, the Imperial Family, members of the council and other lords and ladies.

Not to mention my uncle, the infamous Lord Commander.

He stands there beside me firm as stone, his hand held tightly on the handle of his longsword, ready at any moment.

Dark short hair and a thick, dark beard.

I stand with him.

Uncle and nephew.

I feel immense pride, yet I can feel hateful eyes on me.

Below the huge podium stands other Captains of the Syndicate, they stand at the bottoms of the steps of the Grand Temple around me.

All older and more experienced than me.

 No wonder they give me hateful stares as I stand proudly on the podium with the Imperial Family, and amongst other nobility.

And standing beside me, none other than the Lord Commander himself; it certainly draws their ire.

They all vied for his favour and disliked how I seemed to just have it because of blood ties.

I can see them whispering about me.

No doubt about how the only reason I'm favoured is because I'm family.

If I was not the Lord Commanders nephew, then I would not stand by his side in public affairs.

The rumours have swirled ever since I first took my Initiation.

And so, I trained hard, passing every physical exam I could.

I practised every day for hours with longsword and short, spear and mace, war-hammer and morning star, throwing Saerillian blades and even the use of my special Saerillian Spike.

A Saerillian Spike being a small object, the size of a small dagger, when pressing a button on the side it shoots out a needle, the tip being dipped in Saerillian Silver.

It's used to quickly incapacitate a witch, you simply stab the witch with the needle, the Saerillian Silver quickly gocs to work in their bloodstream, rendering them unconscious almost immediately.

It matters little where you stab the witch, the affects are the same.

Not to mention the use of wooden Black Oak stakes.

Black Oak being the only wood to kill a vampire.

Saerillian Silver is good for inflicting damage and pain.

Even beheading or fire can work too.

However, the best way to truly and permanently put down a vampire is Black Oak to the heart.

The same wood I had carved Tristan's mini sword necklace with, I think fondly.

Imperial Guards gathered around the Imperial Family who were sat comfortably, as well as the other lords and ladies, they all almost had a drink in their hands or were already under the influence of several drinks.

The council of course was there too.

Consisting of Ladies Eleanor and Mavis, and Lords Wyatt and Brandon.

Defenders surrounded the platform and that of the Grand Temple, with tens of rows of them standing guard between the small folk and the platform where he stands.

Claudius…

Here I stand in full black armour with a dark red sun, a black stake through it.
Other Slayers stand proudly wearing the same.

The armour worn of the Syndicate.

Despite the hatred of others, I still stand with pride.
I feel no pride in what is about to happen, however.
Yet those on the podium seem not to notice.
They drink, feast, jest and laugh.
Theodore and his cronies, in particular.
The Crown Prince and his vile friends.
They shout, swear and grab at passing serving girls.
I look upon them in disgust.

The Imperial Dynasty has been around for just over three centuries.
A grand Dynasty which has thrived despite monsters claiming half the lands…
And to think all that history and preservation, a proud and long lineage was about to fall into the hands of… **Him.**

He would be a terrible king, truly monstrous.
He had no sense of right and wrong, and he shirks his responsibilities as that of Crown Prince.
No interest in politics or war, only drinking and raping.
It is not openly discussed of course, but what Theodore and his friends get up to both within the Imperium and Capital is truly horrific.
Talks of young maidens murdered brutally…
All covered up of course, by none other than Claudius.
And the Council have a hand in it too I suppose, after all I do not imagine they want the future king's true nature to come to light.
God save us, with him as King we shall all surely die due to his stupidity and depravity.

And to think I was meant to be his friend also… Our fathers being best friends, they wanted the same for us…

We were born nearly half a year apart.

The assassination attempt on the whole Imperial Family happened in 299ID, just days before the celebration of the Year 300ID.

They had travelled to the Magic Realm to celebrate the new century, however they never returned.

Having all been slaughtered by the Dark Lord himself.

Claudius apparently went crazy with religious rants and condemnation of witches being the cause of the attack.

He apparently left for some weeks however, to spread more hatred across the Realm.

And then returned with the abandoned child who he kept and raised as his own who is now known as Connor.

Only the old king survived the assassination attempt and as the only Imperial left, he was forced to quickly marry and sire children.

And that's exactly what he did.

He was married within weeks and his wife, the late Queen got pregnant almost instantly.

And thus, Theodore was born in the late summer of the Year 300ID.

I was born in the early months of Year 301ID.

My father, a young man had returned to the Capital shortly after the massacre of the Imperial Family.

He had short relations for some months with my mother before he once again left, leaving me in her belly.

With me and Theodore born not long apart, we were supposed to be fast friends like our own fathers.

However, I just couldn't; we were the same age and from as early as I can remember I always hated him.

Tristan and Isabella were born a year after me, also born in the early months, albeit being the year 302ID, they already celebrated their nineteenth name day some time ago and would not celebrate another for a while.

And ever since Tristan was born, only a year after me, we have always been close.

Raised together, we simply fell in love.

We were also raised with Claudius children, despite him being sent away.

His children became wards of the Council.

Claudia, Claudio and Connor.

Claudia however is older than all of us, being twenty-five.

And Connor was born and found in 300ID and with Claudio who was also born in the year 300ID, although later in the year during winter, only mere months before my own birth.

I continue looking around.

I also spot the Princess Isabella, a beautiful yet sad creature.

In public she maintains a social life with the other ladies of court, but really, she prefers the company of her two female slaves.

The Princess, bless her for her kindness, calls them her faithful companions.

She gifted them nice clothing, and yet I can still see the collars around their necks.

Around the Princess' neck was a beautiful gold chain with huge blue sapphires which complimented her blue eyes.

Oddly enough, Tristan and Isabella were twins and yet they had different coloured eyes.

No doubt another present from Claudius.

That will surely piss off Tristan even more.

Tristan has long had his suspicious, as have me and others.

Claudius has been looking and leering over her for the years now.
But to actually be sending her presents… And expensive jewels too,
It's simply absurd.

Looking elsewhere, that's when finally, my eyes come to him.

Tristan.
My Little Prince.
My Love.

I have not seen him since the early hours of this morning when I
departed his rooms in secret.

I had barely managed to sneak back into the Inner Spiral and creep into
my bed without waking the others.
Yet… I could not shake that feeling of being followed…
Ludicrous, surely.
I checked over my shoulder several times and always kept alert, surely,
I would notice if I had been followed.
The feeling still remains.

At least I managed to avoid being seen before the slaves saw me.
Truthfully, I think I only slept a handful of hours, and I feel it deep in
my bones.
I have been trying with all my might to suppress my yawns.

But I would happily be tired if it meant being able to be with Tristan.
Thankfully the Inner Spiral is close to Tristan's tower, his idea of
course, and one I happily went along with.

Tristan looks beautiful as always, with his short blonde hair, the sides
and back neatly shaved.
His fringe touching his delicate eyebrows.

And pretty pink, full lips.
Not to mention those eyes.

Those beautiful emeralds.
A deep, sea of green.

Above all those sat upon the podium, Tristan is the one who stands out the most.

Or perhaps I simply think that because I love him so.

Upon looking closer, he has some redness around the eyes and his short hair is a tussled mess upon his head, as if he has not slept.

And his lips… **Moving**… Yet he does not seem to be talking to anyone in particular.

Even though we had shared in passionate lovemaking, we had left things on a sour note.

A lover's quarrel… Easily remedied.

ARE YOU SO SURE ABOUT THAT?
YOU KNOW AS OF LATE THINGS BETWEEN YOU AND HIM
HAVE SOURED.

No, Tristan might be angry, but it never lasted.
He wanted things to change, I loved him for that.
But right now, was not the right time.

Yes, I despise the villainy that has befallen the Human Realm.
And I detest Claudius and every single one of his damned Defenders.
Yet we cannot risk a civil war within the Human Realm whilst fighting at the BorderLands too.

What was left of the Imperial Army got sealed in the Realm of Magic after the Great Cleansing began.

Without what was left of the army to be sent as reinforcements, I don't doubt that those trapped, brave men are all but dead now.

A sad thought indeed…

And the Imperial Soldiers who were stationed within and throughout the Human Realm either abandoned their posts or even joined the Defenders.

Truthfully, the Defenders right now are the only real army within the Human Realm.

That in itself is a dark and dangerous thought.

The Imperial Army should have been kept up, they should have kept recruiting, instead Claudius let it fall into disarray and instead focused on his army of so-called Faith.

And more Slayers are killed every day… It appears we are in dire trouble.

And yet, with all this, the Council do nothing.

Claudius does nothing.

Nor the Lords and Ladies of the Realm.

It's as if they are completely ignoring the impending doom.

None of this would have happened of course if the Great Cleansing had never begun.

Humans and witches did better when we worked together against a common enemy.

The vampires.

And yes, whilst plenty of witches go dark and align themselves with the demons, that doesn't mean all witches are the same.

Many good people, good witches lived here happily.

Never did any harm, they simply only wanted to live peacefully.

Sure, they have always had prejudice against them, and over the centuries there have been murders, but an all-out genocide was something entirely different.

DID THE SYNDICATE NOT USED TO BRAND THEM?
AND KEEP DOCUMENTS OF WHO THEY WERE, WHERE THEY LIVED...

Yes, the Syndicate did do that.

The documenting of them I thought was perhaps a good idea, but the branding was something I never agreed with.

But then again, when and after the Cleansing started, I had always found it odd how these Defenders knew exactly which homes to attack and what people to burn throughout the Realm.

But how could that be...

Claudius pulls me from these thoughts as he rises from his chair and stands there tall and proud.

He wears the common yellow robes of the High Pope of our faith, yet he has an air of supreme authority.

OR THAT OF A KING...

A thought I must admit seems obvious... A lot happened within these last three years.

The attack on me and Tristan was the start in which led to a chain reaction.

The death of the King, the Great Cleansing of witches.

Yet, Claudius gained a huge following and despite being exiled for some years, he returned like a rat and continued his hatred and quickly regained friends or followers in the Imperium and Capital that he had beforehand.

And somehow, somehow when the King died, he got complete and utter control.

Perhaps because he spearheaded the Cleanse and thus everyone saw him as the leader…

And the rest of the Council simply stood by…

But why?!

The Council tried where they could I suppose, yet it seems as if Claudius ultimately had the final say.

Take this execution in the heart of the Capital with thousands of eyes upon us; you're asking for rioting.

It should have been done in the discretion of the Imperial Island, within the castle ground.

To at least attempt to try and hide these horrors, to pretend they weren't really happening.

But no, Claudius just loved to put on a show of his faith.

He wanted this massive, macabre audience to witness the Cleansing of souls.

Claudius stands there ready to speak, beside him his adopted son, Connor, who always stands motionless and voiceless beside him.

A child of war found abandoned by Claudius on his travels over two decades ago.

Older than the rest of us.

 Yet, it is odd how his adopted son always stands by him, and yet never his son by blood.

He's ashamed of his birth son, who sits with Theodore, drunk too.

There is also Claudius' daughter, Claudia.

Dressed in yellow robes too, a Daughter of the Faith.

A sweet and shy woman of twenty-five years old.

Yet his adopted son Connor stands there proudly…
An oddity of sort, he looks… Different.
He has a pale complexion and yet… He has features… Well, similar
to that of the slaves.

Of black people.

Yet that could not be right?
Could it.

He was also very tall and muscular, similar to me.

He shouts out for silence as Claudius clears his throat, finally ready to
speak.
The crowd, as well as that of the nobility on this cursed podium come
to a silence.

AND SO, IT BEGINS…

"CITIZENS OF THE CAPITAL, I JOIN YOU HERE TODAY IN WHAT
SHALL BE ANOTHER SHOW OF FAITH.
WITCHES ARE CURSED AND EVIL CREATURES THAT THREATEN
OUR VERY WAY OF LIFE!
OUR VERY GOODNESS, OUR VERY SOULS.
BUT THEY HAVE BEEN FOUND.
FOUND AND CONDEMNED AS ALL WITCHES SHOULD!"

The crowd remains silent.

Odd, usually you had the odd person cry out for mercy or justice.

Yet not today it would seem.
I suppose after three long years, any spark of rebellion they may have
held in their hearts is long dead.

It's as if Claudius can hear my thoughts for the next words out of his mouth begin with loud shouting.

"I KNOW THAT WITHIN THE CAPITAL THERE ARE SYMPATHISERS, THOSE WHO WANT TO HELP AND HIDE THE WITCHES.

I IMPLORE YOU; THIS WILL ONLY BRING ABOUT THE DAMNATION OF YOUR SOUL.

A SOULLESS BEING WILL BRING ABOUT DESTRUCTION OF YOUR OWN.

AND WITHOUT A SOUL, HOW DO YOU EXPECT TO FIND PARADISE?

SO TODAY, I WILL CLEANSE THE CAPITAL ONCE AGAIN, THUS SAVING US ALL.

FOR YOUR SOULS TO KNOW GOD'S LOVE AND ETERNAL LIGHT TO SHINE ON YOU IS ALL I TRULY CARE FOR."

Bullshit, every word was bullshit.

Claudius was the furthest thing from Holy.

And besides, we had lived alongside witches for hundreds of years without a problem.
Sure, some of them lived in the Dark Realm and fought for the Witch Queen, yet most of them were just normal, kind people.
They worked jobs and lived lives the same as the rest of us.

DO NOT BE SILLY!
WITCHES HAVE NEVER LIVED THE SAME AS YOU!
CERTAINLY NOT IN THE HUMAN REALM!
THEY WERE DENIED THE ABILITY TO CAST!
THEY HAVE ALWAYS BEEN PERSECUTED AND HUNTED AND MURDERED.

It was true witches were persecuted, hunted and even murdered before the Great Cleanse, but those who committed those crimes were always duly dealt with.

Yet now, no one dealt with it.
They are persecuted, hunted and murdered freely.
The ultimate execution.
Annihilation and extermination to all.
Ripped out root and stem.

The Defenders around the courtyard and around us burst into thunderous applause, every single one of them.
But only perhaps half of the people in the crowds.
The high lords and ladies of the podium seemed divided also.

Scattered applause amongst them all of them.

THE PEOPLE ARE DIVIDED.

Claudius has a wide smile upon his lips, only hearing the thunderous applause of his Defenders.
Ignoring the people are clearly divided.
My eyes flutter from his as I can see Tristan, his is face furious… And his lips… **Moving?**
Perhaps he is muttering to himself?
Probably swearing and saying curses under his breath.
I would gaze further but then Claudius continues.

"Call out the condemned."

He orders.

Several makeshift pyres stand erect in front of us.

A Defender stands on the podium and begins to call out their names.

"Samantha, who has been condemned for witchcraft.
She was seen Casting small rocks in the air."

Dying for playing with rocks, this is surely lunacy.

She is tied to the pyre as they call out the second.

"Daryl, who has been condemned for witchcraft.
He was caught Casting flames on candles."

This leaves a knot in my stomach.
Tristan had done the very same last night.
But what harm was there really?
It was only pretty lights.

And yet you can die for it.

No matter what happens, I will never let this be Tristan's fate.

I look back to him then.

His lips still moving, albeit quicker… Who is he talking too?

More names get called, more get tied to the pyres.
No, I certainly will not let this be his fate.

AND HOW SHALL YOU ASSURE THIS?
WILL YOU CUT DOWN PEASANTS LIKE IN YOUR DREAM?
WILL YOU SLAUGHTER INNOCENTS TO SAVE YOUR LOVE?
WHAT ABOUT YOUR HONOUR?

No.
I will never allow him to be hurt.
I'll kill anyone who dares try to harm him.
On my honour, I will protect him.

SILLY ME, YOU HAVE NO HONOUR.
YOU ABANDONED THAT LONG AGO…
YOU ARE A CAPTAIN OF THE SLAYER SYNDICATE, AND
YOU'RE FUCKING THE IMPERIAL PRINCE!
WHAT HONOUR DO YOU SPEAK OF?

No, I love him.
And so, what if I'm a Slayer.
Does that mean I cannot love?

Besides, we slay vampires.

ARE YOU SURE ABOUT THAT?
THINK ABOUT IT, THINK ABOUT IT PROPERLY…

So, I do, I think back…

Witches have always lived in the Human Realm… And yet, despite them living here, Casting always had been looked as unfavourable and with distaste.
Because of this, many chose to not Cast whatsoever.
They kept their powers hidden.

They had to act normal… And yes, I suppose they were persecuted and murdered…

I think back to the histories of the Syndicate which I have read numerous times.

Slayers have indeed killed witches over the centuries…
But mainly Dark Witches, those found on the battlefield or lurking in the shadows.

After all, every witch who lived in the Human Realm was documented and listed.
We keep records of it within the Grand Spiral itself.
Just in case any stray witches used their Chaos for the dark they could be easier to locate.
Yet, it hardly ever happened.

Up until three years ago, of course.

THINKING ABOUT IT… HOW DID THE DEFENDERS KNOW WHO TO MURDER AND WHAT HOMES TO BURN?

I'm pulled from this as then remember the poor man I had executed several weeks past.
He too, much like those condemned today, were murdered unjustly.
I had tried to make it painless and swift as possible.
Beheading him in one quick swing.

But it wasn't my fault… My hand had been forced…

The Defenders had caught him Casting.
I just happened to be walking by.
I tried to intervene; I really did.
To attempt to save the man.

Shame Tristan did not see that part, however.

Nor did he see the Defenders tell me that it was business of the Faith, not the Syndicate.

And yet, a crowd had gathered.
They called upon me to slay the man, whilst others cried for mercy.
The Defenders told me this was my job, to slay the Soulless.
But he didn't seem without a soul, he seemed scared.
Scared of what was happening, scared for his screaming wife and daughters who were being dragged from the house also.

It was all too much, voices in every direction.
I should have saved him, but I didn't.

Too many called for his death.

And so that's what I did.

I pulled my longsword and struck his head clean off in one strike.
His wife spat at me, and his daughters cried as they were carted off.
They had been burned to death a few days later.

And Tristan… Tristan had seen what I had done.

I should not have done it, of course.
We were forbidden from participating in what was deemed as aiding the Great Cleansing.
However, I knew that the Defenders or worse even, the crowds were going to violently and mercilessly rip him apart.
That is the only reason I did what I did… To give him a quick and painless death.

But that's not what anyone else saw, and especially not Tristan.
I'll never remember the shame in his beautiful green eyes.
He had never looked at me like that before, and it shattered me.
I looked once more to him, ignoring the Defender still calling out names on the parchment.

I focus my gaze solely on him and not the witches being tied to the pyres.
I do not want to see this.

This madness.
This horror.

I just want to look at Tristan.

Only Tristan.

I want to see beauty instead of death.
To feel love instead of hate.

His lips are still moving I notice… **And with incredible speed.**

What is he doing?

Overhead, long dark shadows begin to cast over us.
I look up and the sky has amassed into a swirling matter of dark greys.
What little sun was there is long gone.
It appears almost as night is upon us, despite it being the middle of the day.

It appears as if Claudius has not recognised however, too involved in his so-called righteous speech.

"THESE SENTENCED HERE ARE NOW ABOUT TO DIE.
WITNESS THE CLEANSING OF THEIR SOULS.
AND MAY GOD HAVE MERCY ON THEM FOR THEIR SINFUL LIVES."

I turn quickly to look at the witches' tied to the pyres.
Defenders with torches begin to walk towards them.

I then again look quickly back over to Tristan; his lips are still moving at incredible speed…

No, he cannot be doing what I think he is…

HE IS DOING EXACTLY WHAT YOU THINK HE IS…

No, he wouldn't, not my Little Prince, he is not that stupid.

The sky erupts in an awful cracking noise, as if it is being split in two. I look up, as do thousands of others.

And then rain.

It lashes downwards, a heavy downpour.

"QUICKLY YOU FOOLS!
 LIGHT THE PYRES AND CLEANSE THEM,"

I hear Claudius shout at the Defenders holding their torches, their gazes averted to the sky.

They quickly run to the pyres and attempt to light them.
It is no use; the torches are quickly extinguished.
The rain bounces off my armour with force.
Several of the high lords and ladies also begin to shout and yell at the thought of their precious clothing getting wet and begin to stand and take their leave.

"NO, NO!
WHERE ARE YOU GOING?!"

Shouts Claudius.

He is ignored as several lords and ladies begin walking down either side of the podium, taking the wooden steps and directly into their carriages.

Claudius cannot physically keep them here of course, watching the execution was not mandatory for the lords and ladies, and that of the public, for thousands upon thousands more of citizens still went about their business in the rest of the Capital.

I am not even needed to stay here, being a Slayer, this is not much of my business, but my uncle wants to always be present so therefore I am too.

I do not know why he wants to attend these executions, it is hardly our business, this being a matter of the Faith and we are that of the Syndicate.

I notice that the witches on the pyres all stand with smiles on their faces.

As if the Old Gods saved them.

BUT THE OLD GODS DID NOTHING!
YOU KNOW EXACTLY WHO DID IT.

No, no, he would not…

YOU KNOW AS WELL AS ANYONE HOW HE FEELS ABOUT
THESE EXECUTIONS…
HE SAVED THEM…

I look back to Tristan, rain has drenched him.
A red, wet line pours from his nose.
His lips have stopped moving, instead replaced with a smile…
A smile I had not seen before…

It was… **Almost evil.**
Beautifully evil.

IT SCARES YOU…
WHAT HE CAN DO…
WHAT HE IS CAPABLE OF…

No, I was not scared of Tristan.
I love him.
Magic is not evil…
These people are not evil…

THESE PEOPLE HAVE THE POWER OF AN INSECT!
CASTING ROCKS IN THE AIR AND LIGHTING CANDLES.
MERE CHILDS PLAY!
HE DID NOT JUST CREATE A STORM; HE IS THE STORM!

But Tristan Casts to light candles too.
And I've seen him play with rocks.

BECAUSE YOU WILL NOT LET HIM BE HIMSELF!
HE SUPPRESSES HIS POWERS IN FRONT OF YOU!
YOU ALWAYS GET ANGRY…

It is true… I do often get angry with Tristan whenever he Casts.
I do not mean too, I merely want to protect him.

Defenders crawl everywhere, and the people mostly hate witches, it's
simply not safe within the Human Realm…

THAT IS NOT THE ONLY REASON!
YOU KNOW THAT IF HE GOT TO PRACTISE, HE WOULD
REALISE JUST HOW POWERFUL HE REALLY IS!

THAT IS IF HE DOES NOT ALREADY REALISE…
BUT YOU'VE KNOWN FOR A WHILE NOW, HAVEN'T YOU…
HOW POWERFUL HE IS…

Yes… Tristan is powerful.

As a Slayer I have immense knowledge of witches, reading many books and scriptures about them, dating hundreds of years.
Magic is both used for wonder and destruction, depending on who is the Caster and how they use their Chaos.
Although, over the centuries the magic has been dwindling here in Human Realm.
Witches here have had to suppress their powers or stop Casting whatsoever therefore over time they end up not casting at all.
Wanting to fit in with humans and evade prejudice and persecution they decided to try and act like everyone else, and therefore they did not teach their descendants.
Yes, children and grandchildren and so forth through the centuries have not Cast, or have forgotten.
Their magic has laid dormant, yet still accessible.
A lot of people end up casting accidentally and often uncontrollably through emotion.
And because they don't know how to control it, it often is unleashed in horrific ways.

Perhaps that is why they are so hated…

And yet you get the odd family that did cast through the centuries, in secret, therefore their magic stayed alive and well trained.
And thankfully they are able to control their Chaos.

Yet despite a witch knowing or not knowing how to control their Chaos was one thing, however magic still dwindled.
Witches nowadays were barely able to cast anything of significance.

Mere playing with rocks or casting lights…

And yet Tristan…

HE CAN MAKE FLOWERS GROW, AND SNOW FALL…
AND NOW HE CAN MAKE A STORM APPEAR…

These things were clear and evident signs that Tristan was no regular witch…
He was indeed very powerful.

At least here in the Human Realm, and yet also in the Realm of Magic I wager with the right training and influence he certainly has the potential to be even more powerful than the Council of Covens…

Maybe even…
No…That would be suicide.

He can't fight her; I won't let him.

I want to keep Tristan away from this war.

SILLY MAN!
HE IS THE WAR ITSELF!
THE FINAL WAR…
IT HAS ALREADY BEGUN…

The final war?
What on earth?

Claudius stands tall and proud, his yellow robes soaked yet he bellows loud and clear.

"CITIZENS, FEAR NOT.

RAIN SHALL NOT PREVENT GOD FROM CLEANSING THESE SOULLESS."

There was little point of shouting, only those closest, like myself, could hear him clearly.
The thunder still crackled loudly.
And the thousands of crowds had all but dispersed, only hundreds remaining.

The poor witches tied to the pyre look confused.

They thought they had been saved…
But they should have known they never would have gotten to live…

And Tristan must have surely known this too…
He only prolonged the inevitable.
However, by the looks of his confused face, I can tell Tristan genuinely thought he had saved them.
His lips stop moving, and as they do the thunderous sky seizes almost instantaneously.
And the once heavy rain begins to lighten considerably.
Tristan looks exhausted.
He wipes what blood remains from his nose and begins to wearily stand.

"Untie and behead them!
Witches are Soulless, now execute them!"

Shouts Claudius.

Defenders begin to untie them from the pyres.
There are several of them, they begin to cry and beg.
They genuinely thought they were safe… Poor bastards.

Tristan finally manages to stand upright, his face full of fury.

THIS WILL NOT BE GOOD.

I am supposed to stand faithfully by my uncle's side and not move and yet I move all the same.
I hear my uncle call out my name and yet I ignore him.
I walk directly to Tristan, trying to intercede.
However, he is still furious, and Tristan merely pushes past me and straight towards Claudius.

"Why can't you just free them."

He seethes at him.

Claudius simply looks him up and down with little interest.
He ignores him and looks back to the crowds.
I lean in close and whisper.

"Come on, Tris, let us find a seat."

I point to the seats and tables.
They are wet yet drying.
The storm is all but gone, the heavy clouds dissolved.
I notice yet another drop of blood fall from his nose, he wipes it away quickly.
He has exerted himself... It happens when Casters use too much Chaos.
It weakens and tires them, can even make them sick or die.

"Tris, you're bleeding,"

I whisper to him.

He doesn't listen to me, his face still locked on Claudius.
He looks as if he wants to kill him right there and then, in front of half
the court and what remains of the crowds, still numbering hundreds of
capital residents.
His nose continues to bleed.
I use my thumb and gently wipe the blood from his nose.
He looks at me then, his green eyes darken.

"Tris, please,"

I whisper again, more urgent this time.

For a brief moment it feels like we are the only two standing here.
Just me and my Little Prince.
Him, an injured doe, and me, a brave warrior tending to him.
A hard hand claps my shoulder, and I notice instantly who it is.

My Uncle.

I quickly remember where I am, and step back from Tristan; I look
around and notice that several lords and ladies who remained are
looking at us… They begin to whisper.

Fuck.

I turn to face my uncle, my Lord Commander.
A hardened gruff man.
His face is blank, it always was hard to read him.
Yet I can sense anger… But for some reason, it does not seem directed
at me.

"Perhaps take the prince back to the castle, nephew."

He tells me, his eyes however never coming off Tristan.

"Yes, come on.
Let's leave."

 I urge.

Tristan ignores me.
Ignores my uncle.
He turns away from us and walks to Claudius.
He goes to the brink of the platform, standing directly beside Claudius himself.
Claudius is clearly taken aback; he turns and faces us, wondering what's going on.
I do not have time to stop him before Tristan loudly shouts out to the crowd.

"LET THEM BE FREE!"

It feels in that instant as if the world suddenly stops.
All motion, sound or thought.
They all cease for the briefest of seconds as Tristan's words hang heavy in the air like a thick fog.

The crowd is deathly quiet.
As are the lords and ladies who remain.
Everywhere nothing but silence.

Never before has this happened.
In three years, Claudius has had unchecked power and control, not once has he been so openly defied.

I could not quite believe it.
I knew Tristan has his views on this subject but to so publicly shout this in front of so many people…

What in the name of Light is he doing?!

The council look uneasy, a couple even standing.
Claudius grabs Tristan by the arm and roughly turns him from the crowd.
Anger shoots through me.

How dare he put his hands on him.

"Release him."

My voice is stone.
Claudius head shoots in my direction, his eyes black with anger.

"What did you say."

 He seethes back.

I don't know what takes over me.
I stride towards him, my body towering over his as it does everyone else.
My eyes firmly locked on him.

"I said release him.
NOW!"

Claudius audibly gulps but does as he's told, releasing his grasp on Tristan.
That's when my uncle intervenes.

"Hush boy."

He says to me, pushing me easily aside before turning to Claudius.

"May I remind you all that we are stood in front of the Capital here.
There are too many eyes upon us right now.
Perhaps we should just simply return to the Imperium where we can
solve matters privately."

My uncle is calm, speaking rationally.
However, Claudius does not see it this way.
He angrily replies.

"You do not command here, I do!
Not you and certainly not these boys!"

He points angrily at Tristan, then at me.

"But yes, take the prince back to the castle!
I have no time for disobedience in front of my people!"

I wish he had not said that.
Tristan immediately speaks up.

"Your people?!
They are not yours!
I am an Imperial of the House Imperium!
My bloodline has ruled for centuries and will continue to rule for
centuries to come!
And who exactly are you?!
Some nothing from nowhere!"

Tristan has never spoken like this before.
What has gotten into him?
Claudius looks almost as if he might burst.
Connor then speaks up, although his voice solemn.

"How dare you, this is your High Pope!"

He speaks, defending Claudius.

"You be quiet, you're nothing but a freak."

Tristan barks back.

I take his arm then.

"Tristan, let's go."

I say firmly.

I don't give him a choice, I turn to leave, pulling him with me.
If only things had ended there.
They did not.
Theodore has noticed the commotion in between his many cups, and swaggers towards us.
He comes to a halt, yet as he stands, he still sways from side to side.

"Perhaps you should sit back down, Crown Prince."

 My uncle suggests.

Theodore waves his hand away at his comment before belching.

"I – I – I a – am f – fine."

He stammers, deeply inebriated.

Shameful.

"What… what is going on here then?"

 He gargles.

"Crown Prince, I am just returning your brother to the Imperium."

I answer.

His eyes almost light up at the sound of that.
And a devious glint appears in the irises.

"Ahh yes… My little brother."

He shouts, his eyes fixing on Tristan.
He points at him and stammers.

"S – stop c – causing t – trouble a – and s – sit d – down."

"I'm leaving."

Replies Tristan trying to walk past.

However, Theodore does not let him.
He outstretches his hand and stops Tristan from leaving.

"I am your Crown Prince, and you leave when I say!
And I did not tell you to leave!
I told you to sit down!"

He barks, his voice getting angrier yet clearer.
I can see Claudius and Connor both smiling widely.

"Let us stop this, we are in public!"

My uncle pleads.

I mutter agreement with him, however Theodore does not.

He shouts at my uncle.

"This has nothing to do with you, Lord Commander!
This is between the Imperial Family!"

He snubbers.

Both me and my uncle sigh.

He really is a disgrace.
He is as repugnant on the inside as he is beautiful on the outside.

He looks much like Tristan.
His hair cut short, the same smooth and delicate features, the same beauty, but his eyes are blue like their sister, Isabella.
Only Tristan has those glorious green eyes.

"ENOUGH OF THIS!
ON WITH THE EXECUTION!"

Claudius shouts.

The Defenders force one of the witches to their knees.
The several others are huddled together, tied and shivering.

A sword is drawn.
I can see it hang high in the air.

"Please, stop this."

Tristan begs me, his eyes begin to wet with tears.
I feel a pang of pain in my heart, I hate seeing him upset.

But what can I do?

The sword comes whooshing down and I see a head roll across the
courtyard.
Blood sprays and the crowd begins to cheer.
Not all of the crowd however, some finally begin to cry out for mercy.
Tristan stands there, tears flow heavy down his cheeks.
How I long to pull him in my arms.
To kiss his tears away.

Yet I can not.
Not with so many eyes on us.

I just wish I could take him from here, somewhere only we knew.
Somewhere just for us, away from everyone and anything.

Yet, we have never been alone.
Not really.
We have always been watched.
By everyone.

If only we had been born commoners.
If only we had no ties to the throne or crown or court.

If only...

I long to take him further away from this place to some distant land. Somewhere we can start anew.

Just me and him, without a care in the world.
Just me and him, against the world.

Theodore laughing loudly pulls me from my thoughts of me and Tristan running away to freedom.
His eyes are transfixed on the executions.
He laughs manically as the next witch is beheaded, and then the next.
Blood sprays and sprays, the crowd cheers and cries.
The Defenders use their shields to hold the line.
Again, and again another head is chopped off, rolling away.

Finally, after what seems like an age, it is done.

Bodies of decapitated witches laid in a pile, a huge amount of blood pooling around them.
Tristan is frozen, his eyes locked on the horror sight.

"There, it is done."

My uncle barks.

"Let us go."

He finishes.

Theodore continues to laugh, however.
Like Tristan, he too is staring directly at the blood, however he is finding glee in the horror and death.
And this is supposed to be our future King?

Tristan on the other hand looks utterly destroyed.
Theodore manages to stop laughing for a second to say.

"Shame there weren't more, I do love a good execution."

He bellows.

Tristan turns on him then, his green eyes dark with wild fury.

"So, you find this funny?
How is this funny?
This is horrifying!"

Tristan shouts, his finger pointing at Theodore.

The crowd cheers and cries begin to die down, they can see the commotion unfolding before them and they evidently want to see and hear the drama between the two Imperial Prince's.

"What's the matter, they are nothing."

 He remarks off the cuff, clearly uninterested.

Tristan loses his temper then.
Thankfully not magically, however.

He extends his arms outwards and shoves Theodore.
It's a hard shove, and yet if he had maybe not been so drunk, he may not have fallen straight on his arse.
The crowd at the front who have the best view begin to chuckle and laugh.

"Enough of this!

The both of you!
Get back to the castle at once!"

Claudius barks.

My uncle agrees.
Imperial Guard come forward, ready to lead us safely to the carriages.
However, before any of that can happen Theodore erupts in anger.
He still sits on the floor, writhing and screaming.

"HOW DARE YOU!
DO YOU KNOW WHO I AM!"

He manages to drag himself to his knees; he points at Tristan.

"I AM THE CROWN PRINCE!
I AM THE NEXT FUCKING KING!
I AM THE HEIR.
YOU ARE NOTHING BUT THE SPARE!"

The crowd once again fell silent, everyone did.
I could see the council quickly moving then, as well as the remaining lords and ladies.
Even the Princess is escorted with her slaves, all walking down the stairs of the scaffold and into their carriages.

Clearly, they do not want to be part of this.

Multiple guards following them, they can sense danger and want away from it.
Claudius takes a look of longing at the Princess as she's hurried into a carriage.
My uncle is waving toward some men, signalling them to remove the princes.

Theodore tries to drag himself to his feet but falls straight on his face.
He begins screaming like a child, punching and kicking the air.

"I HATE YOU. I HATE YOU. I HATE YOU!"

He screams over and over.

Poor, pitiful creature.

Tristan turns away from him and addresses the crowd once last time.
The crowd itself deathly silent, all eager to hear what he has to say.
Also shocked by what is happening.
Claudius and my uncle are too occupied trying to drag Theodore to his
feet to notice as Tristan takes his chance.

"CITIZENS OF THE CAPITAL, LOOK AT YOUR SUPPOSED
RULERS!"

He begins.

Claudius head snaps round so quickly you can almost hear it snap.
His face angered and shocked.

"WILL YOU CONTINUE TO BE RULED BY AN OPPRESSOR?!"
A HATEFUL, FANATICAL FOOL!"

Claudius is too flabbergasted to speak, he stands there holding
Theodore upright.

My uncle turns to me

"STOP HIM NOW!"

He shouts at me.

I remain silent.

I dare not interfere with his speech, not now.

Tristan points behind him, at Theodore.

"AND AFTER THIS OPPRESSOR, WHEN MY BROTHER IS CROWNED, ARE YOU READY TO BE RULED BY THIS DRUNK BULLY OF A CHILD!"

The crowd began to shout no and neigh.

They are agreeing with Tristan.

"WE NEED CHANGE!

YOU, THE PEOPLE, DESERVE BETTER!

WE NEED A RULER TO UNITE THE PEOPLE!"

The speech is already treasonous, although where his speech is heading, it will certainly mean death.

He has called the succession itself into question!

That will definitely earn him some sort of punishment.

However, if he mentions magic…

I reach and grab him then and begin to pull him away roughly.

Tristan writhes and squirms, attempting to break free, but I do not allow him.

My grip on him is firm.

A small book falls from his person.

I notice it's a book of Light, a small prayer book.

I had seen him with it before many times in his tower.

I ignore it as I begin to half drag, half carry him across the platform, down the wooden stairs and towards his own Imperial carriage.

As I do, the crown behind us erupts.

It starts off as just one voice.

However, that voice is joined by dozens of others, which quickly turns to hundreds.

They begin to chant a name…

TRISTAN.

More chime in, growing and growing.

Over and over again, it grows louder and louder.

Tristan stops squirming and I stop moving.

We stand there, facing the crowd.

They continue chant his name over and over.

"Stop them!

Stop them now!"

Claudius orders his Defenders.

The front lines of Defenders begin to pull out wooden clubs.

The crowds begin to scream as they are beaten back.

"NO, STOP!"

Tristan pleads as he once again begins to fight against my grasp.

I can see Claudius and Theodore share an evil smile as the small folk are beaten.

The crowd begins to turn into a panicked mess.

That's when it happens.

Several citizens brandish small knifes, they begin to stab at the Defenders.

More and more small folk join in, they brandish more knives and even throw rocks.

It turns into utter chaos; the crowd begins to grow back to thousands, where there are only perhaps a hundred Defenders standing guard.

As the small folk stab wildly, they continue to chant Tristan's name.

I can see that the smile from Claudius mouth is gone.

Claudius is furious whilst Theodore shrieks and quickly runs away, he seems to have sobered almost instantly as he leaps off the podium and jumps into a random carriage which soon takes off.

I pick Tristan up then, throwing him over my shoulder.

"Put me down."

He cries.

I ignore him.

I run down the stairs and directly for the Imperial Carriage.

I can hear the chaos behind us, the small folk have turned into a huge riot.

I hear my uncle calling upon the captains, warning them to take no action.

I can hear Claudius curse and shout he needs all the men he can and yet Slayers of the Syndicate cannot take part in the matters of the Realm.

And my Uncle, being staunchly against the Great Cleansing to begin with, he will certainly not aid the Defenders in butchering citizens.

However, this also means he cannot save those same citizens either.

No, he can do nothing.

No worry, for I see a spattering of Imperial Soldiers quickly arrive on horses too.

The cavalry called I suppose.

I ignore the madness as I get to the carriage and forcefully push Tristan inside.

I enter the carriage too and pin him roughly to the seat.

"WHAT THE HELL WAS THAT?!"

I shout at him angrily.

He sobs and sobs.
Outside the carriage I can hear the chaos getting louder, the sounds of screams and death.
And yet, I can still hear the chanting of the same name.

I even hear some call him King…

"I just wanted to help,"

He cries.

I sigh deeply, sticking my head out of the carriage, I scream to the driver.

"RIDE ON!"

The carriage comes alive and speeds away, away from the Grand Square and through the many streets.
As we get away, the sounds of screams and deaths die down.

Yet the chanting does not.
I can still hear it even now.
Repeated over and over again.

TRISTAN!
TRISTAN!
TRISTAN!

I look at him.
My breath heavy, his own shallow.

"WHY HAVE YOU DONE THIS?"

I shout in despair.

He begins to take control of his breathing, his eyes quickly drying.
In fact, he suddenly looks relaxed and calm, all traces of anger and fear
gone.
A smile spreads across his face, and it is a smile I do not like.
He leans forward, his lips almost touching mine.
He utters a singular answer.

"Power."

THE NEXT MORNING

IMPERIAL APARTMENTS

A PRINCESS'S PLEA

PRINCESS ISABELLA

I could not stand the series of events that transpired yesterday.

Indeed, the whole of yesterday had been one unfortunate event after another.

From watching Tristan in his tower with his lover and illuminating lights, and then receiving another gift from Claudius shortly after One and Two's arrival.

Having to fix a fake smile as I took my carriage across the Grand Bridge to the Capital.

Keeping that smile fixed on my face despite how awful I felt.

Despite the fact I was riding to witness an execution.

Theodore is always drunk and violent, whilst Tristan is angry and reckless.

I love them both, yet someone from the Imperial Family has to act with some sort of sensibility for the people.

YES, THE PEOPLE DO ADORE YOU.
THE SAD, SMILING PRINCESS.
AND YET, YOU DID NOT SEE WHAT HAPPENED.
YOU HAD LEFT BEFORE THEN.
SPIRITED AWAY IN THE SAFETY OF A CARRIAGE.

This was true, I had indeed left shortly before the supposed spectacle.
And I am grateful for that.
From the rumour that has swirled all night, the riot turned into nothing
but carnage and chaos.

CARNAGE AND CHAOS!
CARNAGE AND CHAOS!
CARNAGE AND CHAOS!

And whilst I might have not seen that, there was something I did see…
And hear…

A lowered whisper…

YES, WHAT DID YOU HEAR?

I still cannot understand it.
It sounded like nonsense at first… A jumble of ramblings, words that
made no sense.
But as it continued, I started to think that perhaps it could have been a
language?
But if it was a language, it was one I had never heard before.
I had tried not to listen, to turn my attention elsewhere, but he had been
sat right next to me.

YES, AND WHO WAS IT THAT WAS WHISPERING?

Tristan.

That's when it happened… An awful rumble in the sky.
The clouds darkened, and heavy rain began to fall.
Tristan had smiled then, I noticed.
Yet not a smile that he usually did.
Warm and kind, no, this was a different smile.

It looked… **almost Sinister.**

It scared me… And Tristan has never scared me before.
Not once.
I noticed blood drip from Tristan's nose, yet the rain quickly washed it away.
Most of the lords and ladies quickly departed, away in their guarded carriages.
However, I stayed… As did others, and Claudius quickly called for the accused witches to be untied and promptly beheaded.
Tristan had jumped up then, angry and despaired.
The rain had stopped then, I noticed.
The once heavy drops turned to the faintest of drizzles.
It had only lasted perhaps a mere moment.
Yet I could hear the carriages of the departed already racing away.
I had thought at first that they had been too quick to leave.
They should have known that nothing would have stopped the execution.
And it didn't…
Tristan had cried for them to be set free… A silly thing to have shouted.
Yet nothing worked, the accused were quickly beheaded.
Theodore had then gotten involved, beyond drunk.
That is when the council moved, and they even got me to depart.
I was led down the stairs and away into one of the Imperial carriages and whisked away.

I had also noticed that during all of that, Kaleb and Tristan had shared a tender moment.
One that will surely not have gone unnoticed by others also.

However, being led away, I did not really see what happened between my brothers, or afterwards.

I knew Theodore had interrupted Tristan, but beyond that I had not
seen anything with my own eyes.

But since yesterday the rumours had swirled around the Imperium and
Capital.

I was raced back to the Imperium, and even though I was urged inside
the Imperium for my safety, I stayed in the castle courtyard, waiting.

Theodore had come back first, drunk and falling out of the carriage,
scared and frightened.

He quickly ran inside the castle with the rest of his monstrous friends.

And Tristan, the second he arrived he was duly taken by the Guards.

I could see Kaleb grow fierce with anger, he looked almost ready to
kill for Tristan, at the thought of anyone daring to touch him.

But I saw the look Tristan gave Kaleb, and he softened instantly.

Tristan was led away then, I tried to reach him, but I too was held back.

I called out for him, but he did not answer.

That was yesterday afternoon, and now it was the next morning.

I lay here in my bed.

I had hardly slept, spent most of the night pacing back and forth,
debating on what to do.

I knew Claudius had come back late last night, along with armed
Defenders.

That's the last information I really had, and I only had that because I
sent One and Two out to spy for me.

They returned to my rooms late last night, and they stayed with me.

They comforted me during the night as I cried, paced, and despaired.

I just wanted to make sure my brother was okay.

NOT BROTHERS?
YOU ONLY CARE FOR TRISTAN?

I thought about that.

I loved both my brothers, but Theodore was cruel and drunk
constantly.

Tristan on the other hand, he was different.

He possessed a profound kindness to him, a want to change the world and that around it.

Yet, he was rash and quick to anger.

And a Caster who is emotional can use their Chaos in tremendous and dark ways.

Yesterday's actions were not the right way to go about it.

I knew Tristan had the gift of magic, but I thought it was minor.

Simply trickery with the lights.

But I was almost certain that the sudden storm was none other than Tristan.

It was quick.

The storm came and went within a mere moment or two.

But was this really bad?

After all, he was trying to save those condemned.

And if I had noticed him and heard him whispering then surely others must have too?

This was dangerous.

To Cast in his tower was one thing, but in the Grand Square…

And when that did not work, he apparently caused a spectacle in front of thousands…

And however much I hated to admit it, Tristan had caused the riot.

By all accounts, if he had not addressed the crowd, nor argued in front of them, they would not have risen up…

But there was one thing that had happened that sent a thousand shivers through my body.

It was only a rumour, a rumour One and Two told me last night, a rumour I dismissed as idle gossip and not real fact.

Tristan… Well, apparently after I had left and the departure of many others, apparently, he addressed the crowds once more and asked them if this is what they wanted.

If they continued to want Claudius.

He even asked them if he thought Theodore should be King?

But that is just a vicious lie, surely not.

Tristan would not be so foolish as to shout to the public asking for them to choose…
And what would he even be implying by asking if they wanted Claudius or Theodore…
Surely, he was not meaning for the crowd to instead… **Choose him?**
No, that was preposterous.
And treasonous…
No, I could not believe it, I won't.
But then, how else did the riot start?
All these thoughts were just too much to bear.
I could not stand this any longer, I had to do something about it.
Staying in my rooms, driving myself mad with worry was not doing me any help.
And neither was it helping Tristan.
From what I could gather, he must have been led to his tower.
Confined there… this I found most disagreeable.
An Imperial should not be confined.
We are a sacred bloodline, closer to gods, so they say.
Tristan should be set free.

Closer to gods, yet plagued with madness…

PERHAPS THE SACRED BLOOD IS POLLUTED.

That too was something that had often been on my mind.
I could not deny it, these histories of Imperials are plagued with madness… And I often wondered, as only three of us were left, which of us would be plagued too.
Theodore definitely already had the madness.

He was vicious, cruel, and a coward.
Not a good mix.

And Tristan… **Did Tristan have the madness?**

YOUR FAITH WOULD CALL HIM SOULLESS…

I did not participate in the views of this… New Faith.
I called it New Faith because it changed three years ago.
I always found the book of Light to be about love.
And yet, Claudius had twisted it, turned it into fear and death.

*HUMANS HAVE ALWAYS FEARED WITCHES, THEY'VE
PERSECUTED AND MURDERED FOR CENTURIES…*

But those individuals would always be duly dealt with by guards, or
soldiers or Slayers.
They would be imprisoned or executed.

*NOT ALL!
THERE ARE PLENTY IMPERIAL SOLDIERS WHO ARE JUST AS
PREJUDICED…
THEY MAY WEAR THE ARMOUR,
BUT UNDERNEATH NOT ALL ARE MEN.
MANY ARE MONSTERS.*

This was true, men could be monsters.
Even more so than the supposed actual monsters.
The Red Eyed demons.
But witches… They were not monsters, were they?

Many witches are good, lovers of nature and balance.
But witches have power, and that power can create tremendous chaos.

Enough of this!
Enough of these thoughts.
I have to do something.
And I have to do it now.

I pull myself from my bed then, and I decide there and there to leave
the sadness and tears behind.
I have to be strong right now, for Tristan.

He is confined, I may not be able to free him, but I will surely visit
him.

HE MAY NOT ALLOW IT...

HE of course being Claudius.

I would have to go to him...

There was fear inside of me at the thought of that...
Claudius ruled in all but name, a powerful and tyrannical man.
It would be foolish not to be afraid.

*PERHAPS YOU NEED NOT FEAR, HAS HE NOT BEEN
SENDING YOU NUMEROUS GIFTS?
FOR MONTHS NOW, HE CLEARLY LIKES YOU...*

I suppose he does like me.
I did not know if that made me even more fearful.

*YOU ARE AN IMPERIAL.
YOU HAVE POWER.*

But I am just a woman, and he is a man.

Power holds no desire over me.
I merely want to keep Tristan safe.

"Prepare a bath and fetch me that white dress with the white lace.
The one with no sleeves."

I tell One and Two.

They share a curious look with each other.

"And my jewels, fetch me the pearl necklace, bracelets and earrings."

They were all white.

I knew from previous experience that Claudius liked me in white…

One and Two quickly get to their duties.

Once bathed, I have scents rubbed over my naked body.
My white dress slips over my body; it clings tightly to my bodice.
Not only that, but it is completely sleeveless.
It reveals my shoulders, my full arms and left little to the imagination
in the ways of my breasts, nearly bursting from the fabric.

I take a look at myself as my hair is brushed from tangles.
I looked beautiful… My young body is ripe and firm, my breasts full
and my waist slim, only accentuated by this tight dress.
And my long hair, it flows down my back in a cascade of tousled
yellow.

And my eyes, a bright blue.
One and Two quickly add my jewellery.
My necklace, my earrings and bracelets, all made from pearls.
All shiny and white, they still smell like the sea.
It is invigorating.
One and Two share another glance.

"Are you sure you want to do this, my Lady?"

Asks One.

"Yes, your brother shall surely be fine.
He is an Imperial after all.
He shall surely only be in confinement for a short time."

Chimes in Two.

"It is not about wanting to do this.
I need to do this.
My brother is a part of me, we were born together, I cannot be away from him, and I have to make sure he is safe.
He has started to play a very dangerous game, and I fear what will happen if he loses."

In truth, I also fear what could happen if he won.

He could Cast, and yet no witch had ever sat on the Imperial Throne.
Nor from as much knowledge as I know has there been an Imperial that could Cast.
This was indeed a precarious and dangerous situation.
So much prejudice, hate and fear for people like him, many in the Realm will surely turn against him.

And then there's Kaleb… The Realm will never accept two men as lovers.

There are too many negatives.

 I love my brother, but the world is too dangerous as it is and if Tristan continues down this path, I can see it being disastrous.

I have to speak with him… To calm him.
Make him see reason and sense.

But first, Claudius.

"I'm ready."

 I tell One and Two.

They both nod their heads.
And with that, I depart.

After a long walk from the Imperial Apartments to Claudius chambers, I brace myself for the several Defenders at the door.
They stand right in front of the big wooden doors, supposedly standing guard but more just standing idly, making conversation with each other.

As I walk towards them, they turn their heads, and I can feel all their eyes on me.
Supposed men of God, and yet many were recruited from the darkest, most depraved parts of the Human Realm.
Vicious bullies that want pretty robes and the ability to abuse and murder without question.
They are a terror everywhere they go.
No, these are not men of God, they are monsters.
They look at me and my exposed flesh as if I am a mere piece of meat.

Anger swells inside me – how dare they!

I am an Imperial Princess, and thus shall be treated as such.
I straighten my back and stand tall and proud.
However, standing straight only pushes my breasts out further, causing
the men before me to all direct their eyes to them.
I ignore them and state clearly.

"I am here to see Claudius."

"Do you have an appointment,"

One of them sniggers causing the others to laugh.

I take a step closer and their smiles slowly drop.

"I am Isabella of the Imperium Dynasty, your Princess.
And you are a mere servant.
If I tell you I have an appointment, you smile and open the door.
Do you understand me?"

I muster up as much courage as I possibly can.

But none of them dare question me.
They all grumble apologies and move aside, opening the doors.
I walk past them quickly, wanting away from them.
Entering Claudius apartments, I hear a slave announce me.

"PRINCESS ISABELLA OF HOUSE IMPERIUM."

With my name being called I find strength fill me.
I shall show no meekness or cowardice, only bravery and confidence.

Claudius's rooms are vast, much like the Imperial Apartments themselves.

This is only the ground floor; twin staircases lead to a first and second floor.

High wooden beams and chandeliers, and many candles fill the space.

A huge wooden table, big enough to seat at least twenty.

And a much smaller table, perhaps for six people.

Tapestries and paintings of the Lord of Light fill the room.

The white sun with a sword on nearly all of them.

A great hearth lies toward the back of the room.

I walk over to it and stand in front of it.

The heat feels good, especially given the coldness of today.

I extend my palms outstretched, enjoying the flames.

It begins to do its job, warming my body.

"Princess."

I hear a singular confused and worried voice emanate from behind me, the voice contains just a hint of… Excitement?

I turn and see Claudius standing on the stairs, book in hand.

I'm taken aback and let out a small gasp.

He is not wearing his usual robes, that being the robes of his religion.

Instead, he wears tight fitted leather pants, and a tight white shirt that is neatly tucked in.

He has evident muscles under his shirt, and his leather trousers leave an impression of his evident manhood.

I quickly look away and pray that he has not noticed.

"Your Holiness."

I say, giving a courteous curtesy.

"Please, please, no need for such formalities."

He mutters quickly, that hint of excitement remains.

He stares at me then, as if trying out work out if I'm real or his imagination.
He smiles then and walks down the remaining steps.
He gestures towards the smaller table.

"Will you sit with me, Princess."

He asks of me.

His voice has a slight tremble to it, which surprises me.

HE ALWAYS SOUNDS SO COMMANDING BEFORE.
HE LUSTS FOR YOU, HE HAS FOR A WHILE.

I smile at him and straighten out my dress.
Claudius' eyes hover over me, drinking me in.
He clearly lusts after me.
I have seen the same look that I see on his face right now.
I have seen it on the faces of so many other men before.
And yet, of all the men who had looked at me this way, Claudius was the only one who didn't make me feel disgusted.

"Forgive me for saying Princess, but you look positively illuminating standing there by the fire."

The gifts had been one thing, but to openly and so forward give me a compliment was another.
I simply smile at him again and walk to the table he has gestured to.

A hint of sadness covers his eyes, as if me smiling and not replying at the compliment upset him.
He pulls a chair out for me, and as I sit, he graciously pushes it inwards.

"Thank you."

I tell him.

He sits beside me and claps his hands.
Several slaves come forward, they place fresh fruit, bread and cheese on the table as well as two glasses and several bottles of wine.
A slave begins to pour wine into two goblets when Claudius stops them.

"I can take it from here.
Leave us."

He then waves his hands at them, waving them away.
They all bow and leave quickly their chains rattle as they do.
I hear them all leave and as the doors close I feel uneasy.
As a Princess, I should never not be unaccompanied, especially not left alone with a man.
Yet here I am, completely alone with him.
It is indeed inappropriate, perhaps he has done it to get the upper hand, to make me feel uneasy and uncertain.

I will not allow it.

REMEMBER WHO YOU ARE!

I push all these thoughts aside as I brace myself for another conversation.
Yet it appears he beats me to it.

"Are you hungry, Princess?"

He gestures to the food.

I pick a grape, chew and swallow.
A smile of approval appears across his face as I eat another.

"So, your Holiness."

"Please, Princess, call me Claudius."

I am once again taken aback; he has never asked this of me before.
Nor have I ever called him by his name, not once.

We have always used each other's titles, but now he wants me to call
him by his name, awfully personal.

THIS WILL GET MORE PERSONAL THAN YOU KNOW...

I suppose you could try and use this to my advantage.

"C – Claudius."

I mumble, it feels weird saying his name.
Like tasting bad wine.
I ignore it.

He shows me another smile, his teeth are clear and white.

"Claudius."

I repeat, this time with confidence.

"I came here to talk on behalf of my brother, Tristan."

His smile fades at the mention of Tristan's name.
He takes a moment to think, before answering.

"Princess, I have great admiration that you came here by yourself, and in his defence, but your brother has caused me great trouble.
He has always caused me trouble.
I did not mind when it was within the Imperial, I can contain that.
But this was in the Grand Square, in front of the citizens, and there were thousands of them.
Scores of people rioted."

"And they died for it.
Your Defenders killed them."

My voice flat and serious.

This time it is Claudius who is taken aback, I suppose he had not expected me to speak to him like this.

"It was not just my Defenders."

"By all account, yes it was, Claudius."

The saying of his name is made slightly easier with my anger.
I continue.

"I have heard rumours too, the Imperial Guard merely tried to contain it from spreading, the Soldiers would dare not murder our own people.
Your Defenders however murdered without impunity."

"It was not murder, Princess.
They rioted, and we had to contain it.
They brandished knives and threw rocks."

"Perhaps you should not have been cutting off heads in front of them.
Violence begets violence."

Claudius chuckles at this.

"You have spirit, Princess.
 I like that."

He gives me a look a look then, a longing look.

"You have no idea,"

 I answer confidently.

This brings another chuckle from him.

"My brother is a good person.
I'm sure he did not mean to cause any harm.
He should not be confined, he's the prince after all, he has Imperial blood in his veins.
This castle and island are his home, it should not be his prison."

Truth was that this castle and island have always been our prison.
At least for me.
At least one of us should be free, why not Tristan.

"Princess, you left in a carriage before you really saw anything.
I was there; however, I stood and saw it all unfold.

Your brothers, Theodore and Tristan shared words of anger, and Tristan shoved Theodore so hard he fell over.
He then addressed the crowd, and he asked them if this is what they wanted for their King.
He called in the line of succession into question, and he did so in front of the people!
Doing so privately is one thing, but to do so publicly, do you realise just how treasonous this is?
Forgive me, Princess, but confinement is nothing compared to what others would have done to him."

He answers.

The rumours One and Two had told me, the ones I did not want to believe…
 I still do not want to believe.

"Tristan… No, he wouldn't.
He wouldn't be that stupid, he wouldn't do that to Theodore,"

"Well, it appears as if Tristan does not believe that Theodore should be King.
Nor does he think I should rule, which I do not, I am merely a servant of God, after all."

This is a lie.

Claudius might be a servant of God, but he rules with an iron fist.
The Council, which includes himself is supposed to share the stewardship until such time as Theodore comes of age.
This however is not the case; it is Claudius who really rules.

"I will not believe this, not until Tristan tell me so himself.

I want to see him.”

He goes quiet at this.

“If you will not let him out of his confinement, then at least let me see him.”

“I’m sorry Princess, but I am not sure if this is wise.”

Anger swells inside me.

“What you say has only hints of truth to it, Claudius.
If I am to call you by your name, then show me the respect I deserve.
I may be just a girl, but I’m not stupid.
We both know that it is you who rules.
You can deny it all you want, but if you do, just know that I will be insulted.”

I lean forward then, my breasts touching the table.
His eyes are fixated on them, he shifts in his chair uncomfortably.

“Yes, Tristan has caused trouble in the past, but we both know you have caused more than trouble.
Three years and how many have died?”

“Witches, Princess,”

He tries to interject.

I raise my hand to him to silence him.
He is stunned by this.

“I will not get into that, for that is not why I am here.

346

Tristan is not just my brother; he is my twin.
We grew together inside my mother's womb; we were born together.
We are but two sides of the same coin.
I love him greatly, and I implore you to change your mind about me seeing him."

It is he who leans forward then.

"And why would I do that, Princess?"

His eyes are full of intrigue.
I need to change the subject quickly; I want to catch him off guard.

"You have been sending me presents, yes?"

I say, which makes him instantly look uncomfortable.
He seems to stutter, trying to figure out what to say.

"I thought we were talking about Tristan?"

"We will continue, but I want to know why you've been sending them, firstly.
 Do you perhaps have an attraction to me, Claudius?"

His eyes nearly bulge out his head at my brazen asking.
When he does not continue, I do it for him.

"If you do, then surely you will do this for me?
I have never asked you for anything, but I ask you this."

He takes another moment to gather himself before answering.

"Princess, perhaps we should talk about other subjects.

How goes your needlework?"

NEEDLEWORK?!

"I did not come here to talk of NEEDLEWORK!"

I am so angry I could spit.

"Why all the gifts, will you not even tell me that?
You have sent dresses, shoes and even expensive jewels.
And I have come to understand no one else knows about this?
The Council, mainly."

He seems to go almost rigid.
He knows full well that his role here is already precarious.
He may rule through fear but even he knows full well that sending gifts
to me, well, that is beyond the line, and I doubt even the fearful Council
would be happy to know.

"Princess."

"I am not finished!"

I snap.

His eyes start to rapidly blink, looking stupefied… And yet, aroused?
He is looking at me as if he could have…
Well, perhaps a lady shouldn't mention those things.

***HE WANTS TO GRAB YOU, THROW YOU ON THIS TABLE AND
FUCK YOU GOOD.***

Even the notion!

"Tristan hates these executions, as do many others.
Including myself.
And yet you continue to do them.
It's as if you are asking to be hated.
Whereas Tristan, Tristan is beloved.
The people applaud and cherish him, they always have.
And you have had him locked away in his tower, further damaging your reputation."

I grab another grape and chew as I let him process what I say.

"And why would you care about my reputation?"

He ponders.

This question throws me.
I do not care about his reputation, why would I?
This evil, murdering man.

AND YET, IS HE NOT HANDSOME?
DO YOU NOT SEE THE OUTLINE OF HIS MANHOOD?
HIS FATHER MUST HAVE BEEN A HORSE.

Enough!
Ladies. Especially Princesses do not think on such things.

And yet, as I too process his question, I look at him properly for perhaps the first time in my life.
Dressed plainly, and in the comfort of his own apartments, I cannot help but realise he is a comely man.
Yes, he is twice my age, and yet he does not look remarkably older.
In fact, he looks very well for his age.
He has short, cropped hair, like most men at court, and thick yet shaped eyebrows.

His lips are neither big nor small, just the right size.
And he is clearly muscular, his tight clothing only accentuates this.

I realise I have been staring at him and quickly look away.
When I look back, ready to answer, he is grinning widely.

I grab my goblet and take several deep gulps, finishing it.
I place it on the table and tell him.

"Another."

He raises an eyebrow.

"I said pour me another."

He seems to like that.
He duly pours me another, filling the goblet.
I take a sip then answer.

"I care about the stability of this Realm.
We are at war, and you have not helped things.
And yet, neither has Tristan.
You both are doing the wrong thing."

He seems more and more intrigued as the moments pass.

"And how exactly would we do the right thing?"

"These executions have to stop,"

 I say bluntly.

"You say it is for religious reasons, you are cleansing souls but we both know many you have sentenced to death have been innocent.

And regardless of whether they are witches or not, you show incredible cruelty to others as well.

You have had people executed for simple things as common theft.

Or if anyone is remotely different, they are imprisoned.

And if you don't execute them, they usually rot away in some dungeon.

Broken and forgotten.

The people have dealt with this for three years, but they will not put up with it forever.

That riot yesterday was not the first, and it shall not be the last.

But if you stop this, if you stop this violence and cruelty, perhaps, just perhaps the people will start to hate you less."

Claudius listens to every single word I speak with intent.

For this, at least, I appreciate him.

Women are not usually allowed to speak, let alone so freely and bluntly.

And in truth, I have never spoken so freely or bluntly before, yet I feel empowered.

And the fact he seems to be actually listening…

I know many men, both high and low would harm women for even daring to speak their minds, let alone speak how I have.

But then again, a woman has always been servant to a man.

Whether it be her husband, brother or father, we all were ruled somehow.

Yet I decided that is not how I will live.

I shall think and say and do what I choose, not a man.

Claudius leans forward, his features warm.

"You have incredible spirit."

The warmth of him still remains, his compliment makes me feel good.
And the way he continues to look at me…

"You wondered why I send you gifts, yes?
All these months and you have not said a word.
Not mentioned it, ever."
And yet, now, here you are, and positively seem to be full of words."

"Am I speaking too much for you?"

My anger rising once again.

"Not at all, in fact, I like it when you talk.
I find it rather refreshing.
No one else dares speak to me the way you have.
I like it greatly."

He has a glint in his eye, one that makes me feel a small flutter.

What is happening?

"Well, most men would not like their princesses talking so much,"

"I am not most men, and I did not realise you were MY PRINCESS,"

The way he says, 'MY PRINCESS' gives me another flutter.

"I am everyone's Princess."

I answer, trying to dodge what he said.

A glow of sadness seems to come over him.

"A shame."

He admits.

I do not know why, but I feel guilty.
I had never thought I would feel guilt for him, tyrannical as he is.
However, despite perhaps seeing him in a different light did not change why I came here.
And yet, I realise I also needed to quell the anger rising in the people, and the animosity between Tristan and Claudius.

I reach across the table and take his hand.
He immediately sits upright, his eyes locked on me.
He then takes his hand and places it gently upon my cheek.
He shudders and my own heart quickens, I have never been touched so.

Not by a man, not like this.

He removes his hand, and I feel disappointed.
Yet he places it on top of my hand which is holding his.
He envelops his hands around mine, holding them firmly yet gently.
His eyes continue to be locked on me.

If anyone was to walk in right now, and see us holding hands like this, it would spell nothing but disaster.

"So, Princess, I suppose you have a plan?
To make me… Less hated?"

"Give back to the people."

I say honestly and gently.

"Give them a break, stop the fear and executions.
Stop making people cower and cry in the streets.
Rein in the men you have unleashed upon the Realm.
They are poor and starving and have enough troubles without all this unnecessary cruelty."

"And so, what would you propose?"

"I propose that you take some money from the treasury.
I know it is more than full.
Donate it to the people.
Many in the Capital, especially in the lower city, they have nothing.
Less than nothing.
Most do not even have proper homes; they live in wooden shacks.
So, what if we give them coin.
Coin to buy food, to feed themselves and their families.
They can even buy tools and make repairs; they could even make proper homes.
Mothers can buy medicine for their sick children and babes.
And we can hand out fresh bread also.
Show the people compassion, show them you care."

Claudius looks taken in by me.
That smile never wavers.
And his eyes still bore into me deeply.

HE IS MORE THAN INTRIGUED BY YOU.
CONTINUE!
SHOW HIM WHAT YOU CAN DO.

"Princess, you clearly have a gentle heart, and you care deeply for the people.
These make you a good Princess.

A good woman.”

“You are kind to say so, most just see me as a silly girl.”

His eyes linger over me then, and his hand squeezes mine gently but kindly.

“Trust me, Princess.
You are definitely a woman.”

His eyes linger over my shoulders and bare arms, they focus on my breasts momentarily before looking me back in the eyes.
He knows that I know he is looking, yet he does not attempt to hide it.

HE WANTS YOU.
HE WANTS YOU BADLY.

“But, the people, you really think given them coin and bread will stop them hating me?”

“No, not immediately.
But if you and Tristan go down there.”

He seems to have a flash of anger at the mention of Tristan once again, he sighs and moves backwards in his seat, taking his hands away from mine.

“Princess, after yesterday, the last thing I need is sending him back into the Capital.
To the very people he incites to riot.”

“It has to be you and Tristan; do you not see?
After yesterday, you need to show the people now more than ever that you are united.

That there is no bad blood between you.

That there is no bad blood between that of the Imperial Family and the Faith.

The Defenders shall be there, as shall the Imperial Guard, together, united, we shall show the people the love and compassion they so desperately deserve.

And if the people see us united, perhaps it will stop all those silly notions and rumours about jeopardising the succession.

Do this and we can finally stop all this infighting and terror.

We have enough monsters and death already trying to turn our land dark, we should not be doing it for them instead."

His face is a flush with emotions, I can see him debating internally what I have said.

He takes a drink of his wine, and I find myself doing the same.

My head begins to swim, I am not much of a drinker.

It is however, I guess, helping with my confidence, and also loosening my tongue.

I make a mental note not to drink anymore.

This is a delicate matter; I should not be inebriated.

I cannot read which emotion he will settle on, however I continue to hold his gaze, I will not look away nor back down.

"The idea… The idea is wonderful, Princess.

The idea of giving back to the people, giving them coin and bread, showing a united front, it all sounds good.

However, Tristan is a loose cannon.

No one knows what he is about to say or do next, especially himself.

He cannot control himself, and I do not want him enticing more riots."

"Then let me see him.

Let me go to him and talk to him, to calm him and make him see sense.

As I said before, we are two sides of the same coin, he will listen to me.

I know my brother; he does not want to incite riots or call into question the succession which is already settled.

He loves the people and wants to help them, so let me go forth and present him with this plan.

Giving coin and bread to the people, helping them, he shall surely cherish the idea.

So please, let me see him.

And please, end this confinement too.”

“I suppose… Giving coin and bread would be considered a charitable event, and I think God would like that very much.”

“Not just God, but I would like it too.

More than anything.”

“Well, if it really means so much to you… Then yes, I shall organise this event.

And… And you may see your brother.

However, he shall remain confined… Just temporarily.

Until I know for certain he is entirely calm and reasonable.”

Thank the Light!

“I shall have all the details arranged, but please Princess, be warned, it is not so easy to extinguish hate.

And this… Event… might not go as you plan it too.”

I wave this motion away.

“Preposterous, this will work, you shall see, and you will be a better man for it.

In the eyes of the people… And in mine.”

I had not meant to say the last part, and I blamed the wine entirely.

“Well, then I shall do my best.”

He whispers.

I smile and begin to stand.

He looks worried and saddened; he stands too.

“Leaving so soon, Princess?
I was enjoying our talk…”

“Me too, but I really should go and see Tristan.”

He nods at this, understanding, but the sadness still lingers.

“I could return… To continue talking.
If you wish?”

His eyes light back up at this.

“Really, you will come back?”

“If you prove to me that you can change, if you can show compassion
instead of cruelty, love instead of hate, then yes, I shall come back.”

“Thank you. Princess.”

I can tell he means it, I only hope that he will prove himself.
I curtesy then, and I can hear another shudder emote from him.

With that, I take my leave.

I am Isabella Imperial, and I have shown what I am capable of.
I may not have secured my brother's immediate release, however I
have gotten visiting rights, not to mention I have ensured that the
poorest of our citizens will get coin and bread which they so surely
deserve.
Yes, I have done well for an afternoon's work.

YOU HAVE ALSO MADE CLAUDIUS FALL IN LOVE WITH YOU!

That is ludicrous, no, he does not love me.

*HE DESIRED YOU BEFORE, AND NOW YOU HAVE COME TO
HIM, DRESSED SO BEAUTIFULLY!
AND YOUR BREASTS SO EVIDENT, YOUR HEART SO FIERCE,
AND NOW HE LOVES YOU.*

I push these thoughts aside; I will not even think of that.
I came here for a purpose and did what I had to do.
If that included flattery and flirtation, then so be it.

I have done well.

*YES, YOU HAVE DONE WELL INDEED!
YOU GOT VISITS TO SEE YOUR BROTHER, AND YOU GOT
COIN AND BREAD FOR THE PEOPLE.
AND YOU'VE GOTTEN FEELINGS FOR CLAUDIUS!*

No, I cannot… I will not.
I am the Princess, and he is the High Pope.

*HE IS A MAN, AND YOU ARE A WOMAN.
IT CAN MOST CERTAINLY HAPPEN.*

IT CAN, AND YOU WILL.

No, no, not Claudius.

THE MORE YOU DENY, THE MORE EVIDENT IT BECOMES.
TRISTAN WILL NOT BE HAPPY WITH YOU…

Tristan does not need to know.

SILLY PRINCESS, YOU THINK YOU HAVE HELPED.
TO THINK THAT YOU SOMEHOW WILL UNITE THE PEOPLE,
BUT YOU CANNOT DO THAT WITH CHARITY, COIN AND
BREAD!
NO!
ONLY BLOOD, FIRE AND DEATH SHALL MAKE THE PEOPLE
UNITE!
YOU HAVE NOT HELPED; YOU HAVE MERELY MADE
MATTERS WORSE THAN YOU COULD IMAGINE.

But how could things get worse.

WAR IS HERE!

We are already at war.

BUT THIS IS THE LAST WAR!
THE WAR THAT SHALL DETERMINE EVERYTHING.
THE REALMS WILL BLEED, ALL THREE OF THEM.
HUMANS, WITCHES AND VAMPIRES ALIKE WILL BURN AND
DIE.
SO MANY WILL DIE…
AND THE WORLD AS YOU KNOW IT WILL BE FIRE!
JUST WAIT AND SEE!

I feel dread come over me instead of happiness, and I cannot shake it as I walk to my brother's tower.
No, war is not here.
I will not believe it.
And I will not believe that I have made things worse.

How could I have?

Surely everything shall fall into place, and everything shall be fine.
Fine and wonderful, you'll see.

> ***SILLY PRINCESS, IT IS YOU WHO SHALL SEE!***
> ***YOUR WORLD IS ABOUT TO BURN!***
> ***EVERYTHING AND EVERYONE YOU LOVE WILL DIE!***
> ***YOUR LIFE AS YOU KNOW IT IS ABOUT TO BECOME ONE***
> ***ENDLESS TRAGEDY!***

But will I burn with the world?
Will I too die?
Or will I survive the fires and my fate…

I guess I shall just have to wait and see.

LATER THAT DAY

TRISTAN'S TOWER

BRING HIM TO ME

TRISTAN

I stand at the second and highest floor of my tower, staring out at the violent sea, its waves thrash recklessly and madly.

Waves against waves, waves against rocks, waves everywhere.

It is wild and terrifying… And yet, it is exhilarating and fills me with unpaired joy.

Much like what happened back in the Grand Square…

That had been wild and terrifying…

To take a stand against Claudius and my brother, against all this pain and death.

Kaleb had been furious with me… Tried to stop me, yet I had not allowed him.

I have been quiet for too long now.

Three long years of enduring this.

But even before that.

Always having to endure.

Endure not being myself, not being able to openly express my love for Kaleb, not being able to Cast at will.

I will not be quiet anymore, I refuse to be.

And why should I continue to put up with this?

And the people, should they not live how they wish also?

So yes, I called to them… And how the crowd had cheered.
It too very much like these waves had been exhilarating and filled me
with joy also.
They cried my name, they shouted and hollered for me…
I had even heard some call me King…

Oh, how wonderful it had been.

IT IS TREASON.

No, it is true.
I should be King.

King Tristan…

Had it been wise to call out the crowds?!
Had I acted unwisely and boldly and rashly, yes, of course I had.

I know for certainty I should never have taken my Grimoire.
This is something that does indeed frighten me slightly.
I had been writing and working on it for years, all my magic knowledge
and own Casting spells that I have done… Yes, I managed to disguise
it as a Book of Light, but I do not know yet know how to make the
pages invisible…
It had indeed been foolish travelling with it, but I needed to reread my
spell before I Cast it.
I wanted to make sure I would create a rough and good storm.
And I had… Although the storm came as quickly as it went.
I lost focus and couldn't Cast much more.

But in the future… In the future the storm will be as long as I want.

I'll make sure of it.

But one thing was certain, I had to get my Grimoire back, if it was not lost.
I only hope whoever picked it up will see it as a prayer book and leave it alone.
I hope they will not pick it up and read it.

Whilst it of course could not be directly linked to me, if Claudius or any of his Defenders find such a thing they will be hunting the streets of the Capital like dogs, and I do not want the people to be hurt anymore.

But how can I find it whilst being confined here I do not know.
It's not exactly like I can ask Kaleb, he does not even know about it…
And he would be furious if he did.

So yes, that had been unwise.
But aside from that, how the crowds cheered and hollered and fought for me…

It truly had been exhilarating.

Should I have called into question the Succession… Perhaps not.
But did I care?
No, no I did not.
I wanted them to rise up.
I wanted them to call my name.
I wanted them to see I was the better option.

The only option.

Claudius is nothing other than a zealous, evil tyrant.
And Theodore, he is nothing more than a vicious, stupid fool.
Neither are fit to rule this country.

BUT YOU ARE!

Yes, yes, I am.
And rule I shall.
The crown, the throne, it belongs to me.

Then take it…
Wear the crown, sit upon the Imperial Throne.

But it was never the Imperial crown nor throne that my visions showed me.
As I think upon it, the vision comes to me again.

Of me.
Beautiful and powerful.
Crowned and throned.
The crown bejewelled with the greenest emeralds and most crimson of rubies.
And the throne, dark and mysterious.
But neither were the Imperial Crown or Throne.
No, these were different.
And fire… **Fire everywhere.**

The flames danced and licked, yet they did not scare me.
No, fire could not scare me, I was the fire.
I will be the one to unite the country.
All will love and worship me.

LOVE AND WORSHIP!
LOVE AND WORSHIP!

But another vision still plagues me… **Those Red Eyes.**

I had forgotten it for so long… But it has been coming back to me, clearer and clearer.

Those Red Eyes poking from the brown bark and greenery of the trees. One question remains though… One that has been forgotten and unanswered.

How did the Red Eye Demon get on this Island?

It is a strong question, a question that has apparently been asked again and again…

But with my father's sudden death and the beginning of the Great Cleansing, it seems that important question has been pushed aside.

Even I had been foolish enough to let it slip past my mind and let it be lost these last three years.

Perhaps, it would have been lost forever.

However, it will not be lost now.

No, I will make sure it will not.

This confinement at first had angered me greatly.

Yes, when arriving back to the castle I had willingly been escorted to my rooms; I even stopped Kaleb from stopping the Defenders who brought me to my tower…

Yes, I had been angry.

But now, I realise it had been a good thing.

Here, in the confinement of my tower I have had the pleasure of my own thoughts since yesterday.

And those thoughts brought me to think and think and think again.

About questions.

All sorts of questions.
All sorts of thoughts.

ALL SORTS OF MADNESS!

Am I mad?
Perhaps I am.
Perhaps I am not.
Is not madness and greatness the same?!
Simply two sides of the same coin.

MADNESS AND GREATNESS!
MADNESS AND GREATNESS!
MADNESS AND GREATNESS!
TWO SIDES OF THE SAME COIN!

Yes, maybe I am mad indeed.
But I am also great.
Of that, I am sure.
And I shall show the world exactly what I mean.

BURN IT!
BURN IT!
BURN IT!

The words ring in my ears as they have many times before.

Should I burn it all down?
Is that perhaps the only way I can rebuild?
No, I do not want to slaughter thousands…

BUT THE ARMY OF DEFENDERS NUMBERS THOUSANDS!
SURELY YOU WILL HAVE TO KILL THEM?

Ok.
Maybe slaughtering those thousands would be good…
But only them.

OF COURSE, BUT WHAT ABOUT OTHERS WHO MAY OPPOSE YOU?

I suppose they will need to be slaughtered too…

YES, KILL EVERYONE…

**No, not everyone.
Just Claudius and his Defenders…**

I begin to laugh then.
The waves continue with their violent ways, and I continue with my laughter.

Yes, maybe I am mad indeed.

*YES, YOU ARE MAD!
THE PEOPLE WILL SEE THAT TOO.*

The people will do as they are told.

My laughter continues.
Claudius, I guess, plans to keep me here for a while, and from what I gather no one will be visiting me.
No, surely, I will be left to my solitude in my tower.
And yet, when I am free, I must visit the Capital.
 I have to find the Secret Court; I just have too.
I know they are out there; the witches captured were executed yesterday and they must be hiding somewhere… More importantly, coming from somewhere.

Yes, somewhere out there, just over the water, deep within the Capital is a nest of hidden witches and I intend on finding them.

I must find them.

I will surely need their help to unite the people.

Staring back out into these beautiful, violent waves, I find it so calming.

I had hoped to have peaceful solitude, but alas, that does not appear to be the case.

A large knock raps the door.

Most likely one of the guards.

Claudius it seems has either let me keep my ordinary guards or forgotten to place Defenders at my door.

Or maybe he just doesn't care.

My regular guards, they are good men, and no doubt I can trust them.

They may not be strongest or bravest, and even slightly dim witted, yet they quickly told the Defenders who escorted me here last night to unhand their Prince.

Yes, they are indeed loyal.

I ignore the knock.

I'm too busy staring at the waves.

The door opens, a voice calls out.

Not that of the guard, or even that of a man, but a soft, tender voice.

That of a woman.

A familiar voice.

My sister.

I do not answer her, I continue to stare out into the deep blue.

Footsteps creaking on the stairs, one after the other.
Again, and again and again.
She has to walk all the way up, right to the top of the tower where I have so often fondly sat to read, write and gaze at the views.
Not to mention, I have a small balcony up here, albeit smaller than my balcony on the ground floor, however it allows my owl to fly in and out as he wishes.
Plus, the higher up, the better the view.

"Brother."

A pleading voice calls to me.

I manage to drag my eyes from the sea, there my sister stands, at the top of the staircase.

"Brother."

She calls out again.

I knew she would come, but how has she?

Perhaps the guards simply let her pass.
They must have done for surely Claudius would not allow me any visitors.

So, how did she get here?

"Brother."

She calls out for a third time.

I must answer her, yet I do not know what to say.

I simply just look at her, and her at me.
I turn from the waves, and I walk towards her.
Not a word is uttered, only the sound of the sea and echoes of seagulls.
As I walk toward her, she jumps and wraps her arms tightly around me.

"Oh, sweet brother!"

 She gasps.

"What happened?!
I can't believe any of this!"

She continues as her hug continues also.

I hug her back tightly then.
I do not want to answer, I just want to hold her.
The hug eventually finishes.
She looks fit to say something but there is only one word that I utter.

"Kaleb."

She gasps yet again and takes a step backwards.

"I come here, and you ask for him?!"

Her voice is upset.

I had not meant to upset her, I love her, and yet, it is not her I want right now.
I want Kaleb, always Kaleb, only ever Kaleb.

"Sister, I mean no offence, but I need Kaleb.
Will you bring him to me?"

 I ask of her.

She looks as if I had slapped her.
Her face growing angry, she finally speaks up.

"I waited for you in the courtyard… I saw you taken by Defenders…
I have stayed awake all night doing nothing other than pacing back and
forth, frantic with worry.
And finally, finally I come to see you.
And you ask for him?!"

There are tears on her cheeks.
I feel guilty, yet that doesn't change the fact of who I need.

"You don't understand."

I try to reason with her, until she cuts me off.

"No, you don't understand!"

She fires back.

"I have been worried sick!
Will you not speak with me?
Spend even a moment with your own sister before calling for your,"

"For my what?!"

I question sharply.

She looks at me, her anger subsides.

"Tristan, I know."

I feel as if I have run straight into a stone wall.
And yet, I am not fearful.
She is nothing to fear.

"Before you insult me by denying it, remember I am not just your sister, but I am your twin.
I know you better than anyone, better than you know yourself."

I chuckle at this.
She is fiery today, not often a quality my sister expresses.
No, usually she is quiet and reclusive.

What has got into her?

More questions it seems I don't have the answers too.

QUESTIONS, QUESTIONS, QUESTIONS.
BUT WHERE ARE ALL THESE ANSWERS YOU NEED?

"It is the truth; I know you better then yourself!
And I know that you and Kaleb are… Intimate."

She almost whispers that part.

"What of it?"

I answer back curtly.

My off the cuff comment clearly rattles her.

"What of if?!"

She repeats, bewildered.

"You and Kaleb are both men!"

She cries!

"Do you have any idea what the Faith do to men that sleep together? They are."

"You dare tell me about this?!
As if you even have the slightest idea."

 I say, my voice raising.

I take a step closer, my anger growing.

"You dare lecture me?!
Warn me?!
Tell me about myself?!
I know the ramifications of what me and Kaleb's relationship entails!
I know the consequences of our love!

I shout.

"Tris, I did not mean."

I ignore her, cutting sharply

"Do you think I asked for this, Isabella!
To be born like this!

To have these feelings!

Her face softens greatly, she tries to reason with me, to apologise, but I won't let her.

"The Faith punishes and prosecutes people like me.
And do you know what, sweet sister.
I say fuck it.
Fuck Claudius, fuck the God of Eternal Light and fuck every single person who follows the Faith!"

Her eyes widen at this statement.

"I love Kaleb, and he loves me.
I do not care what your Faith says.
Being in love is not a sin.
And if my love means my death, then I will happily consign myself to the flames."

She says nothing, her body trembles and her eyes stay widened.
I realise I am breathing hard.
I turn away from her and look out back at the sea.
The waves are even more violent.
I place my hands firmly on the stone.
My feet edge between the stone floor of the tower and that of the jutting balcony.
I only need run a few paces and fling myself off the side.

To end it all.

To be part of the crazed sea.

Am I crazy?!

Perhaps I am.
Perhaps I am not.

"You would really die for him?"

She asks of me.
I continue to look out, but I do answer her.

"Yes… I would die for Kaleb…"

Red Eyes appear in my mind once again.

But it's different this time, I do not just see it appearing from the greenery of the trees.
I see it moving toward us…

It wears yellow rags… They look so familiar?

And Kaleb, he draws his Saerillian Silver.
He pushes me aside, harshly, yet manages to make sure I land in the softness of the snow.

The Red Eye Demon and my love battle…

But I realise, as I suppose I did then, that the demon never wanted to fight Kaleb…
No, the creature clearly wanted me…

And Kaleb, he got in the way…

The vision ends abruptly and leaves me gasping, holding on tighter to the stone, so hard in fact I can feel the stickiness of blood in my palms.

"Tristan, Tristan are you okay?!"

My whole body is shuddering, shaking, almost convulsing.
But now, now I realise how it charged forward…
It wanted me and Kaleb defended me, like he always has, like he
always will.

Because he loves me.
And I love him, entirely.
And I need him, I need him now.

My sister continues to pat my back, trying to calm me, but the shakes
do not stop.
I remember more than what I have these last three years…

"K – Kaleb,"

 I chatter.

"B – bring m – me K – Kaleb,"

 I chatter on.

My sister, without argument immediately dashes off.
I barely notice the loud creaks of the stairs as she runs downward.
I can't focus, I feel like the epiphany has just made me madder.

Am I mad?!
Perhaps, perhaps not.

> *YOU WOULD NOT BE THE FIRST MAD IMPERIAL,*
> *DO NOT WORRY.*

I know the histories of my ancestors, and madness plagued many of us it seems.
And it never ended well.
Not for a single one of them.
But none of them had magic like me…

MAGIC AND MADNESS!
WHAT A BEAUTIFUL MATCH!

I had heard stories of madness and magic.
That too did not seem to end well.

Casting Chaos requires many things.
Focus, respect, determination, emotion and clear thought to channel clearly.
However, madness and emotions make magic wild and terrifying if the Caster falls to darkness.

WITH MADNESS, THERE IS NO CONTROL!
WITHOUT CONTROL, CHAOS RUNS RIOT!
CHAOS AND MADNESS!
CHAOS AND MADNESS!
CHAOS AND MADNESS!

The vision returns.
I'm cold, sat in the snow.
Bells in the distance… They distract the demon…
Kaleb plunges his sword deep into its mutated body…
It lets out an otherworldly shriek, and then turns on Kaleb…
He gets hit hard by sharp wings… He flies into the air, hitting a tree with tremendous force.

He lays there, broken and bloody.

Anger surges through me, and I… And I…

The vision once again blows away as if on the strong winds.

My head feels woozy, tears stain my cheeks, I can feel blood even drip
from my nose.
I fall, hard, straight on to the hard, stone flooring.

I'm wide awake though.
My gaze transfixed upwards.
Half of my view is the wooden and stone rooftop of my tower; the
other half of my view is of the outside storm clouds and sea gulls.
I see my beloved owl flying amongst them.

Another voice appears…

Has the vision started again?!
Or am I sleeping and dreaming?!
Or am I even dead…

"Tristan… Tristan… Tristan."

It's the voice of my heart.
Strong arms lift me from the ground and to my feet.
I see his face.
The face I had seen since before I can remember.
His strong jaw, his dark stubble, those dark, brooding eyes.

If I am dead, then surely, I am in Paradise.
But I never went past the Iron Gates…
I was never judged by the Confessor…

The Iron gates being where apparently our souls are sent too after we die, according to our Faith of Eternal Light, however.
And we are judged by the Confessor, who deems whether we have been good or bad and are allowed past the Iron Gates and into Paradise.

"TRISTAN, TRISTAN, TRISTAN!
WAKE UP! WAKE UP! WAKE UP!"

I hear a shout.

I thought I was awake?!
Am I awake?!

My senses seem to come back, I feel more in touch with reality. . .
My legs feel weak however, yet I need not mind, Kaleb keeps me firmly stood.
His eyes are full of worry.

I had so thought his eyes would be full of anger, but they are not.

"Kaleb."

I whisper through the haze.

"I'm here, my love.
I'm here."

He reassures me.

Yes, he is always here, always for me.

I use what strength and send it to my feet,

I push upward, my arms envelop around his neck, and I place my lips on his.
The kiss is soft, tender, so full of sweetness.
His stubble, like always scratches my supple skin.
And I can smell his strong scent.
I feel utterly, utterly amazed.

A loud, audible gasp pulls us both from our own world.

I look over, once again my sister stands at the top of the stairs.
She saw us, saw everything.
I cannot read her expression, it's one I have never seen before.

She looks away, out into the sea I had long stared at.
She finally looks back and speaks.

"You're bleeding."

She notes.

I suppose she does not want to speak about what she witnessed.

"Princess."

Kaleb says panicked.

She holds her hand up, silencing him.

"Captain, as I told my brother, do not insult me by lying.
Especially when I have just seen this with my own eyes."

Kaleb looks scared… A look I did not see on his face often.
He was a warrior, after all.

"Do not worry, my love."

I reassure him.

"My sister knows and shall not say a word."

They both look at me.
I ignore them both.
I can hear Kaleb gulp, and Isabella sigh, but I pay little attention.

Now is not the time; the time is for action.

I turn to Kaleb.

"Keep your eyes and ears out, I need to know everything that happens in this castle whilst I remain here."

 I tell him.

His eyes widen, shocked at my flat tone.

"I've seen what I thought I had forgot.
You protected me, like you always have.
 Like you always will."

I stare sweetly at him; he really is a good man.

My man.

"I will do anything for you,"

He confirms.

It seems as if my sister has had enough, because she calls out firmly.

"You two really are in love, aren't you?"

She asks of us.

It is Kaleb who answers her.
He takes his eyes briefly from mine, stands straight and looks Isabella directly.

"Princess, I have loved your brother since before I can remember.
Since we were mere children.
Over the years, that love has only ever intensified."

"You were called away to the frontlines to be with your father.
You always refused, and when you did finally go, you were gone not even two moons, and raced back here…
I always wondered why… I guess I shouldn't have.
You went straight to Tristan didn't you…
You creep into this very tower most nights, don't you?"

She gestures down below.

"Down there, on that bed, you make love, don't you?
And then you leave, you always leave way before morning."

This shocks me and angers me too.

"Have you been spying on us?"

I glare.

"I can see the lights."

She answers simply.

"The brightest, strongest lights I have ever seen.
No mere candles can do that, nor torches.
And it's always when he comes,"

She points at Kaleb.

Before I can get angrier, Kaleb intervenes.

"I told you that these lights of yours were dangerous, my love."

He tells me.

"My friends have seen them too."

He concludes.

"What friends?!"

I question, sharply.

Kaleb looks affronted by this.

"Tris, they patrol at night sometimes, they can't help what their eyes
see."

What he says make sense, yet I can't stop my anger.

"Well, then maybe they should not have eyes!"

I growl.

They both gasp at this.
More gasps, I'm sick of it.

"Tris, you do not mean that."

Kaleb answers.

His eyes search mine, and I stare at him firmly.
He looks away, and I turn to Isabella.

I had not noticed before when I first saw her, but she looked stunningly beautiful.
She wears a gorgeous white dress, tight, to accentuate her figure.
It is completely sleeveless, her breasts nearly spill out of the corset.
And she wears white pearls.
Necklace, bracelets and earrings to match.

"You look very beautiful, Isabella.
And the white dress… And the pearls… I can only guess whom you wore that for."

Her head hangs low.
I can feel my anger rising once again.

"You went to Claudius, didn't you?"

Her head does not rise.

"He put me here, Isabella?!
He has confined me to this tower!
And you went to him!

You even dressed up for him!”

I accuse, angrily.

“So, I could come and see you!
To make sure that you were, okay!
And you didn't even want me!
You wanted him!”

She points to Kaleb and begins to cry.

“At least **HE** has not betrayed me?”

I fire back.

“Betrayed?!”

She stutters.

“Tris, you're misplacing your anger.
Isabella, ignore him,”

Kaleb pleads.

“No, I will not ignore it.
I have committed no betrayal!”

She points her finger at me and says angrily.

“You were the one who created an outburst at the execution!
And the rumours that have swirled and circulated since yesterday, they
say that you questioned the succession?!
That you asked the people if they wanted Theodore as king?!

What possessed you?
How could you?!"

She accuses wilfully.

She is coming out of her shell… I dislike it.
I dislike it intensely.

"And so, what if I had?"

I answer.

She scoffs at me madly, clearly not happy with my answer.

"Tris, this isn't you.
Surely, surely you realise the damage you are causing?"

"My love, your sister speaks truthfully.
Questioning the succession so publicly was not a good move."

Kaleb interjects.

I can't believe either of them.
Do they not see that I had to question the succession.
I had to ask the people directly who they wanted.
It was obvious they hate Claudius and Theodore too,
Whereas me… No, I have always had the love of the people.

YOU SHALL NOT JUST BE LOVED BUT WORSHIPPED.
YESTERDAY, DOZENS CHEERED FOR YOU.
DOZENS QUICKLY BECAME HUNDREDS IN THE RIOT.
AND SOON, SOON IT SHALL BE THOUSANDS!
THEN TENS OF THOUSANDS,
HUNDREDS OF THOUSANDS!

Yes, I shall rule over everyone and over everything.

I look between the love of my life, and my beloved sister, and state simply.

"Do either of you honestly think Theodore would be a good king?
Do either of you honestly think that he would rule well?
That the Realm would benefit under his reign?
If so, then speak it now."

They both go silent, both thinking.

Isabella answers.

"He is our brother."

I roll my eyes at this.

"It does not matter that he is our brother,"

I answer.

"If that is true, then does it matter that we are siblings?!"

She is angry.

She takes a step closer to me.

"You might think little of Theodore, and in truth, I think the same, however whether you like it or not, he is our brother, our blood!
And he is the eldest, therefore the Imperial Throne is his by right.

Tristan, we are all that's left of this dynasty.
A dynasty that despite everything, has somehow survived for three centuries.
If you do this, if you try and question the succession again, I shall not support you."

This shocks me and enrages me fully.

"Then leave,"

I state.

"Tristan, Princess, I think perhaps we should all take a moment to cool down."

Isabella ignores Kaleb, as do I.

"Brother, I love you.
More than you know.
But if you continue down this path, you will cause civil war.
Turn our Lords and Ladies against each other.
And the people, they will turn against each other.
Blood will be spilled; more blood than you can know.
Brother against brother… My brothers.
And I cannot bear the thought of you two… That you might kill each other."

There are tears in her eyes, they fall down her cheeks freely.

TEARS ARE WEAKNESS.

"If I continue down this path, I will succeed.
You need not worry about war, it shall not last long.

Theodore is hated and I am beloved, everyone will fight for me."

I am sure of this.

"Tristan, my love, it will not work that simply.
Despite what people think of Theodore, despite the fact they know of his cruelty, despite the fact they know he will be an awful king, they will still fight for his right to succeed as king.
He is after all the firstborn son of your late father.
The Imperial dynasty has been unbroken for three centuries.
Father to son, and so forth.
Never has a second son, a younger brother stolen the throne and crown from under the elders' feet.
They will dislike the idea of usurpation.
And what of the rest of the Realm?
Second sons across the Realm would get the idea they can take lordships and lands from their elder brothers.
It will not set a good precedent.
Not everyone shall follow you."

Kaleb's answer is simple, and yet incredibly truthful.

*DO NOT LISTEN TO THEM… THEY MEAN TO CONFUSE YOU!
OF COURSE THE PEOPLE WILL FOLLOW YOU, THE NOBILITY
AND SMALL-FOLK.
ALL OF THEM!
DO NOT LISTEN TO THEM!*

**But are they not being honest?
Are they not giving good advice?
Do they not love me?**

*DO NOT LISTEN TO THEM!
THEY MEAN TO CONFUSE YOU!*

DO NOT LET THEM!

But what if they are speaking the truth?
What if it truly will just cause more death and destruction?
Maybe Theodore should be King…
And I could support and help the Realm as best I can.

*THEODORE COULD HAVE ALL THE HELP IN THE COUNTRY,
IT WILL NOT STOP HIS NATURE…*

But what of my nature?
**Am I not the one who is willing to murder his brother for the
throne?**
I must admit, the thought of power is tantalising.
And I need more of that feeling.
Maybe I am mad…

IT IS NOT MADNESS TO DEPOSE A WEAK RULER.
IT IS NOT MADNESS TO REPLACE A FOOL WITH A GOD!
REMEMBER WHO YOU ARE!
YOU ARE NOT JUST AN IMPERIAL, YOU ARE A WITCH!
THE ONLY ONE WHO CAN UNITE THE PEOPLE!

And to unite the people, first, I must clean house.
Theodore is not fit to rule… And those who would follow him,
well they are foolish and not worthy of living in the new,
united Realm.
A new land free of terror and death.
A world of chaos and love.
And I shall rule it all!

"I love you both, but I shall continue down whatever path I see fit.
Isabella, you have made your choice.

So, I suggest you stay out of the way, I do not want you caught in the ensuing fight."

Her tears freeze on her cheeks at this, and her face becomes beyond shocked.
She shakes her head in disbelief.

"Very well, brother.
Enjoy your confinement."

Before she turns to leave, she says one last thing.

"I went to Claudius not only to see you, but to smooth things over.
I have proposed an idea to Claudius about a charity cause.
About you both going into the Capital and giving coin and bread to the people.
It would show a united front with the Faith and the Imperial Family.
I thought it could help heal and defuse the situation.
At least think on it, brother."

She says bitterly before leaving.

I can still hear her footsteps creaking downwards as I turn to Kaleb.

"It seems as only you are on my side, my Brave Captain,"

 I sigh to him.

Before he answers, I hear the slamming of the door down below.

Kaleb doesn't know where to look, his gaze turning from me to the stairs.

"Tris, please, stop this.
I – I can bring Isabella back; you can apologise and make up.
W – We can sort this out."

I feel as if slapped.

"Kaleb, you are on my side, are you not?!"

He looks at me, searching my face… He looks as if he cannot find it.

"I thought… I thought yesterday had all been a mistake, that you had just spoken during one of your moods, that you would see sense overnight and realise the ramifications of your actions…
But instead, you choose to continue this folly."

Moods?
Sense?
Folly?

I fire rapidly.

"We have spoken before, have we not?!
How many times have you agreed that Theodore should not rule, and Claudius should be dealt with?!
How many times have I mentioned about being..."

"Being King?"

 He answers cutting me off.

"It was just talk!
Silly talk, I never thought you would actually attempt to take the throne."

"Then you are a fool!"

 I spit.

This time, it is Kaleb who looks as if he has been slapped.

"Tris."

I raise my hand to him, cutting him off.

"Clearly, I have no allies.
Fine, it looks like I shall have to do this alone."

"Tris, please, I love you."

He pleads.

"Leave me, Kaleb.
I have plans to think of,"

 I tell him.

Before he can answer, I turn my back to him and step out into the open
balcony.
I feel bad.
They are just trying to help, but not the way I want.
Even more so, I really should have mentioned my Grimoire… I should
have asked one of them to look for it… And yet, I did not.
I really do hope that no one of important has found it.
I still have ink and more empty journals… Perhaps I can make a new
one?

I sigh deeply at the thought as wind lashes at me wildly, and I can see as far as the eye can see.
Parts of the castle, the ocean, the mainland, and far beyond.
I ignore Kaleb's sigh and retreating footsteps.
I ignore that he has left me, like Isabella.
My lover and sister.

It need not matter; I need them not.

YOU ARE TRISTAN IMPERIAL; YOU ARE A GOD!
YOU DO NOT NEED ANYONE!

But I love them…

YOU DO NOT NEED THEM!

But I still love them…

THEY WILL COME BACK TO YOU!
BUT YOU MUST FOCUS ON WHAT IS IMPORTANT!
GETTING RID OF CLAUDIUS, GETTING RID OF THEODORE,
UNIFYING THE PEOPLE!

But if I do this… I will be causing death.

EVERYONE DIES!
BUT NOT YOU!
NOT GOD!

I continue to look at the view.
Another and final vision comes then.
And I welcome it wholeheartedly.
Me once again crowned with emeralds and rubies as red as crimson.
And a black throne.

Can it really all be mine?

The vision changes then.

I'm in the Capital once again, I'm in the Grand Square.
Fire, fire everywhere…
Burning homes, burning buildings, burning people.
Death is thick in the air.
Yet unlike the first time I saw this, I am not scared.
How can I be?
The flames dance so prettily.
And me… Surrounded by those very flames, powerful and beautiful.

And my green eyes… They too shine brightly.

I snap back to reality.

The vision seems to confirm my suspicions.
It has to burn down to be rebuilt.

YES, BURN IT DOWN!
YOU JUST NEED TO FIGHT!
SPILL BLOOD AND BURN IT ALL DOWN!
AND THEN YOU SHALL EMERGE FROM THE FLAMES,
VICTORIOUS!

So, it is settled.
I know the path to take.

The path of blood and fire.

BLOOD AND FIRE!
BLOOD AND FIRE!
BLOOD AND FIRE!

Yes... It will all be mine.

THE DARK REALM

CRIMSON CASTLE

SHARDS OF TRUTH

HELENA

To say I am furious is an understatement.

Running my hands once again over my handheld mirror, nothing happens.

The mirror handle being wooden, with the glass being made from Saerillian Shards.

It allows witches to communicate with each other.

My brother may have only just recently left for his travel to the Human Realm, yet I itch with anticipation.

I had told the Scarlet Soldiers I sent that this mission is of the upmost important, and one in particular, a rather dashing yet disobedient one was amongst them.

An ex-lover of mine, called Demetrius, he is to keep a particular eye on Marcus and to report to me daily.

Although looking back, I suppose perhaps I should have asked someone else, as Demetrius is not exactly known for following orders, going rogue.

I had hoped he would realise that if he did go rogue it would mean his immediate death.

No, hopefully he wouldn't be that stupid.

And not without rousing Marcus' attention.
And that was something that could not happen.

This operation had to go smoothly, without fault.

THEN PERHAPS YOU SHOULD NOT HAVE SENT HIM!

He is my brother.
He will not fail me.

BUT HE HAS FAILED YOU ALREADY!
HAS HE NOT?
TWENTY-ONE YEARS AGO…

It was lucky however that he failed.
If he hadn't, there would be no chance of continuity.

AND YET, YOU STILL HATE HIM, DON'T YOU?
BUT NOT REALLY HIM,
YOU HATE THAT YOU HAD NEARLY BEEN FOOLED.
NEARLY BEEN KILLED.

Yes, because of that bitch.

PERHAPS YOU SHOULD VISIT HER?
SEE IF SHE CAN SEE THE OUTCOME…

That bitch will do nothing but lie again no doubt.

OR FOOL YOU AGAIN!
SHE WILL DO ANYTHING TO SEE YOU DEAD, AFTER ALL.

And she paid gravely.

YES, ABUSED AND TORTURED!
AS SHE HAS BEEN FOR YEARS ALREADY, SO IT MADE
LITTLE DIFFERENCE.

And it would still make little difference, the bitch is mad.

YES, SHE IS MAD NOW, BUT STILL THE BRILLIANCE IS
THERE.
I SUPPOSE, IF ANYONE CAN OFFER A SLITHER OF TRUTH
TO THE FUTURE… SHE HAD ONCE HAD CLEAR CLARITY,
AND VISIONS OF THE FUTURE!
ONCE A FRIEND…

Yes… She had been my friend once.
But she betrayed me.
She took my…

YES, WHAT DID SHE TAKE…

Nothing.
She took nothing.

I will not speak of it, not now.
Enough has been taken from me, my home, my village, my country.
Brought here on a dark, damp ship.
And then that camp… That awful, disgusting camp…

YOU WERE NOT THERE LONG THOUGH, YOU CAUGHT THE
EYE OF THE KING,
DID YOU NOT?!

Yes, I remember it well.
He had come to check his stock, of course…
As if we were mere cattle.

Checking us over for the best and strongest to build his cities and castles.

And his eyes had fallen on me…

I was swiftly taken to the White Demons Camp.

I was bound and chained, I could not do anything about it.

Every night… Every single night.
He raped me, again and again.

Even back then, even nothing but a young girl, I had still been powerful.

One of the most powerful witches back home in our village.

But I couldn't Cast…

No, they used those cursed Saerillian Silver chains that they had forged especially for us.

They knew of us, our ability to Cast, before they even came to capture us…Their plans to enslave us had obviously been prepared in advance.

But the White Devils and that damned Imperial Family would never admit that, would they.

No, in their histories they mention how we were brought here as guests, how we were the ones who attacked first.

Nonsense, of course.

No, they would never portray themselves as monsters.

Even though that's exactly what they are.

AND MONSTERS BREED MORE MONSTERS.

I had been happy and cheerful once.

Full of light and love.

They took that from me, they took it all from me.

And yet I am the monster for fighting back.
For destroying those who destroyed us.

YES, YOU DESTROYED THEM VERY WELL!
ESPECIALLY WITH THAT POTION YOU BREWED!

It was a spell of immortality.
And I twisted it, made it dark with blood magic.

YES, AND YOU SACRIFICED THE ONE YOU LOVED THE
MOST!

He was dying, I saved him.

DID YOU?
DID YOU REALLY SAVE HIM?
OR DID YOU DESTROY ANY CHANCE HE HAD!

I never wanted to hurt him; I love him.

YOU TURNED HIM INTO A MONTER!
YOU STOLE HIS ABILITY TO CAST AND USE CHAOS!
YOU TURNED HIM INTO A DEMON OF DEATH!

I turned him into a God!
I saved him!
Because of me, he will never be sick or age, never have to die.
He will live forever!

EXACTLY, YOU MADE HIM EVEN MORE POWERFUL THAN
YOU!
EVEN YOU DO NOT POSSESS THE ABILITY TO LIVE
FOREVER!

Not for long though!
Soon, I shall have everything I ever wanted.
It will all be mine.

IT IS ALWAYS BEST TO KNOW OF ANYTHING THAT COULD
HAPPEN THOUGH.
GO TO HER.
SEE IF YOU CAN GUARANTEE YOUR FUTURE!

It has been over twenty-one years since I have seen her last.

I remember all too well the treachery she wrought upon me, once again!

But, despite this, she has a power even I do not possess…

THE POWER OF A SEER.
NOT MANY OF THOSE LEFT, ARE THERE?
YOU SOUGHT TO THAT!

I did what I had to do.

Those with the ability to see the threads of future were indeed dangerous and valuable.

And I will not allow that power to be in the hands of the white devils and the damned Imperial Family.

No, they have to be wiped from the earth.

That in turn has made them even more valuable now they are near enough exterminated.

I had been hasty in that, however.

The soul of a Seer would indeed make me strong and young and beautiful for an age.

I have only done it once, a hundred years ago.

I sucked the soul right from their body, it had tasted divine and increased my longevity.

I did not Cleave them of their magic however, no, that power was a curse and I wanted nothing to do with it.
Their magic simply died with them.

Longevity that is now rapid diminishing.

I have to use more and more girls to retain what youth and beauty I cling to.
No, I need the prince… And I have tasked this mission, a mission which my very existence hangs on into my brothers' hands…

And if he fails…
No, he cannot fail.

But I have to be sure… I would see *HER*, it seems.
And to do that, I would have to enter the very bowels of the castle.

I run my hand over the mirror once more and wait a moment for a reply.

Nothing.

Sighing in frustration, I start the trip to go and see her…

I arrive shortly afterwards.
My skin is covered in goosebumps, I should have brought a cloak.
But instead, my bare arms will have to brace the cold.
It is dark, and damp down here.
Drops of water can be heard from the rocks.
Torches are the only light in this place.

This is of course the Black Doom, the deepest part of the Crimson.
Where the most powerful and dangerous of prisoners are kept.

Many include strong and powerful Soldiers and Slayers from years past, they live whatever remains of their mortal lives to die down here, forgotten.

Not to mention witches too.

Ones who have disobeyed me, betrayed me, or are simply too powerful to not be confined.

And of course, vampires too.

Long desiccated now though, of course, without blood, they just lay and rot.

Yes, many have died down here.

But none of those mattered.

No, there is only one prisoner I am here to see.

Several Scarlet Soldiers are also down here, going about their duties.

I pass several of them.

They guard dutifully.

Screams can be heard down here.

The screams of the tortured, the damned, the forgotten.

Yet, screams are nothing new.

This whole Realm is full of screaming.

And yet, screams comfort me, at least I know that my enemies are getting what they deserve.

YOU MAKE THEM SUFFER!
LIKE YOU SUFFERED!

I do not suffer, I have not for years…

No, I am fine!

KEEP TELLING YOURSELF THAT!

The rocky path leads downwards and downwards, further and further into the chasm of rocks and darkness.
After a few more moments, I arrive.

Two fellow Dark Witches stand down here, guarding the door.
They stand upright at my arrival, and I can see the shock on their faces.
They have guarded this prisoner for years, and for years they have been undisturbed.

It has been over twenty-one years since the last time, after all.

They both wear light armour and dark cloaks, sufficient enough in their powers I presume.
Before me, a large door made of black rock.
The entrance to her cell.

"Move aside."

 I command.

They dutifully do so.
I place my hand upon the rock, it is smooth and sharply cold.
I begin to chant, a deep and yet quick chant.

Words of the Ancients.

Powerful and dark chants, those designed to keep this door magically sealed.
The black rock begins to illuminate, brilliant blue lines appear along the rock, travelling in spirals and various patterns.
It looks as if the black rock has brilliant blue veins.

Once the pattern is complete, a brilliant flash of light appears, before it disappears as quickly as it appeared.

A large, low rumble begins.

The black rock begins to shift and change, it splits into two, revealing a gap of darkness.

I move inwards confidently.

I do not wait for the gap to extend completely; I am too eager for answers.

I shove and squeeze my way through the rocky gap.

As I enter, I am brought to a large cave.

The room fills with light.

Magic of course, there is no natural light down here after all.

Despite the light, it still has dark shadows that cannot escape.

I can see stagnates and all sorts of rock.

There is a dripping sound; in the corner there is a small pool of clean water.

I narrow my eyes, scanning in the gloom for her.

There is nothing but silence.

Then the soft rattle of chains, followed by a loud scream.

A body flies at me from the dark, almost grabbing me.

I see a snarled face.

I take a startled step back and almost fall backwards.

Almost.

The chains rattle and shake heavily, she pulls and wills herself forwards, but the chains fastened to the cave hold her firmly in place.

She continues to wail and scream, her face contorted in anger and fury.

I simply stand there, staring at her.

Her clothes are nothing but rags, her hair a tattered mess.
Her body, absolutely covered in cuts and scratches, not to mention various scars.
And her face… Also covered in scars, but the scariest, she has empty sockets.
Her eyes cut out long ago.

Twenty-one years ago.

HAS SHE NOT SUFFERED ENOUGH?
SHE HAS LIVED HERE ALL THESE YEARS, IN DARKNESS AND DECAY.
SO MANY WOUNDS.
SO MANY SCARS.

She deserves this fate.
She was the one who betrayed me.
If she had been loyal; she could have lived a life of privilege and luxury in my Realm of Darkness.
She could have been a lady and lived for years in bliss.
But this was not to be.

She has dwelt down here for three centuries.
But she was the one who committed betrayal, not me.
She deserves this fate.
She continues to wail and scream, I ignore this, hoping she will eventually give up.
I cannot blame her; the wailing and screaming is warranted.
I have after all imprisoned her for centuries and allowed the abuse suffered upon her.
These conditions only worsened over time, of course.

Her voice is dying down, beginning to cough, she falls to her knees, she would be crying if she had eyes.

"Are you quite finished?"

I ask of her.

She continues to make sobbing sounds, so pitiful.
I circle around her, around the cave, drinking in the darkness.

"It has been a while, Agatha."

She sniggers at this, then spits aimlessly.

"H – how long,"

Her voice is hoarse.

"Not long, only twenty-one years."

She begins to wail again.

"Enough of that."

 I snap at her.

"Do you think those stupid sounds will change anything?!"

I ask of her.

"I – it's b – been c – centuries,"

She speaks.

"W – why w – won't y – you. J – just k – kill m – me."

She stutters.

Her voice has gone dry.

I walk over to the pool of water.
There is a clay cup.
I fill it and walk back over to her.

"Drink."

She does as ordered, drinking the entire cup.

I set it aside and answer her.

"Why would I kill you?
You are valuable, after all."

She begins to laugh at this.
A weak, dry laugh, but a laugh, nonetheless.

It irritates me greatly.

"What are you laughing at?"

 I question her sharply.

She continues to laugh.
I could grab a rock and smash her head in
I could burn her where she kneels.

I could enter her mind and make her scream beyond belief in unimaginable pain if I wanted.
I could make her feel as if her skin was on fire.

NONE OF THIS WILL WORK!
SHE HAS ENDURED TOO MUCH!
NOTHING WILL WORK!

We shall see about that.

"I have a question for you, well, several really."

She looks aimlessly into the dark.

"And why would I help you?
Better yet, why would you even believe me?
I've tricked you before, haven't I?
Or so you say."

A smile appears across her face.
Her teeth broken and blackened.

"And you have suffered and will surely suffer further if you try anything of the sort again."

She chuckles wryly at this.

"You have done everything you can possibly think of, three centuries I have been imprisoned.
What else can you do?
Besides, it is not my fault you were so easily tricked.
You know the prophecy; you were the one who acted a fool."

This infuriates me.

"The prophecy dictated that one born from that fucking Imperial Family would be the prophesied one.
That they would be the one to unite or destroy the people."

"And be the end of you."

She declares.

"Watch yourself,"

I warn her.

She chuckles again.

"You have been murdering them for centuries, yes, trying to find out which one.
And somehow, what happened twenty-one years ago is my fault."

"Because you saw the doom of the Imperial Family!
They were all there, in that fucking carriage, everything was arranged, and…"

"What I saw was true.
The Imperial Family should have died out that day.
I wish it had."

The last part throws me.
She has never wished death on the Imperial Family before?!
I set the thought aside as I hiss at her.

"But they didn't."

I accuse.

"Yes, because your brother, upon seeing the faces of the dead, grew a conscience.
He let that Prince escape.
Your brother growing feelings is not my fault."

"But not seeing it is your fault!"

I blame.

"I do not see everything!"

She spits back.

"Only fragments.
Especially in these chains.
I have told you this so many times.
 I saw what I saw and told you what I saw.
No more, no less."

"Lies!"

I accuse.

"I more than anyone had hoped the Imperial Family would die that day."

She mutters.

Her gaze turns to me then.
Eyeless and blind as she is, I know she can't see me… ***Can she?***
Nevertheless, she looks directly at me.

"If they had finally died, you would have died too!
And I would have thanked the Ancestors!"

I slap her, hard.

"You tricked me!
You wanted me to kill them!
You told me the prophesied was in that carriage!
You lied!"

"And if your brother had done his job, then the line would have died that day.
You wouldn't have had to worry about the prophesied."

"No, I would have killed the only thing that can save me!
You wanted the child not to be born, you wanted him to not exist so I would die too!
You knew I needed him if I had any hope of surviving!"

"And yet the prince escaped and became King.
He sired children and thus the boy was born, and lived, and you waited sixteen years to try and kill him again.
A feral at an island three years past.
Again, it did not work."

This part struck me.
How did she know that?

"Did you forget I'm a seer?"

She laughs.

"You took my eyes, yet I still see.
Even with these damned Saerillian Silver chains I still see, that is how powerful I am.
I know that you plotted the boy's death on the island.
I know you employed that zealot Claudius.
How I wished it had worked, I really hoped the boy would die that day.
And to think, if he had, you would have killed yourself."

She giggles at the mention of his name, as if she knows a secret.

"And yet, you didn't know I was going to take your eyes."

 I reply angrily,

"You were shocked that day, were you not?"

 I ask her maliciously.

"Yes, you stole my eyes because of your brother.
And yet, it is not my fault the men in your life like to betray you.
Your brother, Claudius… And let us not forget that silly boy lover of yours.
The human… Ahh, yes, very handsome wasn't he… And rugged…
What was his name again?"

 She answers coyly, she very well knew his name.

I could have slapped her again.

Yet, I did not.

"And Claudius betrayed you, did he not?
He had the opportunity to kill the boy, yes?

All that time the prince was sleeping, having drained his Chaos.
His throat could have easily been slit or a pillow held over his face.
Poison slipped into his mouth.
And yet, Claudius did not.
He allowed the boy to wake up and recover.
Claudius did however easily take over the Human Realm.
Turned it into a Realm of religion and fear.
He is King in all but name.
I'm guessing that was not part of your plan.
No, you want the humans all dead.
To make the whole country dark.
And yet, your lackey now plays King."

Her words unnerve me.
Yet they are true.
But not for much longer.
I allow Claudius his little reign, and soon enough he will have his orders.
And my brother shall deliver my prize.

"Men are not the only ones who have betrayed me, or do you forget your own transgressions, Agatha?"

She scoffs at this.

"I did what needed to be done… You were out of control, you made monsters out of men…
You were destroying and murdering everyone, even your own!
You had to be stopped."

"And you thought the best way to do that was you, your kid sister, and the rest of that little gaggle of friends go over to the other side?
To join the humans!

You stole my…"

"Yes, what did I steal?

She coos.

No, I would not speak about that… Not now, not ever.

"I never thought what would happen to him would happen… If I had, I would not have stolen him from you… However, the prophesised was made to be born from that bloodline…
So perhaps, if it worked out for the best.
You created your own downfall in your very womb."
I ignore her.
I would not speak of it, not now, not ever.

"Another flourished in your womb, did it not?
Centuries apart, yet still borne from you.
One stolen, the other carelessly given away… Tell me, where did you send him?
It doesn't matter I suppose, motherhood clearly was not meant for you."

I slap her, then again.

Harder than the first time.
It leaves a red mark.
Yet it has the desired affect, for she speaks no more.

"You urged me twenty-one years ago to purge the Imperial line and wipe it out before the prophesised was born, thus ensuring my death.
I assumed it's because he had to be born.
He had to be born so I could be the one to kill him.

To ensure my victory.
Kill or be killed.
To stop the prophecy myself.
And then I realised, I wasn't supposed to kill him at all.
Because I figured it out…
His death means my death.
With his death, his limitless power simply vanishes on the wind."

She looks horrified as she realises I know the truth.

"No, he must not just die.
Not as first, anyhow.
His Chaos must be Cleaved.
I will feast upon his magic."

The horrified expression remains.
Funny, for all she sees, she did not see today it seems.

It had taken me a while to figure it out, to be sure.
And to think, I had nearly killed him and lost the chance to steal his Chaos.
To think that I had nearly ensured my own death, it haunts me.
But not death, not at first, instead Cleaved.

Cleaving one of their magic and Soul Stealing is similar, and yet different.

You Cleave one of their magic to either stop them from their using their immense powers.
I had done it before on witches.
An excruciatingly painful torture.
Taking one's magic destroys a person.
Leaves them an almost empty vessel.

They eat and move, sleep and wake.

Yet they're empty inside.

They say a fate worse than death.

For a witch to be Cleaved of their Chaos is no small thing.

To not use Chaos ever again indeed would leave you feeling empty and hollow.

Once a witch is Cleaved, their magic can either be set loose on the wind, to fade into nothing.

Or it can be feasted upon, and the one who eats gains the powers of the one who is Cleaved.

But to steal someone's actual Soul, that ensures death.

Not only that, but it gives you their life.

Extra years of youth and beauty.

Except in my case, it barely works anymore.

I will have to Cleave him of his Chaos.

I will gain his magic, and immortality finally.

"There is no life for you."

She finally answers.

"Your powers have been waning slowly but surely over these last three centuries.

And ever since the boy was born, that decline became rapid, didn't it?

I may be blind, but I am guessing your longevity spell stopped working the second he was born.

I may not have eyes, but I know this is true.

And three years ago, when he finally tapped into his Chaos and used fire magic, well, he began to realise the powers he wields.

And now, it's even more rapid still.
I may be hidden down here in these dark caves, a prisoner of the centuries, and yet I have never felt more raw power than I do now.
And we both know exactly where it's coming from.
It's coming from him.
And he's recently Cast, I can almost taste his Chaos.
It's immensely strong, and with it, your decay."

I lean down to her once again.

"Feel my face and tell me I am decaying?"

"Do not lie to me, the longevity spell,"

"The spell stopped working, yes, but there are ways around that.
Ways that involve young, beautiful girls and their even more young and beautiful souls."

She gaps and backs away at this.

"That, that is disgusting… Truly vile."

"Nonsense, because of their delicious souls, I stay young and beautiful."

"It will not last."

She declares.

"No, no it will not."

 I confirm.

"Hence why I need his magic.
He's much too precious for death.
Whilst he has magic, anyways.
No, I shall have him Cleaved.
His magic stolen; I will happily eat it.
With his powers as mine, I shall surely make the longevity spell permanent.
I will never need to steal another soul.
And I shall finally be immortal."

It was true, I had been stupid.
I had hunted and murdered the Imperial Family at whim, trying my best to eradicate them.
I had sent my brother twenty-one years ago and he nearly exterminated them.
I sent a feral three years ago and almost killed him again.
All because I stupidly thought that simply killing him would save myself.
But that isn't true, the boy cannot just simply die.

Well, he will die… But first, I must do something.

I crouch back down, facing her.

"You wanted me to kill him so he would die, and his power with him. But instead, I am bringing him here."

I lean closer to her.

"My brother is already on his way to collect him."

 I whisper.

Her facial remarks widen, her mouth turning into an O.

"Yes, you had me nearly kill the very thing that would save me.
All these years.
Turns out I need the boy, his magic at least."

She shakes her head nervously… I guess she never knew I would figure it out.

"It will not matter.
You will never get to him,"

She declares.

"Yes, yes, I will.
My brother is long gone; they are no doubt In the Magic Realm by now.
Slipped past the patrols and barriers."

"They will not simply slip by this time, not after."

"The Imperial slaughter?
Whilst it's true what's left of the Imperial Army and those proud Protectors will be extra on guard, they have been for years now.
However, they need not matter.
 Thankfully for me, I have someone on the inside.
On the very Council of Covens itself."

 I whisper.

"YOU LIE!"

She screams!

"Shh,"

I coo to her.

"Yes, that precious little Council you started when you betrayed me.
Always six of them… Although, there was supposed to be seven,
wasn't there?
You were supposed to be the Head Witch, but you weren't, were you…
No, thankfully you were captured on the night of the betrayal before
you could do any real damage."

Her head hangs low at this.

"No, your sweet little sister got the role instead, didn't she.
She and the other five escaped over the enemy lines that night, after
all."

I let this sink in, despite the fact she knows it already.

"Your line still exists, by the way.
At least your sisters does… The current Head Witch is your great, great
so forth and so forth niece.
Yes, a young girl.
Well, she's actually fifty but we both know that's practically a child
for a powerful witch that can live centuries."

I conclude.

"She's inexperienced, only had the role these last three years, her
mother, another one of your descendants, well she died during the
Great Cleansing.

Not from being slaughtered, no, her heart burst at the deaths of all the others, she felt their pain.
But I guess you saw that, or maybe not."

I shrug.

"I felt her death."

She answers solemnly.

"And yet here you are, alive… If not well.
I can't imagine it though.
Seeing centuries of your family.
Your sister and all her descendants.
Their lives, their loves.
And you, stuck here.
How awful."

I feign guilt.

"Why are you here?"

She bitterly asks.

"To tell me histories I already know?
To gloat and declare proudly that you know you need to steal the boy's Chaos?
Well, you know, and now you've gloated, what else do you need to stand there for?"

I laugh musically at this.

"I want to know what is going to happen."

I ask of her.

"I've managed to deceive you before.
Perhaps you should stop coming to ask me questions."

"You may be right, and yet, you're the only one I know who has the
ability to see the future."

"I've not seen anything as of late.
These chains, I only see fractions…"

She rattles her hands at me then.

This is true, as long as she wore the Saerillian Silver, she is all but
really blind.
Yet she is indeed a powerful witch, to still see even glimpses whilst
wearing the chains.
You have to be incredibly powerful for Saerillian Silver to not work.
And it is extremely rare, doubtful even the humans do not know their
damned silver is not as impregnable as it seems.

SHE HAS BEEN PRACTICALLY BLIND FOR CENTURIES!
NO REAL HARM…
AND YET YOU STILL CARVED OUT HER EYES!

I was angry.
Besides, she should not have lied.
I refuse to feel guilt.

YOU HAD BEEN SO CLOSE ONCE
BUT NOT ANYMORE…

Her own fault.

I wave my hand simply over her.

Her chains unlock at her wrists, clanging on the rocky undergrowth.

You would expect her to attack, but she does not, I knew she would not.

Instead, she bolts upright as if struck by lightning, she lets out a loud gasp, her face pointed above.

She begins to convulse yet stays in place.

She shakes all over as wave after wave of Chaos surges through her.

Chaos and visions.

"Fire! Fire! Fire!"

She proclaims.

"I see a boy… Shrouded in doubt and depression.

Caged, trying so desperately to be set free.

Born a second son, all the power and none of the power.

He wants to unify… But he means to destroy.

And his love… A great love, an undying love, a love that will surpass the tests of time.

A love that will live forever… Even though death comes to all."

What do I care who the boy loves?

I want only his Chaos.

"My brother, will he succeed?

Will he bring the boy to me soon?"

She laughs at this, despite her convulsions.

"You should never have sent your brother…

He will be lost to you.

The boy will claim him.
Devour him.
He will be utterly in his control."

No… No, my brother would never.

"Blood… Fire… Decay… Death… Destruction.
Betrayal, betrayal everywhere.
Many will die.
A war is here… The last war."

The last war?
So that means… This is coming to an end.

"Will I get the boy, yes, or no?!"

I shout sharply.

"There will be a fire in the sky.
A blazing ball that will destroy monsters and humans alike.
I see a demon… One with green eyes.
You should never have sent your brother… You have sealed your own
doom."

"No, no, no,"

 I repeat.

"My brother, he will prevail.
 Surely, he will prevail."

"Your brother is gone, already turned from you, he falls in love soon,
a love that will kill him, and you.

Many will die."

Fear grips me.

"How do I prevent this?!
How do I take his Chaos?!
How do I survive?!"

"You don't."

Is her final answer.

And with that, her convulsions stop, her body goes still.

She slumps backwards, having lost consciousness.
I wave my hand over her, and the chains wrap around her wrists once again.

I debate once again picking up her rock and smashing her skull in…
Yet I decide against it, as I had before.

What she says… It haunts me.

I must prevent it by all means necessary.
My brother; my brother must be returned at once.
I begin to chant in Ancient.
The black rock grows its blue veins once again.
It begins to split into two and I narrowly squeeze through the gap once again.

I come out the other side, nearly walking straight into the Dark Witches who stand guard.
I am panting heavily; they all look at me with concern.

"Your majesty, is everything…"

"SEND OUT SCOUTS, SEND RAVENS, DO SOMETHING!
DO IT NOW!
BRING MY BROTHER BACK, AT ONCE, HE MUST NOT REACH THE
HUMAN REALM!"

I shout quickly.

They all share looks of confusion; they do not know I sent my brother
away.
No one does… Especially not my own Council.

I realise then that I cannot send anyone.
I must not let this mission fail… My brother must get the prince.

But he can't…

Fuck.

"JUST GO!
LEAVE ME!"

I scream.

Wanting them to leave.

They scramble as they run off, leaving me by myself.
The black rock shifts and shuts behind me, a thunderous noise.
She is locked back safely away…

I should never have gone down there; I should never have sought her
advice…

I should never have removed those damned shackles.
I should have kept the Saerillian Silver on her.

SHE HAS BEEN WRONG BEFORE…
SHE WANTED YOU TO KILL THE BOY SO YOU COULD NOT
TAKE HIS POWERS.

And yet, she did not mention taking his powers.
She mentioned my brother falling in love… **Ridiculous.**
No, it must be lies.
My brother has been a solemn, pitiful creature these last two decades.
He will not betray me… Not like that.

AND YET YOU HAVE ALREADY SENT COMMANDS TO HAVE
HIM BROUGHT BACK.

I pull my mirror out once again from a pocket in my dress.
I begin waving my hand over it.

Answer!
Answer!
Answer!

Nothing happens… Demetrius does not appear.
Damned fool, I shall kill him when I get the chance.
Instead, I am left here, stood in the darkness with nothing but fear.

I just need the boy…
And them everything will be fine.

IF THAT IS WHAT YOU HAVE TO TELL YOURSELF.

I stare out into the darkness, the void.
And for a moment, I feel as if it stares back.

I get a flash of a demon…

A demon with green eyes.

What have I done?!

The war is here… It looks as if I am about to find out.

Brother where are you?!
Why did I send him…

What have I done?!

I must get hold of Demetrius…
He must keep a close eye on Marcus…

HE MUST BE EXTERMINATED!
IF WHAT SHE SAYS IS TRULY TRUE…
IF HE MEANS TO BETRAY YOU… AND FOR LOVE?
THEN HE MUST DIE…

He has been my brother for centuries.
I cannot simply kill him.

YOU FORGET, HE ALREADY DIED ONCE!
YOU ALREADY KILLED HIM…

I saved him.
Made him stronger, made him immortal.

IMMORTAL AND INSATIABLE!
THE CONSTANT BLOODLUST…

I needed him to be strong.

YOU COULD HAVE SAVED HIM!
YOU COULD HAVE MADE HIM IMMORTAL WITHOUT
TURNING HIM INTO A MONSTER!

We were surrounded by monsters.
White devils that wanted to enslave us.
So, I created my own monsters.
And fought back.
I helped our people!

NO, YOU DOOMED HIM!
YOU DOOMED YOUR PEOPLE!
AND NOW YOU MUST DOOM YOUR BROTHER ONCE AGAIN!

This isn't just about my brother, it's about me…
My reign, my conquest of this country.
I shall not fail.
It has been my mission for three centuries!
And I will not give that up now, not ever!

Forgive me my brother…
But it is I who must live.

It is I who has the destiny to conquer this land!

YOU STILL NEED THE BOY…

I will get the boy…
I shall steal his Chaos.
And I shall be the Queen of everything and everyone.
I shall cover this land in darkness and demons.
I will trade my black throne, and my bejewelled crown for the Imperial
Throne and Crown.

Everything will be mine.
I must send a raven to Claudius, immediately.

And I will sacrifice anything for that.
Forgive me, my brother.
But I must have my revenge.
I must be Queen of all.
No matter what.

MANY DAYS LATER

THE REALM OF MAGIC

COASTAL CLIFFS

VILLAGE OF ASH

MARCUS

My boots splash mud as I take a step followed by another.

My clothes are equally mud soaked and nearly ruined and I have not been able to bathe for days.

I know however my smell is still attractive.

After all, vampires are meant to not only be horrifying to humans and even witches, we are also meant to be alluring.

Therefore, most find our scent, our appearance, our very stature appealing and attractive.

I had been handsome when I was alive…

And becoming dead made me inhumanly handsome.

My features became more defined, stronger, better.

Many vampires romanced and lured their prey, only to feast upon their blood.

My sister gave us the mission a couple of weeks ago, and like always I did as I was told, leaving the following night.

I had traveled in style to begin with, enjoying the comfort of my carriage which was full of luxurious foods and wines and of course, blood.

And yes, contrary to popular beliefs, vampires can indeed still consume food and alcohol.

And thank the Old Gods for it, I cannot imagine living centuries without good food and, even better, wine.

However, blood is my elixir, without it I would rot away, turning into a monstrous feral…

I had seen it happen to vampires before, mainly at my sister's request.

And it certainly is not a fate I wish to ever endure.

Any of the vampire aristocracy who displeased her, any of the vampire generals in her armies, or even guards she disliked, they were locked away, deprived of blood until they turned feral and eventually desecrated.

She still keeps them locked up, poor fucked up demons imprisoned and kept as pets by my sister.

Until they starve too long and desiccate, anyhow.

And a stark reminder to the rest back in the Crimson Castle or anyone in the Dark Realm for that matter not to mess with her.

Alas, when we got near the BorderLands, I had to give up my carriage, and even my horses.

Left them with Scarlet Soldiers who patrolled the outskirts of the Dark Realm.

We managed to sneak into the BorderLands with relative ease, keeping to the shadows, eventually making our way into the Magic Realm.

Also, thanks to my sister.

She has someone on the inside after all and this person made sure there were no patrols at this area.

We kept to the edge of the country, the cliff sides with the coasts stretching out.

I often wondered, as I walked, how I longed to get a boat and sail back home.

It had been three centuries however, and last I saw of my home it was burned to the ground.

They stole so many of us… Is there anyone even left in my home country?

**Surely, they did not steal or slaughter us all.
Or did they?**

The witches travelling with us also used magic to best mask our vampiric scents.

Powerful witches like the Council of Covens can feel disturbances in nature, they would surely feel the presence of the Dark Lord and several Scarlet Soldiers entering their Kingdom.

Perhaps they already know we are here?

And yet, we have been In the Realm of Magic for a few days now and have yet to be descended upon by Protectors or any remaining Imperial Soldiers.

It is said that when the Witch Cleansing began, the previous High Witch felt the disturbance and pain of all those dead and dying.

It all happened so fast, and all over the Human Realm so rapidly that it made her die from a broken heart.

With her dead, the Council Of Covens was divided, half of them wanting to battle the humans for their betrayal, whilst calmer voices reasoned that witch-kind simply could not fight both the Dark Realm, and the Human Realm.

Therefore, calmer voices of the Council prevailed, and the witches decreed that the Magic Realm therefore banned all humans aside from those of the Slayer Syndicate from ever travelling there.

To keep all witches safe, many who escaped the Human Realm enjoyed the sanctuary of the Magic Realm.

They also decreed if Claudius dared step foot in their Realm or any of his armies of Defenders then the witches would withdraw from helping the fight with the Dark Realm, instead they even threatened to join my sister, and annihilate the Human Realm.

A threat of course, witches would never do that no matter what has happened to their kind, many witches believe much in life and balance, and would never blindly kill…
Well, most of them anyhow.
Plenty of witches dismayed at the humans getting away with their Cleansing instead did leave the Magic Realm, going over to the Dark Realm and joining my sister's ranks.
Yet more than most remained, there an uneasy alliance with the Imperial Army and their strong General.

Indeed, because of the ban on humans these last three years the Imperial Army is all but non-existent.
The General, I knew him well.
He had at least a few thousand men with him when the Cleansing began.
Many wondered why the General and the Soldiers simply did not fight their way out of their imprisonment, and yet, despite numbering thousands they would be no match for witches.

Especially powerful ones.

They knew they would be slaughtered with ease, so therefore they accepted their fate.
The General did not seem to mind anyhow, from what I hear he never liked being in the Human Realm anyways, instead preferring the battlefield over his wife and children.

Yes, much was still uneasy in the world.

Another splash of mud brings me to my surroundings.

Despite having giving up the luxury of the carriage and having to use my own two legs for transport, I find it exhilarating.

I had forgotten how beautiful the world could be, despite all the cruelty and death that plagued the country.

As a vampire, my senses are heightened.

Colours, smells, noises, tastes, everything seems richer and more vibrant.

Despite the fact I am technically in danger, being in the Realm Of Magic, I do not mind.

If Protectors or Imperial Soldiers descended upon us right now, it would be a bloodbath.

I have no doubt I would win, yet it would alert us to others presence.

In my company my sister allocated five witches.

All various ages, yet none of them seem powerful whatsoever.

They wear black dresses and black boots, to show their allegiance.

Yet I often wondered why they showed allegiance in the first place.

Many think that the Dark Realm is safe for witches, but truly it isn't.

Yes, we have cities and towns and villages in the Dark Realm, all of whom witches live in, yet they are duly under the control of my sister's army of Scarlet Soldiers.

Soldiers patrol everywhere, and they strictly keep the witches under their control.

Mostly they are left to mind their own business… However, any witches who show exemplary magical potential are taken…

Stolen from their families and homes.

Most are forced to the frontlines, having to fight and die.

Whilst some… Well, some were brought to the Crimson…

My sister liked to keep a close eye on them.

They may have lived in the castle, but they were not free, and they knew that.

Strictly watched and kept prisoner.

And they all dread the moment when my sister calls them to her rooms…

For when they go there, they never come back out.

Not alive, anyways.

I think back to that poor girl whose soul my sister devoured…

I had just stood there…

YOU'VE ALWAYS JUST STOOD BY!
YOU'VE ALWAYS BEEN UNDER HER COMMAND,
SUCH A GOOD, LOYAL DOG.

These thoughts darken my mood, especially looking at the faces of the witches who accompany me.

They are not powerful, in fact from what I have seen so far, their ability to Cast is dismal and depressing.

If they have been sent here to protect me then it is truly laughable.

They would be killed with relative ease.

I often wondered on our journey why my sister had sent these individuals with me.

To make matters worse, I also have five fellow Scarlet Soldiers with me.

All vampires.

All dressed in black clothing.

And yet they clearly have a favourite…

A male vampire, turned young, same as me.

Dark skinned, good looking with thick dark hair.

I knew him from around the castle, he was young even for a vampire.

Turned several years ago, if that.

Yet he had a reputation for cruelty, and it brought him fame.

And my sister had shown favouritism too, and surely had showed her favouritism on him more than once, yet it was surely fleeting.

He was certainly an ex-lover; his name is Demetrius.

And I'm pretty sure this Demetrius is spying on me… Several days ago, I had seen him suspiciously with a mirror made from Saerillian Silver… He quickly put it away when I noticed it, and therefore most likely did not get a chance to speak, yet it was clear he was a spy for my sister.

I will surely have to kill him soon.

And I'm sure my sister will not mind either.

He is a past lover, after all.

My sister discarded him quickly like she does everything.

No, nothing lasts long with my sister, not since… **Him.**

No, she had not had a real favourite since she corrupted that poor soldier… And look who he is now… If anyone found out… Well, that would surely be beautifully chaotic.

My sister's spell soon broke over him though when he realised, he had helped almost bring the downfall of a Dynasty…

That blunder and my self-imposed exile had cost me the loss of respect, clearly.

So, I am forced to travel with five useless witches and five vampires who hate me.

The only part of our party I do not mind is the several Blood Initiates, white slaves who begged to become vampires and fight in the war for us rather than be forced into the Blood Camps to uncertain horrors.

Yet they will hardly be any help either.

A truly awful company of companions.

My sister could surely have picked better…

ITS BECAUSE SHE WANTS YOU TO BE DEFENCELESS!
BECAUSE IF YOU FAIL THIS MISSION, YOU ARE ON YOUR
OWN!
ON YOUR OWN IN A REALM THAT DESPISES YOU…
BUT WAIT, YOU ARE HATED EVEN IN YOUR OWN REALM!

This is true, I have committed terrible and horrendous things in my long life, and none of them earned me any love.

I earned only fear…

And they have a right to fear me.

I am a demon made flesh.
Not only armed with my beauty, but I also with super strength, the strength of twenty men.
And my speed… I can outrun any human, or even vampire for that matter.
With age, that has only increased.
And as the first vampire to be created from that awful plague, and thus the eldest vampire, I am stronger and faster than the rest.
The beginning of vampires to the world has and always will remain a mystery, I'm sure.

I remember the slave camp, where I had been.
Bound in a collar and chains, along with hundreds of others.
We huddled there, cold and hungry.
Beaten and starved.
There was so many of us, and yet the camp was small.
We were packed in, barely able to move.
Forced to sleep on the hard, cold ground whilst our enslavers enjoyed warm tents and cozy beds.

White demons, they burned down our home and brought us here by ship.

Thousands and thousands of us.

Me and my sister had been at the camp for several weeks, awaiting to be put in many of the cages dragged by carriages to lands we did not know.

We had made port in what was now the Dark Realm.

Slaves were transported to help the construction of buildings, and mainly what is now the Capital and even the Imperium.

Most of them moved out, only a small amount of us remained.

That's when a sickness came over the camp.

Most likely due to our horrid living conditions.

Me and many others were dying, I remember our enslavers being terrified.

Worried they would catch the sickness.

But it seemed as if they were more worried about losing their precious slaves, whom the King wanted to build his kingdom.

There had been a rumour amongst us, that they were going to put us all to the sword the next morning.

They had more ships coming in of course, so they would have been able to kill us, as their bad stock I suppose we were disposable.

My sister had not caught the sickness however, she was well and healthy, having been in the white devil's camp.

The King doing awful, terrible things to her.

I remember her coming to me in the late of night.

I could barely move, and delirium had clearly taken over.

She came to me, like some beautiful angelic creature who nursed me, trying to keep me alive.

I had been so cold, shivering everywhere.

She gave me a potion, to ease my comforts and help me sleep…

I was certain I would be dead, and never wake.
I had looked upon her once last time before my eyes closed.
She was crying… Crying yet beautiful.

She had been so sweet once.
I had been sure I would have died that night… And I suppose I did.
When I awoke, I had an incredible hunger, my throat was red raw.
I did not know what took control over me, it had never happened before.
I attacked the first person I saw; I ripped into their neck and drank heavily.
My first kill was a fellow slave I remember, remorse came over me despite the glorious taste of blood.

It was delicious, I still remember it now.

It intoxicated me, made me feel more alive than I had ever been.
They died of course, but my thirst was still ravenous.
The white demons keeping guard noticed me then.
I soon began feasting and ripping and tearing apart my enslavers.
The bloodlust was high, I even began attacking my fellow countrymen.
They were chained and bound, easy pickings.
I tried my best not to kill them though, merely biting instead.
I just needed blood.

Those who I only bit and did not kill soon to my amazement, turned into the very thing I had turned into.
We ripped through the camps, slaughtering without mercy.
We finally got to the King's tent, the biggest and grandest of them of course.
But when I raced inside, drenched in blood, I found my sister.

And the King, dead.

I still remember when she saw me… Covered in blood, guts and viscera.
Yet oddly, she did not look startled.
I still had the urge to feed, to drink, and yet I did not harm her.

I could not.

Thinking back, the fellow monsters created that day also did not harm her.
Despite our bloodlust, she was safe.

Yet, looking back, perhaps it was best I had killed her.
Perhaps it would have saved us these hundreds of years of death.
But that did not happen, instead she embraced me, and told me everything would be alright.
Outside, screams could be heard in every direction.
We left the King's tent, and she quickly took command, powerful and beautiful.
She gave a speech standing upon the bodies of our captors, and she gave us our mission.

To take revenge upon the white man who stole us.
And that's what we did.

We stayed at the camp for several days, we had to hide in the tents, the ones that were not destroyed, to protect us from the sunlight.

And yet I remember, even as far back as then, the light in the world had already darkened.
As if our mere presence brought a blight over the sun.

The ships arrived, bringing more slaves.
As soon as they docked, we pounced.
We killed all those of white skin we could find, and that's when my sister issued her speech.
She said those who had magic could keep it.
However, any of those who did not, had the opportunity to become a vampire.
My sister had named us that.
I say opportunity lightly.
Of course, none of them wanted to become us.

They looked at us with fear… And hatred.
And confusion, confused as to how we became monsters.

My sister forced them… She commanded me to bite the arm of a woman.

Just a single bite she said.
No more, no less.

I did not want too… I didn't want to hurt the woman.
Even though I had attacked my own people when I first became a monstrous creature, even though I had turned them into monsters also, I felt intense regret and did not want to repeat my mistake.
This woman on the ship was one of us, a poor yet kind faced black woman who had been captured and brought here against her will…

Just like me.

And now I was to turn her into a blood drinking demon like myself and the rest.
Despite not wanting too, I couldn't help myself.
My sister cut the woman's arm and I eagerly sunk my teeth into her.

Yes, I did as my sister obliged.

As always.

It didn't end there though; one by one a slave was dragged before me, and I was forced to bite.
And thus, my sister grew her army.
And those who were magically inclined could do nothing to stop it, they were bound in Saerillian Silver to ensure their loyalty.
And once we amassed enough vampires, we removed their chains, and they dare not attempt any sort of rescue or escape.
They simply followed suit and became known as **'Dark Witches'**
We thus swept through the lands, taking it for ourselves.
We had amassed great and vast lands, ravaging and reaving and raping.
We conquered perhaps a quarter of the country we had originally been enslaved to help build.
And in such short time.
We had destroyed cities and towns and villages.
All fell swiftly and quickly.
But then it happened…
My sister and even myself had become so certain of our victory that we had not realised just how much hatred we had stirred, and not just from the enemy, but from within our own ranks.
A plot was found.
Several witches of extreme power who were displeased with the thought of vampirism and demons and death turned against us.
They had tried to keep it secret, trying to turn against us in the thick of night.
There was originally meant to be seven but one had been captured whilst the others had fled.

She had been captured… **Poor Agatha.**

Her younger sister and the five others managed to escape, in the commotion however, they managed to steal something most valuable…

Perhaps if they hadn't… Perhaps she would not have become so mad.

Nevertheless, they fled in the middle of the night.
And under that pale moon they made a pact with the next and Third Imperial King, the son of the very King who had died back at the camp.

The witches asked for their freedom if they fought against us, against the demons.

And lands of their own.
Lands such as the vastness of the Black Woods which became the Magic Realm.

The young King accepted… And thus, united under uneasy circumstances, they stood their ground.

They fought us back.
Pushed us back.

I still remember it.
Dawn had broken and yet there was no sun to be seen, just dark clouds that had stayed afloat ever since demons came into existence.
Six witches, all powerful, betrayed us.
They fought with the humans.
They were about to use their Chaos, and surely with combined strength of witchcraft and that damned Imperial Army many would have died and it's uncertain who would have won…

Yet, I never got the chance to find out.

My sister it seemed gave up almost instantly… Something in her was broken.

I wanted to fight, to carry on the bloodshed, however she simply left the battlefield.

I did not understand at first… Not until later…

If only they hadn't stolen what was most precious to her…

Perhaps she could have focused on love and given up her hate…

But instead she focused on the cities, towns and villages we had already conquered, focused on building her own kingdom.

Thus, the Dark Realm grew, as did the Realm of Magic, the witches who fought against us building their own kingdom deep in the forest…

And the humans in their Realm were saved.

The war of course still rages over the centuries, a boring stalemate in what is now known as the BorderLands.

A thin stretch of land between the Dark and Magic Realm where the fighting happens.

We passed it quickly and briefly on our way here.

The land itself was dead, littered with bones and corpses.

For over three centuries it has been nothing but death.

Animals do not even venture there, and no plants grow.

It is a barren wasteland.

My sister over the centuries however made sure to have the odd Imperial killed here or there other the centuries.

A grim reminder that she existed and could get to them…

But other than that, she largely remained content in her palace.

And I had participated in this farce of a mission to get some quality time away from my sister.

Not just her, but the past and the Dark Realm.

I continue to walk.

Through the mud and rain, under the shadow of clouds.

This is good, however.

The heavy clouds give us the ability to walk in the day light.

The witches and Blood Initiates needed sleep however, both being human.

Yes, witches are humans.

They were only seen as nonhuman and Soulless because of their ability to Cast.

A power we got from the Ancestors…

A power the white man stole.

Yet even when they stole it, they still feared it…

Persecuted and judged… They truly were awful.

And what they did to this country.

They built big stone buildings, huge cities and to do this they cut down and destroyed nature around them…

Never in my home country would we do this.

We were part of the land, we nourished it, and it nourished us.

Yet these white demons were only interested in destruction.

Can you really blame us that we fought back?

We come to a halt as a Blood Initiate runs toward us.

We had sent this young man out earlier this morning to look ahead for us.

We could not simply leave the Dark Realm and enter the Realm of Magic by just aimlessly walking through.

No, we had to edge around their patrols, keeping close to the cliffs and shores.
The Black Woods stretched for miles around us.
I can hear the sea and the sounds of birds nesting in their coastal cliffs.

The Blood Initiate pants heavily as he manages to say between pants.

"Village, a few miles from here."

He continues to pant hard.

I push past and walk a few steps away from them.
I close my eyes and listen.
I can hear the vibrations, music and laughter.

A small village, yet full of life.

"Brilliant."

Claps Demetrius behind me.

"Time for some fresh blood!"

The others begin to chime in with agreement.

I turn to face them.

"We will leave this village alone.
My sister…"

"Your sister sent us here on a delicate mission, yes, yes, you're very important,"

He interrupts, finishing with a chuckle.

The others laugh along with him.

I could easily rip him to shreds right here and now.

I have centuries on him, he wouldn't last a second against me.
However, I don't, I stand there and remain silent, eager to see what else he brays about.

"With all due respect."

He begins in a tone that shows zero respect.

"Your sister is not here, and we need fresh blood.
That bottled blood isn't doing any of us any favours anymore, it lost its freshness days ago.
We need to have fresh blood, and I can smell fresh blood in that direction."

He finishes, gesturing ahead.

I can see the others begin to sniff heavy at the air.
I can smell it too, it's deep inside my nostrils.

All different blood, all different smells, it is intoxicating.

DOESN'T THAT BLOOD SMELL SO GOOD?
DOESN'T IT JUST MAKE YOU WANT TO TASTE IT.

It is true, all of it.

THE BLOOD SINGS TO ME…
AND MY THROAT BEGINS TO FEEL AS IF IT IS INFLAMED.

My sister would not be happy.
She gave clear instructions, including delivering the Vial and letter to
Claudius the Cunt.
And yet, despite this arrogant nothing saying it, he is right, my sister
is not here.

BUT IF YOU DO THIS, YOU WILL SURELY ALERT OTHERS TO
YOUR PRESENCE!
THEY WILL KNOW VAMPIRES ARE IN THEIR REALM!

Yes, indeed it did have its consequences, and yet to hell with it.

My sister has commanded me long enough!
Why should I not do something I want?

BUT REMEMBER HOW YOU FELT?
THE LAST TIME YOU SLAUGHTERED…

I halt myself there, and remember why I had sent myself into exile in
my rooms in the first place…

I know if I do this, I will hate myself entirely.

YOU ALREADY HATE YOURSELF!
WHAT IS A LITTLE MORE HATE?
A LITTLE MORE BLOOD…
BESIDES, SPILLING THIS BLOOD WILL JUST BE A MERE
DROP IN THE OCEAN OF BLOOD YOU'VE ALREADY SPILLED!

But this needs to stop.
The blood.
The death.

JUST ONCE MORE…
JUST ONE MORE LITTLE TASTE…

Oh, how I long to be able to simply walk away.
To tell those in my company that the bottles of blood was good enough,
fresh or not.
That we will leave this village alone…

And yet, I do not.

The blood continues to sing to me, every syllable making my throat
scratch worse and worse.

   YOU NEED TO FEED!
   FEED NOW!
   FEED NOW!
   FEED NOW!

I look at those around me and simply nod.

May the Ancestors forgive me.
For my plague on humanity.
For the death I am about to inflict.

We slowly walked inwards, into the Black Woods.
The smoke in the distance is easy to see, especially for a vampire.
We stay low and creep forward until finally we are close.
Just ahead, is a sprawling village.
We can hear an abundance of noise.
People talking, people shouting, people laughing.

They seem happy, clearly oblivious to their impending doom.

A mixture of guilt and thirst fills me.

Frenzied thoughts engulf me, the need to drink, to feast, to kill.
I can see the same frenzied thoughts in the red eyes of my fellow companions.
They are much younger and the younger a vampire the less able to control their need to feed.
They snarl and bite at thin air, their fangs protruded.
I let out a low, deep growl.
They may have lost respect for me, but they still know who I am, what I'm capable of, they quickly take obedience… All except Demetrius.
He stays looking at me for a second, before falling back in line.

"You, there!"

I point at the Blood Initiates.

All of them cower in fear, shrinking back like whipped dogs.

"Go forth and pretend you need help, draw as much of their attention as possible.
I don't want any runaways."

Demetrius stands forward, his voice bemused

"And what exactly are they supposed to need help with?"

I hear sniggers from behind the others
I ignore it, smiling softly.

"Oh, that's simple.
One of them is dying of course."

He looks confused, as do the Blood Initiates.

A brave one, stands forth and says,

"But my Lord, none of us are–"

He doesn't get the chance to finish his sentence.
My nails protrude like small daggers, I whirl around in an elegant motion, slashing his throat.
At first nothing happens, the Blood Initiate looks confused, only for a second.
Then the blood starts to pour, and he claps his throat, the deep gashes beginning to appear.
He falls to the ground in shock, blood pooling out of him.

"QUICKLY, TAKE HIM TO THE VILLAGE, NOW!"

I shout.

Some of them begin to cry, such pitiful creatures.
Yet they obey my command, nonetheless.
They gingerly approach, and quickly grab the dying man, dragging him in the direction of the village.

I take a glance at Demetrius, and he looks impressed, and scared.
And the rest of the Scarlet Soldiers, they too seem wary, I smile widely.

Hopefully this will teach them to fall in line.

AND IF IT DOESN'T, YOU CAN ALWAYS SLAUGHTER THEM TOO!

"MOVE OUT, SURROUND THE VILLAGE."

I shout again.

This time, not even Demetrius dares to question or say some smug remark.
He does as told.
They all flit off in different directions, taking their respective positions.
Finally, I look to the witches.

I only hope they can do this.

"There are five of you, so I assume between yourselves you can cast a shield?"

I ask of them.
My tone softer with them.
After all, I needed them to concentrate, and they cannot do that if I terrify them.

The youngest of them, or at least I assume she is young, many witches cast longevity spells, making it nearly impossible to tell their real age, a pretty thing with light eyes and light hair steps forth.

Her black dress soaked in mud stains and a belt of potions around her waist.
A small bag over her shoulder, most likely containing more potions, or at least the ingredients to make them.
I expected her to stutter, or show signs of fear, yet she does not.

She looks at me directly and speaks clearly.

"A shield, my Lord?"

I decide that I like her, she has bravery.

"Yes, a shield."

I answer her.

I turn and gesture to the village.

"Cast a shield around the village.
I want no sounds to be heard past the shield, and none inside can leave.
I want no villagers being able to escape and I want no one who may be nearby to hear the screams.
Do you understand?"

She nods simply, then turns her head to the rest.

"Come, sisters.
Our Dark Lord has given us a command."

This village may be close to the near cliffs and sea, and secluded by the thick trees which make the Black Woods, I have no doubt that this area may still be patrolled from time to time by any Imperial Soldiers or more likely Protectors.

The girls being to speak in the language of the Ancients, and just in time.

I hear that the Blood Initiates have arrived at the village, I can hear the shouts of several villagers shouting to fetch medicine, water and clean rags.

**Good people.
Doomed people.**

I look in the direction of the village, and I can see the shield begin to appear.

Not visible to that of a human eye, however a vampire eye has much clearer view.

It looks almost as if a shimmer, a ray of light.

It travels around the village and begins to travel upwards, as it does the sounds begin to die out.

It works then, I see.

The shield continues to travel around and upwards, finally completely in a dome shape.

They are officially trapped like rats, and they don't even know it.

"Make sure the shield continues to work."

I tell them.

The shield has no effect on me or the rest.

It's Cast to keep the humans in, and yet me and my Scarlet Soldiers can freely enter and leave.

I flit forwards, travelling hundreds of yards within the blink of an eye.

I appear directly in the heart of the village, right where they gather round the dying Blood Initiate.

At first, they do not recognise me.

Then one does.

A man looks at me, before he gets a chance to scream, I grab him, pulling him in close and sink my fangs deep into his neck.

The blood flows like liquid gold.

I throw him dead to the floor, and that's when the rest take notice.

I stand tall however and let out a primal scream.
A terrible, awful scream.
The screams of monsters.
The villagers begin to scream, starting to run in different directions.

They don't get far, for just then Demetrius and the other four Scarlet
Soldiers descend upon them, the screams beginning to grow higher and
louder.

I see blood spray and limbs torn.
I hate to admit it, but the sight is beautiful.

Horrifying and beautiful.

And the smell of blood is thick in the air.
I breathe it in deeply, eagerly, hungrily.
I quickly move on to my next victim, and then my next.
Moving at incredible speed, biting and ripping recklessly, violently.
More and more dead bodies piled on the ground.
Some attempted to Cast, yet in the confusion and bloodshed they don't
really have a chance.
They too are set upon and violently killed.

All around me is blood and death.

BEAUTIFUL BLOOD!
BEAUTIFUL DEATH!

Most of them dead, I stand there drenched in various sorts of body
parts and fluids.
I pant hard, despite not needing breathe.
Reality begins to set in, and a deep pain fills me.

I'm a monster.

These people did nothing.

Yet I'm slaughtering them anyways.

YOU ARE A PLAGUE ON HUMANITY!
BUT THIS IS THE CLOSEST YOU FEEL TO BEING ALIVE!
AND THE BLOOD!
DO NOT DENY HOW DELICIOUS IT IS!

This is true, this is the closest I feel to being alive, and the blood is indeed delicious.

Yet the bloodlust is losing its momentum, I feel nothing but intense guilt.

I look down at the dead bodies.

Men, women, children.

I can only pray that I had not killed the children, and yet it is now nothing but a blur.

The truth is, I cannot remember clearly if I had or not.

This only adds to the guilt.

I say a silent prayer of apologies to the Ancestors, yet I know that they would look upon me in disgust for this horror I've committed.

Truthfully, the Ancestors no doubt turned their backs on me centuries ago.

And I don't blame them, I am indeed Soulless.

Irredeemable, a plague, a monster.

The Blood Initiates stay low during the ordeal, cowering and crying.

I ignore them as I follow the remaining screams.

The screams emulate from toward the back of the village, obviously trying to run away, deeper into either the Black Woods or maybe even towards the cliffs, where no doubt they have boats below on the coast.

Whatever the case, wherever they may chose to run too, they are not able.

The shield makes it impossible for them to escape.

As I walk closer, their panicked screams intensify.

Growing louder, more desperate and desolate.

Yet, for whatever reason, this brings me joy.

I want to deny it, yet I can't.

This is who I am!
A living demon with the beauty of a god.

Inner turmoil aside, I know what needs to be done.

I get toward the back of the village, my fellow Scarlet Soldiers joining.

They stand beside me.

I'm standing on guts, viscera and blood.

The small pool of villagers stand before us, they kick and punch at the shield, yet it appears as if they are striking thin air.

They try throwing themselves against it, but are thrown back every time.

A strong shield indeed.

Perhaps these witches are not as useless as I had originally thought.

Thoughts aside, I hear the scream of one villager.

A pointed finger outstretched toward me; I hear.

"ITS HIM!
IT'S HIM!
THE DARK LORD."

The screams become even more shrill after that; I see my reputation precedes me.

They begin to bash themselves against the shield more wildly, yet it matters not.

Not being able to withstand the sounds of screams any longer, I give my command.

"Put them out of their misery."

They do not need telling twice, they attack instantly.

The screams continue for a painstaking couple more seconds, before finally an eerie silence.

A blissful, macabre silence.

The deed of death done, I want to die myself.

I am nothing but a monster.

Not wanting to face my actions, I want it to simply disappear.

"BURN IT!
BURN IT ALL."

I shout.

Various torches had lit the village, and the Scarlet Soldiers quickly get to work, grabbing whatever torches still held flame to them.
They begin to set fire to the plain huts, simple wood and thatched roofs.

YES, BURN IT!
BURN THE BODIES!
BURN THE HUTS!
BURN IT ALL!

As if burning it would hide the shame I feel.

And yet, in truth, the fire perhaps might be able to mask the fact the
village was massacred.
Surely, at some point this village will be discovered, and it's best that
they think it was a fire that killed these people, and not demons.
The fire spread across the village, burning and destroying as it travels.
Only a little while ago, this village had been a happy, bustling village.
There was laughter and music, warmth and love.
And look at what it was reduced to now, at the hands of myself.

Yes, a plague on humanity.

AND NOW IT IS BLOOD AND BRIMSTONE!
FIRE AND DEATH!

As I turn to leave the horror I caused, I hear a wailing sound.
It fills the air.
It comes from a burning hut beside me.
Fire is on the roof, it burns brightly.
Despite fire being one of the few things able to actually kill a vampire,
I head inside regardless.

A dead man lies at the entrance, I step over him.
A simple hut, broken furniture sprawled around and that of the bodies
of a woman and two children lay dead.

A family.

Their bodies mangled and broken; their clothing bloodstained.

"I'm so sorry,"

I say out loud, tears nearly appearing in my red eyes.

The woman holds a knife in her hand.
She had tried to protect them, the poor woman, but what luck would she have had against vampires.
The wailing sound continues, coming from a crib in the corner, I walk quickly to it.
I lift the sheets back, already knowing what to expect.

A fat babe lay there.

It wails and wails.
I can hear the sound of the roof begin to crash inward, I quickly grab the babe and flit outwards.
I don't stop outside the hut, I stop directly outside the village, the shield having dissipated.
The witches must have broken the shield when they saw the flames.
I shall have to congratulate them.
The babe has stopped its wailing, it's nestled into me.

Odd creature, indeed.

I look down, and it looks up at me.
I can't imagine what this babe must be thinking, me standing there covered in blood, with crimson eyes to match and yet it seems unfazed. As if it doesn't know that its entire family has just been slaughtered, their remains burning away.
I feel intense pity once again.

"I'm so sorry, little one."

I whisper to the babe.

"Want me to take care of that."

Asks Demetrius.

His eyes alive, his fangs sharp.

"NO!"

I growl toward him.

"IT'S MINE."

I state.

"You can't be serious,"

He wants to say more, I do not allow him.

I swipe at him, my hand striking him hard, he is propelled several yards away, falling with a deep thud.

The fellow Scarlet Soldiers appear, although they do not say or do anything.
Demetrius simply gets to his feet, spits blood, curses, shrugs and then walks off, no doubt to clean himself up.

Or to use that damned mirror with the Saerillian Silver to contact my sister…

I have earned his eternal hatred it seems, yet I do not care.
He is no threat to me.
The witches appear then too, along with the Blood Initiates.

They all stand there together, silent.
The smell of burning flesh fills the air, and smoke begins to travel upward toward the sky.

Shit, that will surely be seen.

"Let us leave."

I command.

I want away from this horror I created.
The witches look exhausted, the most exhausted being the young, brave girl who had spoken directly to me.
Sweat covers her, her hair stuck to her brow.
I hear another wail, to my surprise it comes from the Blood Initiate I had gouged with my nails.

How in hell is he still alive?

Yet alive he is, the rest of the Blood Initiates having dragged him back.
Yet I can tell his death is very near, it's a surprise he has lasted this long.
I hand the babe to the young girl.
She looks confused but obliges, taking the babe and beginning to fuss and mull over it.

Women and babies, a mystery indeed.

I walk towards the Blood Initiates, as I do, they creep backward leaving the dying man lying there.
He whimpers as I lean down and whisper.

"Do you want to live?"

"Y – yes."

He gurgles.

So be it.

Kneeling, I take his arm.
I bite down, HARD, then quickly release.
He lets out a brief scream as my venom travels through his bloodstream.
He begins to shake uncontrollably, the venom taking its course.
The slash across his throat begins to heal, not even a scar remains, it becomes instead invisible.
Vampire venom cures all wounds, and it changes a person too.
His features became more defined, more beauty appearing.
His hair looks fuller, his skin begins to pale even more so, his muscles harden and become stronger.
He sputters and shakes one last time, before finally becoming still.

He is dead.

Not half a second later, he lets out a loud, audible gasp.
His once light eyes have now turned to bright red as he is now reborn as a vampire.
One of the witches who witnesses this quickly faints.

ANOTHER BEAUTIFUL CREATION!
I'M SURE HE SHALL BE A FINE ADDITION TO THE REST!

No, this is another travesty.
Another monster added to the world.
One more demon to terrorise and murder the innocent.

GODS HELP US!

I think internally as the newborn monster lets out a guttural scream, the village burning in the background.

BLOOD AND BRIMSTONE!
FIRE AND DEATH!

And all because of me.
Ancestors, forgive me.

A FEW DAYS LATER

THE CITY OF BRIDGES

COUNCIL OF COVENS

ANNETTE

Stood on the balcony, I look out at the wonderful city before me.
Great trees full of green and browns surround me.
And everywhere as far as the eye can see, bridges.
They intertwine and weave, connecting everything together.
And more importantly, connecting and weaving us with nature itself.
The bridges are covered in leaves and beautiful flowers.
Down below on the ground, thousands go about their lives.
There are stalls and markets, people buying and selling.
Children playing merrily.

If only they knew what had recently happened…

A poor village on the outskirts of the Black Woods, right by the sea.
Massacred and burned.
I knew I could feel something was wrong, yet I was not sure what.
Not until it was confirmed shortly ago, and therefore I called upon my
Council who shall be arriving any moment.

Where were the damned Protectors!

Whilst it's true we have regular patrols throughout the entirety of our precious Magic Realm, I have to admit that the Black Woods are vast indeed, and not every village is checked upon as regularly as I would like.

My own fault.

Being the Head Witch, therefore I am in charge.
Not only of this land, but of the people.
It is my responsibility and duty to keep them safe.

I failed.

And not to mention the trouble I can feel brewing in the Human Realm.

The boy was growing stronger by the day…

I'm pulled from these thoughts as I hear the Council enter.
Sighing, I turn away from the beauty of the city and inwards to the Council Chambers.

Fists slam down hard on the table.
As usual, Amrita is flush with anger.
And dressed head to toe in armour.
Her helmet is off, her dark hair stuck to her brow with sweat.

"HOW HAS THIS HAPPENED?!
A WHOLE VILLAGE, MASSACRED!
WHERE THE FUCK WERE THE PATROLS!"

She shouts.

"Calm yourself.
This anger does not help."

Says Phelan.

A more rational member of the council.
He is aged sixty and yet having cast the longevity spell looks much younger.

He sits alongside thc rcst.
Before me is the council, the Council of Covens.
Six council members one of which is the Head Witch.
The Head Witch being me.

"Let us stop this arguing!
We need to think clearly.
We cannot let anger cloud our judgment."

I tell them all.

Amrita is not pleased, her face full of anger.

"A whole village is massacred, and you want us to have cooler heads?
We should have a show of force!
We should fight!"

"Fight who, exactly?
We do not yet know the full situation."

Argues Phelan.

"Are you a fucking idiot?
It's obvious who did this!"

"And let me guess, you think it is the Imperial Soldiers…?"

"That's absurd,"

Replies Sera.

A doe eyed relatively young witch.
Only twenty but looks even younger.
She is the last of her family…
If she does not reproduce, her line and position on the Council will come to an end after three centuries.
In truth, each and every one of us on the Council is a descendant of previous Council members.
Myself, being the daughter of the previous High Witch.

"This is obviously the work of the Red Eye demons."

Amrita throws her head in Sera's direction.

"Red Eyed Demons?
Please, I have constant patrols!
If it was Red Eyed demons, I'd know!
No, Imperial Soldiers have done this!
They have slaughtered them, and then burned it down to cover their evidence!"

"Why would Imperial Soldiers do this?"

 I ask of Amrita.

"Because they are still allowed in our Realm!
They crawl around, everywhere!
Disgusting insects!
And we allow them here!

Look what they have done!
They have been slaughtering us for years now!"

I cannot deny this.
Witches have long been persecuted, feared and murdered…

Even though we have helped.
We have kept the vampires at bay.
We have tried our very hardest.

It was three centuries ago when the pact was made.

Six powerful witches crossed over and met with the Third Imperial King.
I, myself, am a great, great, give a few centuries daughter of the first Head Witch.
She was strong and powerful, yet it was supposed to be her elder sister who ruled.
A seer named Agatha, however captured before the rest fled.
And the rest of the Council are also all direct descendants of the other witches who first crossed.
In return for helping the humans fight the deranged and evil Helena, so called Queen of Witches…
She was no Queen of Witches, not here anyways.

No, she was Queen of demons.

And to call herself a witch… She is an embarrassment and disgrace to the name.
Oh sure, she is powerful beyond means and not to be trifled with, but magic is supposed to be used for good, to do and create wonderful things.
It is a gift, a marvellous beautiful gift.

But Helena, she used the powers she was born with and turned it dark, evil.

She created creatures that had never been seen before, and because of this we have all had to pick up the slack.

Our ancestors had been brave enough to stand up to her, they left her in the dead of night, having stolen something… They made a pact with the Imperial King.

They would fight and help the Imperial Army, and in return the witches would be granted their own lands.

Thus, we partly gained the BorderLands and also the vast, vast Black Woods which became the Realm of Magic.

We lived here, deep in the Black Woods and made our glorious City of Bridges.

Witches and humans were allowed to travel between Realms, as friends and neighbours.

We interbred, became families.

And yet, there have always been fearful humans who hate us regardless.

And this hateful faction, they finally have a name.

'DEFENDERS'

They were called.

As if there was not enough death happening, this deranged army led by an even more deranged ruler, the new High Pope, Claudius.

He had been nothing from what I remember, yet his poisoned tongue had sunk into the ears of many across the land during his travels and thus his army of Defenders ascended across the Human Realm.

They beat, raped and murdered any witch they could get their hands on.

Not that they had not been doing that for centuries anyhow.

Oh sure, the Imperial King of old promised that we would be friends.

That humans and witches would live in peace.

In three centuries, we always kept that peace.

Humans here were not harmed, however the same could not be said all these years for the Casters who wanted to live within the Human Realm.

Many of us have had enough, enough of the humans, many of whom seek to start more war.

This, however, I shall not allow.

They are banned from entering the Realm of Magic, and they have been these last three years.

Except of course the humans who were already here.

Either Imperial Soldiers who we kept here, or children born with non-casting abilities to families who were magically inclined.

Many such Non-Casters joined the ranks of Protectors.

They may not be able to Cast magic to protect the Realm, however they are trained with sword and shield.

And when the Cleansing was decreed it was not just Defenders who attacked across the Human Realm, but many small folks rose in to be part of the violence and bloodshed.

It spread like wildfire.

The last Head Witch, she could feel all the blood and death as if it was happening to her.

She was my own mother, a kind woman who was heavily empathetic, the violence and disturbance of the Realms gave her a quick and early death.

I remember feeling it too.

All that pain.

The blood, the screams.
I may not have been there physically to witness it, but we all felt the great disturbance in nature.
The pain was so great for my mother that she simply died from heartache.

What witches managed to survive fled here, under our protection.
Yet many could not get here, they have had to remain hidden these last three years.

My thoughts are always with them.

Many witches here In the Realm of Magic seek justice, they want war.
I can and will not allow that.

We are already at war.
We have vampires and dark witches constantly battling us at the front lines and sneaking in from the BorderLands.
 I can not face an enemy in front of us, and an enemy behind us.

And yet it seems, we have enemies on both sides regardless.

We are in truth, surrounded.
And yet, I will not cause more bloodshed and violence.
Therefore, I made the decision three years ago to not seek justice or revenge.
Instead, I had the Realm of Magic closed off.
Humans are no longer permitted to visit our lands.
Not even imperial Soldiers, we cut them all off.

And those who were already here, well they are imprisoned in all but name.

Except of course those who already lived here as part of families.

Many Non-Casters were born amongst us in our Realm, and the people were divided about them.

Some witches who believed in purity called those who were born unable to cast as 'Undesirables'.

These very witches believe wholeheartedly that the Magic Realm should only be for those who can Cast, and thus the Undesirables should be thrown out.

Whilst there are others who see nothing wrong it, treating and loving them all the same.

Yet, these last three years the numbers of the Imperial Soldiers have dwindled, and we have had to send more and more of our own kind to battle and death.

The General constantly begs us to still allow aid from the Imperial Army in the Human Realm.

But I will not allow it.

I simply cannot risk it.

We are doing okay just now, yet I know we cannot last forever.

But at least the humans have stayed away, and as long as they stay on their side, they are not a threat as far I'm concerned.

The only humans that are permitted here now are the infamous Slayers of the Syndicate.

Thankfully, the Lord Commander stopped that faction from partaking in the Cleansing.

Of course, some disloyal Slayers did take part, but the Lord Commander had them executed.

Therefore, with his mutual trust, only they are allowed into our Realm.

Not that they get to walk around freely, no, they are sent straight to the frontlines to battle and usually die quickly.

I'm more concerned with the imminent threat, which is indeed the Red Eye demons.

Dark witches are not a threat to me.

Not compared to the vampires who with only one bite can turn us into savage bloodsuckers, taking us out like a plague.

I look at Amrita hard, pulled from my thoughts.

"Amrita, we are not infested whatsoever.

There are barely any Imperial Soldiers left.

You know as well as everyone around this table there are only a few hundred of them left.

They once numbered thousands.

What's left are poor and desolate souls.

The only reason they even continue to fight is because they have no other choice and nowhere else to go.

They are treated well enough whilst they have been here, and the General keeps a firm grip on his men.

I seriously doubt humans were to blame.

However, in truth I would like to know where these patrols are, Amrita."

I ask of her.

She seems shocked by this.

She even stutters.

"I, uh…"

"Amrita, we all know your stance on the Imperial Soldiers still within the Realm of Magic, yet they rarely ever leave the battlefield. However, I know too well that we have our own armed forces. And you, you are their Commander, are you not?"

I gesture towards her, the fact she is dressed head to toe in armour.

"Where were the patrols?
You would know this better than anyone?
Where were the Protectors?"

They, like their name suggests, protects the Realm of Magic, from those who would do it harm.
They are some of our bravest witches, Casting their Chaos to keep us safe.
Not to mention plenty of Non-Casters who were born here, fighting valiantly to protect us.
And yet, where were they when this village was massacred?
Amrita wants us to blame the Imperial Soldiers, but why?
To incite more fear?
To create confusion and division?
Whatever the case, I shall not allow it.

"Well, Amrita, you come here angrily accusing others, sowing further discord, and as commander of the Protectors and you cannot tell me where any of them where?
Why were they not patrolling the area?
Care to explain?"

The rest of the Council look towards her.
She shifts uncomfortably.

"With all due respect, Head Witch, we are stretched thin."

"Because more of us have to fight as whatever Imperial Army is left here has dwindled remarkably, which may I remind you, you were a strong and firm hand in doing so.
Which is why perhaps our forces are stretched thin?
And instead of blaming the obvious, which is clearly the vampires, you blame what little help we still have at our disposal from the humans?"

I say.

We all continue to look at her, she says nothing.
I have a feeling that something is going on… And Amrita is heavily involved.
Yet, without solid proof, I can of course do nothing.
I know how she hates the humans… And will do anything to get rid of what's left of the ones still remaining here…
And this anger of hers… I have a strong feeling it may be a charade.

"Forgive me, Head Witch.
Perhaps I am wrong.
Perhaps it is vampires."

"Indeed, and I suggest perhaps instead of standing here swearing, you go forth and figure out why this village had no protection?"

"Well, there are Casters in every village… They did have protection."

"Do you mean themselves?

They may be able to Cast, but you know as well as I that does not mean they are strong in their Chaos or simply are not made to be warriors. And this village, it's on the outskirts, is it not?"

The question was for the table.

Baranabus and Tatiana, the two other Council members and the eldest look uninterested.

"Indeed, Head Witch.
 The village is near the coastal cliffs.
Far from here, not patrolled often however."

Concludes Sera.

"Hmm, it would seem Amrita that you have only yourself to blame.
So perhaps stop blaming others and I strongly suggest you start patrolling further than just our city."

It is true, our city is heavily patrolled and protected, and not many of our forces are sent to protect those living in the furthest reaches of the Black Woods.

And that is my fault.
And it must be rectified.

"I want the dead buried with dignity and honour.
They deserve that at least, we may not have protected them in life, but I shall make sure they have respect in death."

Amrita shakes her head at this.

"Impossible, I have been there myself, there is nothing left.

The people, they are ripped limb from limb.
And the fires burnt them badly…
There is barely anything left."

"Well, whatever is left you shall make sure is buried with respect."

I conclude.

"That is a waste of precious time.
Time that could be spent."

"Hunting them down?
No point, they are most likely gone by now.
From what reports I've read, they ran to the Human Realm."

"Well, that settles it then.
It's nothing to do with us."

Amrita concludes happily.

"Vampires in the Human Realm… But why?
Why have they snuck past… Something is going on?
 Something dark."

Sera confesses.

The rest mutter words of agreement, as do I.

Yet, I am the only one who it seems to know what is going on…
A secret passed down for these last three hundred years.
A secret only me, my ancestors, and if I have any children, shall ever know.

There is a power coming from the Human Realm… A power that burns brightly, and fiercely.

It surpasses that of any known witch I have ever come across.

If so many of us were not focused on this war perhaps many more would notice it…

I have only ever felt power like this before in one other…

And that is the self-proclaimed Queen of Witches, the dark mistress herself, Helena.

The fact another witch has this same raw power… I do not know whether to be terrified or glad.

This power coming from the Human Realm…

 It has a name.

And the one who bears this name shall surely be the one that was prophesied.

Yet the outcome of what they shall do is uncertain.

They shall either be the light or the dark,

They shall doom the world or save it,

Unleash chaos or learn control.

They will be death, or they will be life.

For all of us.

Yes.

It is the prophesied who shall decide the fate of the world and all of us.

And the prophesied is none other than a young man, and an Imperial no less…

But we always knew it would be, as does Helena.

She has always known it, hence why she has tried over the years to kill them here and there.

But on the eve of the new century, she nearly succeeded in murdering them completely.

There was only a handful of days left of the year 299ID, the Imperial Family had travelled here to celebrate the new century.

They never made it to our City of Bridges, however.

No, they were attacked on the road, deep within the Black Woods.

They had patrols, including our own, but attacked nonetheless they were.

It's now the summer of the year 321ID, but by the end of this year, when winter is here, it would be twenty-two years ago.

Their deaths shocked and rattled both Realms, and with time, the wounds created only deepend.

She did not succeed in her plan, however.

And even two decades later, I still cannot tell if that was a good or bad thing.

Another person who knows about this prophecy is my great, great, give a couple centuries aunt.

Poor Agatha.

It was three centuries ago…

She had been friends with Helena at first, or so I'm told.

They were even brought over on the same ship…

She may have been a seer, but not even a seer could have seen what pain and death Helena was ought to wrought…

No, in fact, she did not get her first vision until months later…

Months after Helena had turned twisted, dark and vile…

Months after she had brought her nightmarish creatures to this land…

'A plague'

They called it…

Yet I know the truth.

The real truth.

The spell used to create the vampires, it's a twisted version of a spell.
A spell that is meant to originally being everlasting life…
Twisted by using blood magic.

Apparently, from what information I managed to gather…
And what information or history they knew about our past was mainly lost.
I suppose those harshly brutalised and brought unwilling across the sea, they most likely did not want to talk and share these horrors with their children and grandchildren.

Thus, much is lost to time.

What I know however is fact, that those who stayed started building this beautiful land of magic.
Our own Realm Of Magic, we thus set about building our glorious City of Bridges, and many neighbouring villages sprung up also.
In time, we flourished slowly but surely, we prospered and did not have to fear persecution.
Not here in our territory.
Our own army of Protectors developed, and thus we not only have powerful Casters and brave Non-Casters on the frontlines, but we have many patrols surrounding the entire Black Forest.

And yet, this village did not have any protection.

Where were the patrols?

And how did the Red Eyed demons manage to get so far into our Realm without being noticed?

Sure, many have snuck into our Realm before, but they've always been swiftly and brutally killed.

No, the Red Eyed demons have not only snuck past, but they kept close to the outskirts of the Black Forest, staying close to the cliff sides and coast.

They knew where to go, which paths to take…
And the only way that could happen is if they had help…

Inside help.

I take a final look at Amrita…
She has always had a strong hatred for the Humans, but did she really hate them enough to betray her own people…

I look at her closely, wondering…

I shall have to keep a close eye on this one.

More concerning, there are vampires and without a doubt aided by Dark Witches, not only have they slipped past our forces, but they are now most likely deep into the Human Realm.

They are after him…

And if they get to him, if they kill him…

No, she won't simply kill him, she could have done that easily by now.

SHE TRIED ONCE, REMEMBER?

Yes, three years ago.

The prince was attacked, more likely nearly assassinated…

And the culprit was a feral vampire, and apparently with the aid of a Dark Witch…

But that last part wasn't true, no, the only witch that day was him.

And the feral… Burnt beyond a crisp according to rumour.
And then he was in a deep slumber for weeks…

HE USED TOO MUCH CHAOS.
HE COULD HAVE KILLED HIMSELF.

And yet, he was not the only one there during the attack…
No, the General's son was there too…
Kaleb the boy is called…

Yes, the accounts that swirled were that Kaleb, the son of the infamous General, valiantly and bravely protected the prince and slew the feral.

And yet, whilst I may not have been there, I know that is not what happened.
Whilst I have no doubt that Kaleb would have protected the prince, it was not he who had slain the beast…
No, he just earned all the credit.
He too sustained an injury I believe… A large, deep cut across his back.

I remember when the letter came with the news…
The General had begged me to let him leave, I had wanted too…
I could hear the pain in his voice, the sadness of his eyes, he only wanted to visit what he thought was his dying son…

And yet, I did not allow it.
The council was firmly against it, and therefore, I could not allow it.

For the safety of the Realm.

NO, YOU KNOW WHY YOU KEPT HIM HERE!
EVEN IF YOU WILL NOT ADMIT IT!

I remember how happy the General had been when Kaleb had finally come to visit last year.

Despite Kaleb's injury three years ago he healed apparently quickly, he however ignored his father's summons for two years.

The General did not want his only son and heir to be a Slayer of the Syndicate.

He had hoped to bring him here and persuade him to instead join the ranks of the Imperial Army.

So, last year, Kaleb finally came here.

The General was overjoyed, he wholly believed his son would do him proud and earn the respect of the men.

Kaleb did all of that and more.

And yet, he earned his father's fury and ire when in the midst of night, he ran away.

Before the General even got a chance to try and change his mind.

He had only been here for a handful of weeks.

And whilst he was fierce on the battlefield and proved his worth, the fact he ran off meant those victories were worthless.

He lost the respect of whatever Imperial Soldiers remained here also.

His father is still dumbfounded to this day, and he still does not know why his son left.

YET YOU DO…
YOU COULD SENSE HIS PAIN, HIS LONGING…
HIS LOVE…

Yes, the power of clairvoyance.
Clear and utter clarity.

I knew the young man had honour, had impressive battle skills, and not to mention rugged good looks.

Just like his father.

Yes, many witches here, both male and female had desire for the General, despite him being human.
And when Kaleb came to visit, many young witches and Non-Casters alike also found him equally desirable.

Yet Kaleb showed no interest… No.
His heart belonged to only one.
A strong, good heart.
And despite his honour, he will give it up every time for his love.

For him…

And if the General had any idea that his son…

No, I doubt that would end well.

In my thoughts, I realise the Council are all staring at me.

"We need to send an owl to the Human Realm."

I confirm.

Amrita looks in utter disbelief.

"They have left our Realm, who cares what they do in the Human Realm,"

Yes, her hatred is strong.

I look at her intently.
Has she betrayed us all?

"Amrita, your judgement is clouded.
All those vampires have to do is bite a single person, and so on and so forth before the whole Human Realm would be nothing but Red Eyed demons.
Tell me, how do you expect to fight vampires on both sides?
We would be surrounded!"

Amrita slams her fist down on the table again.

"We are already surrounded.
Demons on one side, and monstrous humans on the other.
Even disgusting humans in our realm.
Why do we keep them here?
Why do we simply not kill them all?"

Phelan, Sera, Baranabus and Tatiana all mutter furiously amongst themselves.
It seems as if they are divided.
I stand then, having had enough of this.

"ENOUGH!
AMRITA, YOU ARE OUT OF LINE!
I SUGGEST YOU GO AND SEE TO YOUR PATROLS."

I shout.

She goes to leave, furious.
However, before she can leave, I finish with this.

"And Amrita, I want a report of why this village was not patrolled.
I also want to know which Protectors were supposed to be there.
I'd like to speak to them personally."

She freezes at this, she turns to me, her face clearly nervous.

"It… Will take some time,"

She answers.

Meaning she probably needs time to cover her tracks.

"Make it quick."

 I remind her sharply.

Yes, I shall have to keep a close eye on this.

She bows her head, clearly disturbed and takes her leave.
I turn to the rest of the council.

"Please, ignore Amrita's outburst, we all know she is fuelled by anger.
We shall not be touching any humans who stay here, and we shall be
sending an owl to the Human Realm.
They need to be warned what's in their lands."

Baranabus speaks up then

An old man with a white beard.

Unlike the calm Phelan, he is more prone to being hot-headed also like Amrita.

Tatiana stays silent, she too is old and extremely wise.

Her white hair covered in flowers; it flows to her waist.

She remains silent however like usual, preferring to listen instead.

"With all due respect, High Witch, but sending an owl might not be in our best interest."

Baranabus tells me.

"And why is that?"

I question.

"Because quite simply they hate us.

Sending them news that Red Eyed Demons have somehow evaded our forces and slipped into the Human Realm, they will more likely blame us than thank us.

They will use this information to create more hatred and fear, they will spread the news that somehow, we are to blame."

Sera adds to this.

"I agree, High Witch, everyone around this table and everyone in our Realm knows the hatred they have for us.

They've always hated us, and now they slaughter us without impunity.

We have to be careful; they shall surely blame us."

Baranabus concludes.

I take what they have to say on board, listening carefully.
What they say is true, the Council would surely blame us, and without a doubt Claudius would use this to fuel the fire.
But a warning still needs to be sent, they need to know what's going on.

And he must be protected at all costs.

YOU MEAN TO PROTECT SOMEONE WHO COULD DESTROY YOU ALL…

Or someone who will save us all.

But the news cannot be sent to Claudius or the council…
No, someone else that is trusted.

"What about the General's brother, the Lord Commander of the Syndicate?

I announce.

The room goes silent, they all share uneasy glances.

"High Witch, surely you cannot be serious?!"

"Yes, you want to send this information to the Lord Commander of the Syndicate?"

"They slay vampires.
Over the years the Syndicate and witches have been fast friends, and they did not partake in the Great Cleansing neither.

Besides, the current Lord Commander is the General's own brother, do you not think they speak via owl or raven?
Besides, I have wrote back and forth many times with the Lord Commander.
He has a strong sense of duty and honour.
I think he would be best suited to speak too."

"Yes, I suppose the Lord Commander is a good man."

Mutters Phelan.

"The Lord Commander may have banned the Syndicate from partaking, yet we all know there were rogue Slayers who happily partook in the slaughter."

Baranabus speaks up.

"And these Slayers were duly executed."

I retort.

"Yes, but do you think that there are not Slayers who do not share the same views of hatred of witches?
You say we have always been fast friends but even Slayers before the Cleansing would kill witches for fun too.
There are many Slayers who wholly believe that they should slay witches too.
Many believe in the Faith of Eternal Light and have gotten swept up in this persecution and fear also.
The Syndicate is divided and conflicted, High Witch.
We cannot send an owl or raven to the Lord Commander."

I listened carefully to what he says, and I too am conflicted.

The Lord Commander was a hard man, prideful and stern.

However, he was honourable and smart like his brother, the General.

If a letter must be sent to anyone, it had to be him.

His Syndicate could really help track these vampires and destroy them.

BUT NOT ALL THOSE AT THE SYNDICATE ARE TO BE TRUSTED...

This was true.

The Capital is a dangerous place, and despite the Great Cleansing, I know that there is a Secret Court hidden within the Capital, or should I say under it.

Hidden away deep in the sewers, I make contact when I can, and they do the same.

They send me reports from time to time.

This is true, also.

And yet, I have to trust that the Lord Commander knows who to trust.

BUT WILL YOU REVEAL THE TRUTH ABOUT THE BOY?

That however is something I cannot do; I do not think it would end well...

The boy is just as easily prophesied to destroy the world as save it...

And if the Lord Commander of the Syndicate, for a second, thought that this boy would bring fire and death to the Realms then he would surely kill the boy...

Or die in the process.

But then again, the Lord Commander is a smart man... **Perhaps he already knows**?

No… If he knows then certainly the boy would be dead.
Or perhaps the Lord Commander does know and can't kill him.

Because if he kills him… Then surely, he would destroy his own nephew…

Kaleb.

And yet, this Imperial Prince has powers beyond belief, and from what rumours I've heard he wants nothing more than to unite the people…
But these reports and rumours from the Secret Council also tell me of a deep arrogance…
And a strong desire to be throned and crowned.

Even at the displacement of his own elder brother…

Then again, it is true by other reports that the older Crown Prince is a truly vile young man.
He would definitely not be the one to unite the people.
It is true, his displacement would be needed for the prophesied to rule.

And yet, I certainly will not be ordering an assassination on the Crown Prince…
No, the elder brother will surely be dealt with but not by my hand.

Of that, I am sure.

"I am High Witch, and as such I have heard your complaints and cautions, however I have the last say.
And as such I shall send an owl the Lord Commander, despite what misgivings you have about him, you cannot deny he has a strong sense of honour and has protected our kind when he could over the years."

"I suppose it's not too bad, besides, I doubt he will turn it back on us, we have his brother all but imprisoned of course."

Says Phelan.

The others mutter in agreement.
I too smile and nod, although I do not want too.

The doors burst open then, and to my surprise it is none other than the General.
My breathe comes to a halt, and my heart quickens.
He is dressed fully in plain silver armour; the kind worn by the Imperial Army.
On his breastplate, an orange sun with a gold crown.

Baranabus takes a stand and begins to shout.

"How dare you enter these chambers!
You have no right!
No authority!"

The General ignores the cries of the Council and continues to walk straight towards me.
My breathe catches.

> *HE IS VERY HANDSOME, ISN'T HE!*
> *JUST LOOK AT HIM!*
> *SO STRONG, SO MASCULINE!*
> *EVERY INCH A WARRIOR!*
> *EVERY INCH A MAN!*

He stops before me and speaks, his voice rough and loud.

And extremely sexy…

"Annette, I promise you, neither I nor my men had anything to do with
the massacre."

He tells me.

His eyes are honest and true.

Baranabus begins to shout once again.

"How dare you address the High Witch, and by her first name no less!
Have you no decency?
No honour?!"

This angers the General

"You would insult my honour?"

He looks straight at Baranabus.

"Do you have any idea who I am?!
What I have done?!
I have fought on the frontlines more times than I can count!"
I have fought and bled and nearly died a thousand times over!
I have fought alongside my men, alongside fellow witches!"

He then points an accusing finger at Baranabus.

"And yet, I have NEVER seen you on the battlefield!
I have not seen you bleed?!
I have not seen you risk your life!
Where is your honour?"

Baranabus stares in total disbelief.

"Shall I take off my armour, and you your precious robes!
Shall we get naked and count each other's scars?!
Because I can promise you, I am covered in battle scars.
Whereas I doubt you have even a scratch on your dainty, weak body."

This infuriates Baranabus.

"WEAK?!
YOU WOULD CALL ME WEAK?!
I'LL SHOW YOU WEAK, YOU PITIFUL HUMAN."

He shouts back.

A huge fireball appears in Baranabus hand, and the General immediately pulls his sword from its scabbard.

They would fight, surely if I allow it.

And yet, I shall NOT allow it!

I wave my hand, and the fireball dissipates immediately.
Baranabus looks at his hand in shock.
The General also looks confused.

Baranabus looks as if he is about to create another fireball, and the General lifts his sword again.

"ENOUGH!"

I shout.

As I do, I slam my hands together, and then outwards.

A strong gust of wind blows both of them backwards, on to the floor.

The rest of the council quickly stand up.
The General and Baranabus then both gruffly pick themselves off the
floor.

"THE NEXT PERSON TO ATTEMPT VIOLENCE IN THIS CHAMBER
SHALL BE HARSHLY DEALT WITH."

I shout.

They both pick themselves from the floor, the General is calm,
however Baranabus mutters words of annoyance.
Neither of them dares question my authority, however.
The rest of the Council glance toward me, with various looks on their
faces.

"I think we have had enough excitement for one Council meeting.
I suggest this meeting comes to an end, and we all clear our thoughts
from violence."

I announce.

They all mutter at themselves, and each other, but one by one they take
their leave.
Baranabus looks at me, anger in his eyes, but he too takes his leave.

The General goes to leave also, until I quickly say.

"Not you."

He flashes a look at me, but he does as I ask, and he stays.
The rest take their leave.

I look at him, and he looks at me.
For a moment, nothing is said between us.

"You enter this Council, you call me by my name, and you call a member of this council weak?"

As I say all of this, I walk towards him.

As I continue to walk towards him, his eyes do not move from mine.
I get close to him, so close I can smell him.

THE SMELL OF A MAN...

"You even unsheathed your sword.
Do you deny it?"

I am right in front of him, I am smaller than him, so I look up at him and yet, we both know who casts a longer shadow.
His eyes are dark and brooding, he looks at me sternly.
And yet, he does not answer.

"Do you deny it, General?"

I ask of him again, this time my tone firmer.

He continues not to answer, instead, he grabs me roughly and kisses me firmly.
I allow him, the strength of his muscles holding me tightly.
I lean upwards into the kiss; it feels rough and passionate.
The kiss ends, as they always do, it leaves us both breathless.
I look up at him, and he down at me, and his eyes become saddened.

He takes a step back, shame filling his face, his gaze no longer meets mine.

In fact, he wants to look anywhere but me.

It is the same story, time after time.

He feels guilty about us.

He is a man of honour, and yet, by being with me, he is dishonouring his lady wife.

We never meant it to happen, this thing between us.

I have known him since the first day he came to this Realm.

He was a young boy then, a squire of his father, along with his younger brother.

He fought here, became a Captain, so handsome and strong.

His younger brother left to take his vows and oaths as a Slayer of the Syndicate.

But he stayed… He stayed and fought…

And then it happened.

That awful, terrible slaughter.

It had been on our land… The Imperial Family… All but nearly wiped out.

Six of them were in that carriage… Only one survived.

In nearly tore the Realms of Magic and Humans apart, thankfully, the one remaining Imperial had survived.

And he had survived thanks to our fierce and loyal Protectors…

And the General was of course shaken to the core by all of this.

He was a mere soldier back then, on guard, the one to be guarding the Imperial Carriage that day… And yet, somehow, despite his tactics and strategy, despite the fact he was well trained in his duties, and also armed with two dozen other guards, not to mention our own Protectors, and yet… And yet, despite all of that, he still attacked…

The Dark Lord himself.

If he had not been saved by our own Protectors, surely, we would have been blamed.

And yet… Despite him being saved, the animosity grew…

The boy became King and thankfully decreed that no harm would come to us.
He recanted on this of course, when yet another attack on the Imperial Family happened.

Three years ago, and this time the attack was on the King's son, and with his dying breathe, the Cleansing began.
It was only a matter of time of course; I am shocked it hadn't happened sooner.
It took three centuries but the humans finally committed the genocide they had so eagerly wanted.

And then there was him… The vilest, darkest, twisted demon that ever walked this earth.
His atrocities and war crimes, his blood and death, his violence and rape, he is one monstrous creature.

HE CAME HERE ONCE TO COMMIT A MASSACRE…
PERHAPS HE HAS COME AGAIN?!

A shiver runs down me, and my blood turns to ice in my veins.
He snuck into this Realm before, could he have done so again…
My body shudders and shakes, I take several dazed steps backwards.

No… No… No

Surely… Surely, he is not back?!

WHO ELSE WOULD THE WRETCHED QUEEN SEND OTHER THEN HER PRIZED BROTHER…

But if it is him…
And if he is in the Human Realm…
It can only be for one reason.
He is going for the boy!
She has sent him to capture the prophesied.
She must have finally figured out she needs him not dead, but instead she needs his magic.
And if she gets her hands on him… Surely death for us all.

ALL THESE CENTURIES OF PROTECTING THE IMPERIAL FAMILY…
SO MANY OF YOU'RE ANCESTORS WHO DID THEIR JOB WELL, AND YOU…
YOU HAVE MESSED UP GREATLY!
DURING YOUR REIGN AS HEAD WITCH, YOU HAVE DONE NOTHING OF VALUE!
AND NOW, YOU HAVE LET THE MOST DANGEROUS DEMON SIMPLY WALK THROUGH YOUR REALM!
UNSCATHED, UNCHECKED, AND UNSEEN.
AND NOW… NOW THE BOY MAY BE LOST!
THE CHANCE OF UNITY… ALL RUINED, BECAUSE OF YOU!

No… No… No.

I have to stop this!

And I have to stop this now!

"Annette, Annette what is it?!"

His voice is not that of the firm General, but of sweetness and softness.
The voice of my lover, Aaron.
His voice full of concern.

"Your brother, you must write to your brother immediately!"

"Why, what is it?!"

He asks, his voice growing more and more concerned.

"Death."

I answer simply.

"Death for us all."

MEANWHILE IN THE HUMAN REALM

THE GRAND SPIRAL

DARK WORDS

KALEB

I am doing the same walk I have done thousands of times.
The walk to him, to Tristan.

He has been confined now for several weeks, and surely it must be coming to a close.
And yet, I am not entirely sure if that is a good thing or not.
I hate myself for even thinking it, but a small part of me thinks perhaps this confinement is a good thing…
God, I really do hate myself.

Tristan is my everything, the love of my life.

But, despite that, I am not completely blind.
Perhaps I had been blind before, for many years, but recently, well let's just say I am seeing clearer.

Tristan is becoming… **Not himself.**

I've always known he is passionate.
He wants change.

He wants to end a great deal of things, especially that of the continued Cleansing.

Not only that, but to rid the Realm of Claudius and even his own brother, Theodore.

He wants to do too much.

And he is going about it the wrong way, completely the wrong way.

And the Great Cleansing, that is something that cannot be changed anytime soon, and even less so overnight.

It is centuries of prejudice and hate, only these last three years has it been legally able to do so.

I do not see people getting over their fear and hate of witchcraft, less so the Lords and Ladies of the Realm.

Too many are scared of Claudius.

But then again, it seems as if that is what Tristan wants.

He wants to end the persecution of witches, but it doesn't seem possible.

Not just one man.

A young man at that.

It will lead to chaos.

And then ending Claudius and Theodore, that will cause even more chaos.

We are already at war for Light's sake, the evil Witch Queen and her hordes of demons forever threatening to plunge what's left of humanity into eternal darkness.

And now Tristan wants to cause civil war…

I love him, more than anyone, more than anything, but I am less blind now, and I am seeing danger coming.

Incredible, awful danger.
Destruction and death.

War has nearly destroyed humanity as it is, civil war will surely destroy it completely.

And yet my love does not seem to notice this, he thinks as if everything will simply work out and he will rise to the top, unharmed and unscathed.

He is folly in this thought.
I know war, I have seen it first-hand.
I have been there, on the frontlines.

It was last year.
I could not disobey my father forever, despite the fact I wanted to stay with Tristan, I couldn't do so indefinitely.

So, away I went.

When I arrived, my father had beamed proudly, although I got a rather cold reception from the Imperial Soldiers.
I suppose because I had disobeyed my father, who they worshipped.
But my father was kind and happy, unusually so.
Despite the fact that my mother mentioned that three years ago if I had gone my father was going to try and talk me out of my newly Syndicate Initiation.
However, upon my arrival last year, he did not utter a word about it.
Perhaps he changed his mind, if only he could tell that to mother.

I still can't get over the words she said… **Marriage.**

Did she not understand that there is only one person I would ever want.

And it's certainly not some girl.

Shuddering, I think back to my father, and think perhaps he did mean to persuade me to forgo my oath as a Slayer of the Syndicate last year and take on the rightful Lordship of House Umpire.
Yet he made no actual mention of it whilst there, perhaps because I only stayed for three weeks.
And during those three weeks, I fought on that battlefield.
I faced vampires and Dark Witches, and I killed them alike.
There's nothing like being on an actual battlefield.
I had trained hard in the Imperium courtyard and in the Syndicate, yet that was nothing to reality.
When on that field, you're always a half second away from death at any point.
I had nearly lost my life and limbs several times.
I had slain monsters, and earned respect, and my father had told me that night he wanted to ask me something… I suppose looking back at it now, I suppose that was the night he was going to ask me to forgo being a Slayer and become a Lord.
But I never met him that night, instead I left.
Three weeks, that's all I could take, all I could suffer without Tristan.
I had snuck out from the camp like a thief in the night, taking my horse and riding hard and fast away.
As a Slayer, I was not stopped by the Protectors or any of the patrols, I rode straight away from the frontlines and camp and through the Black Woods, escaping with ease and returning to the Human Realm.

It took me a couple weeks to get back, I had made it back in less than half the usual time, and in doing so very nearly killed my beloved horse.

But I just had to get away.

I just had to get to Tristan.

I knew that word had gotten out of my betrayal, of my leaving the battlefield.

I surely and knowingly lost all respect I had gained from the Imperial Soldiers.

And I had without a doubt lost the respect of my father.

And very most likely, also his love.

But I had arrived at the Capital.

I rode hard and fast through there too, evading anyone who sought me out, no doubt fellow Slayers who were commanded so by my uncle, or the Imperial Guard.

I evaded them all and went straight over the Grand Bridge.

I got to the Island, and up to the Imperium, jumping off my horse in the castle courtyard and rushing straight to Tristan's tower…

I arrived panting hard and sweaty, yet the second I saw Tristan I forgot about all that.

It all seemed worth it, we approached each other and made wild, beautiful love right there on the floor.

It had been glorious, and without lying, awfully quick.

Afterwards, I hurriedly left his tower and walked from the castle, getting away as quickly as possible.

I didn't want to be found near his tower, I knew people would put two and two together.

Yet found I was, and it did not stop the whispers.

I had been escorted to the Syndicate, and I could see it on everyone's faces, it ws as if they knew exactly why I left, who I went too, and what I did.

Whether it was genuine or extreme paranoia I could not say, but it certainly felt as if they all knew.

Surprisingly, my uncle forgave me, in front of hundreds present.

He shouldn't have.

He should have scolded me, or at least whipped me for my recklessness, or even exiled me from the Syndicate.

A small part of me even wanted him too, I think.

Being a Slayer is tremendously important to me… But Tristan even more so.

Yet my uncle did none of those things.
 He simply forgave me with open arms.

He had meant it out of kindness and love I suppose but he didn't realise that it set me up for hatred amongst the others.

Sure, there were some in the Syndicate I had befriended and gained loyalty from, but there were still many who detested me.

Especially the older members of the Syndicate, and more so the elder captains.

Yes, I gained that hatred.

And the whispers continued, and alas, I knew for a fact at least some people knew, and it would be foolish of me to think otherwise.

Me and Tristan constantly danced on the cusp of the pyre.

We had danced so close for years now.
Slowly but surely getting closer to the flames.

No!
No matter what happened, I would not let Tristan burn.

BUT WHAT ABOUT YOURSELF?
WILL YOU LET YOURSELF BURN?

If I had to… Then yes.
I will burn for him.

But I already knew that.
I had known it for years.
I would do anything for him, absolutely anything.

BUT YOU HAVE ALREADY SACRIFICED SO MUCH!
YOU DISOBEYED YOUR FATHER FOR TWO YEARS!
YOU LEFT A BATTLEFIELD AND SNUCK AWAY LIKE A THIEF!
YOU DISGRACED YOURSELF!
YOU DISGRACED YOURSELF IN THE EYES OF YOUR
FATHER!
THE IMPERIAL SOLDIERS!
AND EVEN YOUR FELLOW SLAYERS!
WHY DO YOU KEEP SACRIFICING?

It does not matter, I love him.
When you love someone, you do anything for them.
Anything to keep them safe.

BUT WHAT ABOUT THAT VERY FIRST SACRIFICE?
THE ONE HE DOES NOT EVEN KNOW ABOUT?
THEN AGAIN, WAS IT A SACRIFICE?
OR WAS IT FEAR?

No, it had not been fear, I had fought bravely last year.

Three years ago, I battled and slew a feral.
I had no fear then, either.

No, I would not think on that.

After all, I am an Umpire.
The son of a General.
Nephew of the Lord Commander.
I come from a long line of warriors.
Descended even from the Imperial line itself.
I have no fear.

The only fear I have is for Tristan.
Fear of losing him.
His death.

No, no I am not losing him.

Am I?

He is changing…

Becoming, not himself, and yet, I am not losing him.

I will not, I will do anything to stop that.

YOU HAVE SACRIFICED SO MUCH!
THEREFORE, YOU WILL CLING TO HIM!
A LIFE SUPPORT IN A VIOLENT SEA!
YET IT WILL NOT SAVE YOU!
NOT REALLY.

Enough!

COME ON, ADMIT WHAT THE FIRST SACRIFICE WAS!
WHAT IT STILL IS…

No, I chose this life.

I chose it.

Me!

No one else.

It was not a sacrifice.

BUT YOU WERE MEANT TO FOLLOW IN YOUR FATHER'S
FOOTSTEPS.
YOU WERE MEANT TO BE THE NEXT LORD OF HOUSE OF
UMPIRE.
TO FIND A WIFE AND SIRE CHILDREN.
YOU WERE MEANT TO BE IN THE RANKS OF THE IMPERIAL
ARMY.
YOU WERE SUPPOSED TO SUCCEED YOUR FATHER AS
GENERAL.
AND WITH HIM GONE, HIS PLACE ON THE COUNCIL.

But instead… Instead, I gave it all up.

I went to my uncle and begged to become an Initiate of the Syndicate.

And my uncle, thank the Eternal Light, he let me do so.

Despite the fact I had not slain a vampire.

He broke three centuries of rules and let me become one of them.

And in doing so, of course earned the ire or many.

But I did it.

I gave up my lordship and titles.

Any wealth or land.

Gave up the chance of a wife and children.

AND WHY DID YOU DO IT?

WHY DID YOU GIVE IT ALL UP?

I said enough!

It was my choice, always my choice.

AND YOU MADE IT FOR HIM…

YOU BECAME A SLAYER ONLY BECAUSE YOU THOUGHT IT WOULD MEAN YOU COULD STAY AT THE IMPERIUM WITH TRISTAN.

YOU KNEW YOUR UNCLE WOULD WANT TO KEEP YOU CLOSE.

YOU KNEW EXACTLY WHAT YOU WERE DOING…

It need not matter now.

I made my choice, and I have to live with that.

These last weeks had been hellish, ever since that execution.

It was foolish of course, to execute those people in front of thousands of onlookers.

The execution should have been done privately, like usual, done in the castle courtyard, but instead Claudius made it a spectacle.

No doubt with the upcoming coronation, Claudius could feel his power slipping, so he wanted to show a force of power.

Foolish really, Claudius has no choice but to give up what power he has, once Theodore is coronated, it will be him who holds all the power.

A scary thought indeed, Theodore as king…

He is nothing but a bully.
Him and his vile friends constantly preying on girls, beating and raping them as they see fit.
And who can stop them?

And they want to give that sort of man a throne and a crown, and give him unlimited power?
It does not feel right, but then again, it does not feel right to try and supplant him either.

By all rights of laws and men Theodore is naturally the successor.
He comes from an unbroken line, father to son, a line that hasn't been broken in three centuries, and now, now that might change…

Tristan wants to be King; he wants to take the throne and crown.

Yet, he has no right to it, not unless Theodore dies of course…

But would Tristan really go that far?

The brothers never got along, hated each other in fact, but would Tristan really kill him?
And Theodore, would Theodore kill Tristan?
Honestly, despite his cruelties, I doubt he would actually harm Tristan.

But Tristan… Tristan can get… Emotional.
These emotions can cause plenty of controversy.
Always shouting his opinions, in places he should not be.
And calling out to the crowd, directly challenging Claudius and
Theodore and even the succession, to ask the public what they think…
That does not bode well either.

These thoughts get pushed aside as a servant approaches.
The same servant boy I had told I would practise sword craft with on
the morning of the execution.
Due to everything that's happened, I haven't had the chance.
I feel a pang of guilt as he sullenly passes me a note.

"I'm sorry I haven't been able to train you.
There has been a lot going on lately.
But I promise, I'll come find you when the dust has settled."

The boy seems to seem less upset as I say this, in fact, he starts to look
happy.
He gives me a half smile before walking off.

I then open the note, it reads as follows.

NEPHEW,
COME TO THE GRAND SPIRAL AT ONCE.
YOU ARE NEEDED.

Sighing deeply, I debate whether to actually go.
I have gone to Tristan every single night since his confinement, always
at the same time, and yet I cannot so outwardly disobey my uncle.

Sighing deeply once more, I turn and instead make my way to the Grand Spiral.

Sometime later, having crossed the Grand Drawbridge and making my way through the Capital, I venture into the Grand Spiral.
It had taken me over an hour, since receiving that blasted note to get here.

As I reach the Hallway of Commanders, I look with pride and wonder before me.
It is a hallway I have walked plenty of times.
And yet, I still love walking through it each and every time.
It contains a portrait of each and every Lord Commander to have had the position over these last three centuries.
Some of the greatest and worst men graced these hallways.
Many of the portraits were of young men, for the life of a Slayer was never long, especially when a Lord Commander such as those of the past went to the frontlines themselves.
The hallway comes to a close.
I look and see a portrait of my uncle, albeit a younger version painted in his own portrait.
In front of me, two guards, fellow brothers.
They are fully armed and armoured and stand there with great pride and duty.
Neither gives me a look of joy upon seeing me, yet they open the door regardless.

I ignore the looks on their faces, I care not if they like me.

MAYBE YOU SHOULD, IF YOU ARE TO BE THE NEXT LORD COMMANDER!
THEN YOU NEED THEM TO LIKE YOU!
TO RESPECT YOU!
TO WANT TO FOLLOW YOU!

This is true, I suppose.

And yet, I cannot do much in the ways of getting them to like me.
Becoming an Initiate without having slain a vampire was one thing,
but also having left the battlefield like I did, running away…
And then to not even be punished, yes, I lost much respect.

Respect I would need to win, and yet, I am not sure how.
Besides, it's doubtful I will be going back to the frontlines anytime
soon, or ever.
No, I will stay here.
I have to stay here.
With the threat of Tristan wanting to alter the succession and even kill
there is every chance of a civil war looming.
I have every hope that Tristan is just angry, that he will see sense and
calm his thoughts.
Tristan is still an Imperial after all.
He could take a seat on the Council and try to make a positive change
by being a great advisor and Lord.
He could have power and influence, money and lands.
He could live comfortably.

We could both stay here, safe.
In love.
Grow old together even.

And Tristan could slowly but surely make these great changes that he
wants to make, with time.
And if the current Council get replaced with even more likeminded
people, then perhaps the Cleansing of witches and all the rest will cease
to exist.

It only takes time; I just wish Tristan would see this.
Be happy and content with his position as a second son, happy and content being a Councillor and Lord, to be happy and content with me.

Arriving at the room I see my uncle, naturally standing at the round table, along with several other Captains.
They are huddled over the table, looking at various maps.

My uncle sees me, as do the others, they all stop talking immediately.
Most of the captains look at me as if bored by my mere presence, which is nothing unusual.
But my uncle smiles warmly and greets me ever warmer.

"Laddie, how are you?"

He says cheerfully.

"I'm good, uncle.
And yourself?"

"Well, not really.
Come take a look."

He gestures to the table.

I walk over and the other captains shuffle aside.
I see the maps laid out on the table, mainly ones concerning the stretch of land known as the Realm of Magic.

"New news from the war?"

I ponder.

"Yes, and no."

My uncle replies.

Confusing.

"Tell me more."

I enquire.

My uncle points to the maps, his finger settling on the edge of the
Black Forest, near cliffs and coasts.

"Here, there is a village.
As you know there are many villages throughout the Black Woods, but
this one was mainly hidden away.
On the rim of the country, near the cliffs and coast.
It happened a couple weeks back now, but we only just found out about
it."

The village itself wasn't actually on the map, it was just drawings of
trees next to cliffs and the sea.
In fact, a lot of the villages in the Black Forest are undocumented and
unknown, many in the Realm of Magic are.
Witches are known to be bohemian and even nomads, they prefer
nature and like to live quiet, simple lives.
In fact, there is only one city in the Realm Of Magic, and that is the
famous City of Bridges.
Then again, it is not a city in the usual regard.
No high walls or stone, instead they use trees as wooded gates, and
they have many wooden constructions build into the trees themselves,
with thousands of bridges intertwined with each other, all leading to
various parts.

They live off the land, and worship balance.
Magic is practised and they Cast there regularly.
 It is the Realm of Magic after all.
I had ridden through it last year; it was truly a different world entirely despite being part of the same country which we all live on.
I only caught glimpses, focused on what lies ahead, but what I did see was amazing, and terrifying.
The things they could do, both of beauty and destruction.

Tristan would love it there, I realise.

He is a witch, after all.
If only he could be around his own people, perhaps he would flourish and be happy.

I attempt to think upon it further when my uncle speaks.

"This village was massacred.
Every single man, woman and child was slaughtered."

He says gruffly.

I stare at the map and pray for the lost souls.

"How did it happen?"

 I ask.

I realise then that the room goes deathly silent, all the fellow captains share looks of uncertainty.

"What's the matter,"

I question.

My uncle folds his arms across his chest and huffs.

"It appears as if the captains are on disagreement."

He speaks.

"They all think different things."

He finishes.

I look around the table at the captains, it seems none want to speak, or even want to meet my gaze for that matter.

"Well, tell the laddie."

My uncle beckons.

A Captain clears his throat, Captain Matthew.
A good yet ageing man, and one of those who doesn't actually hate me.
Not outwardly, anyways.

He answers as follows.

"The inhabitants of this village were not simply slaughtered by sword; they were ripped apart.
Even though most of the village was destroyed by flames, we were told that of what did remain of some of the bodies many had missing limbs and heads.
Not to mention blood everywhere.

It's clear that the only thing that could commit such a monstrosity are vampires."

He speaks clearly.

My brow furrows at this, for this did not seem good.

A massacre done by vampires in the Realm of Magic… That was certainly not good.
How, and more so, why?

"But could vampires get past the Protectors?"

I question.

The Protectors being the name for the faction of their warriors.
A mix of Casters and Non-Casters alike.
All of whom called the Black Woods home.

They had routine patrols and some of the best and finest witches in their ranks, they actively kept the Realm of Magic safe and secure.
They kept vampires and Dark Witches at bay from the east, and these last three years humans to the west.
Yes, they were isolated and surrounded on both sides, yet their Protectors and ability for Casting Chaos was legendary, and there was little doubt that a group vampires could so easily wander through that Realm.
Sure, one or two can slip past perhaps and go unnoticed. . . But a massacre like this would usually mean a group.

"I say it's a trick."

Declares Captain Griffin.

A Captain who unlike Matthew, does outwardly hate me.
A stocky fellow.

"How so?"

I ask.

"This will be good,"

I hear my uncle say in the background.

"Well, isn't it obvious?
The witches are in league with the vampires."

He announces proudly.

"The witches have been in league with the vampires for centuries, we all know that already, ya daft bastard."

Speaks Captain Matthew

I decide I like him.

"Aye, Dark Witches, Matthew, but don't you see, they are all dark witches!"

He shouts the last part.

This leads to bickering between the captains and even some laughter.
Both in agreement and disagreement.
My uncle does not look happy, not one bit.

"Laugh all you want!"

He shouts again.

"But they are all wretched, vile, soulless, abominations!"

He shouts again.

This angers me.
Angers me greatly.
There were many good people who were witches.

And Tristan, my love… He is a witch.

And he is not wretched or vile or soulless, and he certainly is not an abomination.

"I think you should watch what you say."

I say strongly, my glare pointed at Captain Griffin.

His eyes widen, offended that I have even spoken, and also spoken to him in such a way.

"How dare you tell me that I should watch what I say!"

He seethes.

"I'm twice your age, BOY, and I can say what I damn well want!"

I stand up straight then, easily towering over him and every other man in the room.

"As a Slayer of the Syndicate you should know that all of us are barred from taking part in the Great Cleansing, as set forth by my uncle. Therefore, your thoughts are not warranted, they only add to the prejudice and fear these people already go through."

The men mutter in agreement, and my uncle looks proud.
I have spoken well, it seems.

He stutters at this, then collects himself.

"The law stops us from joining the Cleansing and killing them on sight, however it does not stop us from having our own thoughts.
I am a free man, a Captain of the Syndicate, my thoughts are my own and I can share them how I see fit."

He spits.

I ignore him, turning to the rest.

"Look here."

I point back to the part of the map where the village supposedly is.

"This is some ways away from the frontlines, they would have had to sneak through, keeping to the edges of the Realm.
And this village, it's miles and miles away from the frontlines, it's halfway through the Black Forest and just next to the cliff sides."

I tell them.

They listen and look intently.

"Whilst vampires have snuck past before, they usually attack whatever nearby village or people they can.
Or they simply hide and skulk around, causing mischief.
Yet this is no simple skulking nor mischief.
And there was no such attack between the frontlines and this village, therefore they must have been keeping low, trying not to draw attention.
And if they're trying not to draw attention, then clearly, they are up to something.
They must be on a mission, but I do not know what that might be."

 I conclude.

The captains all look at each other, their faces full of concern.

Captain Griffin scoffs at this.

"Preposterous, what mission could they possibly have?!
And if they were trying to stay low, why massacre a village?
If you ask me, this is a trap, those damned witches mean to lure us there and kill us too."

He rambles.

Everyone, including my uncle looks to me.

I keep standing tall, unafraid to back down to this idiotic, prejudiced fool.

"Do you not know of our histories, Captain?
Anytime vampires have snuck across the Borders it has always caused trouble.
Trouble and death.

Usually, when they do come here, it's because they mean to kill an Imperial.
The Witch Queen has done it for centuries, every so often knocking off an Imperial member.
Forever playing a game with them.
It was twenty-one years ago she almost completely wiped them out.
Do you not remember?"

I ask firmly.

He looks shocked, looking to the other Captains and my uncle for help, and yet he does not receive it.

I decide to press on.

"And only three years ago a vampire even got to Imperium Island, and almost killed Prince Tristan."

 I add.

"So, therefore, Captain, knowing what we know about our past, we know that any time those Red Eyed demons sneak across the Borders, across the Realms, it means trouble and death.
And with Theodore's upcoming coronation, it makes perfect sense why they would strike now."

The men all look at me, hanging onto my every word.

"Men, I believe the Witch Queen has plans to assassinate the Crown Prince, Theodore."

I am certain they mean to ruin the coronation.
What other reason would they be here for?

Captain Griffin then speaks up again.

"You've said it yourself.
It's the WITCH QUEEN who plots.
A dark and evil bitch, and all those who Cast are equally dangerous!"

The room erupts into loud, harsh talking, which leads to arguments.
All of them are shocked, all of them agree with me it seems, even Captain Griffin must know I am right, a look of resignation in his face.

My Uncle shouts, commanding silence.

"My nephew has spoken well and spoken truthfully.
My brother has sent warning, and my nephew has spoken sense.
Therefore, tomorrow at the Council Meeting, I shall be going to the Imperium, and I will make myself known and speak what I have learned, what I have been told from my brother.
I have already sent a letter to Claudius and the rest of the council."

He declares.

This shocks me.

Uncle had received a raven from father?
Not even me or mother or even little Violet have received one for months.
And now he sends one to uncle about a village.

Whilst I know the importance of vampires secretly travelling across Realms, and whilst I felt immense pity for those who were butchered, I cannot however shake the anger I feel at not having received a letter from my own Lord Father.

Setting aside my anger, I speak up.

"Uncle, fellow Captains, we must be on high alert.
The Imperial Dynasty is of the upmost importance, we cannot allow one of them to be assassinated under our watch."

The men all mutter in agreement, all but Captain Griffin.

"It is our Oath to not partake in the Realms of men, I say apart from warning the Council, we do not need to do anything."

This angers everyone, and this time my uncle speaks up.

"You may have anger for my nephew, but do not let that cloud your judgement.
Whilst it is true that we are not to interfere in the business of men, we do however have a responsibility to protect the Realm against vampires.
Is has been our duty for three centuries, and it continues to be so."

"And now our duty appears to be risking our lives to save the Imperial Dynasty."

Captain Griffin seethes back.

"How dare you speak like this; do you want harm to befall the Imperial House?"

536

I ask angrily.

"Well, Kaleb… Not all of us Slayers have such personal relationships with the Imperial Family."

My body goes rigid at the mere mention of this, and for a brief moment, the entire room is silent.

Until I throw a chair aside and lunge for Captain Griffin.

Despite my quickness, I do not reach him.
The other captains quickly grab hold of me, restraining me.
They shout words to calm me down, but all I feel is anger.

How dare he say that, and so callously.
To question that I have a personal relationship with…

BUT IT IS TRUE, IS IT NOT?
DO YOU REGULARLY NOT FUCK THE PRINCE?
HAVE YOU NOT SACRIFICED SO MUCH FOR YOUR LOVE FOR HIM?
AND RIGHT NOW, YOU EMBARRASS YOURSELF WITH YOU'RE ANGER!
AND IN DOING SO, YOU ONLY CONFIRM THE TRUTH!

The fellow Captains continue to restrain me, whilst Captain Griffin simply smiles.

God be damned, I have only confirmed his suspicions, everyone's suspicions.
I try to calm myself, I stand still, and stop fighting against the restraint.
The captains slowly but surely let me go, and the room is full of tension for a moment.

My uncle looks disappointed.
Incredibly so.

"LEAVE US!
 RIGHT NOW."

He commands, his voice gravely solemn.

I know in that moment I have fucked up.
Fucked up monumentally.

I had spoken well, gained their attention and even perhaps their respect, if only for the briefest of fleeting moments.

And then Captain Griffin said one off-hand comment and I flew off the handle.

ONCE AGAIN, YOU DISHONOUR YOURSELF!
AND IT IS ALL FOR HIM...

The captains all quickly leave the Lord Commanders chamber, they all give me various looks as they depart, with Captain Griffin smiling broadly.

I want to smash his face against the floor until it's nothing but a bloody pulp.

Yet I hold myself as best I can.

SUCH ANGER!
SUCH FEROCITY!
UNLEASH YOUR FURY!

No, not now.

But maybe later.

It is a dark thought.

One that I should not have, and yet I do.
I feel shame, and quickly push the dark thought aside.

That's not the man I want to be.

BUT IT MAY BE THE MAN YOU END UP BECOMING…

I push that aside too as I hear the captains all take their leave, and the doors close behind us.

It is now just me and my uncle.

But by the look on his face, he is not going to be my uncle right now, but the Lord Commander.

"What was that, laddie?!
You make a spectacle of yourself, once again!"

He says, angrily.

The fact that he says **'once again'** hurts.

"Uncle."

 I try to speak.

"DO NOT UNCLE ME!"

He bellows.

He however conforms himself, before sighing deeply.

"I thought… I thought that once you would do good.
You have so many good qualities, Kaleb… But that anger of yours…
To actually try to attack another Captain, and in front of the others!
In front of me!"

"You heard what he said,"

I try to intervene.

"So what if he made an offhand comment!
You be a man and ignore it!
Besides, why be angry if there's no truth to it?"

He finishes.

I hang my head then.

I can feel him staring at me.
His eyes bore into me, feeling sharp as a sword.

"Look at me, laddie."

He asks.

I look up from the floor and meet his gaze, which is intensifying by the second.
He takes steps towards me, until his face is directly in front of mine, albeit shorter.

"There is not any truth in it… Is there, laddie?"

He says sternly.

I completely freeze.
Never, not once in my entire life had my uncle ever asked me this.
I have absolutely no idea how to respond.
I also can't believe it.
Surely, I must be dreaming, this cannot be real.
But yet here we are, with him right in front of me, asking me the question.

HE KNOWS!
KNOWS ABOUT YOU!
WHAT YOU DO!
HOW YOU DISHONOUR YOURSELF!
AND WITH THE PRINCE, NO LESS!
YOU BRING SHAME TO THE HOUSE OF UMPIRE!
TO THE SYNDICATE!
TO THE IMPERIAL FAMILY!

"I asked you a question, laddie.
Is there any truth to it?"

He says, even more sternly.

"N – No."

I stammer, more of a mere mumble really.

LIES!

I regret it instantly; I wish I had been honest.

I am supposed to be a warrior, brave and proud.

Yet when the moment finally comes, when my uncle asks me, I fold and lie.

I am ashamed.

Of myself, always of myself.

YES, SUCH DEEP SHAME!
YOU HAVE SHAMED YOURSELF!
YOUR FATHER, YOUR FAMILY!
YOU SHAME EVERYONE!

My uncle continues to stare at me, as if by looking at me I will somehow change my answer.

But I am resolute in my decision.

Whilst I love my uncle, and whilst I know he may forgive me for my past transgressions, he surely would not forgive this.

It would be impossible for him to.

Nor I doubt understand it.
Many can't understand it.

Whilst the Slayer Syndicate disallows marriage or children, there are many loopholes to this.

For instance, there have been times when a person who has slain a vampire has been offered a role in the Syndicate, and they may already be married and have begotten children, and therefore they are allowed to continue their marriage and roles of a parent.

Many of them return to their village, town or city and keep stationed there, protecting that area.

It also does not exclude love, many in the Syndicate have known love.

In the past, the present and no doubt the future.

Many Slayers have lovers.

And many even once joining the Syndicate marry in secret and have secret children.

However, I am no ordinary Slayer.

I am Kaleb Umpire, supposed next to be Lord Commander, and I am in love with him.

Not just with anyone.

No, I could not have fallen in love with a commoner or even some small Lord, no I went and fell in love with none other than Tristan.

A Prince of the Imperial Dynasty.

And a Prince that wants to tear the Human Realm apart to build it all over again…

And he wants my help to do it.

Tristan dances closer and closer to the flames.

And it seems that I must be the one to save him.

I look my uncle hard in the eye, clear my throat and say strongly

"NO."

"Hmph."

Is his reply

He runs over his cropped black hair, then turns to me.

"I have done what I can, to try and turn you into a man, but you do not make it easy, laddie.

From your choice to join the Syndicate in the first place, the ire it caused from your father.

But you begged and begged, so against my better thinking I made you an Initiate, much to the ire of the fellow Captains and any other Slayer or Initiate who has graced these halls and earned their right through slaying a vampire.”

“But I did slay a vampire.”

I argue.

“YOU KILLED ONE AFTER I MADE YOU AN INITIATE, AND NOT EVEN WHEN YOU BLOODY THINK.”

My uncle starts to shout but stops himself there, as if he shouldn’t have said that.

But he did say that.

What does he mean?
I never killed a vampire when I think I did?!

“Uncle, I slew my first vampire protecting Prince Tristan, only weeks after you made me an Initiate, and only days before I was going to be sent to the frontlines, where I would surely have killed one then too, had I gone.”

I answer.

My uncle sighs deeply, running his hand through his hair once again.

“Uncle, what do you mean I never slew a vampire when I think?”

My uncle looks away, continually running hand his through his hair.

“UNCLE!”

I shout.

He turns to me then, his eye squinting at me angrily.

"Watch your tone laddie, we may be blood but I am your Lord Commander and you will show me respect."

I take several steps towards him.

"Then respectfully tell me what you meant, I have the right to know, SIR,"

 I emphasis the last part.

Calling my uncle **'sir'** has hurt him, I can see that.

"I cannot,"

He tells me.

He looks to the maps then, staring intently.

He cannot tell me?
He blurts out that I didn't kill a vampire when I thought I did, and his answer it only that he cannot tell me?!

HE KNOWS SOMETHING!
THE TRUTH!
OF WHAT HAPPENED THAT DAY...
HE MUST DO!

"With all due respect, that is not good enough."

I state harshly.

He looks up to me then, with anger in his eye… But also, a modicum of love.

"I'm not telling you for your own good, trust me, laddie."

"I am a man grown.
Let me decide what is for my own good,"
 I tell him.

He waves his hand at me, exasperated, as if he wants me to go away.

I will however not simply walk off.

"Uncle, I'm not leaving until you tell me the truth."

 I demand.

He turns back to me then, and huffs loudly.

"Fine, you want to know, I'll tell you, but you won't like this, laddie.
Not one bit."

I cross my arms and wait for him to speak.

He sighs loudly.

"Fine, fine…"

He gives him a moment to compose himself.

"That night, or shall we say early hours, I was here.
Standing right in this room, reading actually.
I cannot remember what, but that does not matter.

I heard the bells, you see, coming from Imperium Island.

Then the bells started to ring here too, in the Capital.

Anyways, I immediately went about asking what was going on, and such, and I even asked as to your whereabouts.

Being stuck here I could not do much, besides the Imperium at the time was better defended then, by better men, before the Imperial Guard and Soldiers fell into decay.

Or so I thought…

Before a lot of things…"

He trails off.

"Eventually, in the early hours, news came, and it was grave.

An assassination attempt on the prince, that he was gravely injured.

And you… You too were gravely injured.

Naturally, I rode hard to the Grand Bridge, along with a guard of other Slayers.

However, when I reached the Capital side of the Grand Bridge, I found it closed.

The Imperium Island was entirely closed off.

I tried several times to persuade the guards to stand aside, that they had no authority."

"But they would have been Imperial Guards at the Grand Bridge, and they do have right to close the Grand Bridge if it comes from the Council or the old King."

"Yet, they weren't Imperial Guard."

My uncle tells me.

"What do you mean, they weren't Imperial Guard?"

"They were dressed like Imperial Guard, and I suppose they were Imperial Guard, but… Well, they had small pins on them."

"Pins?"

I repeat, confused.

"Yes, they had tried to conceal it with cloaks, and yet, the wind was heavy, and it blew them aside and that's when I saw it.
Now the Imperial Guard, much like us have a strict dress code.
Simple tunics and silver armour.
They had these pins, you see."

"But the Imperial Guard have always wore pins on their tunics or cloaks.
It's on their armour too."

My uncle rubs his temples, exasperating loudly.

"If only I had known then, if only I had taken more interest in it…
 Perhaps I could have prevented things."

My uncle continues to stare at the maps.

Prevented what?

THIS IS VERY INTERESTING!
INTERESTING INDEED…

"Uncle, what in the name of Light are you on about?!"

He chuckles then.

"The pins… It's exactly the same as all the rest.

They are everywhere… On signs and sigils, on tapestries and books.”

I'm as confused as ever; my uncle makes no sense.

“Don't you see, laddie?
The pins, they were a white sun… With a sword through it.”

“But the Imperial Guard, their pins they wear are orange suns, with a gold crown circled around it.
The same as on the breastplate of their armour and on their tunics.”

 I profess.

“Yes, indeed they do… I thought perhaps it was some sort of new pin, some sort of new accessory I did not yet know of, I did not expect the worst.
I should have fought, I should have pulled my sword and run them through.
I should have charged the entire Syndicate into the Imperium… I could have stopped it all.”

Charging the Syndicate into the Imperium?!

That would have been unprecedented, and would have surely sparked a war…
After all, we have no say in the matters of the Realm.
We are Slayers, we slay monsters and guard the Realm of men, but we take no matters in the goings on.
We have no say in courts, trials or whatever the lords, ladies and Imperial Family get up too.
We only protect and slay.
A man as honourable as my uncle, as responsible to himself and his duty, he would not march on the Capital for no reason.

"Uncle, just spit it out, you are speaking in riddles and nonsense."

"I already told you, laddie.
White suns… With a sword… Think…"

That's when it dawns on me.

He already told me a second ago, but I had been too confused to realise.
Now he has repeated it… And I feel terror rung up my spine.

My uncle was true, you do see it everywhere.

Especially on the tunics, armour and cloaks and their little pins… And newly made on Temples.

I can't even think it, it makes me sick.
The white sun… That has only ever appeared on Temples and on the clothing of Holy Men, for three centuries.
Until… Until three years ago, when that damned sword got added.

And that had never been seen before, not since The Great Cleansing began.
Not since the old king made his decree and Claudius enforced it, spreading terror through the land.
But… The attack on me and Tristan, that was a few days before the King died, and the Cleansing which began the very next day after that…"

So how did my uncle see these pins mere hours after the attack on Tristan and me.

"Uncle, you must be mistaken… The white sun, with the sword… That did not appear until the beginning of the."

"The Great Cleansing."

My uncle finishes grimly.

I step back, my mind a swirl with thoughts.

HOW COULD THAT BLASTED WHITE SUN WITH IT'S BLASTED SWORD BE SEEN BEFORE THE CLEANSING BEGAN?!
IT MADE NO SENSE…

"Are you saying that… That the Defenders already existed before the Cleansing?
Before the assassination attempt?"

My uncle sits down in a chair then, once again running his hand through his short black hair.

"Aye, laddie, it would appear so."

He looks to me then, and talks.

"I should have seen it; I should have done something…
Even after the attack, the entire time the Island was on lockdown…
With you there, injured…
I should have stormed the damned Grand Bridge…"

"That could have caused a civil war, uncle.
You would have been seen as attacking the Imperial Dynasty itself.
Imperial Guard and Slayers fighting, it would have been madness."

"Madness,"

He repeats with another chuckle.

"This land is already full of madness, it's everywhere.
Aye, perhaps marching wouldn't have been the best thing, perhaps it may have even been seen as treason, but if I had done it… I could have nipped it all in the bud.
The Cleansing, and Claudius' takeover…
But then again, perhaps I couldn't have done anything."

He pauses then and takes a sip of wine from a nearby glass.

"Claudius has always been a snake…
I've never liked him, not in all the years I've known him.
And that's been many years.
He has always been controversial, always highly opinionated and offensive.
So full of anger and hate.
And all directed straight at witches.
He barely gives a damn about vampires, but witches…
The mere mention drives him mad with fury.
He started from humble beginnings you know, some small village somewhere.
A simple Holy man at first, yet always with these thoughts and opinions and hate.
He made his way to the Capital and came under the tutelage of the old High Pope.
The old Pope was a good man, a kind man, who never had hate for anyone.
He knew that witches were hated and feared, yet he encouraged their presence, tried to make good between men and witches.
He simply wanted peace…

Something not many High Popes have been known for.

But he was different, and many disliked it.

As you know, witches have always been hated, hunted and murdered.

But it was always kept under control.

That is until Claudius came along.

I remember it, he would stand in the Grand Square preaching his vile opinions.

And there was nothing I could do.

Just stand there and watch as he gained bigger and bigger crowds.

Men, women and even children agreeing with him wholeheartedly.

They too shared their hate of witches, the fear of it.

The High Pope noticed this and sent Claudius away.

I had hoped by doing this, that would be the last I heard of Claudius.

But it wasn't…

Even after he was sent away, the crowds he had infected with his madness stayed…

And there were reports.

Claudius might had been sent away, but he was still preaching his fear and hate for years all across the Realm.

I should have realised…"

"Realised what, uncle?"

I press him.

"Realised that he had been growing an army of followers, and army that became none other then."

"THE DEFENDERS."

I finish.

"Yes."

He replies again grimly.

"And even some weeks before the attack, I had seen people around the Capital, men and even women wearing that damned pin.
I thought nothing of it, and I had even seen it on several Imperial Guards.
He had recruited armed guards for the sake of Light!
I should have paid more attention… It was staring at me for weeks!

"So… These Defenders, they already existed way before the assassination attempt?"

"Aye, they already existed, although they had not been named.
How do you think the Cleansing happened so easily, he had hundreds upon hundreds of recruits all throughout the Realm…
He had only needed to wait to strike and strike he did.
And don't you think it's odd that he was the one who found you and Tristan?
Did you know, there was a Slayer who went missing that night also."

"Missing?"

I question.

"Aye, a young lad, still a kid really.
The sad truth, I cannot even remember his name.
There are so many of us, after all.
The night of the attack, he went missing.
Nowhere to be found.
I always wondered what happened to him…"

He looks away into the distance then.

A missing Slayer was odd indeed… And on the same night of the attack.

Surely this cannot just be a coincidence.

"I never really saw it…

The Cleansing, I mean.

When I woke up, I was locked in a room.

For days, weeks, I could not say.

When I finally broke free, I was trapped within the Imperium.

But I could tell something was wrong, I could hear the screams and smell the smoke, even from the island."

I confess.

"Count yourself lucky, laddie.

I saw it…All of it.

It started in the dead of night, men from all over the Capital sprung up with swords.

They began breaking into homes, the homes of witches, they started murdering them.

Slaughtered in their beds, slaughtered in the streets…

Fire, fire everywhere.

Houses and buildings on fire, some people were even tied to makeshift pyres and simply set on fire.

I remember stepping into the Grand Square, sword in hand, I was going to stop it, to protect the witches from this senseless onslaught… But before I could, these men swarmed me.

Showed me papers, papers with the King's own seal, the wax fresh.

Thus, I could not help them.

I wanted too, Lord of Eternal Light I wanted too, but I could not.

But I knew, I knew right there that I or no one else of the Syndicate would take part, not under my rule.

So, I made my own decree, the Syndicate would take no part of the genocide.
No, I would do no such thing.
Of course, there were the rouge Slayers who disobeyed the orders, and they were swiftly dealt with.
I also made a secret decree, of course, as you know,"

"You told me you wrote to other captains of other Spires."

I speak.

"Aye, I told them to give sanctuary to any witch who seeks it.
I sent it to only trusted Captains, ones I knew that did not share hate in their hearts.
I'm only sad that I couldn't trust all my Captains of all the Spirals, then perhaps more would have been saved.
And I certainly couldn't give sanctuary to anyone here in the Capital, I could not seem to be taking sides.
But I tried, tried to help those throughout the Realm."

"I'm sure you saved plenty."

I speak to him, trying to offer what little comfort I can.

"Aye... but if only I had opened my eyes, seen the threat as it was happening, I could have stopped it.
I could have prevented so much death..."

DO HIS WORDS REMIND YOU OF ANYTHING...

No, why would it...

HE SAW A THREAT AND DID NOT STOP IT IN TIME!
HE LET CLAUDIUS AND HIS DEFENDERS TAKE OVER.

AND WHAT ABOUT TRISTAN…

What about Tristan…

*COME ON, SURELY YOU MORE THEN ANYONE CAN SEE THE
THREAT HE IS!
HE SPEAKS OF UNITY, BUT HE MEANS TO DESTROY!
TO RIP APART THE VERY SUCCESSION…
TO TAKE THE THRONE AND CROWN!
NO MATTER WHAT…*

No, Tristan isn't a threat…
Surely, he gets angry and says things…
Awful things, but he would not really act upon them…
No, no he wouldn't…

I'm sure of it.

NO, YOU ARE NOT…

Claudius will soon be over… He has to give up his power, Theodore
will be crowned.

Then again, if what my uncle says is true, and I wholly believe it is,
then I doubt he does mean to give up his power…
And if that's the case, then Tristan was right… Tristan kept saying all
these years how dangerous Claudius was… And all this time… I never
really listened…

Oh Tristan, forgive me.

"Why are you telling me all of this?"

I question my uncle.

"It has been three long years, why keep it a secret?
Why tell me now… Why keep it secret for so long."

"Because a threat is coming…
Vampires have crossed the Border, and Theodore's coronation is coming up.
It is perfect for an assassination…"

"You did not tell me all of this simply to alert me to an assassination attempt."

I say sharply.

"No, laddie…
That's because I fear there is another threat even closer, a threat that has been here all this time…
A threat that could destroy us all."

"Claudius has already destroyed."

I speak.

"Aye, laddie, he has…
But who said I was speaking of him?"

He mutters.

This takes me aback, if he does not mean Claudius who can he possibly mean?

"Then who?"

I question.

My uncle waves his hands again.

"That does not matter right now, it will soon be settled… It has to be,"

He stares blankly at the floor.

"Claudius is the threat, uncle, for the sake of Eternal Light he has an army of Defenders, they number in the tens of thousands, and that's just in the Capital alone!
Claudius means to destroy us all…
By God… He warned me, he warned me, and I didn't listen."

"Who warned you?"

My uncle asks.

"Nothing."

I reply.

My uncle stands then and takes strides towards me.

"Tell me.
Tell me now."

"I'll tell you, if you tell me who the threat is…
If not Claudius, then who?
Who could it possibly be, uncle?"

He looks away from me then, puffing hard.

“I told you, that will be sorted.
Claudius is not the problem.”

This confuses me greatly, how in the name of Light could Claudius not be the threat.
After everything he has done, and after everything my uncle has revealed to me…
How could he not be?

“But… Claudius,”

I repeat.

Fists are slammed on the table.

“LISTEN TO ME, LADDIE!
CLAUDIUS WILL BE DEALT WITH BUT HE IS NO THREAT!”

“His deception, his murder, his huge army!”

I argue.

“Claudius will be executed, his army disbanded.”
 My uncle speaks, nonchalant.

Executed?!
Disbanded?!

Surely my uncle does not think this will be that easy.

“And how do you plan on that happening?”

"Because I have plans to go to the council, firstly tomorrow to report this massacre."

He gestures back to the same point on the map.

"We must warn them of the threat, and that of Theodore's safety, which is of the upmost importance."

He concludes.

"And Claudius?
Do you mean to tell the Council about him?
About his treachery?
About his deception?
About growing a damned army right under our own noses! ..."

He goes to reply but I do not let him.

"This is simply history you have told me, everyone as old as me knows about Claudius upbringing and how he massed crowds of equally repugnant people.
How he was sent away and preached that repugnance around the Realm.
The Council knows all of this uncle and does not care."
They will do nothing, as they've done nothing for three years!"

"I also mean to speak to Theodore, once he is coronated, to tell him about Claudius, and about the King..."

"The King?"

 I say, even more confused.

"Oh, come on, laddie, you're not stupid.
Everything I've told you…
 The attack on you, on the prince, how the King made his decree and
then suddenly died…
A strong, healthy man, suddenly dies right before the genocide."

"Are you saying…
Are you saying that Claudius killed the King?"

 I say, shocked.

Although, the more I thought on it, the more it didn't shock me, the
more it made sense.

Real sense…

How could I have been so blind?

And how would Tristan take this news.
Any of it…

"But, if this is true, then how is Claudius still even breathing?"

"Because he's a snake that strikes hard, swift and does everything
correctly.
The attack on you, that was merely a diversion, so he could have the
Island locked down, and once that happened, he dripped his poison of
hate into the ear of the King.
A King as you know loved his children dearly, especially Tristan.
So, the King made that awful decree, a decree he surely never would
have made had I been there to speak reason and sense to him.
Sadly… Sadly I was not.

The decree went through, he then killed the King, and the Cleansing
began, and now we've had three years of fanatical hell."

"But Uncle, speaking to Theodore won't work.
Theodore simply does not care about anything.
You know him!
You know what he's like, all the rumours about him!
What he does to women!
And not just him, but he's best friends with Claudius son who equally
enjoys in terrorising women also.
You really expect him to be a good King?
You really think he will listen to you?
He also likes Claudius because Claudius turns a blind eye to all his
misdeeds.
If anything, he's Claudius pet, and he won't simply execute him,"

"He will.
He will have too.
Honour will demand it, for his father."

My uncle speaks.

"Honour?… Uncle, you are sorely mistaken, gravely mistaken.
Theodore, Theodore has no honour…"

"If I tell him of his father's death, and Claudius' role, he will have to
seek justice.
He is an Imperial, he will do what is right,"

"Theodore will do whatever makes Theodore happy.
You weren't there, at the castle during the lockdown… But I was.
And Theodore… Theodore could not care less about the King's death.

Isabella was crying her eyes out and Tristan, Tristan… He was still unconscious…"

A memory flashes into my mind.
A memory of the past, when finally, I had knocked down that damned door and ran to Tristan.
When the bells rang out for the King's death… I ran to Tristan.
I assumed he was dead, but he was unconscious when I found him.
I had never cried so hard before.
I refused to leave his bedside for the weeks he laid in bed.
And outside the Realm burned.
I cared not, only about him.
I even sent servants away.
I locked the doors, leaving only me and him.
I spoke to him despite his slumber.
Even bathed him.
And when he finally did wake… It was me who told him of his fathers' death.
Like I knew he would be, he was destroyed.
So angry, angry enough that he nearly created a fireball that blasted his tower apart.
Thankfully I stopped that, I held him tight and let him cry it out.

But Theodore… Theodore was neither sad nor angry.
In fact, the very opposite.

"Theodore, uncle… Theodore was ecstatic.
He cared not that his father was dead, he cared only about the crown.
In fact, I even heard him ask if he could wear it.
His father was not even dead and cold long, and he wanted to wear the crown.
It disgusted the Council, and they refused, due to his age of course, but also their disgust.

It was evident.
Do not go to Theodore, uncle, he will do nothing.”

“Then I see no way of bringing Claudius down.”

My uncle puffs.

But maybe I did.

Truthfully, Theodore would do nothing about his father's death, a death
he was overjoyed at.
No, he is not the Imperial you go to for justice…

But there is an Imperial who would…

   Tristan.

But would it be justice or more murder?

It went against all sense, and it was treasonous to suggest the change
of succession, but I saw it now…

Tristan had been right all along.

Claudius was a tyrant, and Theodore would be much the same.
No, if we wanted change, if we wanted justice and unity, then there
was only one person.

Tristan.

“There may be a way.”

 I suggest.

My uncle looks up, he is clearly deeply stressed.
And his eyes are dark, I wonder when he last properly slept.
He struggles to keep his eyes open.

"What do you mean."

He questions.

I debate whether I should even say anything, it is treasonous of course.
Extremely treasonous.
But it has to be said, did it not?"

"What about Tristan?"

 I blurt.

My uncle stands straight as an arrow at the mention of this, seeming to
be brighter and alert.

"NO."

He states.

Just one word, a name, and instantaneously, as soon as I mentioned it,
he seems incredibly angry.

"But uncle, Theodore is not the correct choice, whilst Tristan."

"NO."

He says again, sterner this time.

Why is he just saying no?

Tristan is clearly the better option, is he not?

"But uncle."

"But uncle, nothing!"

He replies.

"Tristan is the second son, he will not be King, he can't be."

"But why,"

My uncle sighs once again at this.

"Because he can't be King.
I won't allow it, not in a thousand years."

He is angry, very angry.

It made no sense, why did my uncle feel so strongly about this.
Perhaps because of the succession…

"Uncle, if this is about the succession, I do not mean to displace
Theodore,"

That was a lie.
Theodore would surely have to be displaced, but right now I wanted to
placate my uncle.

"I just meant Tristan would listen and that he would be an Imperial that
cares, he could talk to the Council.
In fact, I've been thinking, he would be good on the Council.

The people love him, people listen to him, he would be a good voice to reason Theodore,"

My uncle waves this all away.

"NO, NO, NO!"

He bellows.

Why was he being like this?
So averse to Tristan, even the mention of talking to him.
This was not like him, not in the slightest.

Or… Perhaps this was exactly like him.
As far as I could remember my uncle always seemed to have a dislike towards Tristan.
He was respectful of course… But the dislike remained.

"Uncle, Tristan is…"

 I begin to say, once again trying to praise Tristan.
To make my uncle see his good qualities, but my uncle alas was having none of it.

"NO!"

He shouts once again, the loudest shout this time.
In doing so, he flips over the table.
Maps, letters and various papers, including several glasses and pitchers all clang and smash to the floor.
I take several steps back, away from the carnage.

And that's when I see it, a letter on the ground.

One that particularly stands out amongst the rest.

Its thick paper, and the words of

"LORD COMMANDER."

Stick out, beautifully written.
But not just this, it is the seal.

The seal has the impression of a white owl.

It can't be… But it is.
I had seen it before, a year ago… I was in my father's tent when he received the letter, and when I asked, he told me.

It was the same paper, same handwriting, same seal.

It's from the Head Witch of the Council of Covens.

Why has she written to my uncle, and why did he not tell me, and why was it not being discussed when the other Captains were here?
My uncle catches my gaze, he follows it to the letter on the floor.
Quick as a flash, he grabs it swiftly.
His reflexes of a Slayer still strong, despite him being older than me.
Perhaps had I not been shocked about the flipping of the table and upon seeing the white owl waxed seal, I might have reacted faster and gotten my hands on the letter instead.

"What is that?"

I shout as my uncle clutches it tightly in his strong hands.

"N – Nothing."

 He mumbles.

This was not like him, not whatsoever.
That letter contained something, something important.

"Uncle…

Why all the secrets?!
Why tell me about Claudius and then not listen to my advice!
Claudius will not leave, Theodore will not get rid of him, you are an honourable man, uncle, but honour has no place here anymore."

His eyes dart to me then.

"You speak to me of honour, laddie, to me?"

He questions.

"You, who begged to become an Initiate, to train as a Slayer.
You, who disobeyed your father, my brother, and refused to go to the frontlines for two years. I know you got injured… But two years?!
And when you got there, you stayed only a handful of weeks to run away in the night!
And when you did that, where did you go?
You rode through the Realms and this Capital like the wind!
And instead of coming to the Spiral, instead of coming back like a man to deal with the consequences, you rode straight to the Imperium.
I had to send men to bring you back!
Tell me, laddie, where did you go?
Who did you leave a battlefield and your honour for?
Who did you disobey your father, and me for?

Huh?”

“You forgave me, you welcome me back with open arms.”

 I protest.

“Aye, because once again I was blinded.
Blinded to the threat of the Defenders, blind to your indiscretions, and blind to the real threat.”

He gaps, clutching the letter even tighter, its contents getting wrinkled and ruined.

What real threat?

*DO YOU REALLY NOT SEE THE THREAT?
OH NO, YOU ARE BLIND TOO…*

**Blind?
How?
How am I blind too?**

YOU WILL SEE, SOON ENOUGH.

“What is the threat, uncle?
Tell me?”

He shivers and shakes.
What has gotten into him?
This is not like him.
 Not like him one bit.

“Leave, laddie.

We will talk no more."

He huffs.

Just like that?
He tells me things about Claudius, awful things, the Defenders being
seen before the Great Cleansing, even saying he killed the King…
And yet, he is not the threat?

I do not move, contemplating these questions.
My uncle grows more annoyed by my presence.

"DID YOU NOT HEAR ME, LADDIE?!
LEAVE!"

He bellows.

I still do not move, my body transfixed with all the questions swirling
in my mind.

"LEAVE!"

He roars wildly.

I look at him then.
And for the first time I do not see the battle-hardened Lord
Commander.
But a terrified man.

This is not like him; this is not my uncle.

I take one last pitiful look at him before departing.
I storm from the chambers, pushing the doors wide as I do.

I feel anger inside me as I stride down the hallway of the Lord Commanders.

I feel their faces on me, dozens upon dozens of them.

Their painted eyes burn into me.

I swear, I even hear them whisper.

OPEN YOUR EYES!
STOP THE THREAT!
YOU ARE A SLAYER, SLAY THE MONSTER!
HE WILL BRING FIRE AND BLOOD!
THE REALM WILL BLEED!
THE COUNTRY WILL BURN!

The voices all become one then, I unison they chant.

DEATH! DEATH! DEATH!

I begin to run then, down the long hallway, but they continue.

STOP THE THREAT!
STOP THE THREAT!
STOP THE THREAT!

I run faster, harder, the hallway nearly at an end.

DEATH! DEATH! DEATH!…

It continues on and on.

I push through the doors at the end of the hallway, I find myself on hands and knees.

Breathing hard as the doors close, and thankfully with them, the voices.

Panting hard, I can feel the sweat under my armour, and my breathe is deeply ragged.

What does my uncle mean… What do the paintings mean?
What am I saying?… The paintings meant nothing.
Paintings can't talk.
Can they?

But something is about to happen, something bad.
And it appears as if all the Lord Commanders of the past want me to stop it…
But what exactly is it?

Claudius is the threat.
He's a fanatical tyrant with an army of armed zealots.
He killed the King and carried out the Great Cleansing…
He has been behind these last three years of misery.
Because of him, my father and his men have been all but imprisoned in the Realm of Magic.
He broke the alliance between humans and witches.

Him.

It was all him.
I do not care what my uncle says, Claudius is the threat.
Tristan was right, he was so right, and I didn't believe him.
I kept trying to reach a diplomatic decision, to always calm him, but I see now that he had every right to be angry.

Tristan, my love, forgive me, you were right.

SILLY BOY!
YOU ARE STILL SO BLIND!
IT WILL BE YOUR DEATH YOU KNOW!

Enough!
Enough is enough.

I am a Slayer of the Syndicate, and whilst I am not supposed to have any matters in the Realm of Men something clearly needs to be done. Even my uncle is about to take matters into his own hands and the paintings in that blasted hallway all but screamed at me to stop the threat.

I am not just a Slayer… I am Kaleb Umpire, son of the Lord and General.
I have already broken my vows being with Tristan, what's breaking more to stop the threat.

Claudius will not step down.
He will use his army and keep power.

As the paintings said.

He will bring fire and blood.
The Realm will bleed.
The country will burn.

Claudius has already done that, with the Great Cleansing, has he not?
But he will surely do much more.

There are vampires crossing the Border, they might even be in the Human Realm as we speak.
They are coming for the coronation… They mean to kill Theodore.
That must be stopped.
But Claudius, how do I stop him?

Tristan wants to kill him…

I COULD LURE CLAUDIUS SOMEWHERE SECRET… AND LET TRISTAN…

Did I really just have that thought?
No, no, I am not an assassin.
I couldn't… I would lose every shred of honour I had.

WHAT HONOUR?
OPEN YOUR EYES!
STOP THE THREAT.

I MUST SPEAK WITH TRISTAN… IMMEDIATELY.

I know my uncle received the letter from my father today about the village, and I can only assume he also received the letter from the Head Witch today also.

But before that, before that I should go to the rookery at the Imperium.
Perhaps another letter was sent for one of the Council, or Claudius…
I can try to intercept it… If it has not already been delivered.
After all, despite the Council having basically lost its real power these last three years, there still were good people who resided in the job.

Ladies Eleanor and Mavis especially.
Both kind and gentle women.
Very similar despite the vast age difference.

Perhaps the Head Witch has sent them a letter… Doubtful but hopeful.

But perhaps with my hope that my uncle was not the only one that the Head Witch trusted, perhaps she also had a friend on the Council?…

Yes…

 Yes, I must get to the rookery.
Scrambling to my feet, I wipe the sweat from my brow and race off
down the various corridors and stairs, leading away from the haunted
hallway of talking portraits and my scared but proud uncle.
As I run, only two thoughts remain in my mind.

I will stop this threat.
And I will forever protect and love Tristan.

No matter what.

MEANWHILE BACK AT THE IMPERIUM

CLAUDIUS CHAMBERS

THE PLOT THICKENS

CLAUDIUS

Hands held together, I begin to bless the meal before myself and my family.

"Lord of Eternal Light, we thank you for this blessing of food we are about to receive.
Lord of Eternal Light, please shine upon us and keep us from darkness.
Burn away all the temptations of this world.
And please, watch my children, keep them pure."

Unclamping my hands, I reopen my eyes and see my son by blood, Claudio.

I may have just prayed for him to be kept pure, however he is the furthest thing from pure.
God surely did not shine his light on this one.
He is depraved, the acts he has committed…
And to think, he participated in this with other young nobles, including the Crown Prince.

The same Crown Prince that made a spectacle of himself at the execution some weeks ago.

He conducted himself in the manner of a screaming drunk infant, and in front of such a crowd no less.

And his brother, that fucking brat.

TRISTAN.

He has always been a nuisance, ever since his eyes reopened three years ago.

He has battled me at every turn.
Every command of mine he has questioned.

ME?
HIS SUPERIOR!

His insolence in the castle was one thing.
Hidden away on this island, I did not care.
But on the mainland, in the heart of the Capital, in front of the citizens, he truly overstepped the mark.

SOMETHING THAT WOULD NOT HAVE HAPPENED HAD YOU SIMPLY CUT HIS THROAT WHEN YOU HAD THE CHANCE. INSTEAD, YOU LET HIM LIVE. YOU DEFIED YOUR QUEEN...

She is not my queen.
And yet, I had listened to her when she came to me. . .
And I had plotted and deceived many to get the position I have now.

A position that is constantly jeopardised by that Imperial brat.

Because of him a riot ensued, a riot which I had to use my Defenders to resort to violence.

Justifiable violence of course, they should not have rioted in the first place.

What I was doing was an act of God, and they turned against me, and all for Tristan.

And what he was implying… That he might be… That he could possibly think… That he would be the next Imperial King.

It was treacherous and treasonous; he had no right.

WHY DOES THIS ANGER YOU SO?
IS IT BECAUSE HE IS GOING TO SCUPPER YOUR PLANS?!

The prince has no chance of ruining my plans, he is just the spare after all.

AND YET HE CLEARLY HAS THE LOVE AND POPULARITY OF THE PEOPLE.
THEY CALLED HIS NAME, THEY FOUGHT FOR HIM…
THEY HAVE NEVER DONE THAT FOR THEODORE, NOR YOU!
AND HE MIGHT BE THE SPARE, BUT WE BOTH KNOW THERE IS MORE THAN MEETS THE EYE WHEN IT COMES TO HIM.

It does not matter; he has no chance of claiming the throne.

BECAUSE YOU HAVE DESIGNS ON THE THRONE FOR YOURSELF!
NOT KING THEODORE!
NOT KING TRISTAN!
BUT KING CLAUDIUS.

And why not?

I am the only one God speaks too.

And the Princes, the pair of them, both depraved in their own ways.

Theodore with his abuse, rape and heaving drinking.

And Tristan, who lays with another man and can Cast.

I have no doubt he caused that infernal storm on the day of the execution.

I noticed blood coming from his nose.

And that damned lover of his.

Not just any lover, no, but the nephew of the damned Lord Commander.

A Slayer and a witch…

Damn.

I think as I tuck into my dinner.

As High Pope, I should be eating a simple meal, to appease God.

However, I have a banquet before me.

Various salted cooked meats.

An array of colourful vegetables, all to be washed down with the finest wines.

YOU EAT LIKE A KING, WHILST PEOPLE STARVE!

And why should I not eat like a King?!

I grew up with nothing and look at me now!

A King in all but name.

Yes, I had nothing, only ever my Faith.

I come from a small village, humble beginnings, Faith is all I had.

AND YOUR HATRED FOR WITCHES…

Yes, and that too.

I came to the Capital a younger man and preached vehemently.

I got recognised by the old High Pope.

He sent me away as if I was nothing.

The Council helped him and look at them now.

My whipped dogs.

Lady Mavis and Lord Wyatt were still on the same council.

Them both being in their elder years.

However, Eleanor and Brandon where newish to the game.

Yet all my pawns now.

And me, with all the power.

And that power I shall use to Cleanse the Witches from this cursed land.

AND YET YOU SAVED THE LIFE OF ONE WITCH!
YOU COULD HAVE CUT HIS THROAT, BUT YOU DID NOT!
WAS THAT NOT DISOBEYING THE COMMAND OF ANOTHER WITCH?!
THE VERY QUEEN OF DARKNESS HERSELF?!

Yes, indeed part of me wishes I had cut his throat.

Perhaps if I had then he would not have caused me so much hindrance.

AND YET YOU KEPT HIM ALIVE FOR A REASON…
REMEMBER?

Yes, I had indeed kept him alive for a reason.

Although, I do not know the reason.

The Witch Queen wanted him dead, therefore I guessed that he must somehow be Important.

HE IS IMPORTANT!
AN IMPERIAL WITH THE POWER OF MAGIC…
HE COULD UNDO EVERYTHING!
UNDO EVERYTHING THE WITCH QUEEN HAS DONE!
EVERYTHING YOU HAVE DONE AND INTEND TO DO!
HE COULD BRING PEACE AND STOP THE WAR.
HE COULD UNITE THEM.

The very idea of uniting humans and witches…
Mixing together as if equals.
I could not allow it.
When Tristan hadn't died like she wanted, I had half expected her to send some assassin in the night, to murder me in some horrible way.

And yet she did not.

I had failed to kill the prince, and she had certainly roared and raved back in her Crimson Castle.

Then she went silent.
And yet, despite that, no assassin in the night was sent.
However, whilst I had failed to kill Tristan, I had quickly got to disposing of the king.

Perhaps that is why she spared me?

The king had always been more interested in war than politics.
He had always been fast friends with the General, and surely would have gone to the frontlines himself had the Council not urged him to otherwise.
After all, before he sired children, he was the only Imperial left after that massacre twenty-one years ago.
He had zero love for God also, yet when he did beget children, he loved them dearly.
He quickly became a family man.
Perhaps because his own was destroyed as a mere boy.
You would have thought that massacre of his own family would have showed him how dangerous these witches are.
After all, the massacre was carried out in the Realm Of Magic.

The Imperial Family had travelled there to celebrate the year 300ID.

It was supposed to cement the unsteady alliance with witches and humans.

It was supposed to be a joyous occasion, however it turned into a bloodbath.

The Imperial Carriage carried six Imperial's that day.

They had not long entered the Black Woods and that of the Realm of Magic when they were set upon.

And none other than one of the darkest and most dangerous creatures to have ever walked the land.

Marcus…

The Witch Queen's own beloved brother.

Yes, I suppose in theory it was not witches that attacked that carriage, it had been the Dark Lord himself.

And yet, where do these damned blood sucking vampires come from if not from witches?

I have read our histories extensively, and surely these witches brought the vampires with them.

Or at least they brought that dirty plague with them, the plague turned their eyes red forever.

They were supposed to be slaves… and yet they brought madness and chaos to this once great land.

Despite all of that, six witches had gone over to the third Imperial King.

They had had enough of the demons too, apparently.

From what history tells us, they snuck across the battle lines to the king.

And in the secret of night, they formed an uneasy alliance.

In return for the six witches giving aid to stop vampires from crossing, and in return for them using their ability to Cast Chaos they thus joined forces with the Imperial Army.

And in return, he promised them to have their own lands.

Thus, the entirety of the Black Woods became the Realm of Magic.

They also gained part of the BorderLands, a thin stretch of land between the Magic and Dark Realm.

A stretch of land where the fighting takes place, where everything there is dead.

A place animals do not even venture.

Absolute madness, the Imperial King gave them a portion of the country, and I cannot fathom what on earth would have possessed him to do so…

Some say that the six witches who went to him Cast some spell over him, and yet no one really knows.

He had already lost hundreds of leagues to those damned vampires that had swept from the east… The lands now known as the Dark Realm.

And then giving the Witches the entirety of the Black Woods, which also spans hundreds of leagues…

We lost more than half of the country in only a handful of months…

For three centuries, the Human Realm has been but only a quarter of the country.

Disgraceful.

And something I intend to rectify.

For three centuries these infernal Imperial's have done nothing to reclaim our country.

Whilst some have been religious, holding the Faith of Light tightly to them, they did not shine that Light upon the darkness that infested these lands.

No, we lost most of this beloved country to soulless.

The six witches who had made the alliance with that idiot of an Imperial have become known collectively as the Council of Covens.

Each of them a leader in their own right, with their own special skills which they passed down to future generations.

The current Council of Covens being direct descendants of the originals.

They had indeed built their own Realm, and their impressive City of Bridges.

I have never seen it with my own eyes, having never ventured inside the Black Woods, but by all accounts I had heard it to be beautiful.

And yet, despite begetting these lands, they did not even have the decency to stay in their own bloody Realm.

Instead, they seeped into our Human Realm and began breeding…

Black and white started to mix together.

Disgusting.

It created vile half breeds.

The histories mentioned how the dark-skinned babies were immediately and rightly enslaved.

After all, blacks belong in chains.

Too dangerous otherwise.

The lighter babes however were able to 'pass' as white.

They thus were able to walk free.

With every dark child imprisoned however, it quickly stopped people from mixing.

Or they simply ran back to their silly Magic Realm where they should have stayed.

Not wanting their children to be enslaved I suppose.

Those that could pass still managed to breed, however, the black faded out through the generations.

White humans with black ancestors.

If only I had lived three centuries ago… I would never have allowed this madness to have happened in the first place.
I would have ripped them out root and stem.
Unfortunately, it was not meant to be.
But now it shall be rectified by me.
I will make this country whole again.
I shall Cleanse the land of witches and the Red Eye demons they bring with them.
And thankfully, my chance has finally come.

YOUR CHANCE CAME BECAUSE OF A WITCH…
YOU NEVER WOULD HAVE GOTTEN THE CHANCE TO GET
WHERE YOU ARE NOW WITHOUT HER…

True I suppose… To a certain degree.
However, it was me whom had gathered the army.
I spent years and years gathering crowds of likeminded God-fearing people.
They too held my beliefs that witches are the reason for all our misfortunes.

Yes, it was me who had done all the work.
She simply came at night and whispered words.

It was me who got myself where I am.
Not her.
I will never give credit to a damned witch.

When I returned from failing to kill Tristan, instead becoming his supposed rescuer, I had pleaded and begged with the old King.

Told him about our histories, about how we should never have trusted them, about how they've always lurked in the shadows, waiting to pounce.

And now they had, they had attempted to kill the prince.

The Council tried to argue, to get him to see reason, to say that no good witch had ever attacked the Imperial Family.

That the feral was not the work of witchcraft.

I argued that it's merely because they never got the chance.

I argued that the Witch Queen had come back to once again try and exterminate the Imperial bloodline.

For once and for all.

It was not like she hadn't tried for centuries I had reminded him.

Even bravely reminding him what had happened to his family, and nearly himself years prior.

Not that he needed reminding, I'm sure.

I had begun to shout then, shouting about how we needed to save ourselves.

How we had a threat amongst us, and we needed to cleanse this land, for surely if it continued the Dynasty would fall.

That's when the King had finally listened, his lineage and the continuation of this Dynasty was imperative to him of course because he had seen it nearly destroyed as a youth.

And the fact that his precious son was not waking up, well it was all I needed to gain his ear and trust.

He sent the Council away then from the chambers, and it was just me and him.

I continued to drip poison into his ears of course, and then finally when he signed the decree for the Grand Cleansing, I slipped the poison into his wine.

He quickly died, coughing blood and wheezing.

And yet with the decree in hand, and some lies on my part, I managed to not only become the next High Pope, but also to push the Council aside and gain ultimate power.

They could not say no of course, I had dirt on all of them.
Dirt they did not want aired.
Yet that was for another time.

The sounds of my son chewing loudly on a piece of meat bring me back to the present.
I have been lost in thought for a while it seems, my children having nearly finished their food.
I quickly bring some salted pork to my lips and chew too, trying to catch up, not wanting to draw attention by having barely eaten anything.

But it seems it was noticed.

"Father, is everything okay?"

The sound of her voice is like beautiful music, I turn and smile sweetly.

To my left, is none other than my beautiful daughter, Claudia.
She has delicate features, dark eyes and dark hair, although her hair is always covered by a shroud, as befitting her station as a Daughter of the Faith.

My Defenders may have been my military muscle, but the Daughters were those who regularly gave sermons and prayers, helped feed the poor and nurse the sick.

My daughter, always a good girl, shared my deep love of the Faith.

A kind, sweet girl.
Always wanting to help others.

At first, I had not liked the idea of my beloved daughter being near the poor and desolate, yet she pleaded and begged to help others.
I gave in to her request of course, I had never been able to deny her.
Yet I kept her safe, I did not allow her to travel to the worse and darker parts of the Capital.
I kept her always either on the island or if she did have to go into the Capital, she was instructed to never venture from the Grand Square, and I always made sure loyal Defenders kept a watchful eye over her. Thousands upon thousands of eyes were there every day, at the Magnificent Markets, and I felt certain my daughter would be safe there.

SHE WOULD NOT HAVE BEEN SAFE BEFORE, WHEN THE PEOPLE RIOTED!
IMAGINE IF THOSE DIRTY PEASANTS HAD GOTTEN THEIR HANDS ON YOUR PRECIOUS DAUGHTER!

It was a thought I shuddered at.

AND IF THE PEASANTS DID NOT GET THEIR HANDS ON HER, THEN SURELY WITCHES WOULD TRY.
IMAGINE IF SHE WAS TAKEN BY THE SECRET COURT…

The Secret Court was another matter entirely.
I had all but wiped these damned witches from the land, yet they still seem to pop up like weeds.

We managed to capture some, but there are always more, they must be coming from somewhere.

There is a long-held rumour that they have a hidden base somewhere.

Yet it is not one me nor my Defenders have ever been able to find.

I too push that from thought and answer my beloved daughter.

"Of course, my darling.
Why would I not be?"

Claudio begins to laugh then.
He has been drinking, like usual.

"Perhaps because the Imperial Brat showed you up in front of the whole city,"

I ignore him.

Wiping my mouth with a cloth, I take a deep breath and reply.

"The riot was some weeks ago; besides it was small and contained, those who rebelled were quickly put to the sword, and the rest fell in line like I knew they would.
As for the Imperial Brat as you called him, well, he has been confined to his tower these last weeks.
Only the slaves have been able to attend him."

"Not true, I've heard his sweet sister got to visit him."

DAMN!

I had hoped to keep that quiet, it was true however, the Princess was the only one who was allowed to visit him.
She had come to me, begging me to let her see him.

I still remember how she had stood by the fire, the light illuminating her beauty.

I had gasped when I came down the stairs and saw her stood there.

And entirely shocked.

I had never thought she would be in my apartments, not ever.

However, came she did, and talked about how it was not right to keep siblings apart, especially not ones who were born at the same time.

She was ferocious and smart and spoke her mind.

And her dress which accentuated her breasts – I could not stop from staring at them.

How I wished to touch them, to hold them.

To kiss and nibble at her precious nipples.

She talked of giving bread and coin to the people, a charitable event to show the Imperial Family and the Faith stand as one.

A smart and incredible idea I must say, and just the thing to get the Council and peasants off my back for a while

Indeed, she was so beautiful… I could not say 'no' to her.

YOU LOVE THE PRINCESS…
OR RATHER, WHAT SHE CAN GIVE YOU…

I had sent her many presents these last months, yet she had not responded.

Not until she personally came here.

Begging to see her brother.

The first and only thing she had asked of me, how could I have said no?

YOU COULDN'T SAY NO BECAUSE YOU NEED TO MAKE HER HAPPY!

YOU NEED HER IF YOU HAVE ANY CHANCE OF KEEPING THIS POWER.
AND WITH THE UPCOMING CORONATION, YOU HAVE MERE WEEKS!

Finishing another slice of salted pork, I decide to answer.

"Yes, the Princess has visited.
Her and Tristan are very close, being twins of course.
Besides the Council thought it would be a good idea, and I'm always the diplomat."

I lie.

I had hoped it would be end of it, and yet Claudio continues to laugh.

"Not just the Princess though."

He sniggers.

This catches me of guard, I had left clear instruction with the Imperial Guard to only allow the Princess access to Tristan's tower.

"I'm guessing you didn't know?"

He probes, a smile on his face.

I look at him then, my so-called son.
An abomination, God had surely sent me him to test my faith.

A good-looking boy, with the same features as his sister.

And yet, the things he has done… He is far from God.

The King was a fool.
All the Old Kings were fools.

Centuries came and went, and they did nothing against those who can Cast.

They should never have been allowed to have their own Realm.
They should never have been allowed in our Realm.
I have Cleansed this land as much as I can for the good of God.

Enough!

"Tell me, dear son, what is it you speak of?
Please, enlighten us."

His smile fades then, he tears into a piece of bread, before answering.

"Well, apparently, she only visited once.
However, someone else has been visiting daily…Or shall we say nightly."

Another chuckle escapes his lips.

I do not need to ask for a name.

I already know the name.

Kaleb.

How did this happen?

Damn.

I had to have Imperial Guards at the door and not Defenders.
The Council themselves insisted.

Damn the Council.

I digest what my son tells me, in truth, it was my own fault.
I should have at least had slaves keep an eye, and yet I was too angry
with the prince to care about checking.

And the Princess, I should be angry with her, yet I cannot be angry
with her.
No doubt she knows of their love affair like me and no doubt she cares.
I should have at least checked in on what was happening, and yet I
stayed mainly in my own chambers these last weeks.
The riot in the Grand Square had sent a tremor in me, I knew they hated
me, and we had had riots before, and yet somehow this was different…

The young Prince had always had the hearts of the people, he may be
secluded on the island and yet over the years he has always received a
warm welcome.
I remember three years back when he had been in his deep sleep.
Just days before the Great Cleansing started, thousands upon
thousands came to the mainland gate at the Grand Bridge, they came
with candles and sung songs.

Yes, they had always loved him.
Always him.

Never me or even Theodore.

Perhaps because the people knew what me and Theodore were…

Monsters in our own ways.

Oh yes, I may do God's work but even I understand that murdering thousands earns me the title of monster.

AND YET THE TITLE IS WORTH IT!
FOR GOD.

Theodore on the other hand does not have a cause, just vicious cruelty and tremendous stupidity.

That left the people with the obvious next candidate.

Tristan.

But then again, the people don't know his true nature, do they?
The people hate me and Theodore because they see us, our nature.
And yet they don't see Tristan's.
They do not know that he has a lover.
And not just any lover, no, but a male lover.
And if that is not bad enough, it is with a now Captain of the Syndicate!
And the Lord Commander's nephew to boot!
Exposing their little affair would surely turn people against them.
There are people of God in the Capital, and they would detest the idea of two men sleeping together, they would curse and spit at them.
For any man caught lying with another man is committing an unholy act, a vile act.

They deserve death.

NEITHER THE COUNCIL NOR THE IMPERIAL GUARDS WILL EVER LET YOU EXECUTE AN IMPERIAL!

Perhaps I do not yet have the power to execute an Imperial.
But Kaleb… Well, having taken his oath he cannot inherit any lands or titles.
He is just a Slayer.

THE LORD COMMANDER WOULD STRIKE YOU DOWN FOR EVEN THE THOUGHT…

This is true enough…

Yes, I could not touch Kaleb whilst the Lord Commander breathed.

I keep the plans for another rainy day, when surely, they will be needed.

But for right now, well I am sure I can send a message to both Tristan and Kaleb.
I may not be able to touch either of them as of yet, but surely, I can still send a clear message to them somehow…

I just need two male lovers…
I make a mental note to give orders later for my idea.

"Of course, father knew about it.
There is little father does not know."

My sweet daughter answers.

I smile sweetly at her; she always did come to my defence.

Perhaps not.

"Yes, I knew that Kaleb was visiting.
He and the Prince are fast friends and it's always good of him to accompany and protect the Princess."

I answer.

"Kaleb hasn't been accompanying the Princess though.
And yes, I'm sure Kaleb visits because he and the Prince are just 'friends'".

He emphasised **'friends'**.

My stomach tightens at this.

Fool of a boy.

Yes, it's clear they are lovers, and yet I do not want that knowledge public.
Not yet, anyways.
But perhaps, if even someone as stupid as him can see it, maybe it already is public knowledge?
No, surely if it was public knowledge there would be many more rumours and whispers flying around.
The small folk loved to gossip about their betters, and no doubt the Prince and Captain being intimate would send thousands of tongues wagging.
No, thankfully it seemed those who knew or noticed were within the castle, and they dared not mention it out loud either.

From either loyalty because Tristan is an Imperial or embarrassment
that another Imperial was nothing more than a deviant like so many
others of his wretched family.

I look Claudio directly in the eyes.
I do not take my gaze off him, I stare deeply.

His smile and laughing demeanour go straight away, he sits upright in
his chair uncomfortably.

He knows he has angered me.
I should whip him bloody.
My daughter's hand upon mine softens my anger.

"Father, shall we perhaps pray again?"

Sweet girl.

She always knows the right thing to say.

"Kiss arse."

I hear Claudio say angrily across the table.

Anger sweeps back through me, I stand up, reaching over the table and
back hand him across the face.

He flies backward, his chair going with him.

"I'VE HAD ENOUGH OF YOUR COMMENTS!"

I shout as I stand over him.

I begin to kick at him.

"STUPID, GODLESS BOY!"

I shout again.

My daughter runs round the other side of the table, approaching me.

"Father, stop!"

She cries.

I move to strike him again.
Before I can, she throws herself down on the floor, her body covering her brother's.

I halt myself immediately.
I would never harm my precious girl.
She looks up at me, tears in her eyes.

Tears and disappointment.

I feel regret, I hate disappointing her.
Claudio pushes her off then and drags himself to his feet.
He is bruised and bloody, he looks at me, then looks at Claudia.

"No, you would never harm your darling daughter, would you?!"

He questions, bitterness in his voice.

"She's not that precious you know, ask her about that fucking book she has been keeping."

He screeches before storming out.

Him gone; I look upon my daughter still on the floor.
I outstretch my hand.
I gently pull her to her feet, and I begin to use my hands to dust off her white dress.
As I do, I question her gently.

"What book does he speak of, my daughter?"

She stays silent.

"Sit down."

I tell her, gesturing to my chair.

She does as I tell her; she sits down.
I gently take off her shroud and place it on the table.
Her dark hair falls to her elbows.
I softly weave my fingers through it.
Taking it into three separate parts, I slowly begin to braid her hair.
Her mother had braided her hair, when she was alive.

A good woman.
The love of my life.
 Her death is something that will haunt me forever.

My daughter always loved it when her mother did this, it was something they did together.
When she died, I taught myself how to do it, I wanted to keep my daughter happy after all.
I could not do it for long however, I had been sent away for years and I left the children here.
I had too, of course.

The open road is no place for children.
And yet, I learned all the same, and upon returning three years ago I have braided her hair constantly once again.

Anything for my girl.

"What book?"

I ask again, my voice still gentle.

I weave her hair as she finally answers.

"A – a book… It's about,"

"About?"

 I repeat.

"I'm not sure what it is, really.
A journal, perhaps?
But it has… It has,"

"Yes, it has what, darling,"

 I mutter, as I finish her braid.

I tie it neatly with a piece of white ribbon from my pocket.
I always carried white ribbons for her hair.

"Magic."

She breathes.

I release her neatly tied hair and stand back.

"LEAVE US,"

I shout out, loud enough for those to hear above.

I was not talking to her; I was talking to the slaves who were present.
They all bowed before taking their leave, their chains rattling as they
went.
I had to wait an extra moment for the slaves to leave from upstairs,
from two levels, they walked down the wooden staircase solemnly,
their heads hung low.
All departed, and the huge wooden doors closed, I sit beside her.

"I would like you to hand me this book over, darling."

 I tell her.

"Father, as I said, it's more of a journal.
And just copied histories."

She says quietly.

"Copied histories."

I repeat.

"Yes, the book has written texts, copied from most likely other books.
Restricted books… Histories about magic."

This was true, anything that even mentioned magic had been
prohibited these last three years.

And anyone caught with such an item will suffer the punishment of death.

From spell books to texts and histories, anything with the mere mention of magic.

All strictly forbidden.

BUT YOUR DAUGHTER HAS SUCH A BOOK.
WILL HER PUNISHMENT BE DEATH?

Of course not!

YOU ARE A HYPOCRITE!

So, it seems someone has been reading forbidden books and copying it down in their own book.

And yet, my daughter said it was more of a journal and thus it is personal and will most likely reveal the writer.

"Anything else in this journal?"

I question

"Well… It's weird.

It looks like the Book of Light.

That's why I picked it up, I thought it was a prayer book.

But then I opened it and… Well, it's a secret journal.

And there are some… Some spells.

All sorts, being able to move things with the mind, or hands, being able to lift and move objects at whim, and creating things like small balls of fire to light candles and even bigger balls of flames to light a hearth."

I realised as she spoke that she was… Excited?

I sighed deeply.

I had prayed and prayed and prayed that my precious daughter would
never read such a book.
Such things give way to ideas, and ideas are dangerous.
They infect the mind and make it ungodly.

"And where exactly did you find this secret journal?"

She goes silent then for a moment, before saying.

"I've never seen magic."

She concludes, my question going unanswered.

"Even before the Cleansing, witches weren't allowed to cast in the
Human Realm.
Not publicly, anyways.
I'm sure many still Cast privately however."

She mentions.

This was most likely true; many would have practised hidden away.
I waited for her to finish, for she clearly had more on her mind.

"As I said, I've not seen magic.
But you have, right father?
You've seen magic?
Is it really true, like the book says?
Can people really move things with their minds, and can they control
fire and other elements too?"

She gasps.

I say a silent prayer to the Lord of Eternal Light, I had never wanted to have this conversation.

"Yes, yes, I have seen magic."

I answer, my voice sad.

"And yes, I have seen many witches do many things, and some people… Some people find wonder in it, but really it should be fear. It's dangerous and unnatural, only God should be able to do such things, not"

"Not people?"

She questions.

"Witches are not people, they are abominable."

I answer her.

"Remember what you've been taught."

I remind her.

My daughter notices this and her eyebrows furrow.

"Witches killed mother, didn't they?"

She answers.

It was not something we had discussed before.

We spoke about her mother often, especially me, forever wanting to
keep her memory alive, and yet we did not talk about her death.
I think carefully about what to say.

DID WITCHES REALLY KILL HER?
OR WAS IT YOU...
YOUR HATRED FOR THEM SO GREAT, IT OVERPOWERED
YOUR LOVE FOR HER!

No!
Magic killed her!
Witchcraft killed her!

LIES, YOU KNOW WHAT YOU SAW!
YOU KNOW WHAT YOU DID!

"How did she die?"

I look at her and smile grimly.

"Magic is what killed her, my darling.
It's dark and twisted and it consumes people, makes them evil."

I answer.

UTTER LIES!
YOUR WIFE WAS KIND AND LOVING,
TOO GOOD FOR YOU...
PERHAPS IT WAS NOT THE MAGIC!

Enough!

"Magic is something that should have died a long time ago.
And yet like a disease, it spread and took roots.

It has cursed this land.
Ruined it, and because of magic we have lost more than half of our own country.
Witches brought Red Eyed Demons, they set them upon us, vicious savage monsters that rip you limb from limb and drain your blood dry."

Claudia gasps as this.

She knew about vampires, there was not a human alive that did not, however I usually did not speak so honestly about the brutality of these monsters.
Wanting to spare her, to protect her innocent and sweet nature.

"But… But father, did not the first Imperial King send his son to find other people.
He set sail to distant lands… And he found people."

She speaks.

"He did, indeed.
The slaves are from there."

"And yet… They were not slaves originally.
They were people, unchained and free…
But they attacked us, so we enslaved them."

Her voice is full of sadness.

I suppose this was truth enough.

"Perhaps, perhaps if we had left them alone… To live in peace, if we had not brought them here…
Then maybe none of it would have happened.

The witches and magic and vampires and the war, all of it.
Perhaps… Perhaps it is our own fault."

She says the last part silently, her head hung low.
As if she was scared of what I might say in return.

She had never voiced these sorts of opinions before.
Usually always an obedient and quiet girl.

Just goes to show, when one is exposed to those books, it sets a disease in the mind.

"There is only one group to blame for this travesty.
And that is… The Imperial Dynasty."

I say to her.

She gulps at this.

Speaking badly of the Imperial Family is treasonous, yet I carried on.

"You are right, we did sail to distant lands, and we did come upon the land in which the slaves are from.
And yes, they did turn on us, so we enslaved them.
But it was the Imperial's who did this.
They brought the witches and Red Eyed Demons here; they are to blame entirely."

"But if the dynasty is to blame, why do we still serve them?
Why are they still beloved?"

She ponders.

"Old habits die hard, I suppose.
And when this madness began, we needed stability, and the Imperial Family offered that I guess.
They ruled before, they rule now."

I choose carefully what to say next.

"But… Perhaps, perhaps they might not rule for ever."

I let the comment hang in the air.

My beloved daughter looks at me confused.

"But… But why would they not rule?"

I take her hand.

"You are a smart girl.
A smart woman."

The term woman being more truthful, she was the eldest of my three children.

Being twenty-five, she should be married and have her own children by now, yet I cannot let her go.

*AND YET YOU DID LET HER GO…
ABANDONED FOR YEARS WHISLT YOU GREW A FANATICAL
ARMY AT THE BEHEST OF THE WITCH QUEEN.*

Yet that was not my fault, I did not want too.

I did not want to leave whatsoever; I was forced too.
And it was the Witch Queen who found me… She came to me as a younger man.
Seduced me with lucrative promises of power and the death of her own kind.

Something they will still pay dearly for.

BESIDES, HER MARRIAGE MAY BE PROFITABLE IN THE FUTURE!
YOU CAN MARRY HER OFF TO SECURE AN ALLIANCE!

No, my daughter was not some bargaining chip…She was precious to me.

SHE LOOKS JUST LIKE HER MOTHER.
DOES IT NOT REMIND YOU OF WHAT YOU DID?
AND JUST BEFORE YOU WERE EXILED TOO.

My wife had just died, it was in the year of 300ID.
She had given birth to Claudio…

BUT HOW EXACTLY DID YOUR WIFE DIE AGAIN…

I would not think on that.
My wife died and they still sent me away… Claudia just a small girl,
Connor still a babe also and Claudio just born.
God forgive me.
Use your light to Cleanse my sins and make me whole.

Thinking of Connor especially… How he came to be in my care…
How **SHE** had given him to me…

I push the thought aside.

Instead focusing on what I need to finish saying.

I need to make her realise how bad those who rule us are.

And yet, I cannot speak openly of treason, not until I am entirely sure that she would have faith in my judgement.

The judgement of God.

For he has already judged the Imperial Family.

They need to die.

They brought this plague upon us.

They need to answer for it.

IT IS YOU WHO PASSES JUDGEMENT,
IT IS YOU WHO BARES A GRUDGE, NOT GOD!

"You know the princes."

An obvious answer.

"Of course."

She replies, like I knew she would.

"I have known them since they were born.
 I think I still remember when the late Queen carried the twins."

She answers.

"Really? You remember that?"

I had not thought she would have; she was young still when the twins were born.

I had been gone a year by then.

Exiled and forgotten… Or so they thought.
I had missed the Imperial Birth and yet heard of on it my travels.
It was still a great celebration despite the Queens death.
And the mentioning of the late Queen was not something that had been uttered in a while.
A shame, from what I remember she was a good woman.

A SHAME WHAT HAPPENED TO HER.
MAYBE THAT IS WHY THE KING LISTENED TO YOU?
BOTH YOUR WIVES DYING IN SUCH HORRIBLE WAYS.
A BOND OF GRIEF, PERHAPS.

"What do you think of them?"

I ask of her, trying to silence my thoughts.

She goes silent again, trying to think.

"Theodore… Theodore, um…"

I can tell she did not want to speak badly about him, yet it is the truth.
And we needed to face the truth.

"What about Theodore?
You can speak freely.
What do you think of him."

She looks up at me, biting her lip.

"Well, he was a cute baby, and a cuter infant, but as he grew up…
Well, he was, and is, mean.
Him and Claudio… As they grew, I suppose I became distant from them.
They did not want anything to do with me, anyhow.

614

Theodore and Claudio… They both were cruel as children, pulling pranks on the rest of us.
On me, on Tristan and even Kaleb, and always on Connor."

The mention of Connor reminds me that I had not seen my adopted son today.
Not unusual, however, he often preferred his own company.

"I suppose I do not know Theodore anymore… He hardly takes notice of me,"

She concludes.

"And you should thank God for that."

 I reply.

"I know, father… The girls he does take interest in, well, I've heard stories.
Rumours around the Imperium.
Rumours in the Capital.
I think… I think once I even heard screaming come from his chambers."

She admits.

Yes, Theodore was despicable.
As an Imperial Prince, he thought he had right over anyone in the castle, especially any nearby unexpected girls.
He usually targeted slaves, thankfully, but he had also attacked serving girls.
And in the Capital, he likes to visit whore houses, and he's even vicious there too.

"I think… I think Claudio joins in… He hurts people too."

She confides.

Yes, this was true too.
My son, my blood, often joined in with abuse and rape.
They both found it fun, them and their other group of young lords who felt the same.
As if their titles and power entitled them to whatever they wanted.

"And yet you protect him from my blows."

 I remind her of earlier.

"Because despite what he does, I love him, he's my brother.
But he would not make a good Lord…"

Yes, Claudio had often wondered when I would gift him land and a castle, to rule as his own, and yet I can't, something as impulsive and cruel as him needs to be kept close.
I do not need more parts of the Human Realm knowing I sired such depravity and ungodliness.

"And Theodore, I do not think Theodore would be a good King."

She finishes.

She has spoken plainly and honestly, I am proud of her.

"Good, I am glad you can see the truth.
Theodore should not be King."

I answer her.

"So, Tristan should be King?"

She asks, innocently.

This angers me, yet I do not show it.

HA!

"No, sweetheart, I do not think Tristan should be King."

I tell her.

She looks confused once again.
Not surprising, this was a confusing conversation.
A conversation we had not partaken in before.

"But, after Theodore, the crown and throne pass to Tristan.
He's the next in line after all."

"And yet, do you think he would be a good King either?"

She takes a moment to think, before she can answer however there is
a loud knock on the door.

Damn!

I would surely whip whoever is behind that door!
I was so close, so close to persuading her that perhaps there could be a
new King.
One that was not an Imperial.

True, I am nothing, born from nothing.

And yet you stayed strong to your Faith.
That Faith got you to the Capital, albeit briefly.
You earned attention and followers.
Like minded individuals who hate witches like yourself.

Yes, I was young then, and the High Pope grew concerned, and sent me away on my missions.
And yet, I turned that to my advantage.
Being able to spread my truth throughout the Human Realm, in all different villages, towns and cities.
I was gone for years and years.
But I came back eventually.
I should never have been allowed to set foot past the Capital Gates…
Because during those years is when *SHE* found me.
Truth is, we had known each other for years.
I was 'working' for her for years.
And gave me something special indeed.
She handed me something back in 300ID.
Something I have looked after to the best of my ability.
I push the thought deep down, not wanting to think on it.

The door knocks again.

"ENTER."

My voice annoyed.

The door creaks as it opens slightly, a slave gingerly steps inside.

"What is it?"

 I bark at him.

"S – Sorry My Lord, b – but I work in the rookery.
We received a raven with a message for you.
You told me to come straight away if you ever get a letter.
I do not recognise the seal, though."

He looks down at the letter, it's sealed with wax.
He may not know who that seal is, but I immediately do.

It is **HER**…

I quickly stand to my feet, the chair scraping behind me.

"Father, what's wrong."

 My daughter asks.

"Go to your room, darling, and remember, I want that book.
And I want to know where you found it."

 I remind her.

"Yes, Father."

She stands, curtesy's and begins to ascend the wooden stairs, all the
way to the to her bedroom.
My family's rooms being at the top.

I hear the creaking of wood get quieter as she ascends.
I hear her door open, and then close.

I immediately rush over to the slave.
I grab the letter from his hand and walk away, past the table and
towards the hearth.

Her seal.

Stamped with what resembles a black bat.
The wax is the deepest of black.

I tear away at the wax; it crumbles away beneath my fingers.

She had never sent a letter before… Ever

And to send one so brazenly to the castle rookery…
Letter opened; I realise it is blank.
It's hidden with blood magic; like so many letters before, I know I
must use my blood.
I quickly slit my finger on the paper and drop blood on the paper.
I hold my breath as I read what it says.
Line after line, I can feel myself filling with dread with every passing
word.

No.

No, this surely cannot be serious.
How could she…

I feel as if I cannot breathe.

YOU KNOW SHE WANTED ALL THIS COUNTRY, WHY DOES
THIS SURPRISE YOU?
THE TIME HAS COME!
AS YOU KNEW IT ALWAYS WOULD!

Yes, I had known this day would come.

Eventually… But right now.

Am I ready?

PERHAPS YOU SHOULD SIMPLY FOLLOW HER RULE.
SHE PROMISED YOU AND YOUR CHILDREN'S SAFETY IN
HER NEW WORLD…

A world of blood and death.
Humans forced into those awful camps.
The Devil would rule, and God would perish.
No, this will not happen.
I will not let it.
Yes, I had been lured in by her.
Yes, I had followed her commands.
But she was so sure of herself.
She had no idea that someone like me would betray her.
Stupid bitch.

In truth, I had every intention of betraying her.
I had nodded my head and smiled, and I had been allured by her
promises of power, and yet, it was all to be only temporary.

Eventually, she would come sweeping in and take control.

But she could only do that if I followed her commands to the letter.
She has a plot she wants me to form.
She has called it

'The Ruby Red Plot.'

A wicked, awful plot.
Involving the deaths of thousands, destroying the Capital completely from within.
No, I would not allow that.
I will carry out this plot, but I shall make my own personal alterations.
Alterations that fit only me.

For I have been planning this from the beginning.

Yes, she gave me the ability to take control.
Telling me personal secrets about the General and the Council…
About what really happened that day of the Imperial Family massacre.

And she did supply me with the poison for the King, and even the High Pope.
This gave me ultimate control, and I have every intention of keeping it.

Certainly not handing it over to her…
And neither the princes, either of them.
No, this shall belong to me.

The throne.
The crown.
The castle.

The capital.
The whole country.

I have been growing my armies, they number in the tens of thousands across the Realm.

And I am five thousand strong in the Capital alone, it rivals any Imperial Soldiers that may be here instead of the front lines.

It even rivals that of the Slayer Syndicate.

The Grand Spiral may be a monstrous building which can host in the thousands, and yet only a couple hundred Slayers are in the city.

The rest spread throughout the Realm and at the frontlines.

I also have roughly a couple hundred of my Defenders stationed in the Imperium.

I would need to call more in, it would seem.

Just to be safe.

And both the princes… **They will need dealt with.**

And the princess… **My plans with her will need to start immediately.**

All of this needs to start right now.

She wants this Ruby Red Plot carried out as soon as possible.

The Capital and Imperium are already ablaze due to Theodore's twenty first birthday, and the day of his upcoming coronation.

Many letters have been sent from around the Realm, announcing the impending arrival of lords and ladies.

The castle has been getting prepared and ready for a while now.

All the important lords and ladies of the Realm… Under one roof of the castle…

That may be very good for me.

If I have them here, I can control them.

SO, YOU ARE REALLY DOING THIS…
YOU ARE REALLY GOING TO TRY AND TAKE THE THRONE.
TAKE THE CROWN…

I am not just going to try; I am going to make sure I succeed.
Because if I do not, surely what's left of the Human Realm will fall
into darkness.
To magic and vampires.
I will not let God and his Eternal Light be diminished.

Mind firmly set; I turn to the slave.
He stands there awkwardly, waiting for a response.

"Has anyone else seen this letter, this seal?"

I ask of him.

"No, my Lord. I received it shortly ago and brought it straight here.
No one else has seen or touched it."

He confirms.

Good, this was good.
Only one person knew about this letter that shouldn't…

"Are you hungry?"

 I ask the slave.

He seems surprised, most likely never been asked this question in his
life.
He doesn't answer, most likely too stunned to speak.

"Please, eat what you like."

I gesture to the food.

The slave looks confused slightly, then quickly darts toward the table.
As he tucks into some food, I slowly and quietly walk behind him.
Reaching into my pocket, I pick out another white ribbon.
The same I use to tie my daughter's beautiful hair after braiding it.
I outstretch the ribbon, holding it firmly in both my hands.
I come up right behind the slave, I quickly loop the ribbon around his neck and pull hard.
He gasps and chokes, kicking out startled.
I quickly pull him to the floor; I don't want him kicking chairs over and alerting my daughter upstairs to the noise.

He falls onto his front; I firmly sit on top of his back.
I grip harder and harder, the ribbon tightening around his throat, I can see the skin going dark purple.
He tries to pull himself away, yet he is chained hand and foot, he can't do much.
I pull harder one last time, the ribbon cutting into my hand.
I can feel the slickness of blood, yet I do not release my grasp.
Finally, the slave has the good courtesy to die.

Breathing hard, I release the ribbon.
It's now stained red with my blood.
Shakily, I stand up.
I quickly look upwards.
No sign of my daughter.
Good.

I grab his legs and drag him over to the many comfy chairs by the hearth.
A huge chest sits there.
I drop his legs and open the chest.
It only contains a few books; I quickly empty it.
I pick up his body and push it into the chest.
Closing the trunk, I quickly lock it.
I then take the ribbon and grab the letter and throw them into the hearth, they both crackle as they burn away to nothing.

It is time for my plan.

I smiled upon realising this.
I shall play along for only a short while longer, but as of now, I plan on taking them all down.

The Dynasty, the Council, that damned Syndicate and even the Witch Queen herself.
Only me, my armies of Defenders and God's Light shall remain.

Here comes King Claudius…

Yes, I like the thought of that as I smile into the fire.

MEANWHILE ACROSS THE CASTLE

TRISTAN'S TOWER

TIME TO BE FREE

TRISTAN

I stare out at the violent sea, as I have now for many days.
Days or weeks?
Surely, it must be weeks by now.
Waves against waves.
Waves against rocks.
Waves everywhere.

Always the same.

My only company has been Kaleb.
My sister came only but once…

And I scared her off…

SHE SIMPLY CANNOT HANDLE THE TRUTH!

But I am right… Theodore is not fit to be King.
The coronation is now only a moons turn away.

High in the sky, a beautiful full moon.
It is large, larger than usual.

The waves underneath thrash so wildly that I cannot even see the moon's reflection.

My balcony has been my haven, the only place where I feel I can breathe.

I've often stood or sat here, staring out at the ever-changing tides and moons.

And yet, I find solace in it.

And also my books, I have done more than my fair share of reading, endless reading.

I have been brushing up on the histories of the Imperial Family, as much as I can.

I'll be honest, despite the fact the Imperial Dynasty has been revered and renowned throughout time, I cannot say it is for the right or good reasons.

This land was originally nothing but clans and tribes.

It was the very first Imperial King who spent the majority of his youth and adulthood fighting endless battles and defeating many others, slowly but surely gaining more land and more men to fight for him.

Finally, once his army was in the tens of thousands, he eradicated and destroyed what remained of anyone who opposed him.

When that was done, he was finally the undisputed and only man to be King.

Thus, the Imperial Dynasty was born.

He soon set about building a castle for himself.

However, the first Imperial King, who was by now reaching the end of his life knew that this would take many years of hard work and labour.

He begun designs on building the capital first.

The work was slow in the beginning, and he realised he needed more money and more men.

Our country, being completely surrounded by sea, meant fishing quickly became the main source of food and profit.

But this was not enough, from what I gather anyways and we sought, and discovered, a new land with its own inhabitants.

The histories are muddled after that, not much more information.

The King sent his son, who would be the second Imperial King.

Apparently, according to histories a friendship tried to blossom between these two countries, however when they were eventually brought here on the ships as honoured guests, they attacked us shortly after arriving here.

They unleashed Red Eyed monsters from the deepest of hells to plague us.

The King was quickly killed, and his camp destroyed.

A war soon erupted, and many battles were fought.

Many died, and many were taken prisoner on both sides.

It seemed that we would lose despite what wins we had, after all, only a single bite from one of those monsters would turn you into a monster yourself.

But the recorded history does not make sense.

Why would they attack us when we offered friendship?

Something did not seem right.

And yet, three centuries later and their descendants in this Realm are nothing but slaves.

A cruel fate indeed.

However, there was a small group of witches who for whatever reasons did not agree with the vampires, or the self-proclaimed Witch Queen.

Thus, they made an uneasy alliance with the Third Imperial King.

Not much history is mentioned thereafter.

All I do know, is that despite the fact the Third Imperial King relented and gave a portion of what lands he had left, the lands themselves being the Black Woods, he would not relent on the prisoners that had been captured.

No, he decided these would be kept.
And thus, they were chained and beaten, used for the hard manual labour that went into building the Capital and the continuation of the building of the Imperium and the Grand Bridge.
They were kept and even bred like animals, thus getting further generations of slaves.

Generations of chains.

It was not right, and yet, it was apparently the norm.

*YOU HAVE ALWAYS BEEN KNOWN FOR YOUR KINDNESS CONCERNING THEM.
A WHOLE FACTION OF PEOPLE…
AN ARMY…*

An army of slaves.
No, I must free them.

BUT WHO CAN GUARANTEE THAT ONCE FREED THEY WILL FIGHT FOR YOU?!

It does not matter; they must be freed regardless.

*YES, PERHAPS IF YOU FREE THEM THEN THEY WILL INDEED FIGHT FOR YOU!
MORE PEOPLE TO BOW AND WORSHIP YOU!*

Yes, surely if I free them, I will earn their undying loyalty and gratitude.
And of course, their worship!

But one thing at a time, for we cannot afford to free anyone before I first deal with Claudius and Theodore.

SO, YOU REALLY ARE PREPARED TO KILL YOUR OWN BROTHER...

This In truth I am hesitant about, despite what I feel about him, and whatever I do feel about him is not good, he is still my brother.
My blood.

And he should be my King.

Yes, law decrees that he is by all rights next in line for the throne, but he is completely wrong for it.
He will be another vicious tyrant; he will only hurt the people.

AND WILL YOU NOT HURT PEOPLE?
IN THIS WORLD OF UNITY, DO YOU NOT NEED TO FIRST DESTROY?!
TO MURDER AND BURN...

Out with the old, in with the new.

And I mean to usher in a new age of magic and beauty, of unity for all.
Anyone who is different will be welcome.

And I will be the King of it all...

No, not just a King...

But a God.

***I DO BELIEVE THIS CONFINEMENT HAS MADE YOU QUITE
MAD!***

Am I mad?
Perhaps.
Perhaps not.
No, it is true.
I should be King.

King Tristan.

A part of me still wonders if I had been wise to call out to the crowds?!
Had I acted unwisely and boldly and rashly?
Yes, of course I had.
I knew that already, but the people needed to be awakened, not just
them, but the nobility also.
Whilst it was true most of them left before things got too bad, I heard
my name had been swirling around the castle as of late.
And of course, the Capital.

***BUT WHERE ARE ALL THESE FINE PEOPLE YOU MENTION?
I SEE NO LORDS ASSEMBLING ARMIES?
NO ONE TO COME AND RESCUE YOU!
YOUR SISTER HAS NOT EVEN RETURNED…***

No, only one remained.

Kaleb.

But surely, that day of the execution I had started a small ember, and
now it only needed to go up in flames.
I wanted them to rise up.

I wanted them to call my name.
I wanted them to see I was the better option.

The only option.

I am right, I am surely right.
Claudius is nothing other than a tyrant.
And Theodore, he is nothing more than a fool and a vicious one at that.

And yet, what would that make me?

If I really am to do this, if I really am to take a stand, and I intend too, then that involves fire and blood.
Claudius, Theodore, they will both need to die.

Claudius, I have no regrets over, I am more than happy to watch him die and shall surely do so with a smile on my face.
But Theodore, I hate him yes, but… I suppose, in my own way, I also love him.
He is my brother after all, my only brother.

AND YOUR RIGHTFUL KING…
REMEMBER, YOU ARE JUST A SECOND SON.

Yes, that is what I most certainly am.
The universe must surely have being playing a mad game.
To make me the second son and not the first.
But then again, perhaps it was just random circumstance.
However it happened, it was still wrong.
What is happening is wrong.
And it needs to stop.

And the only way for that to happen is with destruction and death.

But firstly, for any of this to happen, I must leave the confines of this tower.

As it stands, the supposed coronation is only one moon's turn from now.

Right now, Lords and Ladies from throughout the Realm are pooling into the Capital for the upcoming celebration.

And only more will arrive as it grows closer to the time.

Now is my chance to get out of here and try my best to speak to these Lords and Ladies, to try and get their loyalty.

THEY COME HERE FOR A CORONATION, NOT A WAR.

But then again, we are already at war.

YES, AND NOW YOU MEAN TO ALSO HAVE A CIVIL WAR. WHO IS GOING TO FIGHT FOR YOU?

That was something I pondered.

I needed men, an army.

There is of course the Imperial Army, what is left of it, and what is left of it hasn't got much chance.

When the Cleansing began, the Realm of Magic was sealed off and most of the army was there, imprisoned in all but name.

The Council of Covens declared that if Claudius and his Defenders dared march on them, they would slaughter the army and even join the side of the Dark Realm.

So, Claudius held off.

Not because he wanted too of course, but because our own Council forced him too.

The only sensible thing they have done.

With most of the Imperial Army trapped, and with three years of them fighting there with no help or recruits, I doubt there's very many left.

And what army remains here, they've fallen into a stupor.

Claudius is too busy with his own army of faithful Defenders, an army which continues to grow into the thousands.

He has no need for the soldiers that remain of the Imperial Army, thus they have fallen to the wayside.

Many spend their days drinking and whoring away in the Capital, some have even left to venture back to their respective homes throughout the Realm.

So, the Imperial Army is weak and ineffective.

Sure, we have Imperial Guard, employed within the Imperium but they only numbered a couple hundred at most.

And as far as it stands, the only ones that now enter and leave between Realms are the Slayers of the Syndicate.

SLAYERS OF THE SYNDICATE…
THERE MIGHT BE SOMETHING THERE?

Is there something there?

The Syndicate was a prestigious faction, borne shortly after the Rising.

The Rising being a name for when the Red Eyed Demons first came to undead life.

I read it in a book only earlier.

The Red Eyed demons are incredibly strong and fast, and killing them is no easy feat.

However, it is possible.

The first man to slay a vampire was a strong man indeed.

He was the one who got the idea to start the Syndicate.

Eventually more had slain vampires, and thus the numbers grew.

It's almost as old as the Imperial Dynasty themselves.

Many do not even pass Initiation.

Most died young.

It was rare to see an elderly Slayer.

They are also famous for their rigorous training.

Even taking special potions and herbs to increase their stamina and strength, potions created originally by witches.

The Syndicate had much to do with magic and demons of course, and many wondered if they were in league themselves.

Ridiculous of course.

They knew much more and used potions because they knew to fight monsters who had become monsters.

And as such, the Slayers themselves were incredibly strong and fast too.

The best human army to ever be seen.

They had to be.

But how could they help me?

After all, the Syndicate have oaths, oaths which involve not involving themselves in the matters of men.

They cannot hold lordships or titles or have any say in regard to the Imperial Family.

So how could there be something there?!

Perhaps I am just fooling myself.

I have no help, not really.

I am alone in this tower.

But surely not for long, no, I cannot simply let it all slip away.

I cannot just sit idly by and let Theodore be crowned.

No, it is me who should be crowned…

And I shall be.

The crown.
The throne.
It belongs to me.

Only me.

THEN TAKE IT…
WEAR THE CROWN AND SIT UPON THE IMPERIAL THRONE!

But then again, my vision did not show the Imperial Crown or Throne.
No, the Imperial Throne was made of silver.
The crown simple gold.
Beautiful in its simplicity.

No, the throne I saw was dark as night.
The crown also dark, bejewelled with crimson rubies and the greenest emeralds.

As I think on it, the vision appears again.
Of me.
Beautiful and powerful.
Seated on a throne and crowned.
And fire… There is always fire, fire everywhere.

The flames dance and lick, dance and lick.
Again, and again and again.
They comfort me.

No, fire cannot scare me, I am the fire.

I am the one who will burn it all down and rise from the ashes.
I will be the one to unite the country.
All will love and worship me.

Love and worship.
Love and worship.
Love and worship.

Yes, I must leave this place.

This tower.

I have had enough; I need to walk freely.

I need to spread the word.

The word of me.

And there are questions, questions that need answering.

Important questions, ones that have not been addressed…

Ones that have been forgotten and unanswered.

Mainly, the one I keep coming back to, is how did the Red Eyed Demon get on this Island…

The island is separated from the mainland.

The only way across is the Grand Bridge.

It was built to keep us safe.

A feral vampire could not have simply gone unnoticed.

And the Imperium and the island itself have always been well guarded.

So how in the name of Light did the infernal creature get here?

Unless… **Someone brought it here?**

It is a strong question, a question that I cannot get out of my mind, and it apparently goes on and on.

Again, and again…

But it's never been answered, not with my father's sudden death and the beginning of the Great Cleansing, incidents that coincide so well.

And yes, I have been foolish enough to let it slip my mind and let it be lost these last three years.

It seems everyone has.

But I mean to breathe life back into these questions.
Enough of this confinement, that is indeed something I am certain of.
However, if I am to really leave, and without so called permission, I
must do so with a valid reason.
Ridiculous, that I would even need permission…
I am an Imperial, and Claudius is a nothing.

However, if I am to get people on my side, I must perhaps use honey
instead of salt.
I need to be diplomatic and sweet, not angry and emotional.
I had let anger and emotion rule me the day of the execution.
And it got me here.
No, if I leave, I must tread carefully, and differently.

Show them who I am.

YOU WILL SHOW THEM YOUR MADNESS.
BEAUTIFUL MADNESS.

Am I mad?
Perhaps I am.
Perhaps I am not.
Are not madness and greatness the same?
Simply two sides of the same coin.

MADNESS AND GREATNESS!
MADNESS AND GREATNESS!
MADNESS AND GREATNESS!
TWO SIDES OF THE SAME COIN!

Yes, maybe I am mad indeed.
But I am also great, of that I am sure.

And I shall show the world exactly what I mean.

BURN IT!
BURN IT!
BURN IT!

The words ring in my ears as they have many times these last few weeks.
Should I burn it all down?
Is that perhaps the only way I can rebuild?

NO, YOU DO NOT WANT TO SLAUGHTER THOUSANDS.
BUT THEN AGAIN, THE ARMY OF DEFENDERS NUMBERS THOUSANDS!
SURELY YOU WILL HAVE TO KILL THEM!

Ok, maybe slaughtering those thousands would be good.
But only them.

OF COURSE!
BUT WHAT ABOUT OTHERS WHO MAY OPPOSE?

I suppose they will need to be slaughtered too.

YES, KILL EVERYONE!

No, not everyone.
Maybe just mostly everyone.

I begin to laugh then.
The waves continue with their violent ways, and I continue with my laughter.

Yes, maybe I am indeed mad.

YES, YOU ARE MAD!
THE PEOPLE WILL SEE THAT TOO!

The people will do as they are told.

My laughter continues.
It only stops when I hear the door below open.
The same sound I have heard these last few weeks, and I know exactly who it is.

Kaleb.

Funny, when he first came, I had been on the floor, shaken from the first vision, the vision that showed me more than it had before.
I had expected him to be angry, yet he wasn't.
No, he had lifted me to my feet with love in his eyes.

Always love.

We kissed passionately, ignoring the fact my sister was there too.

She knew of course about us.
She had apparently for a while.
From what she said anyways, before she left never to come again.

My own fault, perhaps.

After all, we had fought, and she left with anger and sadness in her heart.

I will need to apologise.

I hear footsteps coming up the creaking stairs.
Always the same creaks.
Odd, he is later than usual.

I still look at the moon, I do not want to take my gaze from it.
The creaks draw nearer.
I must turn around.
The creaks stop.
I can feel his presence.

I manage to pull my gaze from the captivating moon, and I turn to face him.

My love.

He is dressed fully in armour, he looked glorious.
Tall, strong, and mine.
All mine.
He has his head low, his feet almost shuffling.
His breathing is hard.
Something is up, it is clear.

"Kaleb, my love."

I breathe.

He looks at me, a smile on his face.

"How are you feeling tonight."

He asks of me.

A question he always asks me, every visit.

He had never asked me so many times before, not since the execution
and this damned confinement.
It is beyond annoying.

"I am fine."

I tell him, the same answer as always.

> **HE DOES NOT BELIEVE YOU!**
> **HE NEVER BELIEVES YOU!**

But why will he not believe me?
I am fine, am I not?

> **NO, YOU HAVE GONE QUITE MAD.**
> **HE CAN SEE IT.**

No, I am great.
I have power, incredible power.

"Something is the matter."

I mutter.
It is not a question, but a fact.

"Yes… A few things."

He answers.

His voice is grave, I do not like it.

"Tell me."

I insist.

"It concerns ravens."

 He tells me.

Ravens?
What a confusing thought.
And very intriguing.

"Do tell."

I urge.

"As you know, ravens fly throughout the Realm, they carry messages
and such forth.
Anyways, I was at the Grand Spiral back at the Capital."

"Must have been important for you to come late."

I question, slight anger in my voice.
For the last month he has always come at the same time, and yet he is
late by some hours.

He looks away from me, his gaze turning to the moon and tides.

"Why did you leave?"

I question.

"Just Syndicate business."

He answers.

Unusual.

Usually, Kaleb tells me everything…
This is a too off-the-hand answer for my liking.
Yet, there was more important stuff to talk about right now I guessed.
I will however make sure to circle back to it at another more convenient time.

"So, what happened?"

I probe.

"I went to the Syndicate as the Captains had been called.
Every single Captain in the Capital.
When I got there, the room was already full.
They were looking at various maps.
Maps of the Magic Realm."

Even more intriguing.
It is not often that the Lord Commander calls every Captain present in the Capital.
Surely something must have happened.

"Why were they looking at maps of the Realm of Magic?
Is there news of the war?
Is your father okay."

Kaleb looks back to me and smiles once again.

"My father is in good health I believe.

You're kind for asking.
But it is more what my father said."

"So, it was your father who sent the letter?"

I ask.

Kaleb nods at this.

"Aye, he sent a letter.
Apparently, there was a massacre of some kind."

He confesses.

A massacre?

"At the frontlines?
Have the vampires broken through?
Are we safe?"

Kaleb takes my hand.

"The frontlines are the same as always, I assume.
The fighting goes on as it always has.
But… But there is something happening."

"What is it?
What is happening?"

"As you know, the Realm of Magic is the Black Woods themselves.
And these woods, they span hundreds upon hundreds of miles.
Whilst there is what's left of the Imperial Army and their own
Protectors, they cannot simply cover every mile.

It appears… It appears as if vampires have snuck through the frontlines.”

“Snuck through?
But how?
I know there’s little of the Imperial Army left, but their own Protectors still have large numbers.
And they are known for keeping the vampires strictly out of their Realm.”

“They are indeed, and yet it seems as if it still happened.”

Kaleb answers.

“And this village, it was near the frontlines?”

I ponder.
After all, vampires have known to occasionally get past the frontlines, and they have known to attack anything or anyone they see first, such is their bloodlust.”

“That’s the thing… The village they massacred was deep in the Black Woods.
It was along the coastal cliffs, far away from anything else.
They went undetected for possibly weeks and were never caught.
My guess is they only attacked the village because they needed blood.
But… Well, they’ve not been found as of yet and it is unlikely they will.
And there’s every good chance they are heading this way.”

He confesses.

I take a step back, my mind buzzing with thoughts.

Vampires… Snuck into the Magic Realm… And stayed hidden for weeks?
Not attacking anyone until they had too… Incredibly unusual.
And heading this way?
But why?
What could this possibly mean?!

"There's only one reason they would sneak through the Realms.
They must be planning something."

I conclude.

"Exactly my thoughts… The last time they planned something."

"The Imperial Dynasty nearly got wiped out.
My grandparents, aunts and uncle.
Only my father survived…"

And if they are indeed heading here, or in fact, are already here, then it must surely mean they plan on trying to once again wipe us out.
And with Theodore's upcoming coronation…

Kaleb takes hold of my hands then.

"You mustn't worry my love; they will not come anywhere near you!
I swear it, I swear I'll never let anyone hurt you.
Man, or monster.
I will always protect you."

This touches my heart in a way I cannot describe.
He really would die for me…

And yet, despite his protection, I am not worried…

You'd think vampires crossing the Realms and the risk of them attacking would frighten me, and yet, it does not.

I feel oddly calm.
So much so a giggle even escapes my lips.

Kaleb looks at me with caution.

HE THINKS YOU ARE MAD.

Am I mad?
Perhaps.
Perhaps not.

In truth, I hope the vampires do come… I would love to show them the extent of my powers.

"Tris, are you sure you're okay?"

I hate this question.

"Of course, my love."

I say, trying to reassure him.
Yet it is evident by his face that I have not reassured him.

"Was there anything else that happened?"

I ask, trying to take the focus off myself.
Kaleb looks as if he wants to say something, then changes his mind.

"I had a… Slight disagreement with one of the other captains.
It's fine though, nothing to worry about."

He looks away sheepishly.

"Anyways, after all the captains were sent away, there was another letter, one I was not privy too.
My Uncle would not allow me to see it.
He only kept mentioning a threat."

"A threat?
You mean the vampires?"

"No, I think not… There's a threat closer… A threat here, I believe."

"A threat here?
How so?"

I ask.

"I'm not sure, my uncle would not speak much about it."

"Well, if there's any threat then it's certainly Claudius."

I mention.

Kaleb shakes his head at this.

"No… I do not believe it is Claudius.
Don't get me wrong, Claudius has done much… Yet, it seems my uncle spoke of something else.
Of what though I am not sure."

He concludes.

Odd… Clearly Claudius is the threat?
He always is and always has been.

"Did you per chance see if there was a seal on the letter."

I ponder, trying to change the subject.

Kaleb grows anxious then, very unlike him.
Surely, he knows who the letter is from.

"So, whose seal was it?"

I press him.

"Well, if I'm not mistaken, I only saw it once, last year when I left for
the frontlines.
My father read such a letter once, and it had the same seal.
I believe it's from the Head Witch."

He confesses.

This instantly pricks my ears.

The Head Witch?

*THE HEAD WITCH SENDING A LETTER TO THE LORD
COMMANDER OF THE SYNDICATE, HOW OMINOUS.*

Ominous indeed.

My mind floats with ideas, however I try to calm myself.

Perhaps it is nothing.

After all, the Syndicate did not actively take part in the Great Cleansing and thus only Slayers were admitted to and from Realms to aid in the war.

Therefore, the Lord Commander and the Head Witch would no doubt have corresponded beforehand.

So maybe I shouldn't look to closely into this… However, from what I've also gathered, the Lord Commander is no doubt preparing Kaleb to be his successor.

Everyone knows it, and as such, why would he not allow Kaleb to see this letter?

It's clear that letter contains something valuable.

Information most likely, which can be worth more than gold.

"What do you think it is about?"

I ask.

Kaleb shakes his head, still confused.

"Honestly, no idea.

Perhaps it's about the Imperial Army?!

Maybe they are simply telling us the troop numbers are dwindling further."

He scoffs at this.

"It shouldn't even be called an Army any longer, what's left here is nothing but a shambles."

"Why join the Imperial Army, an army that's all been but disbanded when you have the Defenders?"

I answer.

This was true enough, yes, we still had the Imperial Guard, numbering a couple hundred or so in the castle, and perhaps maybe also a few hundred in the Capital, yet the Imperial Soldiers remain largely unorganised, without proper command of course.
The General having been stuck in the Realm of Magic for some years now.

"If only they had someone to rally behind."

He answers.

This is also true enough and gives me an idea.

The remaining Imperial Army do need someone to rally behind, and who better than an Imperial.

I could rally them, what's left of them.

> *THE IMPERIAL ARMY ARE WITHOUT A DOUBT LOYAL.*
> *THE ONES WHO PARTOOK IN THE GREAT CLEANSING ARE*
> *NOW DEFENDERS, BUT THOSE WHO REMAINED ARE LOYAL*
> *TO A FAULT.*
> *BUT THEIR LOYALTY WOULD LIE WITH THEODORE, WOULD*
> *IT NOT?*

This is also true.

If it came down to it, if battle lines were really drawn, and two Imperial's called them to arms, who would they really follow?

The Crown Prince and next in line to be King…

Or a second son who stands to inherit nothing, and has recently become known for mischief and inciting a riot.

Gods be damned!

But despite that, they also knew of Theodore and what despicable deeds he has done.

EVEN IF THEY DO FOLLOW YOU, THEIR NUMBERS ARE NOTHING COMPARED TO CLAUDIUS AND HIS DEFENDERS…

More truth, I do not like.

I look at Kaleb, but this time I really look at him.

He stands there, tall and proud like usual, in his glorious armour.

He is a captain of the Syndicate, but not only that, he is an Umpire.

His House originates from the Imperial Line itself, although muddled over the last couple centuries.

Despite that, his father is none other than the General of the Imperial Army, a man of fine standing, like his father before him and so forth.

They have always been military inclined, not only that, but Kaleb's uncle is the Lord Commander.

His bloodlines and blood ties are strong.

Incredibly strong.

It is anyone's guess what remnants of the Imperial Army would do concerning which Prince to follow, however if I had the aid of Kaleb, whose own father is their beloved General…

Yes... Yes, surely if me and Kaleb showed a united front then indeed, they would follow me.

And why would we not show a united front?
We love each other after all.

But not just the Imperial Army, no, Kaleb is lined up to be the next Lord Commander...

Thus, he would have a whole Syndicate of Slayers behind him.
The strongest, best warriors to walk the land.

And they could be mine!

NO, THEY WOULD BELONG TO KALEB...

Yes, and Kaleb belongs to me, therefore they would belong to me also.

I feel a bubble of excitement, yes, I could have an army at my back.
Not just a rabble of flimsy Imperial Soldiers, but the prestigious Syndicate itself!
With them at my back, surely the rest of the nobility and the commoners alike will follow suit.

A plan begins to form in my mind.
A brilliant plan.
But I can tell Kaleb has more to say, I can only hope this too is good news.

"Is there more, my love?"

I ask innocently.

"Yes, the rookery in the castle.
With my uncle sending me away from his chambers, I thought perhaps there might be another letter sent to the rookery in the castle.
Perhaps the Head Witch sent a letter to someone on the Council.
However, when I got there, the usual slave who works there and looks after the ravens was gone.
He usually sleeps in there but was nowhere to be seen.
A different slave who I perchance bumped into told me that he had gone to Claudius' chambers.
I searched the castle high and low and could not find him.
That's why I'm late, I've been searching for the slave."
As I said, he's not been seen since going to Claudius."

"CLAUDIUS."

I repeat, even more intrigued.

"Yes, the slave went straight away to hand deliver the letter however the slave never returned."

A letter to the Lord Commander who sends Kaleb away.
And now apparently another letter for Claudius which now involves a missing slave.

Intriguing and more intriguing.

"What shall we do?"

I ask of him.

He looks at me then, and it is a look of love.
Despite what he's just revealed, it feels good, this moment.

Me and Kaleb have felt distant lately in my confinement.
Yes, we had held each other, kissed and cuddled, yet we had not made love.
There has been a distance between us…
But now, right in this moment, it feels as if we are good.
How we should be.

I take a step towards him, and he immediately wraps me in his arms.

"There is something else… Claudius… You were right.
His Defenders, they existed before the attack on us.
Claudius had been recruiting for years all across the Human Realm, when he returned three years ago, he did so with a secret army in place."

This shocks me.

Defenders… Before the Great Cleansing?

And yet… It made sense.
When it began, it did indeed happen fast and swiftly.
The only way to have done that is to have already had the men to carry out the dark deeds.

"He has always been known for those speeches… And he has always drawn crowds…"

I look up at him then.
Please, please let us not argue about this again.
I know I should not bring it up, however I had too.

"I can stop this."

I tell him.

A sigh comes from him, and his body turns rigid.

"Tris, please."

He sighs.

"Just listen to me, please.
Kaleb, Claudius is a tyrant.
Look at what you just told me.
He started the Cleansing, he murdered thousands, and he won't stop there."

Kaleb pulls away, he looks as if ready to walk down the stairs, but I hold onto him tightly.

"Please, Kaleb, do not leave.
Don't you find it weird that Claudius was the one who found us?
That he, of all people found us right after being attacked?"

Kaleb hangs his head then.

"There's more."

He grumbles.

There's more?!

A letter from the General and Head Witch of the Council of Covens.
Also, a letter from Claudius which now involves a missing slave.

And now there's more?!

This is true, all of it.
It makes me feel alive.

Kaleb looks at me then and I can see the internal struggle on his face.
As if he is debating whether to tell me or not.

"Kaleb, please.
Just tell me."

I urge.

Kaleb pulls me in close then, enveloping me into a hug.
I can hear his heartbeat.
It beats loud and strong.

A vision hits me.

The feral is clear as day.
A huge deformed winged form of both man and bat.
With yellow rags which were once robes… Still so familiar.
Kaleb thrusting his sword deep into the beast and it letting out a shrilling scream.
Then the beast hitting Kaleb, sending him slamming into a tree.
Him then lying motionless in the snow.
I can remember how angry it made me.
Incredibly and feverishly angry.
I stretched my palm outwards, and fire projected forward.
It hit the creature fast and hard.

The ferocity of the flames burned it to mere bones and dust within seconds.

I hear a voice then…

"Tristan!
Tristan what's happening?!"

I can't reply, I'm too lost in the vision.

I begin to crawl.
Through the flowers and snow and mud.
Crawling for what seems like an eternity.
And me… Weakened and depleting, yet not caring.
Only wanting to reach Kaleb.
Finally reaching him and seeing all the blood.
A huge wound across his back.
And yet, I used what Chaos I could muster to fix it.
The wound knitted itself within seconds, leaving a large scar.
Then his heart… His heart was slow and fading…

I thought intensely about it beating strongly.
I could feel death approaching for me, and darkness coming over my eyes and yet I continued to Cast my Chaos to save him.
And then his heart… It begun to beat loudly and strongly.

"Tristan!
Tristan what's happening?!"

The voice repeats.

And just like that, I'm pulled from the vision.

I'm back in Kaleb's arms and his heart beats just like it did… When I fixed him?

I nearly collapse then.
Kaleb's arms only keep me upright.

"Woah, Tris, are you okay?"

His voice full of concern as he holds onto me tightly.

Was that real?
Was it a dream?
Or the truth?

For three years the story had been that Kaleb had saved me from the attack…
That he had bravely fought and won against the beast.
But he hadn't done that… He protected me indeed, but it was not he who had slain the vampire… **It was me**.

"Nothing."

I lie.

"Tris, what was that?"

I pull myself away from him then and take one last look at the moon before going for the stairs.
I quickly descend them, reaching the ground floor of the tower where most of my furnishings and bed are.

My guards may be outside, but they can't hear a thing.
My tower has been sound proofed for years now.

"Tristan, don't walk away from me."

I ignore him, reaching for the nearest bottle of wine.
I open it and take several quick swigs.

Kaleb grabs it off me.
I reach for it and yet Kaleb holds his hand above his head.
There's no chance I can reach it.

"Kaleb, give me it back."

"No, not until you tell me."

Instead, I decide to change subject.

"If you tell me what other news you had to share."

I object.

Kaleb stops then.

"You said you had other news, before,"

"Before what."

He says harshly.

We stand there in silence.
It appears as if we have reached an impasse.
The moonlight beams heavily into the room, illuminating us both.
He places the bottle of wine on a nearby small table.

"Then I suppose we both have a secret."

I mutter.

I couldn't tell him about the visions.
How it was me who killed the feral, not him.
How I've seen the Capital nothing more than a burning inferno.
How I've seen myself crowned and throned.
And In truth I had one more secret still aside from the visions, I still hadn't talked about my missing Grimoire.
I had lost it at the execution and have not been able to find out what happened to it since.
I half hoped it had not been found.
After all, it had been a month and surely if it had been discovered then there would have been some sort of gossip or news.

"I don't want there to be secrets."

He concludes.

I wave my hands at this.
I do not have time…

"There is a missing Syndicate member."

He announces.

There's a missing Slayer?

"Not recently, but three years ago.
Apparently, he went missing the same night we were attacked."

The same night we were attacked?!

"Who was it?"

I question.

"I'm not sure… That's all my uncle told me."

He finishes.

A missing slave the night Claudius receives a letter… A missing Slayer the night of the attack three years past… And Claudius was the one who found us…

Everything always points back to him.

"Claudius has always been the problem."

I speak.

Kaleb looks at me, I know he doesn't want to be listening, but I can see on his face that he realises I am making sense.

"We've spoke about this before."

He tells me.

Yes, we have, but Kaleb never seemed to listen to me like he was now. Surely whatever he was going to tell me, but now has decided not too, is important.

"But maybe the slave isn't missing, maybe I just couldn't find him. Perhaps he's even back at the rookery now as we speak."

Kaleb states.

"And the Slayer… He was young, he might have just decided that a life of the Syndicate wasn't for him… We've had runaways before."

He tells me.

"Yes, but they have always been found and executed for desertion. Slayers are incredible hunters and trackers; they always find their prey."

I answer.

"Perhaps this boy is just good at hiding."

Retorts Kaleb.

"We both know you don't believe that.
Please Kaleb, you know what Claudius is capable of, you know what I am saying makes sense.
Please, just believe me."

"FINE."

He snaps.

"So, what if you are right?
What does it matter, Claudius is soon to be gone from here.
His regency ends in just moon's turn."

He points to the open balcony, the moon full and bright like it was upstairs.

I look at it intently.

It had been a full moon when me and Kaleb had made love and quarrelled about me Casting my Chaos to make the enchanting and bright lights.

The very night before the execution.

"He will be gone, Tristan.
I promise you; he will be gone.
And then Theodore will be King.
Everything will be fine, I promise.
And then you won't have to worry."

Won't have to worry?
Can he really be this clueless…
Claudius has no plans to go anywhere, he is not about to simply hand his power over.
And Theodore, he will be nothing more than a puppet.
And yet, Kaleb promises me he that he will be gone with a complete certainty.

And now with vampires coming also…

But perhaps… If they really are coming here, and coming for Theodore's coronation no doubt then maybe just maybe they could sort out my little Theodore problem for me…

An awful, dreadful thought… But it would save me from having to murder my own blood.
Yet, there is something I still do not feel right with.

If there is a safe way of removing Theodore… But I just don't see one.

And Kaleb… Always so certain.

But how can he be so certain?
He clearly hides something.

*IF THEODORE IS KING, IT WILL MEAN UNCERTAINTIES FOR
YOU BOTH!
USE THAT.
MAKE HIM QUESTION HOW MUCH HE REALLY LOVES YOU.*

"But what about me?"

I speak.

I had not meant to say it.
I do not want to test his love, but I can't stop myself.

"If Theodore becomes king, then what happens to me?
What happens to us?"

I ponder.

My voice breaks at this.
Breaking because I am testing him.

Kaleb holds me tightly again.

"Nothing will happen to us, nothing!
I promise you; I will always love you.
I always have, and always will.
Surely, surely you know this."

He asks of me.

I knew this would be his answer, I love him for it, but I need to know more.

"I know you love me."

I reassure him.

"But we are getting older, Kaleb.
Every day that passes, we age.
We aren't children anymore, or those teenage boys kissing and professing their love for each other in the woods.
I'm nineteen now, and you twenty.
People talk, I know they do.
I always ignored it, pretended it wasn't real.
But it is real, people know about us, Kaleb.
They whisper and whisper."

**I should stop.
I am hurting him.**

"Let them whisper."

He speaks.

"They can do no harm.
I will not let them."

His eyes watering.

"You know that isn't true."

I object.

"We could burn for this, Kaleb.
Both of us.
You know this."

I say further, adding more tears to his eyes.

"Theodore hates me, he hates you, when he becomes King, he will surely separate us."

His hand strokes my face, his touch so gentle.

"I won't let that happen, My Little Prince."

He sounds so upset.
I feel so guilty.

"How?
What could you possibly do?
He will be King, and he will command us both.
We will be over."

Kaleb's hands grab tightly onto my shoulders, his grip firm.

"No, no, no!"

He repeats.

"No one!
Not even a King will separate us!"

YOU HAVE LURED HIM!
NOW GO IN FOR THE KILL.

No, I should not be doing this.
He is a good man, an honourable man.
Do not make him forsake himself.

"But if he does separate us, what will do you?
If he sends me away, what will you do Kaleb?
What if he locks me away, like Claudius has now.
Only you may never see me again?"

His face contorts into rage.

"THEN I'LL FUCKING KILL HIM!"

He screams.

The sheer ferocity of his voice scares me, I take a frightened step back.
I can only thank my good senses for soundproofing the tower.

THERE YOU GO, YOU HAVE DONE IT.

"I WILL KILL HIM!
I WILL KILL ANYONE WHO TRIES TO TAKE YOU FROM ME!
ANYONE!"

He is getting angrier and angrier.

I've done this.
I've turned him into this.

I try to console him, to take his hands in mine, regretful of what I've
done.

"Kaleb, Kaleb try to calm yourself."

He is still angry, incredibly so.
I reach for him again, but he grabs me roughly.

"I WILL NOT LET ANYONE TAKE YOU FROM ME!
NEVER!"

"Shh yourself, please, Kaleb, calm yourself.
Please, come back to me."

He grabs me once more and begins speaking fiercely and quickly.

"I love you!
People may whisper and say it's wrong, but I care not!
The Faith may say it's wrong and sinful.
The laws of men may say that too.
But I don't care what the Faith or other men think.
Neither people nor laws or Faith will ever stop me from loving you.
And if I have to burn for that love, if I have to burn for you, then I will
do so."

He professes to me, his body still full of anger.

Gods… He really does love me.

I feel so much guilt, but I still continue to coo to him.

"Please, My Brave Captain, come back to me,"

I lean upwards then, my lips finding his.
He pulls me in tightly, kissing me back with harsh intensity.
We begin to walk backwards, falling onto the bed.
His mouth still on mine, I hear the loud ripping of my clothes.

He quickly removes his armour, myself helping him, it clangs and bangs as it hits the stone floor.

He then quickly pulls his pants down and takes his shirt off.

He lifts one leg onto his shoulder and spits into his hand, quickly rubbing it against my anus.

I barely get a chance to register what is happening before he plunges into me.

Deep and hard.

I'm about to release a shriek when his lips cover mine again.

I melt into the kiss.

Despite the evident pain I wrap my legs around him and pull him tighter to me as he thrusts again and again.

He begins to bite my neck, and I am finally able to let out moans of pleasure as the pain turns to ecstasy.

I have missed him, missed this.

"Yes, yes!
Fuck me, Kaleb."

I plead.

He grabs my throat, his darkened eyes staring into mine.

"YOU... ARE... MINE!"

He annunciates with each thrust.

NOW, DO IT NOW.

"Yes, yes I am yours.
Only yours."

I reassure him through gasps, his hand still tight on my throat.

"NO ONE IS TAKING YOU FROM ME."

He commands.

THIS IS YOUR CHANCE, TAKE IT.

Gods, forgive me.

"Then I must be King."

I cough.

He thrusts wilder, he is coming to a close.

"I… Must… Be… King, Kaleb."

I struggle to say, his hand squeezing my throat tighter and tighter.

"Then nothing will happen to us."

I manage to cough out.

His grip tightens even more, and I can even see black spots.

His eyes grow black.

"YES!
YES!
YOU WILL BE KING!"

He growls roughly before letting out a loud shout as he comes deep inside me.

He shakes uncontrollably on top of me momentarily.
I lay underneath him, my clothes ripped, and my body covered in sweat.
The sex was phenomenal, better than it had been for ages.

And I had gotten confirmation.
I tricked him, I tricked him badly.
But I got confirmation all the same.

Kaleb, my love, my life, will stand by me.

AND HE WILL KILL FOR YOU!
KILL CLAUDIUS!
KILL YOUR BROTHER!
AND MAKE YOU KING.

Kaleb rolls off me and within seconds I hear his light snores.
I turn my head sideways and look out at the full moon, still high and bright in the sky.

As the waves of pleasure ebb away, I smile proudly.

Haven't you heard?!

I will be King.

A FEW HOURS LATER

CLAUDIUS CHAMBERS

ANYTHING FOR HIM

EDGAR

I could not quite contain my incredible feeling of utter joy.

I had started coming here some weeks ago, with the hope of catching a glimpse of him.

And it was not until the morning of that disastrous execution that he had told me to stay away.

That had been a moon's turn ago and I had been kicking myself since.

I thought I had blown any chance I had with him.

All I wanted was to admire and stand in awe of the man who God speaks through.

But all this time and nothing.

I felt almost as if I had been severed from my connection to God itself, and it nearly broke me.

I stayed away from Claudius chambers since, or anywhere near that part of the castle for that matter, and yet I still resided in the Imperium despite the animosity from Kaleb and his little gang of friends.

But I ignored it and stayed regardless, and in doing so I seem to have discovered much.

I had stayed before and after the execution and had noticed just how close the Prince and Kaleb really were.

Despite the fact the wretched prince had all but ruined the godly and just execution, I was glad to see him confined to his tower.

A tower which is suspiciously close to the Inner Spiral…

The prince used to stay in the Imperial Apartments where his father once resided, and his siblings still do.
And yet, three years ago after the attack on them and after the Grand Cleansing started, the prince moved from the Imperial Apartments and chose a spooky, derelict tower that had been long abandoned.
He quickly set about doing work and furnishing it to make it liveable.
He can often be seen from the tower.
Either standing on his main balcony where his living quarters are or higher above on a smaller balcony from which his owl often flies overhead.
But that was not the only thing that could be seen…
No, spectacular and weird lights could be seen emanating from it.
The lights have not been seen since his confinement and yet they had been seen before.
I myself saw them the night before the execution when I was doing my rounds.
The same night that our Captain had vanished…
And ever since the confinement began Kaleb had often wandered off and vanished from sight.
No doubt to see the prince.
Just last night I had seen him wandering into the rookery and afterwards walking through the halls like a madman looking for only the Light knows what.
And then he vanished again, once again without a doubt to see the prince.
It was evident that the boys were lovers, and it sickened me to my core.
Two men as lovers was unnatural and ungodly.

To think our own prince… a sexual deviant.
It disgusts me.

Yet not surprising, his brother is also a deviant.
Attacking and raping many women.

The only sane Imperial seemed to be the Princess Isabella.
She was quiet yet beautiful and seems to have good sense about her.

The thing that irks me the most is that, despite Tristan's confinement that Claudius had set in place, somehow Kaleb still manages to gain access to his tower.
I can only blame those fools of guards that stand before the door.
They are feckless and stupid if you asked me, but they have been loyally guarding the prince for years.
The princess had visited but once according to rumours.
Odd due to how close the Imperial twins usually are.

Pushing these thoughts aside, I finally reach my destination.

Claudius' chambers.

Defenders loyally stand at the door and yet as I walk closer they step aside, opening the doors for me.
They must know of my coming.

That means Claudius would have mentioned me!

Even the thought that he would think of me and better yet, say my name, gives me chills.
Surely God smiles on me.
I can feel his eternal light shining on me.

As the doors fully open, I eagerly step inside.

I have never been in Claudius' apartments before, not even when he had contacted me just over three years ago.

YES, WHEN YOU BETRAYED THE SYNDICATE!
WHEN YOU HELPED CAUSED THE DEATH OF THOUSANDS...

No, I betrayed no one.
I was never friends or never owed loyalty to those godless, Soulless witches.
Walking into the apartments, I am happy to see many tapestries of our Lord of Eternal Light.
Beautiful yellow suns with swords through them.
And there, in the centre of the room by his table is none other than Claudius himself.
He stands there with a worried expression on his brow.

"My Lord, is everything okay?"

I ask as I hear the scraping of the doors close behind me.
He looks at me then, his worried expression remaining.

"Edgar, you are here."

He announces.

I immediately feel as if I am above the clouds at the mention of him saying my name.

"Yes, my Lord.
I came as quickly as I could."

"Good… Good…"

He seems befuddled and confused.
I walk towards him and smile warmly.

"What may I help with, my Lord."

I ask of him.

His eyes bore into me then.

"Ahh, yes… Well, I have a situation… A situation that is most delicate.
And I was wondering, if perhaps you might help me with that?"

Claudius asking for my help!

I could die this instant a happy man.

"Of course, my Lord.
Anything."

His brows furrow at this.
He seems uncertain of my answer.
Yet he should not be, he has my complete loyalty.
Surely, he already knew that when he last called upon my help.

I remember it clearly.
It had been a couple months before the attack on the Prince and Kaleb.
Before the death of the old King and the Great Cleansing.
He had asked for documents… Documents which contained where
every single witch lived… and the High Pope… That was me too.
He was searched for high and low and yet was not found.

LOOK AT WHAT YOU CAUSED!

No, I never caused a thing concerning him.
I merely led him to where I was told.
And all I did was hand over documents, I never knew what would happen… Or did I?

YOU KNOW THAT IS NOT TRUE.
YOU KNEW WHAT WOULD HAPPEN.
YOU KNEW EXACTLY WHAT WOULD HAPPEN THE SECOND CLAUDIUS GOT HIS HANDS ON HIM AND THOSE DOCUMENTS.
YOU MAY FEIGN IGNORANCE, BUT YOU KNOW THE TRUTH!

It need not matter now, what was done was done.
I decide to speak then, to assure Claudius once more.

"My Lord, you know I have done as you asked in the past.
I will not speak it out loud, but you know that you have my utmost loyalty.
Please, just tell me what you need me to do."

His body seems to become more comfortable, his facial expressions less worried.
His composure overall seems to ease.

"I need you to remove something for me.
A chest.
That chest."

He turns and points towards a large, wooden chest.

YES, YOU DID MUCH FOR HIM ALREADY.
YOU CAUSED THE DEATHS OF THOUSANDS!
AND NOW HE WANTS YOU TO JUST REMOVE A CHEST.

True.

I have done what he asked loyally and without question, he was so close to God after all.

And yet, I cannot help but feel somewhat deflated.

I had hoped me coming here would be of some importance and significance and yet he just summoned me here to remove a chest.

How odd...

Claudius notices this it seems and speaks.

"Was there something else you wanted to speak about."

He asks of me.

I stutter before quickly composing myself.

"I'm sorry, My Lord, I had just hoped that perhaps you would have asked something greater of me.

I thought perhaps it was more important."

A flash of anger appears across his face, and I instantly feel regret.

I want to serve him; I shouldn't have questioned him.

If he wants me to remove a chest then I should just do so happily.

"F – forgive me... I spoke out of turn."

I speak.

"Yes, it appears you did."

Answers Claudius.

"Remove the chest and do not make the same mistake again.
I'll call upon you again if I see fit.
You are dismissed."

I immediately want to kick myself.
Once again it seems as if I have blown my chance.
I dutifully nod and do as I am told.
I walk over to the chest he had gestured at and begin to lift.
It's heavy, extremely so.
Yet with years of slaying monsters, I am strong enough to lift it.

Heaving and huffing, I slowly but surely walk away with the chest, the
contents of which is unknown.
As I do, some anger takes hold of me.
I have done as Claudius asked three years ago and yet he has treated
me with disdain.
Does he not realise I would do anything for him?
Perhaps he just needs more confirmation.
The chest feels awfully heavy as I continue to carry it.

Perhaps I should open it?

Perhaps if I know its contents, I can better get to know Claudius.
Yes, yes, surely then he will want to be my friend.

My anger gone, I smile as I carry the chest away from Claudius
chambers and back to the Inner Spiral.
I only hoped that Kaleb and his gang of friends will not be there.
Regardless, nothing else matters.
Only Claudius and God.

Only Claudius and God.

A FEW HOURS LATER

COUNCIL CHAMBERS

LOYALTY AND BETRAYAL

TRISTAN

I stand within the Council Chambers.

A big, wide room.

Open windows on either side.

The guards had looked dumbfounded when I opened the doors and walked past them, yet as an Imperial Prince there was not much they could do to question me.

I knew the guards very well of course, they had guarded the door to my tower for years, and before that they guarded me in my Imperial Apartments.

They are good men.

If not slightly dim witted.

I had simply opened the doors, which surprisingly where not even locked.

I suppose I could have left earlier, but what would have been the point?

In fact, I enjoyed spending the last month in confinement.

The guards of course had stuttered and stumbled and asked me to come back.

That's when my beloved had shown up, like he promised he would.

687

He had fallen asleep after our lovemaking, yet despite wanting to finally get to spend just one night in his arms, I had to instead wake him up and he left shortly after.

And yet he returned at morning light.

His hulking and looming frame silences them.

Perhaps slightly unfair, the guards do not need the threat of a threat, yet I had to be sure that I could leave.

They simply let me pass.

The wind howls loudly through the Council Chambers I notice.

The wooden windows often smash against the stone.

Opening and closing.

And the waves, they are extra violent today.

In front of me, a large rectangular table.

Made from solid dark wood, in front of it lay maps and charts, also letters and messages.

I have been here for the last twenty minutes, reading intently through it all.

I should not even be here, of course.

I probably should not be reading any of this, not being a Council Member, and yet that was about to change.

I will show them exactly who I am and I will take my power with words this time instead of a riot.

While I was supposed to be confined to my tower, I could stay there no longer.

Especially after last night.

Kaleb had come to me, sweaty and panicked.

He told me about what happened at the Grand Spiral, and we talked and argued about what to do.

Not to mention the Head Witch herself sending the Lord Commander a letter.

A letter sadly Kaleb did not manage to read.

I will need to know what that letter contains, of course.

I had wanted to ask Kaleb to fetch it for me, but I did not want to push his boundaries too far.

I had already tricked him into confessions he probably would never have admitted had I not spoken of how our fates could be dire.

He had shouted and swore and furiously told me he would kill anyone for me.

And when he made love to me hard and fast on the bed, he told me I would be King.

I could still feel the pain from last night, I was sore that was true.

But oh, how sweet our love making had been.

And yet, I still did not want to push him anymore.

I love him, and I don't want Kaleb to do any of those things for me.

He is a good, honourable man.

I can't take that away from him by making him my personal executioner.

YOU HAVE ALREADY TAKEN HIS HONOUR!
YOU HAVE DONE IT SINCE THAT VERY NIGHT YOU
PROFESSED LOVE AND KISSED.

No… No, I just didn't want him to go to the frontlines.
I didn't want him to die!

YOU JUST WANTED TO KEEP HIM FOR YOURSELF!

But he got injured.
The feral nearly killed him.

YOU HEALED HIM!
YOU COULD HAVE LET HIM GO… YET YOU DID NOT!

No, it's not my fault.

He wanted to stay.

He loves the Capital, and the Syndicate and his family.

He likes it here.

Besides, he did go to the frontlines, eventually.

BUT YOU MADE HIM STAY… FOR TWO YEARS!
HE IS A WARRIOR WHO SHOULD BE ON THE BATTLEFIELD!
HE CAME BACK FOR YOU AND HAS STAYED SINCE!
THREE YEARS… HE STAYS ONLY FOR YOU.
HE DISHONOURED HIMSELF AGAIN AND AGAIN FOR YOU!

No, no, I do not want to think on it.

YOU DO NOT WISH TO THINK ABOUT IT BECAUSE YOU
KNOW IT IS TRUE!

Well, if it's true then it shall be true no longer.

I will not make Kaleb more dishonourable… I shall not push him any further…

I had decided that I would not tell him that I had slain the vampire…

I could not take that from Kaleb… Not right now, anyhow.

And besides, he clearly was not telling me everything either.

Or will I indeed push him to his limits…

I suppose I always knew he would do anything for me.

After all, it was he who always tried to stop me from revealing my magic.

It was he who always looked out for me and loved me.

Even when I caused a city riot, he still loyally and dutifully visited me every single night.

And yet… All of those nights he did not make love to me…

Not until last night.

I suppose he had been angry, yet his love outweighed it.

I only hope this is true.

After all, it was him who told me of this very Council Meeting this morning right before he departed.

Perhaps that was the information he withheld, and yet, I think whatever he held had more importance.
The Council has not had a meeting for a while, and I can only assume it will be about the upcoming threat.
Surely the Lord Commander of the Syndicate must have called the Council?
What with everything Kaleb told me last night, with vampires perhaps being here in the Realm and Theodore's upcoming coronation there must be much to discuss.
Not to mention the various Lords and Ladies who have gotten here and the many more that are travelling throughout the Human Realm to travel towards the Capital.

Or perhaps this meeting is about me.

And if it was going to be about me, I was not going to allow them to talk about me without being here to defend myself.

And yet, as I continue to read, I can judge that it seems this meeting is indeed about the disturbance within the Black Woods, the Realm of Magic.

There seems to be some reports of the frontlines too, the frontlines themselves being outside of the Black Woods, where the BorderLands are.

A thin stretch of land which hangs in the balance the Magic and the Dark Realm on either side.

It appears to be exactly how Kaleb described, a village was massacred and completely burned to the ground, and yet, it was apparent that it was not the fire that killed those poor people.
No, according to reports sent by the General himself, and from what Kaleb told me, the Protectors, an army used by the witches sent scouts that have reported that the corpses had torn bodies, limbs and heads ripped off.

And blood.
Even when the fire had died, there appeared to be blood everywhere.
A massacre indeed it seems.

And by all accounts, no known survivors,
No, they do not usually leave survivors.
I know exactly what was responsible for this.

Vampires.

Thinking about them, a flash of Red Eyes appears before me.
Fangs snarling and massive wings and razor-sharp claws.
And Kaleb… He protects me, as always.

More visions.
More memories.

I had not originally remembered hardly anything from that day, and now over the last few weeks more and more comes to me.

The vision changes suddenly and once again I'm surrounded by fire.
I'm seated on a throne, wearing a bejewelled crown once again.

And the fire licks and dances around me.
It is exhilarating.
It slowly but surely begins to ebb away.
The Council Chambers come back to reality.

I shudder and breathe hard as I grip the table so tightly my hands bleed.

Damn it!

I quickly grab a cloth and begin wiping my hands.
Getting myself under control just in time, I hear the doors open behind me.
They walked in talking, yet upon seeing the back of me they fall silent.

I smile a wide smile, then turn to face them.

"COUNCIL, WELCOME!"

I shout, as cheerily as can be.

They all stand there, mouths agape.
The council consists of Ladies Mavis and Eleanor, and Lords Wyatt and Brandon.
Walking past them, oblivious and muttering to himself is Claudius.
He soon spots me and he too halts, becoming furious.
I wave my hand at him and smile brightly.
This seems to make him even more furious.

Brilliant.

"Why and what are you doing here?"

His emphasis on each word.

"Which question would you like me to answer first?"

I ask sweetly.

A snort comes from Lady Mavis, a kind and elderly woman.
 She hides it quickly, yet a smile remains.

"You are supposed to be in confinement."

He tells me.

"You mean my imprisonment, yes, lovely little time to reflect and read."

I answer.

"However, I decided it was time for it to come to an end.
So, I left and came here."

I shriek the last part in pure happiness, gesturing around the council chambers.

Perhaps I am mad?

Claudius then too stands agape.
I saunter over to him, and close his mouth, then flash him a devilish wink.
Walking back to the table, I take a seat.
In the biggest chair, the chair reserved for the King.

It is no throne, merely a nicer and bigger chair than the rest.

And whilst we did not have a King, I can only assume Claudius usually sits here.

But not today.

This brings shock from them all.
Lord Wyatt, a bumbling and middle-aged man steps forth, stuttering.

"P – prince, t – that I – is C – Claudius' s – seat,"

I'm surprised he's not pissing himself he shakes so much.

Clearly Lord Wyatt Is scared of Claudius.

But why?

"I'm sure Claudius does not mind, do you, Claudius."

I ask of him.

He looks at me, he wants to say something clearly, yet he swallows his anger and answers.

"Of course not, Prince Tristan."

He says each word through gritted teeth.
He takes the seat furthest away from me, at the other side of the table.
We stare at each other intensely.
The Council take their seats nervously.
They all seem scared.
For too long though the council has danced to Claudius' tune, and I have had enough.

I had a long time to think whilst in that confinement, and I had decided there in my deep thought that it was truly time someone actually tried to make a real change.

I am an Imperial.
I have the blood.
The name.
And I have magic, although that is a secret.

Yet eventually a secret that I should and must reveal.

I have had enough of this tyranny, of Claudius.
And in truth, I have had enough of the Witch Queen and this centuries old war.
The people deserve peace, we all do.

AND WHAT HAPPENS WHEN CLAUDIUS IS GONE?
AND THEODORE?
WHEN THE WITCH QUEEN IS GONE?
WHAT SHALL YOU DO?
WHAT SHALL YOU BECOME?

I will be King and bring peace…

IT IS NOT THAT SIMPLE…

I brush these thoughts away.
I know it is not so simple, of course it is not.
After all, I have yet to attain an army.
And yet, hopefully if this meeting goes to plan I can gain some support from the Council.
If I can get even one of them on my side, then they may be extremely helpful in my upcoming plans.

But even if I do dispose of Claudius, deposing Theodore is another thing entirely.

Claudius is a tyrannical, cruel man who many despise and want to be rid of.

They may be too scared to admit it, but it's more than true, many want him dead.

As for Theodore however, well he is a monster also, albeit that's not as well known.

And he is technically the next in line for the throne.

Despite what he is, there are many who will stay loyal to the succession and not waver on that matter.

Yet, if he was to have an accident…

But can I really murder my own brother?

And even if I could… It would have to be done secretly.

I need my succession to go smoothly…

IF YOU WANT THE THRONE AND CROWN YOU NEED TO TAKE IT WITH FIRE AND BLOOD!

Can I really do that though?

This will surely cause civil war…

But if I can avoid fire and blood and get a diplomatic solution than would that not be better?

YOU DO NOT NEED DIPLOMACY.
STAND UP… STAND UP NOW AND SET THE ROOM AFLAME!
KILL THEM ALL AND BECOME KING RIGHT NOW!

No... If I did that, I would be no better than Claudius or the Witch Queen herself.

Speaking of the Witch Queen, I never met her in the flesh of course, yet I have known of her since before I could remember.
She had plagued my family for generations, killing us whenever she could.
In fact, she's responsible either directly or indirectly for having killed the most Imperial members of the Dynasty.
Yet, she never seems to kill us all.
I'm sure she could have wiped out my family ages ago had she truly wanted too, yet she has only killed some of us off throughout the centuries, as if a cat playing with a mouse.
Forever tormenting, yet quite not doing the deed completely.

However, twenty-one years ago she had certainly tried, tried her hardest.
It seemed as if the Imperial Family would fall that day, and yet it did not.
My father survived, and with his survival another three Imperial children came from his loins.
Myself and my siblings.
My father is dead now, however, mother too.
Only the three of us remain.

And yet only one of us can rule.

Theodore is out of the question, and Isabella being a girl is also out of the question.

This leaves me.

I had studied hard during my confinement too, on what I am about to say and do.

I intend to appease and win the Council to my side, I have to get them out from under Claudius' thumb… Or at least some of them; from there surely I can make changes.

EVEN IF YOU DO PUSH ASIDE CLAUDIUS, YOU STILL HAVE THEODORE.
HIS CORONATION IS FAST APPROACHING…
LORDS AND LADIES ALREADY REACH THE CAPITAL.
AND IT MUST BE ON EVERYONE'S LIPS…

This is true enough; we have not had a coronation for years and thousands upon thousands from the Capital and other areas of the Human Realm will travel to witness it.

From the highest Lord to the lowest peasants and slaves.

Thousands will come to bear witness.

But if something happens to Theodore before that then, perhaps they will all be witnessing my coronation?

The mere thought sends a shiver done my spine.

Not a bad shiver though, it feels good.

And yet, it seems as if there is no way of diplomatically getting rid of him…

EVEN MENTIONING THEODORE'S REMOVAL AS KING WOULD BE TREASON.
BUT THEN AGAIN, YOU BASICALLY DID THAT AT THE EXECUTION…

My thoughts get set aside as I realise Claudius stares at me.

I decide to stare back.

We both sit there, staring endlessly at one another.

A power of wills it seems.

He then looks away, and I smile coyly.

I won.

"So, from what I've read here."

I begin.

"You have read this?"

Questions Lord Brandon, a young good-looking man, and if I'm not mistaken, he too secretly likes men.
I have caught him many a time staring at me… And it caused great ire from Kaleb in the past.

"Yes, I've been here for a while."

I answer, nonchalantly.

This time it is Lady Eleanor, a beautiful young woman, who stifles a laugh.

And yet, they do all share uncertain looks with each other at that.

"You have not had a meeting for a while, so I can only assume it is of importance.
Therefore, I brought myself here early to read through this.
It seems as if there's a disturbance in the Magic Realm, the General has written that the bodies were ripped apart as if by animals.
And yet, even an angry bear or pack of wolves could not rip apart an entire village."

I lean forward then.

"And I certainly do not know of animal that can light fires."

I jest.

This brings laughs from the Council; they also look impressed.

And shocked… Very shocked.

Even Claudius has a look of shock, and maybe… Just maybe, he's even impressed too.

I clap my hands then.

"So, what are we to do about this?
I was thinking perhaps we should send aid, perhaps some spare soldiers to help patrol the area."

I go to grab a map I had outlined with a plan and yet Claudius stops me then.

"There are no soldiers to spare.
The majority of the Imperial Army has been stuck in the Black Woods for these last three years.
And what remains are too small and valuable to simply send away.
We have a large Capital, and it needs protecting.
Besides, this has happened in the Realm of Magic.
It should not concern us."

The council share another look, a look of uncertainty.

"Perhaps the Imperial Army would not be stuck in the Realm of Magic had the Great Cleansing not begun."

I note.

Gasps from all around happen.
Claudius has a stone-cold expression.

"The Cleansing was sanctioned and authorised by your own father, the late King.
May the Eternal Light take care of his soul."

"May the Eternal Light take care of his soul."

The rest of the Council mutter in unison.

I do not however share their prayer.

"If only your Defenders could be of use… But I guess you have an army for no reason."

I continue.

Claudius grits his jaw at this.

"Prince, if you are just here to throw taunts then perhaps the confinement should last longer.
As I said, this is of no importance.
It does not concern us."

A veiled threat, of course.
I have no intention of going back to my tower.
Not unless I want too, anyways.

"High Pope, it would seem it should be of every concern to us.
A village has been massacred, bodies ripped apart, this is clearly the work of vampires.
And if vampires have crossed into the Realm of Magic, which I'm sure they have, then they may very well cross into our lands… Vampires here could mean death for us all, we all know only one bite and you become one of them."

Before he gets to interrupt, I continue.

"This threatens the entire Kingdom, do you not think?"

This time, I make sure to emphasise my words.

"Also, if it is of no importance or concern then why even have a Council meeting to begin with?"

I look directly at Claudius; he looks as if for the first time as he does not know what to say.

The council all directly look at him too.

"He has a point, Claudius."

 Says Lord Brandon.

"Yes, indeed the young Prince does."

 Chimes in Lady Mavis.

Claudius looks between them, as if trying to think of what to say.

He does a half smile, stutters then talks.

"Well, yes, I suppose if you point it out like that, yes, it's very dangerous.
Soldiers shall surely be sent."

He confirms.

"When?"

I ask him straightaway.

He looks at me, I can see him growing angry again.

"As soon as I can."

Again, through gritted teeth.

I know this is a lie.
Claudius has no intention of sending soldiers, of that, I'm sure.
I want to press the matter further, when the Council chamber doors are reopened.
I need not look, I know it's the Lord Commander, I can hear him cursing.
He approaches the table and slams his fist down.
Kaleb stands behind him.
He may have met me at my chambers earlier to see that I was definitely able to walk free, and yet he had to leave to report back to his uncle.
And now he is here again.
We share a quick smile with each other.
He notices where I'm sitting, in my father's chair, the chair of a king.
And that's when he shoots me that cheeky smile.

The one that makes my heart melt.

I quickly look away, I do not want too, and yet, I have too.

"What is the meaning of this!
I am the one who sent you a raven last night for this meeting and you do not even bother to wait for me to be here to start!"

He accuses.

Claudius simply looks at him, his face composed.

"It was not I who started this meeting."

He gestures toward me.

"The prince has been here since before us, reading extensively it seems.
And doing the same in his tower.
Perhaps our young Prince might be a scholar one day."

Many would think this is a compliment, but I know better.
It's an insult.

He knows my life is not that of a scholar.

NO, YOU SHALL BE A CONQUEROR!
ALL WILL FEAR AND BOW TO YOU!

But I don't want to rule with fear… Do I?
I want to be loved… Don't I?

A LOT OF THE CITIZENS OF THE HUMAN REALM ARE VERY FAITHFUL!

ONLY A FEW PEOPLE OF TOLERANCE LIVE HERE.
WITCHES ARE HATED!
WITCHES ARE HUNTED!
WHAT DO YOU THINK IS GOING TO HAPPEN TO YOU?!

But I have to try…
I only have a short time.

Claudius and the Lord Commander's argument brings me back to the room.

"THAT IS HORSE SHIT AND YOU KNOW IT!"

He roars.

I stifle a laughter.

I always did like the Lord Commander.

"I'll remind you to watch your tone, sir.
May I remind you whom who are speaking too?"

"Yes, the High Pope."

He replies gruffly.

Silence hangs in the air and the Council members shift uncomfortably once again.

Claudius merely speaks softly back.

"A man can have many titles, and responsibilities.
You are the Lord Commander of the Syndicate for example, and your responsibilities are hunting vampires.

You took a solemn oath.
An oath which includes that you also stay out of the affairs of the Realm.
So, why are you even here?"

The Lord Commander looks as if he could have a fit, he is so angry.
He leans down on the table, looking Claudius directly in the eyes.

"My men and women, brave all of them.
They travel throughout the kingdom, keeping you all safe.
We are on the frontlines; we fight and die for all of us.
I think that's earned me a right in what's going on, especially when it concerns vampires, the very being which my OATH commands me to slay.
And especially seeing as it was me who told you."

Claudius sips some wine from his cup.

He simply replies

"Well, you know now.
You sent me a raven telling me about what happened, and we are now discussing what to do.
You have done your responsibilities, Lord Commander.
You may leave."

He says it so callously, as if not realising he is speaking to one of the greatest warriors in the Realm.

The Lord Commander steps back, throwing his hands in the air.
He walks over the window, holding open one of the swinging wooden shutters.
He stays there, taking in the air, trying to ease his anger I suppose.

Kaleb looks furious.

"My uncle speaks the truth.
We protect the Human Realm, we protect everyone.
And we cannot do that if we are not informed of what you plan to do."

I smile then; he has spoken well.

Claudius doesn't even bother to look at Kaleb, instead he focuses on some parchment before him.

"Well, as I said.
Your uncle told us of the situation and now we mean to handle it.
We have agreed on sending some Imperial Soldiers, if we can find any that is."

I can see a half smile on his face at the mention of this.
He likes the fact the Imperial Army is all but gone.

He stops for a moment then, and his smile spreads even wider.

"Actually… Imperial Soldiers will not be sent."

He answers.

He then looks at me, and back at Kaleb.
I get an unnerving feeling in the pit of my stomach.

"Instead of Imperial Soldiers who are already dwindling, then perhaps the best solution would be to send Slayers.
After all, the Syndicate is the only humans permitted to enter the Black Woods anymore.

The room goes quiet, the Lord Commander turns at this though, he obviously heard what Claudius said.

"I mean, after all, as you said, it's your duty.
And I have to wonder, there are already Slayers who should be in the Black Woods and at the BorderLands where the frontlines are.
How come none of these Slayers who patrol came across the monsters who did this."
Perhaps your Syndicate is losing its touch."

The last part makes Kaleb's face turn dark with anger.

Claudius then looks at him.

"As I told your uncle, BOY, you may leave.
Go back to your Spiral and perhaps tell the rest of your Syndicate that they need to do their jobs better."

I cannot stand it any longer, the downright rudeness of it.

And not to Kaleb, not to my love.

"How dare you!"

I spit.

All heads turn to me.

"The Syndicate are a proud and honourable faction; they have guarded us for hundreds of years.
And that 'JOB' as you just called it is no job!
It's a solemn and scared oath, one not taken lightly.

If it was not for them, this country would have surely been covered in darkness centuries ago.
They deserve your respect, not your rudeness.
If you had any decency, you would apologise."

Kaleb smiles brightly at me; I can feel the love.
Claudius stands then.

"This meeting cannot be conducted like this!
There are people who should not even be here, and YOU"

He points accusingly at me.

"YOU should not even be here!
I have too many things to attend too with your brother's upcoming coronation.
As such, I and the Council rule in his stead as I have these last three years."

A downright lie, we all know who really was in charge these last three years.

He says this with a confident smile.

NOW IS THE TIME TO STRIKE.

"And yet, with all due respect, Claudius, as High Pope, may I remind you of your responsibilities.
That is of the Faith, and I cannot see the Faith having any part of this.
Of course, you could always pray for the innocent souls who were ripped apart by beasts."

"And why would I pray for witches…

If they were ripped apart then surely that was God's will."

How could he be so cruel.

"You may be a Council member, but it's clear you have command, and as such it is your upmost responsibility to teach and guide the next Crown Heir, is it not?
Making sure he is ready for his role and duties as King."

His eyes widen at that, as does the council and Kaleb's.
Before anyone gets a chance to speak, I quickly continue.

"And yet, forgive me If I'm wrong, but in these last three years has my brother attended a single Council meeting?
Does he know anything about the politics of this Council, of this court?
Does he have a clue about anything to do with the war?
How many soldiers we have, how many new recruits need trained?
How many Slayers are out in the field?
Does he even know of this meeting?!"

"All good questions, my Prince."

He declares flatly.

"And yet, I still do not think you should be here.
These are matters for myself and the Council.
Perhaps you should focus on other matters."

He is trying to brush me off, make me as if I'm an insignificant child that has no clue, but I have no intention of being turned away.

Not now, not ever.

I decide to do something bold and say in return.

"And does my brother know about the Council of Covens?
Does he have any correspondence with them?
Does he even know their names?"

Even the wind and sea seem as if they have momentarily become lost in silence.

It seems even as time itself has slowed.

People do not talk about magic, or so they say.
But it's ridiculous, the witches and ourselves have had an uneasy alliance for centuries, and surprisingly it did not even sever completely when we commuted our travesties against them.

This is wrong and has to be rectified.

Claudius looks at me as if he is wishing my death.
And the Lord Commander, he looks taken aback.
He did not know I knew about the letter which Kaleb told me about.
In fact, he shoots Kaleb an uneasy glance and I immediately feel bad for having landed him in certain trouble.

"You have gone too far!
You know that the talk of magic…"

Begins Claudius.

"Is strictly forbidden, yes, except of course it must be acceptable at Council meetings, how else would you even have this alliance with them all these years."

Claudius looks uneasy at this.

"The prince is correct, Claudius.
We do discuss magic here, and we do send letters back and forth with
the Council of Covens now and then."

"Only when it is needed, which it is not!
The war is the same as always.
Every day, the same battle.
The same battle every day for centuries.
They attack, we attack, nothing changes."
Everything is fine, and there is no need to discuss magic!"

"And yet everything must change!"

I declare back.

"Whether you like it or not, Claudius, we have had an uneasy alliance
with them for centuries.
Nevertheless, they have always done as they have faithfully said.
They sacrificed and died with us on the field of battle, they've lost just
as many families and friends and neighbours as we have.
They have bled and died with us.
They are allies, possibly our strongest allies.
And if we are ever going to win this war, which we should have every
intend of doing so, then we need magic!"

I let my words hang in the air.

"I think the prince is tired.
He must be, otherwise he surely would not have said what he just said.
Because as the Prince well knows, this talk is treason."

"What do you think, am I speaking treason?
 Or the truth?"

They stay silent whilst Claudius shouts.

"ENOUGH!"

I stand then, the chair scrapping behind me.

"OR IS IT TREASON TO SPEAK TRUTH!"

I shout back.

He looks ready to curse at me, yet I then shout at the council.

"WILL NONE OF YOU SPEAK?
WILL NONE OF YOU SHARE YOUR OPINIONS?!"

They say nothing.
They look like they want too.
Desperately want too.
Yet they do not.

THEY DO NOT CARE.
THEY ARE ALL TOO SCARED…

But why?!

I look desperately at all of them.

Will they really not say anything?
Will they really not see sense?
Why am I the only one who speaks the sanest and yet sounds the maddest?

HE MUST HAVE SECRETS ON ALL OF THEM…
SECRETS YOU NEED TO FIND OUT…

Yes.
Perhaps if I can find out what it is that keeps them under Claudius' control, then perhaps I can fix it.

OR YOU COULD USE IT TO MAKE THEM GIVE YOU LOYALTY.

No, I will not blackmail the Council like Claudius has all these years.

WHY NOT, IT CLEARLY WORKS.

I then look at Kaleb.
He looks desperately back at me.
He goes to speak, but the Lord Commander places his hand on his shoulder and Kaleb silences.

"You want something to happen, then fine.
We shall not send Imperial Soldiers, but we shall send a retinue of Slayers."

He turns to the Lord Commander.

"Can you muster some good warriors to send and report back."

"Aye, I can indeed."

Answers the Lord Commander gruffly.

Claudius looks at Kaleb then and smiles again.

"Perhaps your nephew could lead them."

I feel as if I have been hit by a bolt of lightning.

Kaleb… Kaleb leading them?

But that would mean…

"NO!"

I shout loudly.

All eyes immediately turn on me.

"Something the matter, my Prince?"

Asks Claudius coyly.

"You wanted me to do something, well I've just done it."
Lord Commander, pick your finest Slayers and your strong nephew of course."

He then turns to the rest of us.

"I say we reconvene this meeting of the Council at a more convenient time.
And next time, let us make sure that no one BUT COUNCIL MEMBERS attend."

With that, the council quickly move from their seats and take their leave.

Claudius too stands from the table and begins to walk.
As he gets to me, he pauses briefly and speaks

"Perhaps you can stay here and continue to read.
A scholar in the making, yes."

He then takes a step closer and whispers.

"Nice try."

Before walking off.

Anger surges deep inside of me, I feel my fingers tingle.
Heat begins to develop.

TURN THE CUNT INTO A HUMAN FIREBALL!

The anger continues to surge, I begin to raise my hand and the faintest
sound of a crackle can be heard.

Claudius is right there…

Before I can do anything further, Kaleb grabs my hands roughly and
squeezes.
He winces loudly as the sound of the crackles dissipates.
We stare into each other's eyes.
He continues to hold onto my hands tightly, continuing to wince.
Thankfully, neither the Council nor the Claudius look back to see us,
they simply leave the chambers, and the doors are closed.

The Lord Commander seems to have noticed, however.
He looks at me and Kaleb.
His hands on mine, our eyes locked in embrace.
We quickly notice and step apart.
As I do, I notice Kaleb has small burn marks on his hands.
I hurt him… I never meant too, but I felt like I could die in that instant
for hurting him.
The Lord Commander continues to stare deeply at me.

It makes me feel uncomfortable.

HE KNOWS

No… Surely, surely, he could not.

HE KNOWS EVERYTHING!

He then breaks his stare and quickly walks away.
The Imperial Guards open the doors and close for him.

"Leave us" I command.

They bow their heads in respect, yet it is obvious they too noticed.
They take their leave.
Just me and Kaleb remain.
I begin breathing hard.
I reach for Kaleb and at once turn his hands over, inspecting his palms.
They are red and blistered.
Not severely burned enough to leave a scar, yet still burned, nonetheless.
Yet he stands there without a hint of pain.

A true warrior.

I had nearly just set fire to Claudius.
I had nearly just revealed myself.

BUT HOW DID IT FEEL!
EVEN FOR THAT BRIEF SECOND!
THAT POWER, DID IT NOT FEEL GLORIOUS!

It did feel good.

I had been angry, and still am, and yet for the briefest second when I had imagined him as a fireball, when I heard the small crackle at my fingertips, I felt…

YES, WHAT DID IT FEEL LIKE?

It felt amazing.

AND HOW DID YOU FEEL?

I felt powerful.

YOU ARE POWERFUL.

Yes… Yes, I am powerful.

Another Image flashes through my mind.
Me, throned and crowned.
Yet, as noticed before, not the Imperial Throne, nor the Imperial Crown.
So what throne is this?
What crown?
I looked so beautiful, so powerful.
And all around me, a raging inferno.
It looks so beautiful.
But then the image changes.
I am no longer on a throne, and I am no longer wearing a crown.
I am stood… I am stood in the Capital… The fire is everywhere.
All around me is nothing but flames.
Buildings, homes, even people.
There are screams.
Thousands upon thousands.
And eyes… So many eyes… **All bright red.**

"TRISTAN!"

I hear Kaleb say loudly.

The fire stops, I am no longer in the Capital, I can no longer see the red eyes.
I am back within the Council Chambers.
My breathing becomes so ragged, so torrid,

"Tristan, Tristan are you okay?"

I push away from him and walk towards the open window the Lord Commander had left.

"I-I c-can't b-breathe."

I gasp.

 I stick my head out the window, trying to suck in as much air as I possibly can.
After a moment, my breathe starts to return to normal.
But what was that?
Why do I keep seeing this?
Is it a dream?
A memory?
No, it cannot be a memory.
It feels as if it has not yet happened.
So… Does that mean… Is that the future?
Did I just see the future?
But how?
And why does the future involve the Capital burning down to nothing but cinders.

TO MAKE THE WORLD ANEW, IT MUST BURN!

No, I only need to bring the Council to my side.
With their support… Perhaps a peaceful takeover…
But why the red eyes?

Only vampires have red eyes…

Does that mean. . . **Are they already here?**

THAT WILL NEVER WORK!
THEY WILL NEVER WILLINGLY LISTEN!
YOU WILL HAVE TO MAKE THEM!
WITH FIRE AND BLOOD!
YOU NEED TO BURN IT DOWN!
BURN IT ALL!

I feel hands on my back.
Despite the fact he is burned, he still gently massages my back.
I feel instantly calmer.
I turn to face him; he looks at me with such longing.
I take his hands once again and turn his palms upwards.
I close my eyes and begin to focus.
I focus on his hands, the burns, the flesh.
I imagine it healed, the skin becoming smooth and soft.
I hear an audible gasp, and I smile.
Eyes open, I can see Kaleb staring at his healed hands with awe.

"I tried Kaleb, I tried so hard.
They will not listen; it is as I feared.
They do not want to help fix this place, to fix the world."

I confide with sadness.

"Fixing the world doesn't happen overnight."

He answers.

"At this rate it will not be fixed whatsoever.
Claudius needs to go."

“I agree.
Finally, I do agree.
He cares not for the Realms, only his power.
There is little we can do, my love.
But Claudius will not be here for much longer, anyways, his regency
is nearly over.
Theodore.”

“THEODORE IS NOT GOING TO BE THE FUCKING KING!”

I snap.
I had not meant too, yet I did.
Kaleb looks hurt, and I immediately feel bad.

“I’m sorry.”

I whisper.

“But he cannot be King, he will not be King.
And you said last night.”

“I know what I said.”

He confirms.

I smile warmly.

“Kaleb, do you not see, Claudius is never going to let go of his power.”
“Yes, he needs to go.
But… I do not think we can just kill him.”

Kaleb answers.

“But last night.”

"I know what I said last night."

His head hangs low.

"Tris, I do not know what came over me… I should never of said those things… About killing everyone for you."

I am taken aback.
I was certain after last night he was completely and undoubtedly on my side.
And yet here he stood, seeming to go back on his words.

"But how else will we get rid of him?
He will not simply walk away!
And if Theodore is coronated and crowned, he will just be a puppet, dancing to Claudius strings.
And even if Theodore was brave enough to step against Claudius, which we both know he is not, he will be a terrible ruler.
He acts like a child with a vicious temper, he knows nothing of war or ruling.
Of tactics and strategies, he knows nothing."

"And I suppose you do?"

Kaleb barks back.

"You've never ruled, and you've never been in battle either, you do not know these things either."

His tone angry.

"And yet unlike my brother I am willing to learn.
I read, I read all the time.
And I learn, I learn constantly."

"Yes, but books and real life are different."

He answers.

"Different, yes.
But I am going to get experience."

Kaleb's voice raises even higher then."

"How?!
How will you?!"

He questions.

He takes my hands then.

"Tristan, I love you.
I love you more than anything.
I always have and always will.
But perhaps you need to accept that you will not rule.
But I promise, Claudius will not rule forever, and I'm sure that even though the Council did not say anything, they were throughly Impressed with you.
With time, I'm sure you could have a real seat at the Council.
And as a Council member, you could make a real change.
As I said, fixing the world does not happen overnight, it may take years.
And yet, I'm sure you will do it.
Slight changes at first, but with time, bigger changes too.
I believe in you, Tris."

His words were sweet.
Sweet like sugared honey.
A position on the Council one day?
Perhaps that would be nice.
And yes, I am sure with time I would make changes.
But what Kaleb is taking about is years in the making. . . And I simply do not have years.
And besides, it was not a seat that I envisioned myself sitting on.

Not a seat, but a throne.

I place my hand upon Kaleb's cheek.

"A part of me… A part of me wishes I were not a Prince.
And that you were not a Slayer.
I wish that my father was not a King, I wish your father were not the General.
I wish your uncle were not the Lord Commander.
Sometimes, sometimes I wish we were born as commoners.
Then we would be free… Me and you could be together.
Together properly."

It was a wishful dream.

Kaleb wraps his arms around me.

"We could get land one day and build a beautiful house together.
We could have animals.
Cows, sheep, pigs, and chickens.
And of course, horses.
We would go riding every day."

"But the animals won't be for food, they will be beloved pets."

I confirm to him.

"Ha, and where would we get meat to eat then?"

"Why of course, my big strong man would go hunting."

My hands rub across his firm chest.
His muscles so hard under his tunic.

"And we would make love every night."

He whispers.

“Yes, every single night.”

I whisper back.

“And after we can hold each other all night, wake up to each other.”

“Oh, how I’ve longed for the night you would stay.”

And with that we kiss.
A beautiful, soft kiss.
Oh, how I wish we could both be free…
The thought of us growing old together, away from everything.
The thought of us having our own home and land and pets and lives.

It was such a beautiful dream.

But a dream was all it was…

The kiss, like always, does not last forever.
But wouldn’t it be so sweet if it did?
I know what I am about to say will ruin the moment, I know it may
create a rift, and yet I have to say it.

“Kaleb, what you said was lovely.
And I am sure if I ever did get a Council seat, I would make changes.
And I am sure we could get land, have animals, and go riding every
day and make love every night.
But I am not meant for a simple seat on the Council, I am made for the
throne.”

He steps back from me.

Tears begin to form in his eyes, he harshly brushes them aside.

“But Tristan…”

“I will be King.”

I tell him.

"But… But the life we could have together?
If only you give up this silly desire.
We could still change the world, just slowly.
And we could be happy, so happy!
Please, Tristan… Please see sense."

"My love… It is nothing but a dream."

He looks as if he has been punched.
He stands tall, proud, and angry.

"Then I suppose it is a good thing I am leaving.
As soon as my uncle has gathered the others, I will be heading to the
Realm of Magic!"

"Perhaps you'll get trapped and stay there."

I retort bitterly.

Kaleb looks shocked.

"Tris, my love.
You do not mean what you say."

"I am aware of what I say, my love.
I am telling you that perhaps if you go that you will not come back.
I will not want you for your betrayal."

"Betrayal!"

His voice even more shocked.

"Yes, Kaleb…
If I want to make real changes, if I am really to rule, to unite the
people,"

"RULE? ... UNITE?!"

He looks even more perturbed than before.

"Tris, what are you on about."

"Do you not see!
With Claudius or Theodore in power nothing will change.
The wheel of terror will keep spinning.
The prejudice, the violence, the death, the war.
Maybe a civil war to clean out my threats would be for the best.
Then I can fully turn my focus on to the Magic Realm.
I will meet with the Council of Covens like my predecessor King.
I will unite us, and when I do, when I show them what I can do, when
I rule both the Human Realm and Magic Realm.
I can use all that force to wipe out the Witch Queen and the Dark Lord.
I can conquer this whole country, take it all back.
And me, I will be..."

I do not finish; I see Kaleb's face is that of pure terror.

I knew it would be.

"Then you mean to take the Imperial Throne, and then conquer the
Realm of Magic, and then the Dark Realm?

You mean to conquer everyone?"

"I mean to exterminate the vampires and unite the witches and humans,
yes.
And to do that, I must conquer so I can liberate."

"Conqueror to liberate?!
Are you hearing yourself?"
This will not work.
Your talking of murder, of betrayal and death and civil war.
Please, please tell me you do not mean to do this."

"I will need to learn the secrets of the Council to ascertain what Claudius holds over them.
Bring them into the fold, with the Council I should be able to take the throne."

"Even if you do, you think you're just going to go to the Realm of Magic and what?
The Council of Covens will just hand it over to you?"

"Well, why would they not?
I am an Imperial with magic.
If anyone could unite the people, it would be me."

I say matter of factly.

Why can he not see what I am saying makes sense.
I can do this; I will do this.

**I was born to rule.
I am sure of it.**

*YES, YES, CLAIM YOUR POWER!
UNLEASH YOUR CHAOS!*

Kaleb grabs me roughly then.

"Tris, I do not want to hear about this again.
Do you understand me?
Never, ever speak another word about this."

His words frantic, his eyes searching.

"DO YOU HEAR ME,"

He shouts.

"Let me go."

I bark.

"I am trying to help you!"

He says.

"Help me?!
You couldn't even help me when it really mattered.
You think you saved me, but you're wrong!
It was me who saved me.
And you!
I killed the vampire, me!
You just got in the way."

All the words tumble out of me at once.
I regret it the second I do.
No!
No, why would I say that!

Kaleb becomes still… His grip loosens.

"Kaleb… Kaleb, I did not mean."

His grip becomes strong again, I struggle against him, yet his grip is too strong!

"YOU LIE!
YOU WILL NOT DO THIS!
YOU WILL PUT THESE THOUGHTS TO BED AND LEAVE THEM THERE!
I AM NOT GOING TO LET YOU RISK YOUR LIFE FOR THIS FOLLY!"

He shouts.

"Unifying the people is not folly."

I stutter.

"ENOUGH!"

He shouts louder.
The guards rush in then, their hands on their swords.

"My Prince, are you okay?!"

I ignore them at first, for standing behind the guards is none other than the Lord Commander.

I thought he had left, and all this time he had just been standing outside.

Shit.

Kaleb releases me and walks backwards from me.
I turn to the guards, trying my best to ignore the scowling look from the Lord Commander.

"Of course, I am absolutely fine.
Me and the Captain were just having a spirited debate about politics, that is all."

They look uncertain but they dare not question further.

"I thank you for your concern, but please, if you may exit.
Me and the Captain are not finished with our discussion."

The Lord Commander makes a noise at that.
The guards go to leave when Kaleb speaks up.

"Actually, if you will keep the doors open.
I think me and the Prince have said everything that needs to be said."

Kaleb looks hurt, I can see tears in his eyes once again.
I look at him, hurt and broken.
I do not want him to, not like this.

"Kaleb, please."

I begin to beg, low enough for the guards nor the Lord Commander not to hear.

Kaleb looks at me then.
And then looks away.
For the first time ever, he looks at me in shame.
My heart wanted to break.
He bows respectfully without looking at me, then takes his leave.
The guards leave with him.
The Lord Commander gives me one final glare before too taking his leave.
And once again I am alone, my only company the violent storm that is brewing outside.

DO NOT WORRY!
HE SHALL BE BACK!
HE ALWAYS COMES BACK...

But I am testing his loyalty and faith each and every time.
I speak of murder and civil war and death.

LIE TO HIM!
NEXT TIME YOU SEE HIM, TELL HIM WHAT HE NEEDS TO HEAR.
AND WHEN ALL IS DONE, HE WILL HAVE TO ACCEPT IT.

But will he though?
Or will my play for the throne and crown cost me my love?

LOVE AND POWER DO NOT MIX WELL!
IT IS BEST YOU CHOOSE...
AND I SUGGEST YOU CHOOSE POWER.

But if choosing power means I lose Kaleb, then it is not worth it.

DO NOT WORRY!
ONCE YOU HAVE THE THRONE AND CROWN!
YOU SHALL HAVE YOUR LOVE BACK!
YOU WILL GET EVERYTHING YOU WANT!

It is decided then.
I will make my grab for the throne and crown.
I shall rule.
I shall conquer.
I shall be loved.
First things first, I have been confined too long.
There are people out in the city, my people.
Not the humans, but the witches.
It is time to try and find this Secret Court.

YOU PLAN ON GOING TO THEM?
YOU PLAN ON FINDING THEM?

Yes, that is exactly what I plan to do.
The Council might not listen.
But perhaps they will.
I know witches hide in the Capital; I can sense them.
I can sense them all around.
But I have to find one.
Perhaps I can grow my own army…
An army of secret witches.
Right under the nose of everyone.

So, it is settled…

I have to go to the Capital.

PERHAPS WHILST YOU ARE THERE YOU COULD GET SOME POISON…
IT WOULD BE SO EASY TO SLIP IT INTO SOMEONE'S CUPS.

I must dispose of Claudius, that is fine with me.
I cannot wait to watch him die.

And I have a plan in mind for him.
He really is obsessed with my sister…
And would she not be the perfect person to deliver his death?
I smile wickedly at the mere thought.

SEND HER TO HIM…
PERSUADE HER TO SEDUCE HIM…THEN KILL HIM!

No, I could not sacrifice her like that… Could I?

YOU MAY HAVE TOO…
SACRIFICE YOUR SISTER…
AND MURDER YOUR BROTHER!
ONLY ONE IMPERIAL CAN REMAIN TO WIN THE THRONE.

Doing this to my siblings… My blood, my brother, my sister.
And yet, I do not see any other possibility.
As long as he is alive, he could always be a threat.
And Claudius would surely do anything for Isabella, and I can use
Isabella to get rid of Claudius.

A flash of fire appears again.
Images of The Capital, burning.
And me… I am smiling.
Perhaps it was true.
I really will have to burn it all down to rebuild it.

Kaleb, forgive me.
I love you; you own my heart.
And my siblings, please forgive me too.

But I want the throne.
I want the crown.
I want power.

YOU HAVE MADE YOUR DECISION THEN.

Yes, my mind is set.
I will be King.
I will unite the witches and humans.
And nothing shall stand in my way.

INSIDE THE IMPERIUM
HARD CHOICES

KALEB

The doors swing open as I continue to shake and shout at Tristan.
Guards have their hands on their hilts.
I do not care, for standing behind them is my uncle, the Lord Commander, and he looks furious.

At once I let go of Tristan and take a step backward.
Tristan speaks, yet I do not hear.
I am too busy with my muddled mind.

Tristan not only wants to conquer the world, but he also claims that he was the one who killed the vampire those some years ago.
But surely that is not true.
No, it was me.
I killed the vampire with my Saerillian sword.
Didn't I?
But then again, in these years I have not a single memory of actually slaying the beast.

Tristan mumbles something about that things are fine and for the guards to leave so we can resume our conversation, and yet I have no wish to carry on.

"Actually, if you will keep the doors open.
I think me and the prince have said everything that needs to be said."

With that I respectfully bow before I take my leave, passing the guards and my uncle.
I walk as quickly as my feet can carry, my mind swirling with thoughts.
Is it true?
Did Tristan, and not I, slay the vampire?

ALL ALONG, YOU THOUGHT YOU WERE A HERO.
BUT YOU'RE NOT.

The sound of footsteps behind me pulls me from my thoughts, I try to quicken my pace until I hear a commanding voice bellow behind me.

"Laddie, stay where you are."

I want to ignore, to disobey and continue walking, yet I dare not.
He is not just my uncle, but my Lord Commander.

I pause and take a deep breath before turning around.
There he stands, tall and proud, his face still showing signs of anger.

"Uncle."

I mutter.

At first, he does not answer, instead he stands there just looking at me.
His gaze searching mine for who knows what.

"Show me your hands."

It was not a question.

I immediately become agitated.
Why did he want to see my hands?
Surely, he did not notice Tristan burn me by accident.

BUT WAS IT AN ACCIDENT?
HE WAS GOING TO CAST IN FRONT OF THE ENTIRE
COUNCIL.
HE WAS ABOUT TO KILL CLAUDIUS RIGHT THERE.

But I had stopped him.
I had grabbed his hands with mine and stopped him.

"Your hands."

My uncle says once again.

Begrudgingly I extend my hands towards him.
He quickly grabs them and turns them palms upward.
My hands, like I knew they would be, are perfectly fine.
In fact, I think they might even look better than before.

All thanks to Tristan.

Thinking of him makes my heart feel sorrow, I wish I could walk back
to the Council Chambers and make things right with him.
To hold him and kiss him, to feel him against me.
But there is just no use in talking to him right now.
He is too obsessed with ruling, and he means to sow discord and even
civil war.
I cannot leave him right now.
I mustn't.

My uncle scoffs and lets go of my hands.

"Uncle, about what happened back there, it was nothing."

"Nothing?"

My uncle muses.

"I would not say what happened there was nothing.

After all, you've been picked to go to the Realm of Magic, have you not laddie?"

Again, it was not a question.
Yes, Claudius had decided that I will be leaving, but I cannot.
I cannot leave Tristan in this state, only the Light knows what he might get up too if left to his own devices.

"Uncle, about that… Would it not be wise to send someone more experienced.
Perhaps an older Captain."

I say.

My uncle looks at me sternly, his face still angry.

"You and the Prince… The rumours are true, aren't they?"

It wasn't a question.

I am taken aback, this is the second time my uncle has asked me this question, the first being in the Grand Spiral back in the Lord Commanders chambers.
I had denied it then, just like I intend to do now.

"I don't know what you are talking about."

I answer.

It was stupid of me, of course I knew what he was talking about, it seemed as if everyone lately knew of me and Tristan's secret which doesn't seem to be a secret anymore at all.
And yet, despite dancing close to death, I must protect Tristan where I can.
I will not openly admit it and send him to his death.

HIS DEATH WILL HAPPEN WHETHER YOU WANT IT TOO OR NOT.

YOU CANNOT PROTECT HIM; YOU NEVER HAVE AND NEVER WILL.

No, I will protect him at all costs.
He means more to me than life itself.

MORE THAN THE SYNDICATE, MORE THAN YOUR FAMILY AND DUTIES.
YOU LOSE ALL HONOUR IN LOVING HIM…

I am a Captain of the Syndicate, I love my position, I love my duties and my family.

But I love Tristan… I love him so much more.

"You are lying."

My uncle answers.

Once again, I am taken aback, my uncle had never once accused me of lying.
Am I losing his trust?
Am I losing his respect and love?

IN LOVING TRISTAN, YOU LOSE EVERYTHING AND EVERYONE…
YOUR UNCLE WILL TURN AGAINST YOU.

"Uncle, I swear."

"Swear nothing to me, laddie.
Do not lie to me regarding what I can see with my own eyes.
You two shared a moment back there, one of thousands you have shared.
Have you lost your mind, laddie!
Have you any idea what you are doing?!"

I have no idea how to reply, so I instead remain silent.

Perhaps if I say nothing, he will drop it.
My hopes are dashed however when he reaches into his breastplate and pulls out a small piece of parchment.
He unfolds it before looking at me once again.

"I have been in contact with your mother as of late."

This shocks me, I had not known they had been in contact lately, it worries me deeply.

"Your mother mentions how she plans to have you married off.
How she plans to have you leave the Syndicate altogether, to become the head of your House, to become the Lord of the House of Umpire.
To sire children and continue your family line."

This reminds me of the conversation I had with my mother some weeks ago, how she wanted me to marry and leave the Syndicate, and to leave Tristan.
It seems now that my uncle is wanting the same thing.

"I cannot leave the Syndicate, uncle.
I have taken solemn vows, I will not break them."

"You have broken them already by being with the prince!"

He says angrily.

"How could you be so stupid laddie?!
You are a Captain of the Syndicate!
He is the bloody Prince, what on earth are you the pair of you thinking!"

I stay quiet, I have no idea what to say, I cannot believe this is happening.

"I'll tell you what, you are leaving and going to the Realm of Magic.
You are going to search for these damned vampires and slay them if you do find them.

I'll stay here and await the upcoming coronation."

Leave?!
I cannot leave.
Not leave Tristan, not like this.
Tristan is heading down a dark and dangerous path, I cannot simply leave and let him be unsupervised.
I have to try and stop him.
To make him see sense.

"Uncle, I cannot just leave, Tristan is…"

"Do not dare say his name!"

My uncle glares.

"You must leave, this silly affair between you two shall end.
I will not have you anywhere near the Prince anymore, it is dangerous.
He is dangerous!
More dangerous than anything or anyone."

This confuses me, my uncle speaks like he did back In the Grand Spiral not long ago.
Tristan could be untamed and wild, but dangerous…

HE IS DANGEROUS THOUGH… HE WANTS TO KILL CLAUDIUS, USUPRP HIS BROTHER AND TAKE THE THRONE AND CROWN…

This is true… But he wants to unify the people, to create a new world for humans and witches alike.

YOU FOOL YOURSELF, YOU KNOW HOW DANGEROUS HE IS, THE POWER HE HAS…

Tristan has power, that is certain.
And what he intends to do with that power…

No, I love him.
I know he will listen to me; he will see sense if I can just get through to him.
I'm certain of it, but to do that I must stay.

"Uncle, I cannot leave.
I cannot leave him."

My uncle scoffs.

I take a deep breath, and with that I finally intend to tell the truth.

"Uncle, I love him.
I've always loved him; I always have and always will."

Saying it out loud feels as if a huge weight has been lifted from my chest.
To finally be honest and truthful.
To actually admit my love out loud, it feels incredible.

My uncle takes a step towards me.

"I care not laddie; I am putting a stop to this.
You have a choice.
Do your duty, do as your told, go on this mission, leave the Prince and you will have a bright future.
But if you stay… If you stay I will have you banished from the Syndicate, not only that but I will wholeheartedly support your mother's decision to have you married
Married and sent to our ancestral home."

This shocks me so much I let out an audible gasp.

Banished from the Syndicate?
Married and sent away…

Surely my uncle cannot be serious…

My head begins to spin, what shall I do?

I love Tristan, I cannot be apart from him, especially now… But to be banished from the Syndicate, forced to marry…

Perhaps if I do this, do what my uncle wants, I'll soon return… Return back to Tristan…

Perhaps if I'm more secretive next time, perhaps my mother and uncle won't notice…

DON'T BE A FOOL… YOU ARE CAUGHT… SO WHAT SHALL IT BE…?

I cannot be banished from the Syndicate, but I cannot leave Tristan either.

It's not exactly like Tristan wants me around right now anyhow.. But to leave him like this, I dare say I'm scared of what he might do…

But if I don't leave, I'll be banished and married… Forced to be apart from Tristan…

If I leave for a short while… Let Tristan calm down, do my duty, stay a Captain of the Syndicate… Perhaps I can have it all.

"Fine uncle, I will leave, on the condition that you will speak to my mother and put an end to any talk of marriage, that I can stay a Captain of the Syndicate, and that when I return, you will mind your own business and let me do as I wish."

My uncle scoffs once again.

"I'll agree to putting an end to marriage talk, I'll agree to letting you stay a Captain, but I will not agree to you pursuing this ridiculous affair with the Prince."

"Then banish me."

I say firmly.

My uncle stares at me for a long moment, before finally sighing and speaking.

"That boy… You have no idea… He will be the death of you."

He states.

He is not the first to say this, nor will he be the last I'm sure…
But I already know this.
I'm happy to die if it means loving Tristan, I already resigned myself to this fate long ago.

"I know uncle, and I don't care.
I love him, since before I can remember, he is my heart, and if it means my death, then so be it."

My uncle stares at me hard before finally saying

"Suit yourself, laddie, but don't say I did not warn you.
And do not ask me to watch you die.
Now get out of my sight and prepare yourself for your mission.
You leave immediately."

With that I stand tall and salute my uncle, my Lord Commander and take my leave.

I only hope this mission is not only successful but short, I have not even left and already I miss Tristan.
I must be back for the coronation in a moon's turn, I cannot miss it.
Besides, Tristan surely was speaking nonsense, he does not really intend to kill Claudius and usurp the throne.
Anyway, he cannot do it alone and he knows it.
Perhaps my leaving will give him some perspective.

OR PERHAPS HE WILL GROW EVEN MADDER AND CARRY OUT HIS PLANS WITHOUT YOU THERE TO STOP HIM…

No, Tristan will surely settle… He must…

And if I don't leave, I'll lose him forever.
Married off and sent away to the ancestral home to sire children.
I cannot… Will not let that happen.

Forgive me my love, but it will only be for a short while, and when I
return we can be together again… I'm sure of it.

WE SHALL SEE…

Yes… Yes we shall.

LATER THAT NIGHT

INSIDE THE CAPITAL CITY

LET THE SEARCH BEGIN

MARCUS

We are finally within the Capital.

It had taken us a little longer to get here than expected.

We had to hide, something which I do not enjoy.

We left the massacred village with relative ease.

After a few days however, just as we were on the verge of escaping the Black Woods, we had Protecters hot on our heels.

I told the rest to leave whilst I stayed behind and let them catch up with me.

They charged hard on horseback, and when I saw their approach, I let out a gut-wrenching growl.

Their horses fell backwards, crushing some of the backs and legs of the witches sat upon them.

The rest galloped off, terrified.

And those poor bastards with broken bones on that dirt road…

Well, let's just say their blood was delicious.

No longer followed, the rest having firmly doubled back.

No doubt to tell their superiors that we had managed to get into the Human Realm.

Or perhaps they would not say anything at all, most likely terrified for having not continued to give chase.

And terrified to admit they did not fight and die with honour.

In fact, they had left their fellow comrades to die, broken on the road.

No, I doubt they had said anything at all.

I am certain we are safe here.

Once we had entered the Human Realm, the witches used their magic to change my appearance and that of my fellow Scarlet Soldiers.

Most importantly, our eye colour.

From my red eyes to the blue I'd had when I was a human.

However not as light as they used to be.

It was a darker blue however, the red tones still present underneath.

Magic is only so strong on demons it seems.

The witches changed the colour of their dresses too, from darkest of blacks to pale grey and beige dresses which are now more like rags.

We could not however change the colour of our skin.

A stupid Blood Initiate had suggested that he try and find some chains and collars.

He quickly got a snapped neck for that suggestion.

Instead, we have to wear dark cloaks.

We managed to get horses however in a passing village.

We stayed away from any of the towns or cities.

Kept on horseback, we rode hard and arrived at the castle gates of the Capital.

The place was crawling with these so called

'Defenders.'

Righteous bullies by all accounts.

An army grown by Claudius the Cunt.

And the ones responsible for carrying out the Cleansing of Witches.

And yet, we got through with relative ease.

With the Crown Prince's upcoming coronation, it seems as if hundreds are arriving from all over the Human Realm, a coronation not having happened for years.
The streets seem alive, there is plenty of cheer and laughter.
Many are drunk, even more drunk than they should be.
The guards are clearly too busy to even notice us simply walking in.
Once past the gates, we stick close to the outskirts.
Keeping to the very worse of the city, the slums and shacks where thousands of slaves live and citizens who are just shit poor.
Yet everyone seems lively, apart from the slaves of course.
I halt when I first see them... My people, still in chains.

Centuries of chains.

It breaks my already dead heart.
This should not have continued.
They should never have been enslaved; we should have saved them.
Maddening, all these humans cheering and partying, I can hear them outside this ugly little house we found abandoned.
Well, almost abandoned.
Several dregs of society were passed out.
Not wanting to drink dirty blood, we dragged their bodies and threw them out on the street.
I quickly put the Blood Initiates to work.
Clearing the ugly, dirty house as best they can.
The wooden floorboards creak.
They are covered in a thick layer of dust.
The windows, if you can call them that, are extremely dirty too.
This house is desolate and disgusting, clearly not lived in.
It seems it's a squatter's house if anything, like many of the ugly houses along these streets.

Demetrius speaks then.

"Surely you can't expect us to actually stay here?"

It seems that slap he received from me after the village massacre was not enough to knock some sense into him.

YOU SHOULD HAVE KILLED HIM WEEKS BACK.

Yet I had not and was not entirely sure why.
Perhaps because the other Scarlet Soldiers seem more loyal to him.
Besides, even though I'm certain I can kill him and the rest with relative ease, I can hardly do it now.
I'm in the Capital and I dare not risk a bloodbath.
Even in this disgusting part of the city where even the guards care little about the goings on.
Indeed, it is perfect for what I am here to do.

"We shall not be here long.
Our mission is simple after all."

"Yes, get the prince.
But how exactly are we supposed to do that?
We aren't even close to him, we are on the wrong side of the Capital for start, and he's not even in the Capital, he and the rest of the fucking Dynasty live on that island for theirs."

He sounded impressed with himself, as if he was sharing news I did not already know.
I am centuries old; I had been there at the very beginning.
I know where the Imperial Family lives, and yet this fool somehow thinks otherwise.

"Thank you for that illustrious lesson you just shared with us."

I say sarcastically, running my finger along a particularly dusty staircase.

"Well, when shall we get him then?
Tonight?"

He is eager…

Yes, too eager.
I did not choose this company; I chose none of them.
My sister chose these, each and every one.

THEY ARE WORKING FOR HER…

Yes, she so desperately wants to get her hands on this Prince and yet she did not reveal to me why.
She instead danced around the question, instead offering promises of peace and freedom.
I intend to find out why this Prince is so badly wanted.
There must be something about him, something in particular.
I will indeed capture the prince, but I have every intention of doing that on my own.

"Not tonight, no."

I answer.

"Why not?"

My anger rising, I swirl to face him.

"Because the closer we get to the castle, the closer we get to being discovered."

I take a step towards him.

"Firstly, I placed us here in this ugly, disgusting house because we are surrounded by drunks, addicts, slaves and various other undesirables. The Imperial Guard and Defenders barely patrol here; therefore, we are secluded.
Also, close to the Capital Gates, if we need a quick exit."

I take another step towards him.

"We need to get to the far side of the Capital, and reach the Grand Bridge, which is heavily guarded on both sides.
And if they suspect us, even if we try to run, the middle section of the Grand Bridge acts as a drawbridge.
We would be trapped, and I do not fancy my chances in the sea, do you?"

I take another step.

I'm directly in front of him.

He gulps.

"So, before we do all of that, we must first do surveillance and monitor the situation.
How many guards at which gates, when they change shifts.
Also, there is a good chance the prince could come to us, here in the Capital.
We might not have to go anywhere near the Grand Bridge or the island."

I stand there, facing down at him.

He bows his head and takes a step back.

The other Scarlet Soldiers duly do so too.

"Tonight, why don't you go out and start your surveillance?
Go to the gates and watch out."

I can tell this is the last thing they want to do.

"Also, go to the taverns and whore houses, and see if there are any important rumours floating about.
Anything about Lords or Ladies but better, information on Council members, Claudius, or the Imperial Family members."

They seem to cheer up at the sound of that.
I know for a fact most of them will not find out anything, they'll go to the taverns and whore houses and have a night of drinking and fucking.
It does not bother me, it gets them out of my way, keeps their watchful eyes from my business.
I'm certain they are watching me, keeping an eye on me.
I've felt their eyes on me the entire journey here.
I am certain they are reporting back to her somehow.

"Well go on then, have fun."

I say enthusiastically.

They do not need telling twice.
They hurry out the door one by one and into the partying streets of the Capital.

The only one who stays is the new recruit, the Blood Initiate I had turned into another monster.
He is fair skinned with dark hair and blue eyes.
As a human, he is average looking, however now changed, he is very comely.
He stands there, unmoved.

"Do you not fancy drinking and whoring?"

I question him.

He shuffles his feet nervously.

"No, my Lord, if that's okay with you.
I… I don't like the others.
They are cruel."

He points out.

"Trust me, I am much crueller.
As is the world, you must get used to it."

I tell him.

He hangs his head low.

"Stay here if you wish, protect the witches and other Initiates.
And keep a watch out for any guard."

He seems cheered by this.

"Yes, yes, of course my Lord.
Thank you, thank you."

He gushes.

I can't help but admit it is cute how excitable he got.

No, I must not get distracted.
Not by another handsome young man.
I go to take my leave of the ugly house then, wanting to get away from
the dust and smell of piss and shit.
As I get my hand on the doorknob, I hear my name called out.

For fuck's sake.

I turn around and there stands the young girl, she still holds the baby.
She has barely put it down since I found it.
A good thing perhaps, after all I do not know much about babies.

WHY DID YOU EVEN SAVE IT?!
I SEE NO POINT.

Because I cannot stand any more death.
Especially not a babe.

"What is it?"

I ask, just wanting to leave.

"The others are asleep."

She is talking about the other four witches.

The Blood Initiates still work around us, trying their best to clear up.

"May I speak with you, my Lord?
In private?"

She gestures towards up the stairs.

I sigh deeply and follow her.
We end up in an abandoned room, adjacent to the room where the I
can hear the fellow witches sleeping softly.

"What is it?"

I ask of her, annoyed.
I could already be out in the Capital right now, finding out real
information.

She continues to sway the babe in her arms, cooing softly.
She looks up at me then,

"My Lord, I know we have only been here for a couple hours, but… I
can sense something."

Her voice is lowered, shrouded in fear.
I am surprised.
I too have felt it, I had felt it before we had even got to the Capital
Gates.
The air here… It is thick with magic.
Strong, potent magic.
The fact she senses it too… Only powerful witches can detect other
powerful witches.
The same goes for vampires, we can detect magic from miles away.
You have to have utter control of your senses, however, you need to
be calm and focused.

Most vampires struggled with this, their only focus ever being on blood.

"What can you sense."

I ask of her.

"I can sense this is an evil place.
Just as evil as the Dark Realm.
The only thing here is death.
So many have died here, I've felt it since we got to the Human Realm.
So many witches, violently murdered.
Tortured and abused.
And plenty of humans too, accused of false witchcraft."

"Can you sense anything else?
Here, in the Capital."

"Yes… there are witches hidden here.
They hide and scurry like rats in the sewers.
I can sense them… I can sense their fear…
But there's something even stronger…
Even stronger than all the witches combined hiding in the shit and piss."

"And where is it coming from?"

I question her further.

I want to see just how good her senses are.
She clearly has good focus, and I suspect it was mainly her who created the shield back at the massacred village, the other witches having little to no magical potential.

But this girl… She's something, she has power.

"There is something here… something incredibly powerful.
It's building… Getting angrier.
It is pure chaos… And zero control.
I can sense… Sense a profound evil."

Her voice is even more scared.
I had sensed it as well.

Something incredibly dark and powerful… And so alluring and beautiful.

"I think it's intoxicating."

I confess.

"Thank you for sharing your thoughts.
You and the babe should get some sleep.
Now, if you don't mind, the hour is late, and I only have few hours till morning.
I am going to go and assess the situation here."

I turn to leave then, but she grabs my hand.

"Don't let it intoxicate you, my Lord.
That kind of power… It will draw you in and kill you."

Her voice is panicked.
She really is scared…
Then again, many were scared of the powerful.
I however have always been drawn to it.

*THAT IS WHY YOU HAVE FOLLOWED YOUR SISTER FOR
CENTURIES!*
DRAWN TO POWER, YET NEVER HAVING IT YOURSELF.

I've commanded armies…

NOT YOUR ARMIES, THOUGH.
YOUR SISTER'S, SHE IS THE ONE ALWAYS IN CONTROL.

Not anymore.
I do not why she wants the prince.
And I do not know where this incredibly powerful magic that resides
here is coming from.
But I need to find out.

*YOUR SISTER GAVE YOU CLEAR ORDERS, TAKE THE PRINCE
AND PORTAL TO HER.*

No, I shall find the prince, and for whatever reason he is wanted, I can
use him as leverage.
I remove her hand from mine.

"Please, do not forget yourself, you are but a servant.
Now go to sleep."

She looks hurt at this, but I have to establish order here.

I am not their friend.
I am no one's friend.
A creature covered in centuries of blood, death and misery and
loneliness.
I finally do what I've been wanting to do since I got into this dank and
damp and dusty house.

Leave it!

I step out into the cool air; the street is littered with drunks and slaves.
I can hear the adjacent streets, all alive and rowdy as well.

I pull my hood down lower, making sure I'm disguised and begin to walk.
Walk out and into the night.

Hidden, cloaked, covered by darkness.
A monster amongst men.

TO BE CONTINUED...

ABOUT THE AUTHOR

From a young age, I was no stranger to hospital rooms, where my imagination became my greatest escape. With endless hours to fill, my mind wandered through worlds of magic and adventure, crafting stories more vibrant than the sterile walls around me.

Living by the sea only fuelled my daydreams. I'd stand by the shore, letting the crashing waves carry my thoughts to distant lands and mythical realms. It was easy to believe that just beyond the horizon, magic awaited.
I grew up enchanted by epic tales like *The Lord of the Rings*, and anything steeped in fantasy instantly captured my heart. I've always wished—perhaps still do—that I could wield a little magic myself.

From those early days, I knew one thing for certain: I wanted to write. I wanted to create my own worlds filled with wonder, magic, and adventure. And now, that dream is becoming a reality.